Soon enough, the guide seemed to decide that
Primrose was nothing more than she appeared.

A grave mistake many had made before, and one that Prim
would certainly count on many making in the future.

The guide's attention returned to Tasherit. Primrose heaved
a sigh of relief and then, along with the rest of the passengers,
emitted an unintended shriek of surprise when a loud bang and
pop reverberated through the quiet night air.

Someone appeared to be shooting at them! This was not part
of her plan.

Then the sky was briefly set afire with a brilliant flash of
sparkling yellow and red.

Someone screamed loudly.

Someone else fainted.

Praise for
Competence

"Carriger excels at wry humor and clever phrasing, and her ensemble cast is thoroughly charming and satisfyingly diverse. There's a genuine sense of whimsy and fun running throughout this story, making it a treat for fans of the series."

—*Publishers Weekly*

Praise for
Imprudence

"Carriger's trademark wit and whimsy are in evidence from the very first sentence, and the result is an inventive madcap adventure."

—*RT Book Reviews*

"The continued fantastical adventures of Prudence Alessandra Maccon Akeldama...are as charming as the first book in the series....For a silly, fun escape from day-to-day dirigible-less doldrums, *Imprudence* is required reading."

—*Oklahoman*

Praise for
Prudence

"Filled with lavish fashions, supernatural high society, and witty dialogue, this story is a fine introduction to a fabulous new series."

—*Booklist*

"The author's humor and affection for her outlandish characters is always appealing. A fun launch."

—*Library Journal*

By Gail Carriger

The Parasol Protectorate
Soulless
Changeless
Blameless
Heartless
Timeless

The Custard Protocol
Prudence
Imprudence
Competence

The Parasol Protectorate Manga
Soulless: The Manga, Vol. 1
Soulless: The Manga, Vol. 2
Soulless: The Manga, Vol. 3

The Finishing School
Etiquette & Espionage
Curtsies & Conspiracies
Waistcoats & Weaponry
Manners & Mutiny

COMPETENCE

THE CUSTARD PROTOCOL: BOOK THREE

GAIL CARRIGER

orbit

www.orbitbooks.net

Copyright © 2018 by Tofa Borregaard
Excerpt from *Soulless* copyright © 2009 by Tofa Borregaard
Excerpt from *The Immortals* copyright © 2016 by Jordanna Max Brodsky

Cover design by Lauren Panepinto
Type design by Chad Roberts
Cover illustration by Don Sipley/Michael Roberts
Cover copyright © 2018 by Hachette Book Group, Inc.

Orbit
Hachette Book Group
1290 Avenue of the Americas
New York, NY 10104
orbitbooks.net

Originally published in hardcover and ebook by Orbit in July 2018
First U.S. trade paperback edition: February 2019

Orbit is an imprint of Hachette Book Group.
The Orbit name and logo are trademarks of Little, Brown Book Group Limited.

The publisher is not responsible for websites (or their content) that are not owned by the publisher.

The Hachette Speakers Bureau provides a wide range of authors for speaking events. To find out more, go to www.hachettespeakersbureau.com or call (866) 376-6591.

Library of Congress Cataloging-in-Publication Data
Names: Carriger, Gail, author.
Title: Competence / Gail Carriger.
Description: First edition. | New York : Orbit, 2018. | Series: The Custard protocol ; book 3
Identifiers: LCCN 2017046503 | ISBN 9780316433884 (hardcover) | ISBN 9780316433877 (ebook (open))
Subjects: LCSH: Werewolves—Fiction. | Vampires—Fiction. | Paranormal fiction. | Steampunk fiction. | GSAFD: Fantasy fiction.
Classification: LCC PS3603.A77448 C66 2018 | DDC 813/.6—dc23
LC record available at https://lccn.loc.gov/2017046503

ISBN: 978-0-316-43385-3

Printed in the United States of America

LSC-C

10 9 8 7 6 5 4 3 2 1

ONE

A Lioness in a Hat and Other Concerns

A *nd to think* – Primrose tried not to be grim – *that only a few moments ago I felt misled by the claim that this is the biggest wheystation in the South Pacific.*

Turns out Singapore's Wheystation Alpha was a lot larger than one liked, when one suddenly had to run all the way across it.

The Honourable Miss Primrose Tunstell hated running. To be honest, she rather loathed exercise of any sort, it being at best heart-palpitatingly incommodious and at worst, well, sticky and stinky. If she was lucky, the most strenuous endeavour she need undertake in any given day was the lifting of a teacup to her lips. Unfortunately, since signing on board *The Spotted Custard*, Prim was rarely so lucky. To wit, the fact that she was right now positively dashing through a crowded wheystation. *Dashing. Well . . . dash it!*

Primrose wasn't stupid, she was wearing her summer-weight stays and her most modish muslin travel gown. Singapore was, after all, quite close to the equator and thus deserving of warm-weather attire, even when not dashing. Yes, it was late December but it was also hot. Unfortunately, even her lightest corsetry wasn't designed for an all-out sprint. *If I'd known, I should have worn my tennis dress.* Except, of course, that Primrose Tunstell would not be caught dead *shopping* in a *tennis dress* of an evening, equator or no! *The very idea!*

Primrose shook her head at her own flights of whimsy – *Tennis dress indeed!* – and put on another burst of speed as the gondola section of *The Spotted Custard*, which had been moored quite safely and respectably above station decks a mere quarter of an hour previous, slowly sank out of sight. *So doth my ship collapse away from me, sad and sagging. I left it too long.*

Of course, the initial impression might be that *The Spotted Custard* was intent on leaving Primrose behind. Or had forgotten about her. This was always a possibility: Captain Prudence Akeldama was anything but prudent and had, on more than one occasion, forgotten about something important. It was unlikely that she would forget about her purser, chief organiser, and best friend, however. Not that Primrose overvalued herself, but really! There was also the fact that Prim was carrying on her person, at that moment, a month's worth of ship's correspondences. Rue might leave Prim behind, but a letter from her adored father? Never.

Also – and this was the meat of it – they'd floated down to the Singapore wheystation specifically because the main balloon had sprung a leak. Sinking, under such circumstances, was rather more likely than not.

I guess they had more difficulty than anticipated in patching it promptly.

Primrose's legs were burning, she couldn't take a proper breath, and she was beginning to feel a little dizzy. But she did not want to be left behind in Singapore. Although, thank heavens, they mainly spoke English. And the shopping was to die for. In one hand Primrose carried the crew's letters but in the other hand she had a cloth-wrapped bundle full of spices and sparkles from a recent market foray. *To die for.*

All of which, including her good self, would be at risk if she were left behind. *I might actually be left dying for it. I don't have an escort. I'm alone and stranded! Worse, if I have to bunk down overnight, I don't even have a change of hat.*

The topmost squeak deck of *The Spotted Custard* was almost

out of sight. Prim could see it sinking through the open bay door as the balloon rigging came into view instead. Spoo was hanging off one rope and waving at her to move faster.

Primrose tried, she really did, but she'd never win a prize for foot speed. It simply wasn't her preferred mode of locomotion. A sedate stroll was more her capacity. Or better yet, a nice float on air or sea.

She nearly ran into a porter.

"Oh, a thousand apologies, good sir," she said, between pants. "But I believe my transport is sinking away without me. I do beg your pardon." She was embarrassed to find herself short of both breath and adequate vocabulary.

The kindly gentleman did not seem to take offence. No doubt he was accustomed to people on a wheystation moving at speed. He nodded, and Primrose resumed her undignified scampering.

I'm not going to make it.

Primrose wasn't given to flights of fancy or overly dramatic reactions to dire situations. Well, not most of the time. She tried to be practical. The pragmatic side of her brain was explaining that, given the restriction in her stride (copious skirts) and in her capacities (laziness meets corset), combined with the distance she still had to traverse, even if she made it, the leap would be more than she could safely undertake.

Nevertheless, she kept running.

Primrose ended up at the edge of the gangplank which had once been connected to the boarding deck of *The Spotted Custard*.

The top of the dirigible's rigging was in front of her and the lower part of the massive red and black spotted balloon that gave the *Custard* her lift. Percy was now steering the craft away from the station, so as to keep the bulging balloon from crashing against it.

Prim crouched down and looked over the edge.

Spoo and Rue looked up at her from the squeak deck.

"Sorry, Prim dear!" That was Rue, her voice high and ridiculous sounding due to the still-unpatched helium leak. "It got worse."

"Yes, indeed," shouted Primrose down at her friend and captain. "So I see."

"Hang tight and we'll come retrieve you as soon as possible."

"Oh, I say! That's very reassuring, Rue darling. Very reassuring."

"I'd give you a time frame but might be difficult to find helium where we're going."

"Oh? And where's that?"

"Down."

"Lovely. I'll wait here then, shall I?"

"I'm sending reinforcements."

"You're too kind."

"You haven't seen whom I'm sending."

"Better do it quickly, darling."

Rue gave a nod and something huge and sleek and golden brown leapt from the crow's nest, which was still well above Primrose's head, to land gracefully on the dock next to Prim. The something resolved itself into the form of a large and quite beautiful lioness wearing a smug expression and an awfully familiar flowered sun hat and holding a large carpetbag in her mouth by its handle.

"Ah," said Primrose politely, "good evening, Miss Sekhmet, nice weather for it?" *Lovely. Now I am stranded in Singapore with a werecat.* "Wait a moment. Is that *my* hat?"

The cat gave a meow-trill around the handle and trotted over, depositing a carpetbag full of, no doubt, useful items for two ladies weathering an undisclosed amount of time alone on a wheystation in a foreign land. Primrose shuddered to imagine what Rue would think important to pack under those circumstances. Certainly there would be plenty of pastries and a change of shoes, but would there be something as sensible as a hair comb or additional banknotes? Her darling Prudence was practical up to a point, about things that interested her, and then she was most decidedly not practical at all about anything else. Hopefully there was also a change of clothing for Miss Sekhmet. At sunrise she'd return to human form whether she liked it or not. Both Prim and the wheystation would see a great deal more of her than decency allowed.

Primrose hoped there was at least a robe. Or come sunrise, she'd be stranded in the main dirigible station of Singapore's famous port with a naked woman. Quite apart from what that might do to Singapore, Primrose had learned (to her deep and continued trauma) that a certain naked werecat, when not a cat, played hell with her own much-vaunted stability and good sense.

Fortunately for all, Tasherit Sekhmet was currently a lioness, which Primrose always found *much* easier to stomach. In this particular state, she was also an excellent form of defensive escort, if perhaps a little more attention-drawing than Primrose preferred.

Prim was never one to skirt credit when due in matters of manners or monetary exchange. So she said politely to the lioness, "It is awfully nice to have you with me. I must admit I wasn't looking forward to being stuck here all alone without escort or protection. You are both."

Miss Sekhmet chirruped at her and nudged the bag in her direction.

Primrose picked it up and put her recent purchases and the stack of letters on the top.

"I suppose we are stuck here for no little while? We should find some place to stay. You'll need protection from sunrise. I believe *Baedeker's* indicated that the best hotel on station is the Raffles Extra High Extenuation, towards the northeastern quadrant. Shall we secure quarters?"

The lioness nodded at her.

"I take it they couldn't fix the leak, and it got worse? I wasn't gone any longer than I said."

The cat meeped an answer.

"Well, there you have it. Is Rue very put out?"

A chirrup at that. It took a lot to upset the captain. It was one of Prudence Akeldama's stronger points that she took everything in stride, easygoing and eager to please. Prim herself would have been annoyed at any delay, even if they really didn't have anywhere urgent to be. Just on principle, because Primrose liked everything in order. Rue, on the other hand, would let the ship sink and figure it all out later without a break in her general good humour.

Ridiculous child. Prim sighed.

"How is it," she asked the cat, "Rue's harebrained schemes always end up with *me* in trouble?"

The cat didn't answer, simply started trotting off across the dock towards the enclosed central residential area of the busy station.

Prim scurried after her. "Slow down, do! Let me tie a ribbon to you at least, so you appear to be under control. You'll cause a panic simply wandering about like that. People will think you're a fearsome wild beast, loose among them."

Tasherit paused, turned on her haunches, and hissed.

"Yes, yes, I know, you are a fearsome wild beast in a hat. But consider appearances, please, do."

The cat paused for Prim to catch up to her. Prim tried to untangle one of her hair ribbons so she might wrap it around the lioness's neck in a mock leash. Unsurprisingly, the cat would have none of it, but moved off again, expecting Primrose to follow.

"Oh, do slow down! Be sensible. I just ran through all this, and I'm not made for this kind of undignified rushing all over the place. And now my hair has fallen!"

Tasherit ignored her.

"Cats!" said Primrose to the station at large.

The station, no doubt, would have agreed with her, if it didn't have its own business to attend to.

Initially, Tasherit snaked through and around the crowds, skirting them in such a way as to have people glance in her direction, wince, and then glance quickly away, no doubt hoping that what they had observed was a remarkably large domesticated dog of some feline persuasion, and not a random lioness wearing a straw bonnet a mile up in the air on a dirigible station.

Then, of course, someone in what proved to be some form of military attire spotted her and blew a decidedly aggressive whistle. Primrose was reminded of the first time they had met Miss Sekhmet. She'd been a lioness then, too, and had eviscerated a perfectly respectable teahouse.

A spot of tea would be lovely right about now, thought Prim, and then, *Oh no, we're running again. Pox.*

The orderly, or policeman, or enforcer, or whatever his official moniker was, was running after Tasherit. So Primrose trundled after him, now laden down with carpetbag and regretting everything about her modern and entirely fashionable marigold gown with leg-of-mutton sleeves and embroidered bodice. It was too warm, too constricting, too noticeable, and it clashed with the bag.

The lioness's straw hat tilted at a jaunty angle. Prim had to hope it was well secured – it was one of her favourites.

Eventually, without too much bother – Miss Sekhmet clearly wasn't trying to cause chaos – the lioness disappeared around or behind or into something and the policeman gave up the chase and his aggressive whistling.

He gave Prim an aggrieved look. "That your lioness, Miss?"

"No," said Prim, primly. Well, Tasherit wasn't hers. They were merely travelling companions.

"Then why are you chasing her, miss? If you don't mind my asking."

"Why are *you* chasing her?"

"Merlion rumours, you know."

"Pardon?"

"Ah, you aren't a local."

Primrose looked down at herself, and then back up at the man. He was a cheerful fellow, round faced and handsome, if you liked that sort. Prim supposed she *ought* to like that sort and so put a concerted effort into flirtation.

"My dear sir, do I *look* local?"

"Singapore's got all sorts," he said proudly.

"Well, as I am clutching a carpetbag on a dirigible whey-station, I'd guess odds are against me being a resident of your fine city."

"Are you alone, young lady?"

"Only temporarily."

"That's not on for your people, is it?"

Primrose baulked. "And whose people is that?"

"English-type females."

Prim tried to dampen a blush. "Ah, well..." *It's a fair accusation.*

The young man straightened. His eyes had a pleasing tilt to them, and, while dark in colour, they twinkled. "Might I escort you to your destination?"

Is he being gentlemanly, or nosy? wondered Prim. *Ah well, in either case I've lost my feline escort. A man in uniform can't be all bad. And I can always bop him with the carpetbag if he becomes impertinent.*

Primrose also possessed, tucked into a secret pocket of her very nice yellow-orange dress, an equally nice .22-calibre pistol. Although perhaps not quite so pretty in colour. Prim didn't like guns, and she didn't like to have to shoot them, but that didn't stop her from being very, very good at it.

"Where are you headed?" enquired Mr Uniform-Twinkle.

"Um, I'm afraid I don't know you at all, so I must decline your kind offer. I assure you, I shall be perfectly topping all on my lonesome."

"But, miss, there's a ruddy great lioness dashing about." The man tilted his head and frowned, looking genuinely concerned for her safety.

"Excellent point."

"What's your interest in the matter anyway, miss? You were chasing her too." The man narrowed his eyes, now more suspicious than concerned. One had to give him credit for persistence.

Primrose shrugged. "I like cats."

He snorted a laugh, recognising her avoidance of the subject, and offered her his arm. "Captain Lu, ma'am, at your service."

Prim took his arm. It was, after all, the polite thing to do. "Miss Hisselpenny." She didn't give her real name. Instead she used one of her more common aliases. Rue would know to look for her under Hisselpenny. They often pretended to be the wealthy and errant Hisselpenny sisters, when out and about. It simply made life easier, most of the time, to be someone else.

The moment she took the young man's arm, however, there came a yowl. Miss Sekhmet reappeared from wherever she'd gone and charged, head butting between them, hissing and spitting.

"Stand back, miss, I'll protect you," said the young gallant.

Well, who would have thought, a true gentleman and not simply a nosy flirt. How refreshing. Prim's faith in the innate kindness of human nature was restored, even if this man's attempt to save her was misapplied. He shoved her to one side and she stumbled, emitting an *oof* noise that if asked about later she would categorically deny.

Primrose straightened and tried a winsome smile on the young man who now faced off against the lioness, brandishing a truncheon.

"Oh, Captain Lu, don't be silly, she's not dangerous. At least, not to me."

"So she *is* yours?" He looked back and forth between them.

Miss Sekhmet, with a cat's impeccable timing, stopped hissing at the officer and glided over to Prim, rubbing against her hip in a possessive manner.

Prim rested one gloved hand on the top of the hat on Tasherit's head. The cat sat down primly and curved her tail around her massive paws. Her un-catlike dark brown eyes narrowed and then she let out a great big yawn, showing all of her wickedly sharp teeth.

Captain Lu flinched.

Tasherit closed her mouth, twitched her whiskers, and looked impossibly pompous.

"What have I said about yawning in public?" admonished

Prim, and then to the young captain: "She is no one's but her own."

"Ah, yes, I see. But you two are together?"

"Theoretically."

The young man straightened. "Well, then, I must insist you have her under some kind of control. At the very least a collar and lead. Frankly, station regulations dictate she be caged."

Primrose bristled and so did Tasherit. "We really are only trying to get to a hotel of some kind. Then we will both be out of your hair."

The captain looked upset until the lioness yawned again. "Oh, very well. Let me escort you to..." He went to offer his arm to Primrose once more, very brave considering how close the cat sat at Prim's side.

Tasherit hissed at him again. She did not want his company.

"I assure you we will be fine." Prim nudged the cat with one foot to stop her from causing any more of a scene.

"Miss..."

"Hisselpenny."

"Miss Hisselpenny, you can't go wandering around alone with an untethered lioness. It's simply not done. Especially with the merlion rumours."

"Again, merlion, what does this word mean?"

Miss Sekhmet cocked her head, also interested.

"A sort of supernatural spirit animal, half lion, half fish. Supposedly one was spotted in the harbour only yesterday."

"And this is connected to us, up here on a dirigible station, how?"

"Well, *that* is a lioness."

"I assure you, she has no tail."

"You're positive?"

Primrose shook her head at the absurdity of this conversation. "Aside from the one you see lashing right at this very moment."

"Well, then..."

"Captain, if I assure you that this lioness is" – Prim searched for a way to be truthful, because she couldn't very well call Miss Sekhmet *tame* – "disciplined and well behaved, could we be allowed to get on? Then we will be safely out of the public eye. We are rather causing a fuss here."

And they were. A crowd had gathered around them in a wide circle to stare curiously at the pretty Englishwoman with the unbound hair, the handsome young station captain, and the lioness in the straw bonnet.

The captain looked about, apparently just noticing their audience. "I feel I ought to fine you or something."

"For having an unlicenced lioness?"

Captain Lu looked embarrassed. "Well, yes."

Primrose shook her head and crossed her arms. "Well, go on then."

The young man whipped out a notepad and began scribbling on it with a stylus.

The crowd, now realising this was devolving into that most common and uninteresting of occurrences, the traffic infraction, began to disperse. Although a few attempted to touch Miss Sekhmet, she hissed at them and they thought better of it. She was, it must be admitted, a great deal less fierce in the straw bonnet. But Prim left it on her, because she had only one free hand as it was, and she needed that for her gun, just in case.

The young man handed her the slip, which Prim glanced down at with interest. It was written in English, which somehow surprised her. She had expected some of those lovely Chinese swirly characters. But she supposed *official language* meant officially *written* language as well.

The fee was nominal and she could have Rue pay it to the station, once *The Spotted Custard* returned to pick her up. If they returned.

At the bottom Captain Lu had scrawled a wheystation quadrant address, possibly his own. *How very presumptuous.*

Prim looked up, blue eyes narrowed. "What's this, then, sir?"

"My direction, miss." He blushed quite red. "I mean to say,

that of my posting station. In case you need further assistance. That's my office. You can find me there most nights, or send a runner."

This was accompanied by what could only be described as puppy dog eyes.

Oh dear, thought Primrose, not too surprised, *I've made a conquest.*

The lioness gave a funny *huff* noise that was likely her version of a snort, and turning, began to trot away once again. Her long tail was held aloft, the white tip twitching only slightly, flag-like.

Primrose nodded a farewell to her erstwhile captain and followed quickly after. "Slow down, you! This is what started the whole mess."

Primrose didn't turn back to see, but she thought she heard the young man laughing.

Well, I guess I brightened up his evening.

Tasherit eventually brought them to the door of a respectable-looking hotel. Full of foreigners, of course, but then again this was a foreign land, so Prim didn't quite know what she was expecting. Everyone seemed nice enough. And who was she to complain, gallivanting about with a lioness?

She ascertained that they had available rooms and accepted pets, ignoring Tasherit's hiss at the use of that word. The hotel staff were not as upset as they ought to be to find Primrose travelling alone as a female, although they were shocked that her pet proved to be a lioness. By the time they noticed this – Tasherit put both massive paws onto the reception bar and then stood on her hind legs to look the clerk in his gobsmacked face – Prim already had key in hand, a room number in mind, and was bustling off. She ignored their cries of "Miss, miss, is that a big cat? Miss, I don't think that qualifies as a p..."

Primrose unlocked their room door, grateful that this strange land did not provide porters or hostesses. It was a novel thing to enter a room without guidance. It was fortuitous, however, because the moment they were alone, Tasherit shifted form.

"Oh, for goodness' sake," said Prim, hiding her face behind her own hands and not watching. She would absolutely not look. Well, maybe just a little peek.

Primrose could never get accustomed to the sound. The wet snapping and crunching of bones and flesh breaking and re-forming itself. The lioness hissed in pain and then, out the other end, whimpered very softly. It had to be agony, for Miss Sekhmet was an incredibly strong woman, to be brought low enough to whimper. It hurt Prim's teeth even thinking about it.

Prim unclenched her jaw but did not drop her hands until she had turned away from the noise. She upended the carpetbag onto the small single bed and ruffled through the contents.

Triumphant, she recognised the pile of fuchsia silk as one of Tasherit's many robes, and went to toss it to her.

Except there was warm breath and golden skin right next to her, and one graceful arm reached around to pluck the robe from her suddenly slack grasp.

"Mine? Thank you."

For the life of her, Primrose could not fathom why the presence of Tasherit in human form had such a profound effect on her breathing. She assumed it was some mixture of awe and terror. After all, Prim had seen the lioness rend asunder more than one man in battle. And yet Prim was not scared of Tasherit in cat form.

Perhaps it was her force of personality? So stubborn and fierce, regal, or worse, playful. Or perhaps it was the way she smelled, of amber and apricots.

Primrose twisted her engagement ring under one glove self-consciously and took a long deep breath, shifting subtly away from proximity to the naked supernatural creature.

Uncaring, Tasherit swung the robe on and belted it with a wide colourful scarf, also from the carpetbag pile.

Prim turned to face her, watching as she combed through her thick straight hair with careless fingers. Prim's own fingers twitched.

Forcing herself to focus elsewhere, Primrose bent over the objects scattered on the bed. *As I predicted, nothing as sensible as a comb. No night-rail either, charming. And what am I meant to sleep in, Rue?*

She plucked up her ribbon-not-leash and went to a nearby metal mirror to fuss her hair back into some semblance of order. Sekhmet handed her the straw bonnet.

"Rue said you'd want something different for when daylight rolls around."

"Well, at least she remembered something important."

"We're stuck here until they determine the source of the problem."

"Percy's ego?" suggested Primrose, pertly.

"I mean, the source of the leak."

"Percy's long-winded explanations?"

"Your brother is not so bad."

"You only say that because you are a cat and he likes cats."

"Mmm. Shall we find some supper before sunrise?"

"You are always hungry."

"You noticed?"

"I'm in charge of ship's stores, of course I noticed."

"It's a cat thing."

Primrose tried to hide a smile. "Of course it is. That's your excuse for everything."

Tasherit lounged on the bed, looking smug and exotic and totally relaxed. One long naked leg sprawled out of the robe. "Well, it's a good excuse when it's true."

Prim glanced away and finished with her hair. *That will have to do for now.*

Prim decided they were in dangerous verbal territory and she ought to change the topic. "Do we have time for me to review my correspondences?"

"Do you have many?"

Prim sorted through the letters she'd collected from the Royal Post drop point. "Three?"

"Oh, very well." The lioness smiled at her and moved over slightly on the bed, making room.

That seemed far too dangerous an invitation, so Primrose pretended not to notice and went with her letters to sit on a tuffet at the vanity instead.

She opened the one from her mother first.

"Tiddles, darling girl! I can't believe you are traipsing off to Singapore. Are you mad? It's savage and full of curry and coconuts and whatnot. Very dangerous things, coconuts. Can't be relied upon at all. Too hard, too rolly, covered in hair, and filled with water. I meant to say, what kind of nut is that? Come home, child, do. Your fiancé is waiting for you. He's been most attentive. Or he was most attentive, now he seems to have vanished, but I'm sure he'll resurface if you return to the bosom of your beloved family."

Primrose frowned and considered said fiancé. Lt Norman Plonks was one in a long line to have held the rather tarnished title of the Honourable Miss Primrose Tunstell's affianced. *Lt Norman Plonks. A good man.* Or so she felt after three consecutive dances and four well-supervised social calls over tea and tiny cakes. The man had excellent taste in flowers – he'd sent her hydrangeas, not primroses. And he proposed using a decent ring, not too big, not too small. No doubt he would be a decent husband. What more had Prim to go on than those truths society permitted her to ascertain? He cut a dashing leg at a ball, could order bouquets with the best of them, and did not slosh his tea. Not a bad way to start married life.

Then again, she would have to go home to marry the blighter. Return to England. And give over adventuring. Primrose Tunstell was beginning to find, much to her own surprise, that she rather enjoyed adventuring. Except for the times when there were shootings and injuries and such. But the rest of it was rather exhilarating – exotic lands and strange foods and new experiences. She'd met supernatural creatures the world didn't know existed, until *The Spotted Custard* spotted them. She'd seen Percy eat a chili pepper, which was fun for everyone – except Percy.

Was Lt Plonks's excellent taste in hydrangeas enough to summon her back home?

Not just yet, I think.

She twisted the ring on her finger again.

"That a letter from your fiancé?" Tasherit's warm voice interrupted, slightly sharpened by irritation.

"No, my mother."

"You're playing with that stupid ring again."

"It's a very nice ring. Now hush and let me finish my letter. You're only grumpy because you're hungry."

"What does she say, your mother?" *Cats, always curious.*

Primrose continued scanning the note. "Nothing of any import or merit. It is, after all, my mother."

Baroness Ivy Tunstell was an accidental vampire queen of unexpected power and influence, considering she was also, frankly, quite silly.

Much of Primrose's own competent nature had developed as a defence against her mother's countless eccentricities. Eccentricities that had, due to Ivy's vastly important position in society as a highly ranked female supernatural, been encouraged and overblown rather than nicely shoved under the carpet where they rightfully belonged. If Primrose had learned anything from her unusual childhood in a vampire hive, it was this: do not give untapped wealth and social influence to a woman whose greatest love in life is increasingly outrageous hats.

Prim continued scanning the letter. "In between the lines, and likely accidentally, Mother relays somewhat interesting gossip. The London pack has relocated to Greenwich and had dealings with some sort of cult. Apparently there was an offensive waistcoat involved. Speaking of waistcoats, Rue's Uncle Lyall has returned home: that will make everyone happy. We met him in India, before you were with us in any official capacity. Nice werewolf. And Mother says something about my great aunt's schoolmate's youngest offspring who might *do for the Custard.* Whatever that means."

"Is it in code?" Tasherit asked, not illogically given the peculiar nature of the information.

"No, sadly, it's my mother's way."

"Wow."

"I find it best to imagine she is inebriated. At all times. She isn't, of course, but..." Prim shrugged. How to explain Ivy Tunstell to those who had never met her before. "It makes her more tolerable. Alternatively, you could imagine *yourself* inebriated, or get that way before having to interact with her. Percy sometimes takes that tactic."

"You and Percy make a great deal more logical sense now."

"Do we?" Primrose put down the ridiculous letter from her mother and picked up the next one, which was from her fiancé. No doubt her mother had told him they were headed to Singapore, if he wished to send along a missive. She rather dreaded it for some reason.

Think of the lovely hydrangeas.

"My dearest Miss Tunstell. My heart aches as I pen this. I am ashamed it must be done via the written word, and not in person, as your good standing and good self might justifiably expect a proper audience." *Oh dear,* thought Prim, *this is a weighty matter. Is he...?* "But with you journeying ever further away from me and our fair isle, I am afraid that I must regretfully inform you that honour compels me to call off our engagement." *Ah, extended exposure to my mother has had its effect. So much for a well-turned leg.*

"Who is that one from?" Tasherit wanted to know as Prim began frowning.

"My fiancé."

Tasherit went quiet, letting her read.

The letter continued. "It's simply too much. You are too much for me, too good, too concerned with weighty matters, too occupied by the condition of the Empire. You deserve a better, more worldly man. Yours, etc., Lt Norman Plonks." *And so, for the first time, a gentleman is throwing me over. How unexpected. What sensation does this engender in me? Am I saddened? Is my heart crushed? No, that's more likely hunger. It's been ages since luncheon. Oh well.*

Prim folded it and tucked it away. Tasherit's liquid brown eyes in her impossibly beautiful face were focused on her with an odd unreadable expression. "And how is your young man?"

Primrose did not feel like telling her the truth. Some strange protective instinct, or her own embarrassment at having entered into the engagement to begin with, held her back from confessing all. "Oh, he is well, sends his regards."

"Not his love?"

"Gentlemen do not speak of such things. They certainly don't write of them!"

"You deserve love, little one."

Prim sniffed. "Don't be daft. Now who's this last from? I don't recognise the hand."

The seal looked somewhat official and the script was a bold one. Primrose cracked and opened the letter, glancing down at the signature to see who it might be.

"Oh, it's from Lady Maccon." Her voice registered only some of her considerable surprise.

"Rue's mother? What could she want with you?" Tasherit's eyebrows went up.

The werecat and the soulless had met and been civil enough, but Rue's mother was a force of nature (or perhaps more accurately, a force of the unnatural), and no cat enjoys that sort of competition. They hadn't exactly been chummy. Plus, most of Lady Maccon's time aboard *The Spotted Custard* had been spent high up in the aether, and the werecat always fell into a deep sleep whenever the ship entered the aetherosphere.

Prim scanned the short letter. Then scanned it again. It was full of inane pleasantries and didn't sound like Lady Maccon at all.

Only one sentence stood out: "Do make a note in the Ledger about extra milk."

The Ledger was Primrose's code name in Lady Maccon's Parasol Protectorate espionage ring.

That phrase meant the whole letter was likely in cypher. Primrose waved it at Tasherit. "Only banalities." The werecat was not a member of that particular club. If Lady Maccon wanted something kept private, Primrose would hold her peace despite those beautiful liquid brown eyes.

"That's not like her."

"No it isn't." Prim shrugged. "But perhaps she has nothing to say, being retired from society and residing in Egypt."

Prim folded the letter carefully and stuck it into her secret skirt pocket next to her gun. It was likely the missive employed the Isinglass code, which meant she needed the book *Sand and Shadows on a Sapphire Sea: My Adventures Abroad* by Honeysuckle Isinglass to decipher what it said. That book was back aboard *The Spotted Custard.*

She glanced through the rest of the letters and noted another one, addressed to Rue, in a similar bold script. She took that one and tucked it down the front of her corset, still sealed. She would *never* read a letter addressed to someone else, but she would keep it as safe as possible.

Tasherit watched this action with interest.

"Shall we find a teahouse or ascertain if the hotel serves after hours?" Prim asked, distracting the cat with food. As you do.

"I've never done very well with teahouses. Let's see what the hotel has on offer."

Tasherit presented her arm, as if she were a gentleman and Primrose a lady. Well, Primrose *was* a lady, but Tasherit was no gentleman. Still, Prim didn't wish to appear churlish, so she took it and together they made their way downstairs to the dining room.

CHAPTER

TWO

A Bad Case of the Dropsies

Professor Percival Tunstell was not having a particularly pleasant evening. First there was the helium leak. Then there was being unable to repair the leak – not that that was his problem, he was navigation, not repairs. Then there was having to leave his sister behind and now, well, this.

"Percy! We are headed straight for the ocean!"

"Yes, Rue, we are sinking. And Singapore is an island. You know, surrounded by water."

"Well, stop it! I can't swim."

"Did you miss the fact that we are sinking? I rather think that is something for you to stop, Captain."

"Well, steer us towards land at least. Isn't that land there?"

Percy did not wish to be condescending – well, to be fair he did wish it, he was excellent at condescension – but he could hardly take the time to explain to his extremely aggravating captain how aeronautics and wind dynamics worked.

"We have caught an offshore breeze, which means, unsurprisingly, that it is taking us *offshore*, Rue."

"So, catch a different breeze."

"It doesn't work like that."

"Percy!"

"Auribus teneo lupum."

"No Latin! You know I can't abide Latin during unsustainable situations!"

"Rue." Percy turned on her. "We catch breezes by going up or down. Up *or down*, Rue. Without vertical movement options, we thus have no choice on lateral direction. We are sinking, and therefore we are drifting as the wind wills it. Right now I am simply trying to keep us from landing directly inside a major shipping lane. While it would improve our chances of being rescued, *The Spotted Custard* would likely be destroyed by a large boat. If we can at least make for calmer waters, we might float for long enough to be rescued."

Rue looked genuinely scared at last. Her pretty face paled as much as her tan complexion allowed, and her odd yellow eyes dilated. "Do we float on water?"

Percy shrugged – he knew how to swim. *I suppose I'll have to rescue her if it comes to that. I wonder if there are any of those handy Bubbles Instant Flotation Apparatuses lying about.* He went back to the task at hand. "I think so. Never tried it. Ask Mr Lefoux, he was part of the design team. Wasn't he?"

Rue picked up the speaking tube and buzzed engineering.

"What!" Percy heard a sharp but deep female voice on the other end.

Bugger, he thought, but didn't say.

"Aggie, get me Quesnel."

Aggie, on the other end of the tube down in the boiler room, muttered a string of insults, or curses or complaints, that Percy couldn't focus on interpreting even if he wanted to. They seemed to have caught some new crosswind and there was a chance, just a chance, he could ride it back towards shore.

"I don't care how busy he is, this is important!"

Tentatively Percy depuffed, sinking them with a lurch faster downwards, so as to nest the collapsing balloon inside the new breeze. It caught them and dragged them back towards Singapore and away from all those huge busy steamers below.

"Fine, well, please ask him if we float on water. Yes, I know you float on water, woman; no one is more filled with oil than you. No, I *know* that I'm funny. Oh, for goodness' sake!"

Rue slammed down the tube and glared at Percy, face flushed. "That woman will be the death of me. Quesnel seems to think that yes, we might float, at least for a bit. But we aren't watertight due to the lower hatches, and if the balloon collapses entirely it will probably tilt us over: the mast and rudder are for aether use, not water."

Percy nodded but did not verbally acknowledge this information. He'd nothing intelligent to add to these details, so he said nothing. A policy he wished the world in general would obey. He bit his lip in concentration, focused on the one breeze he'd managed to find, hoping it didn't peter out.

There was a wide expanse of muddy tropical beach just ahead of them. It looked promising, and at least uninhabited.

He depuffed them again.

The Spotted Custard couldn't really land either. The airship wasn't made to go to ground any more than she was made to float on water. The gondola might shatter or break. He couldn't fill the balloon with air either – that might push the last of the helium out the as-yet untraced leak.

But Percy figured it would be safer for everyone if, when they did crash, they crashed on a nice soft beach, so that's what he aimed for.

Primrose and Tasherit had a respectable meal at their hotel. Tasherit even minded her manners, much to Prim's relief. There had been a time, when the werecat first joined the crew, that she would pick at meat with her fish knife, or wildly stab at rolling fruit.

Prim shuddered at the memory of their first (and only) whole roasted goose with the werecat at table. The woman had actually plucked up a leg and gnawed on it! Holding it in her bare hand

and tearing the flesh off the bone with her teeth, like, well, like an *animal*.

They returned to the rented room prior to sunup. The one bed certainly made things awkward. It wasn't that Prim was so wealthy she'd never shared a bed before. She and Rue, in their younger years, would hide under the covers together giggling and nattering away until they fell asleep. The occasional female cousin came to stay and had shared her room, partly because it meant Prim could keep her out of hive business. Ah, the awkwardness of a vampire queen who had human relations. So very odd, to be related to one's food.

But Tasherit was different. Primrose couldn't articulate it, or didn't want to, not even to herself. Tasherit never treated her like a female friend or relation. Not really.

Tasherit, and there was no more circumspect way of putting it, *flirted* with her. Primrose, who was a consummate flirt, was, as she had soon learned, only consummate when it came to men on the receiving end of her carefully crafted conversation and sweet expressions.

Thus the prospect of sharing bed linens with the werecat floored poor Prim. With no other options or ideas forthcoming, she removed her outer garments and her stays, and left on her combination.

Tasherit gave it a funny look. "What is that garment?"

Primrose looked down at it. It was one of her sensible combinations, muslin and only a little lace in plain cream cotton. It was a little embarrassing that it wasn't finer and silk and flattering, but it didn't have any holes or anything, and it was relatively new.

"This is a perfectly proper combination and we ought not to discuss such things."

"Why are you wearing it?" Tasherit said, suiting her own words to actions and stripping herself bare.

It was startlingly sudden. Primrose jumped and quickly turned away, pretending to lay out her discarded skirts.

Prim liked to think of herself as progressive, and not only in politics. She was a new woman. She'd recently ordered a bicycling ensemble and the latest in high-flying dirigible attire. Both these outfits came with split skirts and bloomers – and were made in America, for goodness' sake! She was modern. These were garments she dare not ever wear in England or anywhere her mother might get wind of them, but she couldn't get away from the sensibleness of split skirts. She was ready for the future. She was open to technological, and fashionable, and supernatural advancements. And she had dealt with Rue's occasionally necessary nudity throughout their long association. Prim's best friend changed into a wolf more often than not, which made clothing inconvenient.

But Tasherit was so very casual about the whole endeavour.

And Tasherit wasn't Rue. Or anyone else for that matter.

Tasherit was all golden limbs and long smooth legs and glossy hair and overmuch naked in a way that Rue simply was *not*. Because, well, Rue was Rue, and Tasherit was Tasherit. If Primrose could be more articulate, she might understand why the one bothered her and the other did not. Especially when the one was about to climb into bed and under the covers in all that golden long-limbed glory.

Primrose kept on her ugly combination as a kind of armour and climbed under the covers and hugged the edge of the narrow bed with single-minded intensity. She tried incredibly hard not to burn and flush in the places where Tasherit touched her. Touch was inevitable in a bed so small, and Tasherit curled into a ball when she slept, for obvious reasons.

Prim worked to slow her breathing, to feign sleep. A tentative hand settled on her hip. It scalded, but in the best possible way.

Primrose hated it for its hesitant possessiveness and loved it for the same reason in equal measure. She was also terrified that it meant more to her than any fervent lip pressed to her wrist by any one of her many fiancés and even more numerous beaux and swains over the years.

She kept very very still and Tasherit, no doubt unaware of Prim's turmoil, fell into a deep deathlike sleep as soon as the first rays of a full warm tropical sun arched above the horizon.

Prim relaxed and tried to sleep herself. She tossed and turned for a while, fell into a fitful doze, and then awoke after midday, starving. There was also a growing buzzing urge to get them off the station and back aboard *The Spotted Custard* as quickly as possible.

Rue, Percy, and the others were no doubt sunk far below. They needed helium, and Primrose realised that it was now her responsibility to get it for them. She was, after all, in charge of supplies and aboard a wheystation.

She dressed quietly, leaving the sleeping werecat to her daytime dreamlessness, and let herself out into the bustling station, heading towards the supplies and munitions area.

They anchored *The Spotted Custard* to some palm trees and somehow managed to remain inflated enough not to actually crash, although it was a near thing. They were only a few feet above the sands.

Spoo, bless her industrious little heart, found the leak at last. Percy had a soft spot for Spoo. This was mainly because Spoo had befriended his young valet, Virgil. And Percy adored Virgil. Not that Virgil, or anyone else for that matter, would ever know such a thing. Percy would never want to be thought of as sentimental – heaven forfend. His mother was mostly sentimental. From what he'd heard, his father had been wholly sentimental. Percy worked hard to be stoic as a countermeasure. Someone had to.

Virgil was a good lad, diligent in his efforts to keep Percy clean, well groomed, and modestly turned out. Percy didn't make it easy on the poor boy and delighted in vexing him with his eccentric academic disregard for attire and chronic misplacement of hats. Virgil, in turn, delighted in chastising his master as if he were the elder and Percy not twice his age. Percy also used Virgil, much as he used Footnote, as a judge of character. Virgil liked Spoo, therefore Spoo must be a decent sort of human. Footnote, his cat, also liked Spoo. Therefore Spoo must be a genuinely good egg. Or possibly eat a great deal of tuna. Footnote couldn't be trusted to be entirely discriminating.

Percy, you see, knew himself to be a supremely bad judge of character. He didn't like *anyone*. Ever. So he needed his pint-sized valet and his tuxedo cat to figure these things out for him, and to pave the way for his own acerbic personality. Everyone liked Virgil, and most people with sense liked Footnote. Therefore they tolerated Percy's eccentricities by extension, his household staff acting as ambassadors, of a kind. Percy's abilities afforded them all a place aboard *The Spotted Custard* that all, particularly Percy, had come to enjoy rather too much. It thus behooved him to make nice, by extension of his employees if not himself. Of course, Percy would never admit such a thing to anyone.

So when it was Spoo who found and patched the extremely problematic helium leak, Percy frowned at her severely and secretly cheered for her small victory. Rue praised the deckling soundly as a genius. Rue was good about giving credit where due. It was part of what made her crew so very loyal. She'd even praised Percy on one or two occasions. Not that he was counting. Not that he needed it, of course. He knew his own worth. Still, it was nice to be appreciated.

I wonder what would happen if I praised someone? Virgil perhaps? He'd likely expire on the spot from the shock.

Rue promised Spoo extra biscuits at tea for her perspicaciousness. *And there you have it; she's never given me extra biscuits for my navigation.*

Virgil grinned (Spoo slotted him one of the bickies) and then turned his eagle eye on Percy's loose cravat. Percy batted him away. Everyone generally relaxed under the realisation that they were all still alive and the leak was fixed.

Now, how to get more helium?

If she had any sense at all, thought Percy, *my sister would come haring down here with a refill tube. That's assuming one would stretch.*

But she hasn't any sense, and it's after sunrise so no doubt Sekhmet is fast asleep and my sister is having kittens over holing up with only the werecat for company.

"Percy, isn't it splendid? We aren't leaking anymore." Rue turned her big broad smile on him.

"Splendid," grumbled Percy.

Then his semi-nemesis, Quesnel Lefoux, the chief engineer, poked his head abovedecks.

Rue ran at him, wrapped her arms about him octopus-like, and then practically picked him up in her enthusiasm. As a general rule, it was Quesnel who liked to twirl Rue about, but with his shoulder currently sporting a bullet hole, it was for Rue to do the lion's share of the twirling.

"We fixed it!" crowed Rue. "Well, Spoo did, but still, it's patched at last."

"So I hear, *chérie*. Good news indeed. Well done, Miss Spoo."

"Thank you, sir."

Quesnel didn't kiss Rue, thank heavens, because they were abovedecks and the whole crew was scattered about – battening down, sewing up, and hatching things or what have you. Percy was grateful for the man's restraint. One didn't expect it from a Frenchman. Percy would rather not witness blatant affections. He knew they occurred, of course. Quesnel and Rue had been, well, *Quesnel and Rue* for going on a month now. It's only that Rue was like a sister to him and, simply put, *no*. It was a little like watching someone eat and enjoy a food you disliked. He was happy *they* enjoyed it, and happy he didn't have to eat it, but that didn't mean he wanted to watch someone else swallow and belch happily.

But Rue, who never stayed still very long anyway, was already back dashing about issuing orders and gesturing for things to be put away and repairs to be undertaken.

"Check over the rest of the balloon as well, please. If that leak went unnoticed for so long, I want to make absolutely certain we have no other squeakers. Willard, draw up a grid rotation and have the decklings climb the entirety, so as not to miss a spot."

Willard, the deckhand, nodded and began barking out orders of his own. Percy wondered why he never used the small amplification cone that dangled from his belt expressly for that purpose. Then he wondered at the dissemination of sound within the grey. He hadn't noticed whether sound was affected by aether immersion, but then he hadn't bothered to conduct tests.

Percy sucked his teeth and tried to communicate mentally with his twin. *Bring us helium.* There was some research to suggest twins had odd supernatural abilities of communication. Percy didn't believe a word of it. He rarely understood what his sister *said* half the time, let alone what she did or thought. But it was worth a try. *Perhaps it only works with identical twins.*

Then Rue rounded on him. "Percy, what are you doing?"

"Hoping my sister grows some sense and thinks to acquire helium and transport it to us. I think it's more likely she'll find it up there than we will down here." He hoped his gesture indicated his contempt for the very pretty, but highly useless, creamy sandy beach over which they now bobbed.

"Oh, that would be nice." Rue looked delighted by the idea of Primrose coming to their rescue. She had unremitting faith in Primrose. It was sweet. *Misplaced, but sweet.*

Percy moved them on from the disappointment no doubt inherent in his sister's future actions, or lack thereof. "Apart from that, I was wondering about sound transference abilities within contained aetherosphere, and whether the same limits exist as imposed by our standard atmosphere on verbal communication ranges."

As always, when he told someone what he was really thinking about, they got flustered and frustrated with him. Or he assumed that's what Rue's slightly bug-eyed expression meant. Percy never understood that. Didn't she find the idea *fascinating?*

He continued rambling, because it *was* quite fascinating. "I should go see if I have a copy of Korbouz's *Treatise on Sound Direction and Reverberations of the Human Cavity* on board. I don't think he thought to test it in aether, possibly because he published before the aetherosphere had been charted, but perhaps he had a follow-up pamphlet with the Royal Society and – "

"Percy!" Rue had *that* tone of voice. The tone that said Percy had drifted and verbalised a great deal more than anyone but he cared to hear.

Self-conscious, he crossed his arms and glared at her. "What?"

"Would you be a doll and check on our prisoner?" Rue gave him her most winning smile. It was a nice smile. She was pretty enough. She wasn't asking too much, was she?

Percy grimaced. Rue kept doing this to him. For some reason, he was the only one who seemed at all able to tolerate Rodrigo Tarabotti, otherwise known as Rue's cousin, otherwise known as their prisoner. This was odd, not the least because, as already mentioned, Percy disliked most everyone. And most everyone disliked Percy. But with Rodrigo – and yes, they were somehow on a first-name basis – this established mutual dislike had proved a foundation of something ... more.

Rodrigo, as it turned out, was disposed to dislike people too. And Percy appreciated that in a man.

Percy sighed. "Fine, if you insist. But I don't see why I have to be the one to do it all the time."

"You're the only one he hasn't tried to kill. Yet."

Percy frowned. "Are you sure? There were a lot of guns shooting during that attack of his. I distinctly remember being fired at."

"Oh, Percy. Just go see if he's bumped or damaged anything serious during our fall from the skies. Or died. We can't have him smelling up the place."

Percy sighed. "If you insist." He paused, remembering his position. "Very good, Captain."

Percy was terrified of most females in the region of his own age – apart from Rue and Prim, of course. That was because, for some strange reason he'd yet to fathom, strange young females always seemed bent on fluttering their eyelashes at him, or trying to talk to him about silly things, or, at the very least, trapping him into an assignation. It's a horrible thing to be the near-constant victim of strategically applied eyelash fluttering. Drove a man to despair over all manner of things, from the state of the universe to the efficaciousness of a pudding course. Percy didn't like to be put off his feed by anything, let alone a misapplied eyelash. *I mean to say, who jolly well would?*

Despite the prevalence of feminine wiles in his social interactions, which had resulted in him becoming hell-bent on avoiding both wiles and society, Percy knew himself well enough to be confident that he preferred the female form. He'd experimented at Eton – who didn't? After all, hypothesis, thesis, and experimentation was the only proper scientific path to truth. Thus he was tolerably certain, after continued observation of Lord Akeldama and his handsome drones, that his own biological preferences lay in the region of internal sexual organs rather than external ones. Not to be clinical, but there it was. Percy had continued modest research to his own satisfaction, and hopefully the satisfaction of those few ladies he'd hired to finalise his studies. Thus Percy supposed he'd have to suck up his eyelash abhorrence and marry at some point, if only to satisfy his mother. He doubted his sister would be providing the grandchildren.

Why am I thinking about this right now? He climbed down the first set of ladders to the corridor that led to where they'd turned the smallest guest room into an improvised prison chamber. *Hannibal ad portas.*

He tapped on the door and then unlocked the dead bolt to let himself inside. The sootie on guard detail nodded at him and then bolted the door behind him, trapping him inside with their resident Italian.

Oh yes, that's why I was thinking it.

If Percy were the type of man to prefer the company of other men, Rodrigo Tarabotti would have tempted him.

To be fair, Rodrigo Tarabotti had *tried* to tempt him on several occasions. He was wily, and one of those wiles was seduction. And an apparent disregard for the gender of the object of said seduction.

Percy had been startled by the approach, and then amused and even a little flattered, but he put a definitive stop to the attempts some two weeks into Rodrigo's imprisonment. However, he could intellectually understand why such wiles might work on a gentleman less confirmed in his preferences.

Rodrigo was a swarthy Italian man, both he and Rue sharing their mutual grandfather's cheekbones, straight fierce eyebrows, dark wavy hair, and tan complexion. Rodrigo's nose was more pronounced and eyes deeper set and brown, not tawny. He had lashes most women would envy. Primrose had actually complained about them. *She would. And here I am, thinking about lashes again.*

"What happened?" the Italian demanded, the moment Percy stepped inside the cell.

Percy shrugged. "Bit of a blunder."

Rodrigo sneered at him. Italians were very good at sneering. Although, truth be told, this was Percy's first Italian, still he felt it was something they ought to be good at.

"*Basta.* What does it mean, this *blunder?*" Rodrigo shook his hands about while he complained. He always seemed to speak almost as much with his hands as his mouth. Percy was grateful; it did help them to understand each other better.

"We sort of, well, fell."

The man's dark eyes widened. "Fell? From where?"

"The sky."

"To where?"

"The beach. Well, almost but not quite."

Rodrigo tilted his head and made a frantic spiral gesture with his fingers around one temple. "Are you *folle?*"

"Crazy? Perhaps. Some have suggested this. But personally, no, I don't think so. And I fail to see what that has to do with this conversation."

"Are we *sicuro?*"

"Define *secure?*" Percy knew he was being difficult, but he did wish others took language and semantics more seriously. Imprecision was so very frustrating.

"We suffer the attack? There is the battle?"

Percy shook his head. "Not since you. No, we sprung a leak. It'll get fixed momentarily."

"When?" Both of Rodrigo's hands came up at this, as if in prayer.

Really, the constant gestures are fascinating. Are there any books on Italian that take into account this aspect of the language? If not, I should write a short paper on the subject. I should need an artist to assist. I wonder if Anitra can sketch? Percy rather liked Anitra, the ship's chief cultural liaison and interpreter (and sometime spy, but everyone has their foibles). She was a sensible girl, rarely said much, and never interrupted him in his library.

"Soon, I hope." Percy answered the man's question, if not his gestures. To be fair, the leak was already fixed, but Rodrigo didn't need details. He was, after all, a prisoner.

The Italian looked oddly relieved that the ship which held him captive was in no grave danger. He was a strange man. To come aboard and attempt to confiscate, or possibly kill, Rue, and then when he lost the battle to acquiesce with relative grace to being kept aboard for no other reason than that Rue had no idea what to do with him next. Technically, he'd attacked her outside the bounds of the British Empire. Being a native Italian, he wasn't really in violation of any laws that Queen Victoria could enforce. Aside, of course, from common human decency and the general feeling that one ought not to go around attempting to kidnap one's cousin all willy-nilly. Rue had turned over his men as poachers to the Germans in Zanzibar. But she met with some resistance when she attempted to confer responsibility for

Rodrigo himself, as ringleader and Templar agent. After much discussion, the German officers agreed to send an aetherogram to the Bureau of Unnatural Registry in London requesting advice. Since a metanatural and a foreign preternatural were involved – thank goodness Major Channing was in charge these days and knew all about Rue – BUR forwarded the correspondence to the Shadow Council. The Shadow Council concluded that this was a family affair and therefore Rodrigo Tarabotti and his disposition were Rue's problem. Which meant he was *The Spotted Custard*'s problem. Which meant he was Percy's problem.

"So where are we now? In the world." The Italian looked curiously out his tiny port window at the top of a palm tree just visible through it.

"Singapore."

"Ah."

"Ah what?" Percy knew that look. Rue wore that look when she was *up to something*.

"Might be good things, if Singapore did not know I am here."

"And why is that, Mr Tarabotti?" *As if we told anyone you were aboard ever.*

"I think I might be – how do you say? – wanted for a kill in Singapore."

"Oh, Mr Tarabotti, have you been murdering people again?"

"It was ... some time ago. But still." He shrugged broad shoulders and raised his hands up.

"As you do."

The man inclined his head.

Percy enquired, without sarcasm and out of genuine interest, "Is there anywhere you aren't wanted for murder?"

"Italy."

"Of course."

"Although ..." Rodrigo let himself trail off and looked thoughtfully down at his own large rough hands.

"Yes?"

"They might want me dead now too."

This was an interesting turn of events. "Why would they want that? I thought you were one of the Templars' best agents."

"Sì, sì, but I am of the soulless. We have the history."

Percy cocked an eyebrow. "Oh yes, what history is that?"

"Of the . . . how do you say? Going to the native. Left away from the Templars too long. We go bad. Or I say, for you, we go less bad. How long have I been here, on little cousin's ship?"

"A month or so."

"Sì. So I think it."

"So you thought," corrected Percy. "But what does that matter?"

"I near the end date."

"You mean, if you are away too long the Templars consider you a traitor to the cause?"

"Sì."

"Because why? Because you turn against their corrupt and evil teachings through exposure to outside influence and logic?"

Rodrigo looked surprised at Percy's vehement interest. "Well, yes. Sì."

Percy considered him in all seriousness. "Do you think it's something you're likely to do?"

"What?"

"Go native."

The Italian stared at Percy for a long moment. "You are – how you say? – a strange poultry, Professor Tunstell. Are you not?"

"An odd duck? Well, I don't think so, but I suppose my opinion doesn't count for much in the matter of other people's impressions of myself. Would you like to talk more about the Templars' philosophical stance on the matter of soulless integration?"

Percy had found in Rodrigo a decent mind and a top-quality philosophical debating partner – aside from the language barrier, of course. Percy spoke only limited Italian, although his Latin was excellent. And Rodrigo wasn't exactly fluent in English. Nevertheless, they'd spent many an evening over the last few weeks debating the general Templar beliefs, impressed upon

Rodrigo from an early age, that preternaturals were a kind of demon. Soulless killing machines meant only to do God's dirty work, at the Templars' request. Percy found this entire philosophy preposterous and was delighted to poke as many holes into the theory as he could, long into the night on several occasions. Rodrigo was a willing partner in such conversation. Or perhaps he simply liked the company. Had to be lonely, being a prisoner. Not that Percy got lonely; he had his books. Which he'd taken to loaning to Rodrigo as well. Which sparked more conversation. They imbibed too many cups of tea and moved on to the general question of balancing science with religion, and whether that was even possible, and from there into theories on the state of the aetherosphere, the universe, and even the rise and fall of civilisations and whether the integration of the supernatural and preternatural was an effective bellwether for cultural longevity.

Percy was no judge of character. His sister had informed him, on more than one occasion, that he was, in fact, decidedly poor at it. He supposed one had to like people in order to really understand them. Yet while Percy, generally, did not like people, he found, despite himself, that he liked Rodrigo Tarabotti.

Oh, he wasn't going to do anything stupid. The man hadn't persuaded him of anything, but he was fun to argue with. It occurred to Percy to wonder, now, if perhaps he had persuaded Rodrigo of something. If perhaps he, Percy, had managed to change the man's general inclination to kill everyone aboard. Or whatever it was he wanted with Rue . . . and the rest of the crew by proxy.

It'd be rather an unexpected perk if I did. Considering it was all unconsciously done and I have never, to my knowledge, effected a profound change on any gentleman's moral fibre. At least, I don't think I have.

Oddly, Percy wished his sister were here. She would know. Primrose could come in and figure out what was going on in this man's head. She was good like that. Persuasive with men.

Rodrigo certainly found her appealing. *Now that's a disgusting thought.*

Unless he prefers men, in which case maybe I could get Quesnel to seduce him to our cause.

Do we have a cause?

Bah, thought Percy, *I'm not good at this kind of thing.*

So he switched topics. "Have you had a chance to read the paper I gave you?"

"Ah, the one on the *moral fibre versus ethical standing as pertains to excess soul and the creative mind?*" Rodrigo read out the English words carefully, pulling the small pamphlet out from under his pillow.

Percy nodded. "What did you think?"

Rodrigo turned to settle back on his bed. Percy, as was his custom, folded himself awkwardly onto the small tuffet that was the only other piece of furniture in the room.

Footnote, his cat, came to sit on his feet. He'd no idea how the cat had got into the cell, but one didn't question Footnote on his feline abilities. So Percy simply reached down to scratch him about the ears.

Primrose had a decidedly civilised lunch at a very international tearoom by herself. It served all forms of tea, but seemed confused by her request for milk to go with the leaf, so eventually she gave up and drank it black. After much menu confusion, she ended up with an array of what appeared from the outside to be small hot cross buns, but which were filled with meat, or fruit paste, or meat paste – odd but not unpalatable. The bun part had a pleasant sweet squishiness to it, and Prim found she rather enjoyed the whole concept. Wonderful how most cultures develop, relatively quickly, a means of transporting a meat item inside a bread item.

She thought fondly of Cornish pasties. And then purchased a dozen more of the little buns to feed the werecat when she awoke. Fortified, she then went off to investigate the refuelling stations. There did appear to be several helium suppliers aboard but they all expected, not illogically, to tube over a supply to a waiting dockside ship, not tank a dose to the surface. Giving up that quest by teatime, Prim turned her attention to simply getting herself and Tasherit groundside, given that then at least they'd be reunited with *The Spotted Custard* and crew.

There seemed to be very few ways to get to the surface. Most of them were independent high-flyer services – a large omnibus dirigible drop left every hour, but stopped running at sundown. The dockworkers used a freight transport, but Prim would need a local licence to board that.

Which left the higher-risk, privately operated dropsies as her only real option. They were odd mushroom-shaped things, helium filled up top (Prim perked up at that), air-ballast filled below, but weight-balanced for the drop. Which is to say they took on a mess of passengers and it was the sheer weight of those passengers that drove them to ground. Once there, the bottom of the transport opened up and everyone inside, except the driver, fell out. Without the weight, the dropsy instantly bobbed right back up to repeat the process over again. The dropsies were tethered loosely to vertical wires, but at their hearts they were rudimentary contraptions. Quesnel would have sneered at the engineering, for marvels of mechanical invention they were *not*. Percy would have sneered at the design, for exemplars of modern scientific theory they were *not*, either. But they were dangerous, which Rue would have enjoyed, and they were practical, which Prim modestly appreciated.

She did not, however, appreciate their general mushroom appearance, or the rough-and-tumble way in which they were operated. They were run by frankly suspicious sorts of people. They were patched-up, dirty, messy-looking creatures, both dropsy and dropsy captain. Untrustworthy, Primrose felt. Still, with no other option...

Also, at her best guess as proud purser of *The Spotted Custard*, one dropsy was probably packing enough helium to load over to the *Custard* and get a rise out of her. Which meant, while Primrose hated to think so poorly of herself, she was already trying to come up with a plan to steal one of them.

Primrose strolled along the edge of the dropsy lineup, trying not to look suspicious. She wished she had a parasol with her, parasols always helped one look less suspicious. The straw hat was doing its best for her, but a parasol was always a great deal more effective. In this part of the wheystation anyone of Prim's dress and mannerisms was a little out of place, but she thought she managed to avoid too much notice.

She found the largest and most disreputable-looking dropsy and met up with the equally large and disreputable individual who appeared to be in charge of passenger drops. She arranged a fare for two adult females, average weight (although she thought Tasherit might be on the denser end of things as a werecat but wasn't going to admit that to anyone), for just after sundown, when the dropsies began running. Prim guessed dropsies waited until the omnibuses stopped and then picked up the fares of those passengers who had missed the last puff down and were desperate for another method of grounding.

Plan at least somewhat in place, Prim then ambled casually off and spent a little more time wandering the station pretending to be a tourist, in case she was followed. She knew she was an odd case, a wealthy young lady better suited to the omnibus – why wait until nighttime transport? So she had to occupy herself with reasons to whittle away the day that might explain the delay. She was self-conscious to be rambling about on her own without escort, but it seemed to be not unusual in this part of the world. She noticed a number of females, in various different types of attire and of ranging ages, alone and without appropriate companions.

After some consideration, Primrose paid a visit to the garment district, where she found a truly lovely iridescent teal-and-blue-taffeta bolt, some needles and thread, and a basket full of lovely large shell buttons of the imitation black pearl variety.

Another teahouse for her afternoon repast and Primrose returned to the hotel, shopping in hand, ideas forming, and a rather crafty grin on her pretty face.

CHAPTER

THREE

A Merlion in a Mushroom

Primrose spent a pleasant afternoon in the hotel, the bellman supplying her with seemingly endless pots of tea in an oddly desperate manner that suggested her approval of said tea was paramount for his continued existence. *Certificate of merit to the bellman*, Primrose felt, bestowing upon him a grateful smile each and every time, which only added to his desperation.

Tasherit remained oblivious to the bellman's antics, the sun confining her to motionlessness. She curled in a silent ball in the exact middle of the bed, on top of the coverlet but under a throw, which Prim had insisted upon for the sake of the bellman (and her own sensibilities, of course). Prim found her presence there oddly comforting, despite the near nudity. The bellman found it confusing.

Primrose (sipping tea) happily measured, stitched, fashioned, pleated, and hummed quietly to herself. It was a rushed job, but it came out better than she might have hoped. She imagined it must have been like this in her pre-memory childhood, when her parents had run a successful acting troupe. No doubt Mr and Mrs Tunstell spent many pleasant afternoons together assembling costumes in anticipation of an evening performance. Aunt Alexia had much to say on the subject of those costumes. *Outrageous*, *scandalous*, and *life altering* were only a few of the words she had used. Primrose believed it. After all, her mother's taste had not altered noticeably with the advent of her father's demise or her vampiric state. It would be impossible to believe Ivy Tunstell had controlled herself when treading the boards.

Not quite sure on size, Primrose chose a drawstring for the waist. She figured no one would look too closely. It would be hidden by fur anyway, if things went according to plan.

The sun eventually set, which Prim noticed only because Tasherit stirred and stretched languidly. Her almond eyes blinked open and she immediately focused on Primrose.

"What are you doing so industriously, little one?"

"Making you a fishtail," said Prim, in a tone of voice that suggested this ought to be perfectly obvious.

"What has happened while I've been sleeping?" The werecat sat up in bed and, in clear deference to Prim's modesty rather than her own, wrapped the throw about her as she sat on the edge.

"There's yummy meat bun things there." Prim pointed to the little cluster she had placed on a low table. "They're cold, I'm afraid, but tasty. And there's tea in the pot, of course, if you wish." Tasherit usually just drank the contents of the creamer, but one should always *offer* tea even if one's guest had questionable beverage habits. It was best to assume that a non-tea drinker might, at any moment, develop refinement. Fortunately, this hotel was accustomed to young ladies who took milk with their black tea. Or at least, did not question the extraordinary affectation.

Tasherit focused in on the small pitcher, licking her plump lips eagerly.

"As we are where we are, do you think I might have pu-erh?" The werecat glanced over at her briefly in question.

Primrose did not try to hide her flinch. "You could, but why would you want to?"

The werecat shrugged. "Developed a taste for it last century. I always liked how it sounded, the name I mean, kind of like *purr*." She made the rumbling noise in her throat.

Primrose tilted her head. "Except that you don't."

Tasherit looked up from enjoying one of the little buns. "Don't what?"

"Purr."

"You noticed?" Those lovely almond eyes crinkled in pleasure. Well, the buns were delicious.

Primrose returned to her shell button decorating, nipping a thread cleanly with her teeth and declining to answer.

"I always thought it'd be fun to purr, but we lions are roaring cats. And one must, of course, be one or the other."

"Why?" Primrose was curious.

The werelioness shrugged. "No idea, it's simply the way it is. So, about this fishtail?"

Prim explained her plan, and their imminent transport to ground, and how the two were tied together with a possible misappropriation of helium.

"Speaking of, we'd better get dressed and settle the hotel account. The dropsy leaves in half an hour and I'd like to get there early enough to choose the right positioning."

Tasherit looked as if she'd like to object to the plan, as after all it required her to make a fool of herself. Cats, as a rule, were opposed to such endeavours. But she clearly could not construct a superior one. Or she could, but hers likely would result in bystanders becoming injured. Primrose's scheme was worth a try, and even if it failed, at least the two of them would be groundside and closer to their friends.

They arrived at the station in good time. Their dropsy couldn't depart until it had sufficient weight allotment, so everyone was being weighed as they boarded. A sort of lever-scale with a funny crank-and-piston arrangement cantilevered a plank outwards that stretched to the basket edge of the dropsy.

Primrose carried her carpetbag. It was now carefully packed full of fishtail as well as correspondences, her daytime straw hat (she'd switched back to her evening one), and wacker. *Wacker* being a crass colloquial name for a particularly delicate and rather expensive augmentation a-directional puffer (advertised as: *ideal for improving upon the old-fashioned balloon in one's life*). She trod the weight plank carefully. It was a great embarrassment to have oneself weighed in public, and no doubt a key reason the omnibus was the preferred transport of the upper crust, but needs must.

Tasherit came after. Whatever she weighed seemed to surprise the guide in charge of the dropsy, because the large female made the werecat get off the plank and then get back on.

Miss Sekhmet said something curt in some language Primrose did not know and the guide waved her aboard.

"You're denser than you look, aren't you?" Prim asked, as they settled into the best positioning for the next stage of her scheme, on the opposite side of the basket from where a strap kept them leashed to the wheystation's guideline.

Miss Sekhmet arched a perfectly shaped eyebrow. "All cats are denser then they look, especially if on top of a human. Which I'd be happy to demonstrate at any time."

Primrose sputtered at the blatancy of that comment, although it was no doubt intended to be seductive. She was struck by the not unpleasant vision of Tasherit sprawled atop her, pressing Prim into some feathered and pillowy bedding, all silks and sweet sandalwood smells.

Of course, Primrose instantly changed the subject. *I really must watch my tongue around this woman. She does take advantage of any opening. And now I'm wondering about tongues.* It wasn't really fair, with a werecat, to think on tongues. *I mean to say, how much of that agile dexterity translates between forms? That's what I'd like to know. Or perhaps that's what I don't want to know. Or really shouldn't be thinking about at all.*

Plan. Fishtails. Stop it, Primrose Tunstell, right now!

Sometimes, around Miss Sekhmet, Prim rather lost track of her own brain, which was not only careless but highly dangerous.

She busied herself watching their fellow passengers climbing aboard, pleased to see they seemed to be mainly locals, or at least not anyone who might cry false on the next stage of her hijacking scheme. This was the kind of situation where an academic or scientist type of Percy's ilk could muck everything up.

But isn't that always the case with schemes?

If Primrose were Rue, she would have jumped right into the dropsy without any kind of plan in place. As it was, Prim had a plan, but she didn't think it was a very good one. Unfortunately, this proved to be the case about halfway through its execution.

She and Tasherit sat in their semi-secluded section of the dropsy basket. Still, they and the other passengers were all rather packed in together, so there was no real privacy of any kind. Thus it was understandably difficult to get a werelioness to look like a merlion without people following what was actually occurring.

Consequently it was imperative that Primrose herself become a distraction. This was not entirely in accordance with her nature. Prim did not consider herself a self-effacing individual. She was not *afraid* to be centre stage; she was simply not *accustomed* to it. After over twenty years of intimacy with Prudence Akeldama, Primrose was usually not the one others gawped at. When one's very best friend in the entire world happens to be a scientific anomaly meets enthusiastic adventurer meets excitable harridan of tiny yet epic proportions, one becomes accustomed to remaining modestly in the background. One also becomes accustomed to cleaning up after a great number of messes, but not causing them oneself.

Primrose took a deep breath. At this moment, life was calling upon her to be profoundly messy.

After assisting a grumpy and decidedly disgruntled Miss Sekhmet to climb into the fishtail – while keeping said tail hidden underneath Tasherit's conveniently full and flowing silk robes – Prim made her way ostentatiously to the opposite side of the basket.

There she arranged herself to look back and up at the station, staring with focused intensity at something that was clearly very upsetting to a woman of her delicate sensibilities. Whatever it was did not exist, but Primrose had learned over the years that if a young lady looked with great interest at nothing at all, eventually most people in the crowd around her wanted to know what she was looking at.

Soon enough she had her dozen or so travelling companions all looking intently in the same direction. Then she made a tiny gasping noise, just a small one – small noises were generally more effective than loud ones – and raised up her gloved hand to point in obvious shock and horror at the continued nothing. Now everyone was looking either at her or whatever it was that had upset her.

Primrose trusted Miss Sekhmet to take that opportunity to drop her robe and shift forms. Now everyone was distracted, including their guide, trying to determine what it was that had their fashionable young female aristocrat passenger so increasingly upset. Primrose pretended to stumble forward. She made yet another small whimpering sound and allowed her pointing hand to shake slightly. She was pleased to note her lavender gloves emphasised the trembling.

The guide moved towards her and said in a cross but not unsympathetic voice, "What is it, young miss? What has upset you so?" She was a large gruff weather-beaten lady who reminded Prim of their head greaser, Aggie Phinkerlington, in attitude if not appearance.

"It appears as if we are losing our attachment to the station, good lady." They weren't, of course, but give Primrose a little time and she would fix that. At the moment, she was merely trying to keep attention away from Tasherit.

The guide leaned next to her and squinted up into the darkness. She even raised a spyglass to one eye. The wheystation proper was now some distance above them. It was relatively well lit with gas lighting and lanterns and the like, but the scaffolding part was not intentionally illuminated. Unlike the Maltese Tower, this wheystation was not occupied with residents and workers all the way up and down its length. It was only about a tenth the size, and situated some considerable distance below the aetherosphere. No one had felt it necessary to light the base of the station – waste of resources.

At this juncture, as per their previous arrangement, Miss Sekhmet let out a great roar. Primrose had never heard her roar so loudly before. It was impressive but also sounded a great deal more like a very loud coughing fit than Prim felt a roar ought to sound. Not precisely threatening so much as worrying in an *imminent expectoration* kind of way. Still, it was good enough to get everybody's attention away from the *possible* threat of drifting slightly off their downward course, focusing instead on the *actual* threat of suddenly occupying their dropsy with a lion. Or more precisely . . . a *merlion*.

At a modest distance – which is what the passengers were currently giving Miss Sekhmet as they backed away, pressing hard against each other – Prim's handiwork in terms of tails was actually not bad. It did, in fact, seem to everyone assembled that they shared their transport with a creature the top part of which was a lioness and the bottom part of which was a shimmering iridescent fish. It wasn't a sensible, or logical, or realistic creature in any way, but if one was prone to believing that a half fish, half lion existed, then this was a pretty decent approximation of said creature's presentation in reality.

Miss Sekhmet had lifted herself up and arranged her body in such a way that the lioness portion was leaning up against the side of the dropsy basket while the fishtail draped gracefully down to the floor.

Primrose suspected that she was the only one to notice that there appeared to be an enthusiastically moving bulge in the back section of the fishtail. No doubt this was the lioness's actual tail, twitching in annoyance. Or perhaps it was lashing at the embarrassment of having been put into such a position.

It was an odd thing, a tail trapped inside a tail. It bore a striking resemblance to what Primrose imagined those ferrets-down-trousers fellows looked like. Or perhaps more a boa constrictor inside a taffeta sack. Nevertheless, the fear over the sudden presence of a roaring lioness-with-a-fishtail distracted from the strange bulging behaviour of said fishtail.

As previously arranged, Primrose seized this opportunity to finally separate the dropsy from its leash to the wheystation drop line. She used a letter opener to accomplish this. It was perhaps not proper for a young lady of Primrose's consequence to gallivant about sporting a letter opener, especially a double-edged one kept impoliticly sharp, but she had found over the years that a small letter opener discreetly tucked about one's person could be endlessly useful. She never regretted carrying one, and always regretted when she didn't.

It was a little *too* easy to slice through the lead that held them to the station line. It had once been made of a sturdy leather but was not well maintained, and repeated exposure to sun and weather had made it weak. This gave Primrose some pause as to the general safety of the dropsy, but there was no going back now.

She popped open her trusty carpetbag, pulled out the wacker, put the device to drape over the edge of the dropsy basket, and pressed the release cord. The wacker was a primitive safety device that she'd purchased at the station that morning. At the release of tension it began a quiet whirring noise and the dropsy began to push away from its previous trajectory. It was one of those devices that required actual manual labour to wind up, but then it exuded power and force as a release of mechanical tension. Quesnel would have sneered at its primitive structure, but it was extremely useful when one didn't have access to steam power. It only worked for twenty minutes before it needed to be wound again, but Primrose had calculated that they shouldn't need more than twenty minutes. Even if they did, the wacker would at least set them in the correct direction.

At this juncture, Miss Sekhmet began to direct them in said direction. They'd prearranged a series of noises she would make.

A roar and Primrose needed to shift them slightly left, a hiss and they needed to jog slightly right, silence and they would stay the course.

This was, of course, where Prim's plan fell apart. Because everything was predicated on the werecat being able to ascertain the location of *The Spotted Custard* below them. They had assumed that their ship's landing was within some short recognisable distance of the station, and they had assumed that said landing would be within a relatively well-lit area of Singapore and civilisation.

Unfortunately, this did not appear to be the case. Firstly, Singapore was a smaller city than Prim previously thought. Its buildings were mainly centred about a large dark harbour, with the strait and the wheystation being more occupied than the port itself. Secondly, it was nighttime, so hard to see anything. Thirdly, the *Custard* had clearly drifted away from the populated area. And, of course, Rue's crew was not inclined to illuminate their actions as a rule.

Prim dug about for her opera glasses and, leaning dangerously over the side, determined that, even assisted, she could not spot the *Custard* in the darkness of beach, plantation, and tropical foliage that made up Singapore's environs. Primrose had no idea what direction they ought to be heading in, and Tasherit certainly didn't either.

Nevertheless, the werecat continued to roar and hiss, guiding Primrose *somewhere*. Prim hoped that at least they were staying over land instead of drifting out over the ocean. The dropsy guide and other occupants of the basket seemed wholly unaware of the fact they were now untethered and entirely adrift as they sank slowly into the darkness.

Percy didn't have a function aboard ship when said ship wasn't in motion, at least not in any official capacity. After all, when

one's ship was grounded and anchored to a palm tree, it's not as
if a navigator could be of much assistance. What would he do,
calculate the bendability of the palm tree? He didn't even have
the next stage of their journey to chart. Rue had yet to tell him
where they were headed after Singapore.

But that was his life under Captain Prudence. Full of uncer-
tainty. It was bally annoying.

After running out of conversation with Rodrigo when the
man became distracted by Anitra bringing in dinner, Percy
went to his library.

The library was Percy's sanctuary. It was crowded with books
and the slightly musty ink smell of knowledge and comfort.
Footnote greeted him upon arrival, the black-and-white tom
rubbing his legs a few times in the classic cat fashion of *this might
be love or this might be attempted murder by tripping cleverly disguised
as affection.* Difficult to tell with cats. Percy, knowing his duty,
gave Footnote the requisite head scratches and received a flop
and minor ankle-nibble for his pains.

Intrigued by his previous rumination on the nature of sound
within aether, Percy went foraging about for any treatises he
might have collected on the subject and became lost in the data
for an unspecified amount of time.

"Sir!"

Percy looked up. Virgil stood next to him. It was also now
dark outside.

"Yes?" Percy did not try to tame the grumpiness in his voice.
He hated to be disturbed while he was reading. Of course, he
was always reading, but that did not signify.

Virgil gave him the *you are in trouble* look developed early
by all good valets. Not the *you are in big trouble because there was
something you were supposed to do as navigator and forgot about, and
now Rue is on the rampage* look, but only the *you are in trouble for
some other silly reason that likely has to do with manners* look.

Primrose, darling sister that she was, called this the universal
why must you be so very Percy? expression.

Percy patted at his own chest and neck. *I'm wearing clothing. I even have on a cravat. Feels a little loose. I appear to have lost my jacket and hat somewhere, but it's a small ship, they can't have gone far, and I'm technically within in the sanctity of my own quarters.* "What is it, Virgil?"

"Did you eat, sir?"

Percy frowned. *Did I eat?* "Anitra brought victuals round to Mr Tarabotti and myself in his, erm, quarters. But I might have left before consuming anything. Can't remember. Conversation had flagged."

"I don't like how friendly you are with that Italian scutter."

"Don't be absurd, Virgil, I'm friendly with no one."

Virgil glared. "You *talk* to him, all the time."

"He's interesting. Odd perspective on the state of the universe. I blame his upbringing."

"He could be corrupting you. Sir." The *sir* was added with great reluctance.

"Funny you should say that, Virgil. I was recently worrying that perhaps I was corrupting *him*."

"What do you mean, sir?"

"He seems to be coming round to my way of thinking. You know..." Percy waved a hand airily.

"He is?" Virgil sounded genuinely shocked.

Percy bristled. "Well, and why shouldn't he? It is, after all, the correct way of thinking."

Virgil looked confused. "It is?"

"Of course it is. It's mine, after all." Percy felt this should be perfectly obvious, even to Virgil.

Which is when the only other person allowed to break the sanctity of Percy's library joined their conversation.

"Preternaturals are ethically malleable," explained Formerly Floote, shimmering into existence through a bookcase in that uncanny way he had. Percy was impressed by ghostly abilities. He thought he'd like to be a ghost one day, although it wasn't likely at all. There was nothing creative about Percy. In fact, he rather abhorred creativity – so illogical. No one would ever accuse Percy of excess soul.

The ghost glided over and began reading over Percy's shoulder. Percy had found this habit rather annoying (not to say rude) at first. But Formerly Floote possessed a keen mind and an active interest in advanced learning, and Percy wasn't one to kick any-one out for that, even if he was dead. Besides, it's not like he could pick up a book and turn the pages himself.

Also, Formerly Floote didn't say much. Percy admired that in a chap. Although the ghost had said something just now. Only Percy forgot what that was.

Virgil looked at the ghost.

So did Percy.

Formerly Floote was in excellent condition for a month-old ghost. Quesnel had stuck him into some kind of advanced pres-ervation tank, developed specifically with him in mind. The tank kept Floote's body in perfect condition during daytime and aether transport, and allowed just enough aetheric connection at night in atmosphere for Formerly Floote to manifest throughout the public areas of the airship. His range, most of the time, was not unlike Footnote's.

Percy remembered the thing about preternaturals and wiggly ethics and asked with interest, "Exactly how malleable are they, morally speaking?"

The ghost shook his head. "No morals."

Percy frowned at this and Virgil looked smug. The little valet didn't trust Mr Tarabotti. Not that Percy did, but Virgil had residual feelings about the Italian trying to shoot his deckling friends. Percy supposed this might make a lad like Virgil, all vibrating energy and young passion, a tad vindictive. Then again, Percy was tolerably certain that Rodrigo had tried to shoot him, Percival Tunstell, twice. Percy had nearly killed Rodrigo as well. But none of these attempts had been at all personal. Frankly, Percy was accustomed to offending people into near murderous rages. When someone actually tried to pot him off, it felt endearingly honest.

Percy narrowed his eyes, considering the ghost's terse words. "Ah yes, because morality is linked to the soul and preternaturals don't have souls."

Formerly Floote nodded. "Hence the importance of an *ethical* grounding. Mr Tarabotti has never had one. Neither did his father. Or his grandfather, for that matter."

"Your original master." Percy considered. "But he changed, did he not, at the end? That first Mr Tarabotti? I mean to say, the story goes that he tried to kill a werewolf gone mad. For the good of society."

Formerly Floote looked thoughtful. His wispy blue-white form drifted as he lost a bit of control over himself in contemplation of the past. "Is that what you believe?"

Percy shrugged. He didn't like the word *believe*. Things were either true or they weren't, there was no *believe*.

"Is that not what happened?" He tested for veracity. Formerly Floote should know. Floote was there.

The valet-turned-butler-turned-secretary-turned-spy-turned-dead merely nodded. "In a way."

Percy shook himself. This was not important, the past was irrelevant. The past was, most of the time, wrong. "So if we give Rodrigo Tarabotti some ethics, will he come around and stop trying to kill or kidnap us?"

Formerly Floote looked even more thoughtful. This was odd, on a ghost, as if his manifestation were trying to access his corporeal brain meats, which were, of course, no longer active. "It's possible."

Virgil glared at Percy. "I hardly think you are the one to do it." He paused, then reluctantly added, "Sir."

Percy thought he ought to be affronted. "Why not? We're oddly friendly, Mr Tarabotti and I."

"Well, sir, no offence, but you're rather shaky with all things moral and ethical yourself."

Percy thought he ought to be even more affronted, but he found this to be more like a compliment than not. It implied that he never allowed his scientific analysis of a situation to be troubled by how the rest of the world thought it ought to be. "I'm a perfectly decent human being."

"You're constantly losing your hat, sir."

Percy sniffed. "I hardly see how hats have any bearing on this situation."

Both Virgil (his valet) and Formerly Floote (once a valet) looked utterly appalled by this statement.

"The height of one's top hat brings you closer to God," intoned Virgil. Which explained why he was always trying to get Percy to wear a stovepipe.

"*Vox nihili*. What a preposterous statement," objected Percy. He straightened his spine, stood up, and went to rummage about in the philosophy and ethics section of his library. Admittedly a small collection, but there were a few good bits on logic from those ancient Greek fellows. Terribly philosophical, of course, and prone to swanning about in their nightshirts, but a solid starter to a quest for ethical stability and in life's mysteries. Might as well begin with them. "I shall give these to Mr Tarabotti next. We will convert him to our side."

Formerly Floote whispered at him, "And how, exactly, would you define *our side*, Professor Tunstell?"

Virgil looked equally intrigued. "Yes, sir, how?"

Percy glared at them. "The superior one, of course. Now stop bothering me, I have aether noise transfers to investigate."

Virgil seemed to recollect himself at that juncture. "Actually, sir, you're wanted on deck."

"I am? But we aren't going anywhere."

"No, but the captain thinks there might be someone coming after us."

"Hardly see how I can be of use."

"You hid it well, sir, but now we all know you're quite handy with a pistol. And there's the multiple language capacity as well."

Percy wrinkled his nose. He was actually also rather handy with his fives, but he'd never tell anyone *that*. Physical exertion of any kind gave him the vapours, and punching someone was so very violent.

Still, an order from his captain was not to be ignored, so he followed Virgil abovedecks dutifully, leaving behind his research with no little regret.

He bumped into Anitra in the hallway. The young lady was looking flustered – odd, as she was generally an admirably unflappable individual. He handed her the Greek logic books. "Would you give these to Mr Tarabotti next time he has a meal?"

She looked at them suspiciously. "Why?"

"Your ghostly grandfather and I were talking, and we thought it might be a good idea to get him started on a proper ethical foundation."

Anitra's dark eyes brightened. "Grandfather suggested it?"

Percy shrugged. "Apparently it's worked well in the past, on other Tarabottis."

Virgil interjected, "That's not exactly what he – "

Percy glared. "Hush, Virgil, no one asked your opinion."

Anitra looked unexpectedly pleased with the prospect. "You think he can be saved?"

Percy looked her up and down. Anitra was a pretty thing, a Drifter by birth and with all the fine strong features, big brown eyes, and tan skin one might expect from those of Ottoman descent. She even had dimples. Percy found her very pleasing, but more for her soundness of mind than her lithe appearance. It mattered not either way, she was without a doubt not interested in him for any kind of liaison. Her eyes were always friendly in their evaluation of his own form, but never hot.

Percy wasn't fussed, he was pleased to have her goodwill over her romantic interest. The former was a great deal more comfortable than the latter. The latter might have involved eyelash fluttering. Anitra had such very long and thick eyelashes, he might not have been able to resist.

"Saved? Saved from what?" wondered Percy.

"The gallows, of course."

Percy frowned. "Oh, I don't think anyone wishes to see Mr Tarabotti strung up, do they?"

Anitra seemed surprised. "Don't they? Isn't that your custom?" She paused. "Not even Mr Lefoux wants it?"

Percy considered this. Quesnel Lefoux had suffered the worst as a result of the Italian's attack. His injury was still not completely healed and there was a good chance he would never regain full use of his right arm. "You understand that there is no love lost between myself and Mr Lefoux, Miss Anitra? But I should never describe Lefoux as a vindictive man. Although he is French, and the French can be quite passionate about...everything."

Anitra seemed to lose her taste for this conversation. Percy wondered if he had stuck his foot into his mouth as per usual. Still, even as her attention drifted, her expression remained pleased, and she was clutching the Greek philosophers to her small bosom in a very ardent manner. Percy supposed there were some who felt ardent about Greek philosophy.

She said, a little breathlessly, "I shall take these to him immediately."

Formerly Floote materialised through the wall at that juncture, looking with ghostly affection at the young lady. "Granddaughter?"

"Grandfather! Professor Tunstell says Greek logic might save Mr Tarabotti and that you suggested this approach. Do you really think it possible?"

The ghost was confused. "Now, now, my child, that's a hasty supposition."

But she was off, trotting gracefully back down the hallway.

Formerly Floote rounded on Percy. "Now look what you've done, gone and raised her hopes!" With which the ghost hurriedly drifted after her.

Percy shook his head in utter confusion. He made his way up top. *Women. Women and ghosts. And now Greeks. What a tangle.*

Abovedecks everyone seemed to be looking at some kind of mushroom which was falling from the wheystation above and headed in their general direction.

Percy wandered over to Rue, who had an articulated spyglass to her eye and was squinting into it in a manner guaranteed to give a girl a headache.

"I see my sister is headed our way," said Percy, casually.

"Do you really think it's her?"

Percy gave his captain *a look*. "Who else would drop a mushroom on us?"

Rue nodded and continued staring through the glass.

Percy said, just in case stating the obvious hadn't already been done yet, "Bet it's a great deal harder for them to see us than it is for us to see them."

The mushroom, after all, was silhouetted perfectly against the brightness of the station above it, but it wasn't headed *directly* at them, and they were sunk into the obscuring darkness of beach and palm trees.

Rue jumped. "Oh, my, yes! How could I be so foolish? Thank you, Percy, we should send up a signal of some kind. Let them know where we are. Quesnel? Quesnel, where are you?"

The handsome Frenchman materialised out of Percy's navigation pit on the poop deck. Percy tensed. *What is he doing in my zone?*

Lefoux ambled over. "Yes, *chérie?*"

Rue said, knowing it would please her lover greatly, "Get out the fireworks, would you, my darling? This situation calls for sparkles."

Mr Lefoux dearly loved blowing things up. Percy found this inclination juvenile. Rue found it utterly charming. Percy supposed it was Rue's opinion that mattered, both as chief officer and semi-spousal affiliation.

"Did you want me for something else, Rue?" he asked, while Lefoux dashed off in pursuit of fireworks.

Rue grinned at him. "I had Quesnel check over the navigation pit. Everything seems to be in good working order."

"As it should be." Percy was affronted. "We sprang a helium leak, Rue, that's nothing to do with navigation."

"Better to be safe than sorry."

"There's no need for platitudes."

"I also wanted to ask you about our little Italian friend."

"Mr Tarabotti? We were just discussing him."

"Oh, were we? What we?"

"Virgil, Formerly Floote, Miss Anitra, and myself. Oh, and Footnote."

"Percy, that's a veritable tea party. You?"

"It wasn't by choice, Rue. Nor was it all at once. Footnote was party to the first, Anitra to the second."

Rue grinned at him, tawny eyes sparkling almost as much as the fireworks soon would. "And what did you conclude?"

"Prevailing opinion seems to be in favour of a possible ethical reform."

"You believe the situation can be salvaged?"

"Why does everyone think I have an opinion on the matter? What on earth would I know about reforming a man's character?"

"You make a very valid point, Percival."

Percy nodded in relief. At least Rue wouldn't overestimate him. "I've sent him into the care of several Greek philosophers."

Rue nodded. "Logic?"

"Yes."

"You'll move him on to the medievalists next?"

"I was thinking Thomas Aquinas."

"And then perhaps *The Higher Common Sense*?"

Percy figured Rue was much better equipped to select a course of study for a soulless killer than he. After all, there was some question as to whether she herself had a soul or simply borrowed other people's on occasion. No matter what, she seemed, to Percy, a generally positive influence on the world. Occasionally a tad enthusiastic in her methods, sometimes lacking in forethought, but her motives were, if not noble, at least affable and not intentionally malicious. She was, in her own bizarre way, a role model.

"I believe I have a copy of Fausse-Maigre somewhere in my library," said Percy, wondering where he'd filed *Common Sense*.

Rue gave him a measured look. "Perhaps you should read it first and discuss it with him."

Percy nodded. And then, "Wait a moment. Was that a *dig* at my expense?"

Rue blinked tawny eyes at him. "Oh, look, Quesnel's brought up the fireworks. I should just go, um, supervise in a captain-type manner."

Percy spared her a sniff and wondered if he should get her to read the bloody books as well.

Primrose liked to think she was a dignified individual. As a result, she cherished a particular preference for floating. It was, when all was said and done, a very dignified mode of travel. One might even call it a civilised pastime. Except for the way Rue did it. But then, while Rue was many things, dignified wasn't one of them. During the more frustrating times in their long friendship, Primrose had even accused Rue of being *uncivilised*. Rue hadn't denied it.

Still, as Primrose leaned perilously over the edge of the slowly sinking mushroom, she did wish – ever so slightly – that they were dropping with a bit less elegance and a great deal more purpose.

Around her, the contents of the mushroom, otherwise known as her fellow passengers in the dropsy, were restless. Their awe at sharing a basket with a merlion, and their confusion at finding said basket no longer heading in the preferred direction – towards the city of Singapore rather than one of its adjacent beaches – were giving way to a general murmur of distress and annoyance. In other words, the rising anger of the dropsy's passengers was outpacing the speed of the dropsy's dropping.

There were many languages being spoken, and such a range of origins guaranteed that some were less awed by a merlion than others. Primrose watched them all covertly, and worried.

The guide tore her eyes away from Miss Sekhmet-the-Fish and regarded Primrose suspiciously. Prim only continued with her subtle steering of the balloon, the artificial propeller dropped well over the edge and out of sight. She leaned carefully against the bearing straps so as to shield them from view. Her massive sleeves, at the very height of fashion, proved extremely useful in this regard. As did the design of her evening hat, which emphasised her constant glancing over the edge, the quivering of its feathers misconstrued as representing the distress of one who fervently wished to be elsewhere. Primrose appeared to be nothing more than a worried wealthy young lady who had sacrificed her safety on the altar of lesser transport and was now reaping the upset of fraternisation with the hoi polloi.

Soon enough, the guide seemed to decide that Primrose was nothing more than she appeared. A grave mistake many had made before, and one that Prim would certainly count on many making in the future.

The guide's attention returned to Tasherit. Primrose heaved a sigh of relief and then, along with the rest of the passengers, emitted an unintended shriek of surprise when a loud bang and pop reverberated through the quiet night air.

Someone appeared to be shooting at them! This was not part of her plan.

Then the sky was briefly set afire with a brilliant flash of sparkling yellow and red.

Someone screamed loudly.

Someone else fainted.

Fireworks.

Rue was fond of fireworks. Quesnel was positively obsessed

with them. *The Spotted Custard* had employed them in the past, for battle or in cases of dire emergency.

The night air lit up again and the bang of the little explosions surrounded them. Prim bent quickly over the edge to take advantage of the illumination, and there, almost directly below them, was *The Spotted Custard*, her balloon slightly deflated but still cheerfully portly and well spotted.

That was when Primrose recalled something Tasherit had casually said shortly after she came aboard – several months ago now. The officers were chatting over dinner, something to do with military training and battle tactics. Not Prim's area of interest, as a rule, so she hadn't paid very close attention. The other officers were busy listing assets and abilities, should it come to combat or a race through a foreign jungle . . . again.

Miss Sekhmet had mentioned that, in her cat form, she wasn't as good with colours as she was in human form, although she could see odd things like scent trails and heat remnants, but she had added that her night vision was substantially superior as a lioness. Rue, who had on several occasions borrowed Tasherit's lioness form herself, corroborated this. Prim, who found herself all too often hungry for information pertaining to their resident werecat (she had no idea why, but she did) had perked up at this odd ability. Which is to say that she now realised Miss Sekhmet had likely seen *The Spotted Custard* below them on the dark deserted beach from the moment she shifted form. Because she had superior visual acuity as a cat in the dark.

Which means my plan was better than I thought initially. Putting Tasherit in charge of guiding us once she became the merlion. How accidentally smart of me! Prim blushed to realise that Miss Sekhmet might have thought Primrose intentional in this regard from her initial explanation of the plan. *And why should I delight in her believing me intelligent? I do not wish for her regard.*

This also meant that they didn't really require Quesnel's fireworks. Still, it was nice of Rue and the others to light the way so Prim could see that her trust in the werecat was not misplaced.

And also, Quesnel was probably enjoying himself immensely. *Let him have his fun.* They were most awfully pretty.

Some of the other passengers, who may not have ever seen such a thing as airborne sparklers, were now in an increased panic. *Random Merlion, loose dropsy, and now fireworks? What is the world coming to!* Primrose grinned. It was a slightly maniacal and faintly vicious grin. Across the basket, Tasherit twitched her whiskers at her in the cat version of a laugh.

Perhaps this is why Rue is so absurd all the time. Causing a ruckus is rather fun.

Primrose hoped no one jumped out of the basket, because the weight balance was so precisely measured there was a good chance they might stop sinking, or at least slow their already glacial descent.

The guide seemed to sense this crisis herself. She began to bark at people in various different languages, finally getting around to English with a "Stay inside the basket!"

Someone next to Prim lurched to the edge.

Primrose grabbed the man's shoulder and pretended to collapse against him. He was a large attractive gentleman with arm muscles the size of coconuts and a beard that looked to be the colour and texture of said coconut's husk. *Russian, perhaps?*

Primrose directed his attention towards an extremely pretty young lady with long black hair and a colourful silken robe who was being pressed in a thoughtless manner against the edge, and looking rather faint. "Oh, sir, do help the poor thing." She pointed for good measure.

Whether he understood English or not was unimportant. He took her meaning and, with a bellow, stopped thinking on his own skin and went to the distressed damsel's rescue. Primrose felt rather like an emergency matchmaker.

Suddenly there was a clunk, followed by a holler from the guide.

Someone had shot a grappling hook at them from the *Custard* and they were being slowly and inexorably dragged towards the downed dirigible.

Once they were within hailing distance, the passengers and the guide all began yelling. Primrose could see Rue, Quesnel, Percy, Anitra, and assorted well-armed decklings and deckhands waiting in tense silence on the *Custard*'s decks.

A general modest chaos persisted, and then several things happened in quick succession.

Miss Sekhmet let forth a particularly loud roar and, despite her fishtail, coiled her magnificent muscles (what Prim could see of them) and leapt over the basket edge and down to land on the deck of the *Custard*. Her back legs were still inside the fishtail, but she managed to land with something resembling grace.

Rue took one look at her and burst into ill-timed hysterics, head back, laughter expansive.

The lack of the lioness's weight caused the dropsy to pause its descent, but the grapple was in place and so they didn't slow too much.

Since it was no longer necessary to man the propeller, Primrose pushed her way to a better observation point, leaning over the edge to watch the doings of her friends below as the dropsy drew closer and closer.

Anitra put a bullhorn to her mouth and began yelling in several languages. When none of these provoked intelligent discourse, she passed the horn to Percy, who commenced his own series of formal greetings.

The guide of the mushroom pulled out a rather large shotgun and pointed it at the collected officers on the *Custard*'s main deck, now plainly visible as their trajectory had shifted and the grapple was bringing them in around and under the massive spotted balloon.

Quesnel grabbed Rue out of the firing line with his good arm.

Primrose began moving closer to the dropsy guide. She tried to remain unobserved and innocent looking.

Spoo and Virgil, manning the Gatling gun with the serious expressions of young people given grave responsibility, swung it up and back as far as it would go and then gave a quick burst of fire. It was well below the mushroom, but it effectively terrified the occupants into more screaming and greater chaos.

Primrose reached the guide's side, and lacking any better options, swung her carpetbag at the woman's burly shoulder as hard as she could. The guide dropped her gun over the edge, and it fired, putting a very large hole into something, as there came a splitting sound. At least it hadn't put a hole into *someone*.

In the resulting panicked madness, Primrose looked over the edge to see the ghostly form of Formerly Floote shimmer up from belowdecks. By pure chance, he rose up directly next to where Tasherit still sat, in her shimmering teal tail, looking annoyed with the world.

The dropsy and its occupants fell into an awed silence.

Primrose wasn't aware of Singapore's official policy on ghostly apparitions. Ghosts were pretty rare, and they never lasted more than a month or so, unless the climate for preservation was particularly extraordinary. It was unheard-of for an airship to carry a ghost, as bodies were customarily burned or buried, not carted about in tanks. Also, it was rare to see a male ghost.

Primrose didn't think it was any of these things that caused the passengers around her to fall silent.

It was the combination of ghost and merlion. Together.

The locals inside the dropsy, at least, seemed to see this as a prophetic revelation, or perhaps such an extraordinary set of visions that they hardly knew what to do with themselves. Everyone went quiet, a few – including the guide – bowed their heads in reverence, three fell to their knees.

Percy put the bullhorn back to his lips, and because he had absolutely no sense of reverence, began repeating his greetings in various languages. Including Latin.

Frankly, Primrose had no idea why he bothered with Latin. *Simply showing off. Ugh, why is my brother so annoying?*

Percy always tried Latin, yet barely anyone spoke it. Except the Italian in their brig.

By this time, the dropsy had been dragged down and fastened tightly to the squeak deck.

Primrose pushed to the very front of the awed occupants, and with great embarrassment, since there was no other way to do it, hoisted herself up to sit on the basket's edge. She then swung herself, and her carpetbag, over to slide down the side and land on the squeak deck of her beloved airship. This was accomplished with very little dignity and necessitated showing both petticoats and ankles to the wide world.

It was humiliating, but she'd experienced worse while aboard the *Custard*, so she managed to carry it off with aplomb. Or at least no loss of limbs.

"Primrose darling!" Rue reappeared on the main deck below and looked up at her with a wide grin. "You brought me a mushroom."

"Yes, dear. Haven't you always wanted one?" *What is she wearing? Is that a cocked sugarloaf? Oh, for goodness' sake. Next it will be a sash and a pirate's hat with an ostrich plume out the back. As if I haven't had to deal with my mother's eccentric hat choices for most of my life, now Rue whips out a sugarloaf.*

"Not as such." Rue didn't stop smiling.

"As such, pah! You love it. Very natty turnout, you'll see. This mushroom is full of helium. Now say thank you like a good girl."

Rue put a hand to her ample bosom. "Oh, darling heart, how thoughtful. You shouldn't have."

"Shouldn't I? Well, if you like it that much, you can reward me by taking off that disastrous hat."

The crew disregarded their silliness. Two of the decklings were already porting down a sipper tube to the top of the dropsy. No doubt they would figure out how to drain the mushroom of its helium in no time.

Rue continued the banter by touching her cocked sugarloaf lovingly. "I wouldn't go that far. Still, the helium is most welcome, thank you, Primrose dear. And the, erm, tail on our lioness?"

Prim slung her carpetbag down to the main deck and began climbing down the ladder between it and the squeaker. Willard, one of the deckhands and a decent sort of chap, came over to help her down. She didn't require assistance, but it was gentlemanly. Tasherit let out a sort of low growling hiss.

Percy and Anitra, between them, seemed to have deduced a way of communicating with the stunned guide. The woman was speaking in low reverent tones and casting constant glances down at Formerly Floote and Miss Sekhmet, who remained motionless and idol-like (aside from the aforementioned growl – from the werecat, mind you, not the dead butler, of course). Clearly they were aware of the powerful impression they were making, and unwilling to break the spell.

Safely on the main deck at last, Primrose let out a sigh of relief. *Home.*

Rue gave her a quick hug. She was a tactile little thing, not very British of her – presumably her father's werewolf pack were to blame.

"So, why's Tash in a tail?" Rue asked, pulling back and smiling happily.

"Long story," said Prim. "I'll tell you over tea, later."

"And this mushroom thing?"

"You know, I think you're better off trying to buy the whole contraption off the guide. Might solve all our problems by throwing money at her."

"Primrose! What a very crass suggestion. How unexpected from you. Brava."

"Thank you, dear. Now, I'm going for my tea. I trust you can take care of things up here?"

"You're leaving me with a dozen angry locals, a stolen mushroom, a lioness dressed as a mermaid, and your brother armed with a bullhorn?"

"That last is entirely your fault."

"True."

"You also gave a Frenchman fireworks."

"Darling boy, he does love them so."

"And Spoo still has the gun." Primrose arched an eyebrow.

"Oh dear, excellent point." Rue turned away from Prim, already back into her bustling captain mode. "Spoo, I don't believe we'll need that anymore this evening. Please go and ensure that the sipping is under control. Virgil, see to your master, do. He doesn't need to *keep* using the bullhorn, they're plenty close enough now. Nor does he need to keep using Latin. Yes, I know he likes to pepper everything with Latin, but a little Latin goes a very long way."

Primrose left her friend to it. Rue would get everything settled and under control while Prim fortified herself with some much-needed nibbles. Once she'd done that, she would return up top and start organising the inevitable fallout that would result from Percy and his bullhorn.

CHAPTER

FOUR

The Premier Floating Philosophy Club

Primrose consumed her well-deserved tea with no little gusto, and by the time she reappeared abovedecks, people were prepared for her to organise. There was very little Primrose loved more in life than organising things. This was probably a grave character flaw, but not in her family. And certainly not aboard *The Spotted Custard*, where she basically got to organise everything.

As it transpired, the dropsy guide had been remarkably amenable to selling them the mushroom and, more important, its helium. For a small additional fee, she'd then led the grumbling passengers off along the beach back to town.

Miss Sekhmet had retreated belowdecks to lick her wounds, figuratively of course, as they were all dignity related.

Primrose didn't ask where the werecat was, but with her usual lack of tact, Rue insisted on telling her.

"She muttered something about bathing. Every time something out of the ordinary happens she seems to want a sponge bath." Rue contemplated the decklings' activities around the helium dispensation without really seeing them. "I suppose it has something to do with cats and washing. Instinctual response to unexpected outside stimuli."

"Good thing for us she doesn't do that in the midst of battle," replied Prim, acerbically.

Prim straightened her sleeves self-consciously and tried not to blush. Hopeless, of course, to keep her own reckless imagination at bay. Thank heavens it was nighttime and Rue couldn't see her rosy cheeks.

Rue turned too-perceptive yellow eyes on Primrose. "I recommend boxes."

Prim was confused. "Pardon?"

"Something large and crate-sized. I'm sure she'd like it."

Prim privately agreed. Tasherit – *Miss Sekhmet to you, my girl* – probably would like a nice big box. Footnote was always inside a hatbox anytime Prim let him into her quarters. Not that lionesses and domestic cats could be directly compared, not within either's hearing.

"Does she have a birthday coming up?"

"That's not why I think you should give her a box," said Rue.

Prim was not going to give her friend the satisfaction of asking why. Rue would say something silly about courting gifts. Rue had odd ideas about relationships. She'd been raised by a male vampire who preferred the company of men. And her lover had been raised by a mother who was practically married to her female companion. Not that anyone said anything about it in public, but in the matter of all things high society, everyone *knew*. Primrose didn't want to be *known*, not like that. Her mother was already infamous, Prim so very much wished to be normal.

She wondered, idly of course, how big a hatbox one might acquire. And then she resolved to write to her French milliner as soon as possible (the situation with her more regular supplier in London was in flux). There were hats to order as well, naturally, she couldn't *only* enquire about massive hat boxes. She'd have to find a way to bring it up off the cuff, so to speak.

Primrose schooled herself and glanced over at the navigation pit. Percy wasn't there, no doubt taking the opportunity to research something obscure and irrelevant and useless.

The decklings dropped down to the squeak deck looking pleased with themselves. Primrose climbed up to examine the deflated dropsy, which now took up most of the squeak deck. Rue followed her up.

"I think we should get rid of the basket," Primrose said to Rue.

"Oh yes?"

"Well, it's bulky and adds weight. If we dump it, we can still use the dropsy itself as an emergency floatation device, rig up some sort of hammock to hold passengers. I'm assuming that's why you want to keep it aboard."

Prim examined the means by which the sipper tube was attached with a spigot valve to the collapsed dropsy. If necessary, the process could be reversed and the smaller aircraft filled with helium sucked from the larger, allowing them to escape the *Custard* in cases of dire emergency. Well, allowing *some* of them to escape. There were over twice as many people aboard *The Spotted Custard* as could safely occupy the dropsy.

Rue grinned at Prim in a slightly pained yet savage manner. No doubt she herself would never employ such an escape measure. Rue was one of those who believed a captain ought to crash with her dirigible. *Not the most sensible of individuals, my Rue.* No, at the moment she was thinking of making certain the decklings and sooties were safe and could use the dropsy as a life craft.

"Of course that's why I want to keep it. Maybe we can catch us a second one as well. I agree about the basket. We can set the decklings to devising a sling next time we're trapped in the grey for any length of time. They're good like that, and it's a good project to keep them occupied and out of mischief."

Prim nodded. She and Rue began to push the basket over towards the edge of the squeak deck.

"So." Primrose panted slightly and decided to wait to ask her next question. This much physical activity in the space of the last twenty-four hours was really rather aggravating.

Basket tipped over the edge and disposed of to the beach below, Prim caught her breath and turned to her friend. "So, was it enough helium? Enough to at least get us back up so we can refill at the wheystation?"

"Yes, dear, you did very well. Now tell me about the tail."

"I'd be delighted."

"Poor Tash was rather upset. But it seemed to do the trick."

Primrose grinned. "I know, wasn't it delightful?"

"You shouldn't tease her so."

"I shouldn't? Why not? And I wasn't teasing, not how you're implying."

"Weren't you?" Rue looked arch. Primrose hated it when she got that way. She'd been doing it more and more since she and Quesnel had begun, for want of a better way of putting it, *sharing quarters*. Primrose hated to admit that her friend now knew a great deal more about bedroom activities than she did, and it was rather unkind of Rue to keep lording it over her. Rue always had to do everything first.

So Prim lashed out. "Rue dear, despite what being raised by Lord Akeldama may have taught you, we aren't all deviants."

Rue frowned. "I don't like that word. And that's your mother talking, not you."

Primrose shivered slightly. Rue really did sound upset. "No offence meant. You know I love your Dama, it's simply that . . ."

Rue got all condescending again. She patted Prim's shoulder in a highly irritating (and sleeve-flattening) manner. "You aren't ready yet. Fine, yes. It always did take you longer to come around. But I do have that book still, if you'd like it. The one with the pictures that Quesnel gave me when we were courting. It has a whole *section*. You know."

Primrose *didn't* know, and she couldn't help giving Rue the satisfaction of asking, "A section on what?"

"Oh, you know . . . *ladies*."

Primrose still didn't quite understand. And wasn't sure if she was dying of curiosity or humiliation. But she decided to do neither and go see how her impossible brother was doing at the moment. Percy was many things, but he never tried to interfere in her life or choices, and for that Primrose was profoundly grateful.

It's a strange day when I seek solace with my brother because my best friend is being too nosy. The world works in mysterious ways. I might be one of the only people on the planet who finds Percival Tunstell restful.

Percy looked up from an article on the nature of sound that was particularly absorbing. He'd have to ask Miss Sekhmet sometime if sounds resonated differently in her ears when she was a lioness. *Or Rue. Rue would be able to tell me not only if they're different as a lioness but if they're different as a wolf. I wonder if they'd allow me to conduct some experiments involving pitch and secondary animal forms?*

His contemplative revelry was disturbed, first by Footnote leaping off his lap in a manner that was just this side of painful to the nether region, and then by the reason for Footnote's excitement: his sister's bustling into the room.

Percy considered the library sacred space, and his quarters *were* attached, so it ought to be treated as a private sanctuary, but no one else gave it reverential treatment, barging in at all hours.

"Percy, you pollock, where are you?"

"Tiddles, must you?"

"Well, aren't you happy to see me safely home and whole and hale and all that rot?"

"You were only away one night."

"Yes, but I might have been stranded there forever. And I came to your rescue with helium."

Percy snorted at her, trying to pretend he wasn't checking her over carefully for signs of distress or injury. "What do you want, sister?" She looked in fine fettle, not a scratch. *As if Tasherit would let anything harm her.*

"I need Isinglass."

Percy grimaced. Isinglass was the Tunstell family's great shame. His mother's widely read and widely critiqued slim travel journal published at great personal expense, and fortunately under a pseudonym. The fact that Lord Akeldama, and then Lady Maccon, and then Rue and his sister insisted on using the horrible little book as a cypher for their secret communiqués was only one more nail in the humiliation coffin.

Could they not leave the awful thing to lie low and be forgotten by all?

Percy gave a mighty sigh and went to retrieve it from its carefully hidden shelf behind the chair in one corner of the library.

"Take it away, do."

Primrose grinned at him. "I love you too, Percy."

"I'm assuming you received a letter of significance?"

Primrose went all prissy. "That's for me to know and you not to know."

Percy dreaded asking but knew she'd gone to retrieve the mail while on the wheystation. "Anything from Mother for me?"

"No. Thank your lucky stars, my boy."

Percy didn't like to take instruction from his sister, but in this instance he followed her order to the letter. Nothing disturbed him more than his mother's notice. The fact that she had not written him a single line was a profound blessing. She was utterly impossible. She was, in fact, the reason he could tolerate Rue and Prim with all their absurd eccentricities. They may be silly, and on occasion even frivolous, but they were never as bad as Ivy Tunstell, vampire queen and Percy's mama.

"I do have these for you, brother dear." Primrose tossed him a few other missives.

Percy flipped through them. One from his publisher. One from a colleague at university. The latest pamphlet from the Royal Society. Nothing urgent.

"Percy? Percy!"

He looked up. "Oh, are you still here?"

"Anything happen while I was away?"

Percy frowned, considering. "I have started Mr Tarabotti on a course of study designed to give him an ethical foundation."

"You have?"

Percy instantly defended himself from his sister's unexpected shock. "Formerly Floote thought it was a sound idea." *I mean really, why should I not teach others? I'm an educated man, and information does no one any benefit if it is not shared.*

Prim blinked at him. "Well, very good then."

"No need to be so startled, I believe his granddaughter may be joining us."

"Anitra wants to, uh, study ethics?"

Percy nodded. "We are starting with the ancient Greeks and logic."

Prim's eyes instantly glazed over, as Percy knew they would. His sister loathed the Greeks. *Bunch of stuffy old men dressed in bed linens talking to each other about mathematics,* she'd once said to a governess.

"I take it you aren't interested in attending the seminars?"

"Discuss dead treatises? With an Italian murderer? I think not." Primrose gave a delicate shudder.

Percy hid his grin of satisfaction. He didn't want her horning in. This was his philosophy club, not to be shared with sisters.

He picked up one of his letters and ostentatiously broke the seal.

Primrose left him to it. "Ta-ta for now, old chump. Bye, Footnote – unless you wanted to come along?"

She held the door open for the cat. Footnote wavered on the threshold and then caught a whiff of something that caused him to hiss, whirl around, and dash at Percy, seeking refuge under his chair.

As the door closed behind his sister, Percy heard Tasherit say, "Happy to be back aboard, are you, little one?" in that particularly warm tone she reserved only for Primrose. Her voice was almost a purr.

Percy wondered how long it would take his sister to realise that their resident werecat was in love with her. Then he
shrugged and went back to his letters.

Primrose pushed into Rue's quarters after only a perfunctory
knock. Quesnel was below in engineering or she wouldn't have
taken the risk. While she was well aware of what her two friends
got up to behind closed doors (in principle if not in specifics),
she in no way wished to witness such an appalling activity. Of
course, the door had a bolt, but Rue always forgot to lock it.

"I have the mail! You forgot to take it from me earlier," Prim
announced, waving the sealed missives about temptingly.

Rue looked up from where she was lounging on her bed,
going over coal consumption reports from the boiler room. "At
last! What took you so long?"

"Well, you did sort of strand me on a wheystation."

"Details, details."

"You've one from your mother."

Rue winced. Her dark eyebrows knitted into a frown. Primrose could feel her mother's commentary in her head. *Don't frown
so, darling heart, you'll end up with lines, and no one looks good in lines.*

Prim added, to share the burden, "I received one from your
mother too."

"Really? How odd."

"And I think we are going to need this." Primrose tossed *Sand
and Shadows on a Sapphire Sea: My Adventures Abroad* by Honeysuckle Isinglass down on the bed next to Rue.

"Oh? Oh! Cypher? Code! Adventure is afloat. How exciting."
Rue brightened considerably and sat up, grabbing her letters
from Prim.

Primrose perched stiffly on the end of the bed. She envied Rue
her flexibility of movement. Rue had announced (some time ago
now) that she no longer wished to be *confined*. With no further

warning she had given over stays and eventually combinations. She'd done this only after securing her father's approval. Not her vampire father, mind you, her *werewolf father.* She'd explained that, as a metanatural, she was safer if shifting forms were easy to do, and stays did not make it easy. Lord Conall Maccon, werewolf Alpha, was a pretty carefree gentleman, unless his daughter's safety was threatened. If corsetry threatened her safety? Well, then, convention, nicety, honour, purity, and riotousness be damned, his little girl did not need to wear a corset. So Rue didn't.

Unless, of course, Quesnel really wanted her to. And then, no doubt, it did not stay on for very long.

It was at times like this, when Rue could positively lounge, catlike and comfortable, on a bed in full day dress, that Primrose envied her this otherwise unacceptable eccentricity of dress. Or not dress.

Primrose *always* wore a corset, and a combination, and stockings, and garters, and all other accoutrements any well-bred English girl ought to wear. However, this did mean that when visiting a friend in her boudoir for a discussion of great secrecy and import, Primrose was unable to lounge in comfort.

Rue dove into reading her mail, teeth nibbling her full bottom lip as she did so. Rue was always moving, shifting, and fidgeting, even if it was only a tiny nibble. It drove many people spare, but Prim had grown accustomed to it over the years. She fancied her friend was rather like a hummingbird. In those few moments of stillness she did allow herself, the whole world took a breath with her and paused to admire her shine. Rue wasn't beautiful, but she was most awfully shiny. It was something in the manner of a master painting where one is drawn into admiring the skill of the brushstrokes rather than the composition as a whole.

In addition to the letter from Lady Maccon in Cairo that Prim suspected was a counter to her own, Rue had one from her vampire father in London, and another from her many times grandniece in Scotland. The grandniece was actually a werewolf and a great deal older than Rue, because family trees got bushy when immortals were involved.

"Dama's very cheeky about us visiting something in Singapore called the *Shrine of Iskander Shah*. I suspect he thinks he's being funny."

Prim frowned, trying to remember if any of the books she'd read had said anything about it. "Do we have time to play tourist?"

Rue shook her head. "It's not *important*. Not in that way that sometimes his frivolous statements can be. I believe we can give it a miss. The rest of his letter is full of gossip. London is rife with rumours since we exposed the world to both werecats and weremonkeys. The gossip rags have new kinds of shifter creatures coming out the woodwork. Selkies have been reported off the Irish coast, bear shifters in the Scandinavian woodlands, and even a fox shifter in Nottingham. Oh, and one very amusing tale of a weregoat breaking into someone's wardrobe and eating all her hats. Dama doesn't give any of them much credence, especially the fox. He says something about Lavoisier's Law."

Primrose nodded. "That makes sense, and it is certainly supported by what we've observed so far. I've been meaning to say, I believe Miss Sekhmet is denser as a human, which is how she manages to be larger as a lioness. Preservation of mass and all that rot."

Rue stared at her. "Primrose darling, what are you on about? You sound like Percy, and how would you know anything about Tash's density? Has she been on top of you recently?"

"What? No!" Primrose hurried on from that. "And Percy *is* my brother, I'd have to have picked up something. You didn't study Lavoisier? He has several interesting papers on the chemical and physical nature of shifter physiology. Originally in French, of course, but the formative ones have been translated."

Rue only frowned at her. Primrose tried for a quote. " 'Nothing is lost, nothing is created, everything is transformed.' "

"Oh, *that* Lavoisier."

Clearly, Rue had never read a word written by the infamous scientist. Prim scoffed. "Really, Prudence, you shift your form regularly – aren't you at all interested in how it works?"

"Not really. Considering that it *does* work. Why mess with a good thing?"

Primrose shook her head. And went back to analysing the coded letter she'd received from Lady Maccon.

Rue resumed reading her correspondences in silence. She left her mother's missive to last. Because, well, Lady Maccon took a lot of preparation, even in letter form. Especially if you were Lady Maccon's daughter.

Prim watched her friend, covertly, when Rue finally did read over her mother's words. Rue's face was a study in small smiles, grimaces, and exasperated eye rolls.

Eventually she came to the end. "Well, they seem to be settling just fine in Cairo. The tea business is taking up a great deal of Mother's time. Although I don't believe that will keep her from interfering."

"Interfering in what?"

"Oh, you know, everything. My mother would spin the world faster, if she felt it more efficient."

Prim grimaced. She didn't like the idea of someone as important as Lady Maccon engaged in trade. It seemed indicative of a general lowering of standards.

Rue had no such scruples. So far as she was concerned, anything that kept her mother occupied was a good thing.

Rue continued. "She's upset to discover she has a brother, dead or not, and wants us to bring Rodrigo to her for a proper introduction, *once we're done with him and he's sufficiently reformed.* Whatever that means. And she says she has *a great deal of faith in our integration abilities.* Integration abilities indeed. Bah."

Prim nodded. "She thinks we can save him from himself and from the Templars. And she knows us well enough to realise we would try."

"My mother is three biscuits short of a trifle."

"Oh no. She's right. I, too, believe we can do it." Primrose nodded her understanding.

Rue glared at her.

Primrose was confused. "What? You mean to say that's not what you've been having Percy and Anitra do with the man?"

"Uh, is it? Am I? What's going on?"

"Oh, Rue. You don't know?"

"What don't I know?"

"Percy has started a sort of book discussion group. I believe Formerly Floote recommended it. To give Mr Tarabotti some ethics, apparently. Anitra has joined in the reformation effort."

"Oh, I say. He might have said something. Or perhaps he did and I didn't notice. You know me and Percy, I was likely thinking of something rather pleasant while he droned on about it. You believe it might work, Percy and ethics?" Rue looked unconvinced.

"Anything is possible when Greek philosophers get involved. Can't stand them myself. But then, you know, they aren't for women."

Rue nodded. "Did you have anything interesting in your letters? I presume you read them yesterday on the station."

Prim nodded. "The usual ridiculousness from my mother. She is exhausting. And then there's this one from your mother, which needs to be decoded."

"Also exhausting."

Prim nodded. "And one from Norman, of course."

"Norman?" Rue squinted her eyes.

Prim rolled her eyes. "My fiancé, remember?"

"Primrose darling, it's terribly difficult to keep track."

"Well, it will continue to be so. He broke it off with me."

Rue looked mixed at this revelation. Delighted, because she hadn't approved of the man (she rarely did), but also horrified and upset on Prim's behalf. "*He* broke it off with *you*? Isn't it customarily the other way around?"

"I know. I didn't think he was that intelligent." *Or had that much gumption. Two reasons I chose him for a husband.* Primrose gave a tiny grimace. She wasn't upset. Her pride was a little bruised, but it wasn't like she'd been in love with the fellow. Love had nothing to do with marriage, every sensible young lady knew that.

"Shocking behaviour. And via a letter no less. I *am* sorry, Prim." Rue, who had a certain generosity of spirit, even looked a little sorry for her.

Primrose did not shrug. She would very much have liked to, but shrugging was not something nice refined young British ladies did. Not even with their best friends when hearts were not broken but perhaps should have been. Instead she said, "These things happen."

Rue nodded. "Have you told Tash about this yet?"

"No, and I very much hope you will not. This is a private matter. It is no one's business but my own." Prim kept her tone of voice firm.

Rue snorted at her. "Oh, for goodness' sake, Primrose, *really!*"

"Stop it, Rue. This is not your concern. Now, I've got this letter from your mother deciphered and I'm afraid it's as I suspected. We have been activated as agents of the Parasol Protectorate. She uses both Ledger and Hot Cross Bun, so the instructions are for the both of us. However, mine is only the first half of the necessary information. She wishes for us to investigate something. Some report or another. Yours is likely the second part, explaining what, precisely, we are to look into. Would it be all right if I . . . ?"

Rue handed over her own Lady Maccon letter with alacrity. Clearly correspondences from her mother were neither sacred nor private.

Primrose began the laborious task of using the Isinglass cypher to break the second part of their code and see whatever it was that Rue's infamous mother actually wanted them to do.

After a long moment she said, "Well, this is odd."

"Go on?" Rue had finished with her own letters and was back to the coal stocks listings. Thus she was eager to be disturbed.

"I believe your mother wishes for us to visit the Andean highlands."

"In South America?" Rue perked up.

Prim nodded. "Where no one of our acquaintance has ever travelled. It's supposed to be" – she cleared her throat delicately – "quite wild."

"How exciting. Are we after reports of more odd shape-shifters then?"

"No. Vampires this time."

Rue snorted. The Indian vampires, the Rakshasas, had been no fun at all, to put it mildly. "Well, if we must."

"I think we must indeed. Your mother seems, well, worried about them."

"That can't be right. Mother never worries about anything."

"I believe this part, here, suggests she thinks they might be dying out. The last of their kind. She wants *us* to *save* them."

Prim frowned, trying to better decipher the meaning. "Or exterminate them. Difficult to tell."

Rue nodded sagely. "Now that does sound like my mother."

Prim frowned in thought (then remembered this wrinkled her forehead most awfully, and stopped). "We're charged with a kind of collect, preserve, and rescue mission. The last of a supernatural species, under grave threat."

Rue wrinkled her nose. "Generally speaking, I'm better at blowing things up. But if that's what we are to do – save a vampire race – then I suppose we'll do it."

Primrose felt compelled to words of caution. Ever her sacred duty around a friend like Rue. "Unfortunately, there's no indication on the nature of the threat or the nuances of the species."

Rue shrugged. "Still, it'll be nice to travel to that part of the world. No one I know has ever been to South America before. The lure of the unknown."

Primrose considered. "I don't think Percy knows the high mountain dialects."

"Or the aetheric currents for that matter. They aren't very well charted over the Pacific."

"He's going to be both delighted and annoyed with this destination."

Rue laughed. "Oh no, he's going to be thrilled. It's a chance for him to make a name for himself. You know, I think by the time I'm done with him, your brother might be one of the world's most renowned aetherographers."

Prim nodded. Her brother had already filed a report on a new current he'd discovered between the Sudan and Zanzibar. They were calling it the Tunstell Passage. Prim felt that sounded ever so slightly rude, but she admitted to the glory of it (when Percy wasn't around to get puffed up about it).

"Anything else from my mother?"

Prim didn't like to have to say this part. "She is warning us to stay away from Europe because of Rodrigo. Her spies in London report that the Templars are after both you and him now."

Rue looked militant. She didn't like to be told what she couldn't do by her mother. She didn't mind being told what she could do, or being sent on quests and adventures, but being told not to return home? That was asking for trouble.

Primrose braced herself.

"Dama didn't say anything!"

"Would he?"

"Not as such." Rue crossed her arms and glared at Prim. As if Prim was responsible for the order and not Lady Maccon.

"Perhaps you should reread his letter for hints." Primrose tried a delicate nudge. "Look, darling, South America is far enough away to be out of everyone's reach and jurisdiction – your parents, the Templars, you know, *everyone*."

Rue looked slightly less militant. "You have a fair point."

"So are we headed there? Parts unknown?"

Rue nodded. "Yes, yes, I think we are. I'll go tell Percy to set a course. I want to talk to him about this book group of his while I'm at it. I don't know how I feel about him turning my ship into a reform school meets university all willy-nilly like that."

Prim did not feel compelled to defend her twin. He could get himself out of his own messes. But she did say, "Oh, you know Percy, I'm sure it wasn't intentional."

Percy was only mildly offended to have his whirlwind of a captain descend upon him with outrageous demands. It was to be expected of Rue, quite frankly. And, after all, he couldn't very well conduct any aether experiments until they were actually back inside the aetherosphere. So when Rue curtly informed him that they were headed to South America and the Andes Mountains, he struggled to hide his pleasure. This would be a fun journey. And they would be a long time inside aether, crossing the oceans and charting new currents.

He rummaged around and set those few charts they did have aside. The first leg, to Port Moresby, was well charted, if not frequently floated by Her Majesty's Airships.

However, it was the second of Rue's attacks that Percy was ill prepared for and found totally unwarranted.

"I say, Rue! You object to my philosophy club?" Why on earth should she? *"Barba non facit philosophum."*

"No Latin, Percy," Rue grumbled at him. "Look, is it safe? How do I know my dear cousin deadly Italian mucky-muck isn't practicing his conniving arts and turning you lot to his side? Greek logic can be easily misapplied."

Are we back on this sides thing again? I blame cricket. Percy huffed. *Why persist in seeing the world in black or white? Isn't that the whole point of philosophy? Besides which, how dare she question my own moral fibre?* "Speaking as the only one in this room with a confirmed soul, I should like it known that I am not at all at risk. In fact, I'm offended you should think me so weak spirited. Besides, whatever powers of persuasion your cousin has, said powers clearly lean towards the physical."

Of course, Rue took offence at that. "Are you implying that my cousin is intellectually inferior?"

Percy snorted. "Compared to me? Of course he is." *Aren't most people?*

He looked to Footnote for support. The little traitor was diving about Rue's feet and purring up a storm. Rue was fond of very fancy shoes and so was Footnote.

"Oh, Percy, you are a chump."

Why is the truth always so difficult for people to accept? "Everyone should know their strengths. I don't believe that Mr Tarabotti would deny that his persuasive powers are not necessarily verbal or mental in nature. Particularly with a language barrier. It's not an insult if it is not his objective. Now do stop being so wilfully obtuse, Prudence Akeldama. You don't even *like* the man." Percy held up a hand when Rue, who was now slightly red in the face, clearly would have persisted. *How can she not realise? None of this is important.*

Blessedly, she stayed silent. Percy pressed on. "If you want to know what's going on, read the books and come to the discussion yourself. Now, let me get these charts in order and set our course."

"Oh, very well," Rue unexpectedly agreed, albeit with ill grace.

Percy blinked at this. *Perhaps I am more persuasive than even I give myself credit for.* "Good then." He cleared his throat. "Well. That is . . . I think we will have our next meeting the evening after next, once we are safely in the grey. Our next hop is a slow current, it will take us two full days to get there from here, lots of reading time. We meet in Mr Tarabotti's, uh, quarters."

Rue crossed her arms and nodded.

"You'll have to collect the Greeks from Anitra, as they are

currently residing with her. She should be done soon, she's an admirably fast reader."

"And my cousin?"

"Oh, not quite so fast. But then English is not his best language and I don't keep things in translation. Although I may have the original Greek. Probably wouldn't work any better. I don't think he speaks Greek. Perhaps in future I might acquire some treatises in Italian. I mean, if he stays aboard, it might improve – "

"Percy, stop. Enough. Fine. I'll talk to Anitra then."

So it was that Rue came along the next time Percy had a philosophical meeting with Rodrigo Tarabotti.

The discussion got heated, but stayed fair, and ranged over the nuances of choice and preference, societal stipulations, and progression of the moral compass. The conversation thus proceeded in a manner that Percy enjoyed immensely, as did, apparently, the cousins. It reminded him of the good old days after hours at university. The spirit of true intellectual debate that might only be improved upon with the addition of small cigars and possibly port. Since he did not think Rue would condone either, Percy resolved to be happy with only conversation.

Eventually the discussion petered out and Rodrigo asked, tentatively, about their situation so far as being stranded in Singapore went.

Rue grinned at her cousin. Rue was not the type of girl to hold attempted kidnapping against a man, which was jolly decent of her, Percy felt. No doubt this confused Rodrigo, but it also seemed to charm him. He became more animated in his engagement, which in turn caused Anitra's lovely dark eyes to go hot. Percy wondered if the seductive quality of Italian men was a measurable phenomenon and if it had anything to do with the hands waving about while talking. Perhaps their motion had a seductive dance effect, like when peacocks shook their tails at their mates.

In answer to the Singapore question, Percy explained that Primrose had come to their rescue with a mushroom.

"Mushroom? What is this word *mushroom?*" Rodrigo mulled it about in his mouth.

Percy searched his Latin and limited Italian for the correct term. "Fungi?" he hazarded.

Rodrigo threw his handsome head back and laughed. "Fungi, like the porcini? The food?"

Percy nodded.

Rue was also amused. "I like it. We shall call our new escape dropsy the *Porcini.*"

Percy didn't think it a great idea that Mr Tarabotti know there was a means of escaping the ship once said ship was fully afloat. But that was Rue for you, smart but not particularly crafty so far as evil was concerned.

Percy said, carefully, "Not that we are keeping it inflated, mind you. It will be for emergency purposes only, so don't go getting any ideas."

The Italian shrugged. "Bah! Is too late now. I cannot go back. Even if I wish it. I find I like it here. You are interesting humans. There is nothing bad with three meals a day and fun *conversazione.* Even if your food, she is *abominevole.*"

Rue bristled. She kept an excellent cook aboard ship. So far as dirigible food was concerned, *The Spotted Custard* offered unprecedented delectables. "How dare you criticise the meals that I have been providing for you! At my expense, I'll have you know, cousin!"

Percy thought that Rue sounded and looked more like her mother when she put on airs.

Rodrigo was not impressed. "You English. You know nothing of food. Do not play the food."

"Play the fool," corrected Percy, quietly.

Rue sneered. "I'd put you to work in the galley, if only I trusted you not to poison us all."

Rodrigo shrugged. "It would be more to do. And then, I should not keep with the eating of such *poltiglia*."

"Percy?" Rue turned on him, imperious.

Percy considered. "Mud?" He hazarded a guess. "Or perhaps, mush?"

"Mush?" Rue fairly shook in her boots, glaring at Rodrigo. And then again, "*Mush!*"

"Sì! It is as I speak it." The Italian glowered, his eyes no longer hot except in anger. Suddenly he and Rue looked very much alike. Both tan, both wilful, both fierce-browed and glowering.

Percy might have tried to mitigate the heat of the argument except he had no idea what to say in times like this. He wasn't any good when passions flew. He was usually the one to cause anger and disagreement, and even then, he didn't know how to stop it. Especially then.

He cleared his throat. "Are we all done with the Greeks, then? Should we move on to Aquinas next? Terribly interesting fellow, Aquinas."

Rodrigo's fierceness softened. "I believe Miss Anitra wishes to join us to talk that book."

"Does she indeed?" The young lady had asked to read some of the Greeks, which Percy understood to be a means of connecting with Rodrigo. Percy supposed Formerly Floote must have given her some instruction. Formerly Floote was her adoptive grandfather, but he had lived and travelled with her and her family long enough to have found the time for epistemology. *I mean to say, who wouldn't?*

Rue looked interested at this addition to their book group. "And how would you know that, cousin?"

Rodrigo Tarabotti grinned at her. "She brings me my meals."

"Oh yes, I did ask her to do that."

"She is *bellissima*, your *aravani*."

Rue looked to Percy for an explanation. They both knew *bellissima* meant *pretty*, but *aravani* was not a word Percy knew in either Italian or Latin. Then again, given their prisoner's clear affection for the girl, it may be a pet name of some kind.

"Aravani?" he pressed.

Rodrigo shrugged. "There is no other word I know for this."

Percy shrugged too. It didn't seem important so they left it at that. "So in a few days we meet again, wherever we are floating, and talk Aquinas? I'll bring the books around shortly."

Rodrigo seemed delighted with the prospect.

Percy didn't know why, but he was pleased as well. This was rather fun, and whatever else it was doing, it certainly seemed to be having an effect on their prisoner. Which is to say, Rodrigo was still annoying, and still Italian, and most likely still evil. But he was warming towards them.

Well, it was hard not to like Rue, she was eminently likeable with all her vivacious enthusiasm. Percy had a suspicion it would be difficult to be evil when Rue was around making it so very easy to have fun. Even if she was arguing.

He hoped the man was being honest with them about his prospects. If he really did have nowhere to go, perhaps he might stay with them voluntarily for a while.

But Aquinas first.

I must see to the nature of this man's soul, Percy charged himself firmly. *Which is laughable. I have become a priest of mercy in my old age. Me. Who'd have thought it?*

FIVE

A Grey and Melancholy Danger

As Percy had indicated, the first leg of their journey to South America was essentially painless. At least for the mortals aboard ship. The aether currents were slow and quiet and the crew subdued and industrious. The immortals, of course, slept.

Primrose always felt a little melancholy within the grey. Being inside the aetherosphere was like being suspended in a dry fog: everything felt muffled, and there was nothing to do or see.

Rue tended towards grumpiness, because she said the grey made her ache and tingle. Percy said that this was likely something to do with the ambient aether interacting with her metanatural abilities. And then he wanted to perform experiments on her. Rue bopped him on the back of his head with a sausage link and told him to mind his own business.

Miss Sekhmet, of course, being a supernatural creature, fell into a deep deathlike sleep. Prim worried that prolonged exposure to the grey wasn't healthy for a werecat. After all, werewolves got horribly airsick, and vampires went insane when immersed in such vast quantities of aether. Tasherit brushed off any concern (expressed by Rue at Prim's request) with a dismissive wave and simply confined herself to her room. Where, no doubt, she curled into a ball and suffered alone, if indeed she

suffered at all. Prim refused to worry further. Which she told
herself firmly every time she walked past Tasherit's closed door
and was tempted to check. Strangely, she found herself walking
by that door a great deal more frequently than her duties ordinarily allowed.

Formerly Floote, being also a creature of aetheric representa-
tion, could not make any appearances. He was trapped inside
his dead body in its Lefoux tank.

Percy muttered something about tethers not existing inside
aether, or being subsumed by aether prevalence, or there being
too many possible tethers or something. Percy found the reactions of the supernatural when exposed to the aetherosphere
rather too fascinating for Prim's comfort. He was always threatening to bring vampires up in the *Custard* and *see what happened*.
This appeared to be a specific objective of her brother's, merely
because the last report of vampire aetherosphere exposure was
over forty years old. Which didn't mean it was a good idea. Poor
vampires! Prim felt a sudden satisfaction that they were floating
to the rescue, as it were.

Fortunately for any vampire foolish enough to take Percy up
on his planned course of experimentation, Rue had put her foot
firmly down on the matter. This came as no surprise considering she had a beloved vampire for an adoptive father. Percy was
not allowed to tender an offer, not even by post to a rove. Nor
could he invite anyone in person. Nor could he slip his request
into conversation when in polite society. Not that he ventured
into polite society all that often. Rue made her wishes explicitly
clear, and did not give Prim's twin any kind of loophole. Rue
was accustomed to dealing with Percy. And this could only be
thought a good thing. Because if Percy went up against vampires, Prim would not wager on the vampires.

Regardless of Percy's thwarted endeavours, with no werecat,
no ghost, and the captain twitchy and maudlin, things were
markedly subdued during their float further eastwards. To
pass the time, Primrose put the decklings and sooties through

lessons. She was teaching them reading, mathematics, social graces, the quadrille, and minor stabbing techniques. Useful things like that. She avoided Percy, because he was a pill, and chatted pleasantly with Quesnel when the opportunity arose.

Primrose rather liked Quesnel, once he stopped flirting with her. He was better off concentrating on and flirting with Rue, who flirted back. Quesnel seemed the only thing able to lift Rue's spirits. He'd rather embraced the role, doing everything he could to put a smile on their captain's face. It was nice to see. And odd, in a love *affaire*. Primrose had never thought humour and genuine affection might be involved in romance. Who would have considered it even possible?

They dropped out of the grey and depuffed over Port Moresby, which was served by a tiny fueling station. However, it was so very rarely used that they were able to top up their helium and even take on a bit of reserve for the *Porcini*. The boiler room also got a full restock of coal.

Primrose, as ship's purser, went in search of supplies in Moresby, only this time she took Quesnel and Tasherit with her. Rue might very well leave any two of them behind, but she wouldn't dare abandon all three.

Primrose found some unfamiliar fresh vegetables that looked tasty – that's assuming they were, in fact, vegetables. If they were actually fruit, she wasn't so certain. Either way, they would likely shock Cook into apoplexy. Cook was very good with pastries, which is why Rue valued him so highly, but he was, to be fair, not exactly fantastic with strange vegetative matter. Percy said that Mr Tarabotti called his cooking *mush*, and Prim half-heartedly agreed with this assessment. It may not be fashionable to prefer her vegetables with a bit of colour and texture to them, but she did. So far as Prim was concerned, the grey need not permeate food as well as atmosphere when they were floating the high currents. That was taking things too far.

She wondered if she might speak with Mr Tarabotti on the subject of food. Perhaps he had thoughts on techniques she might encourage Cook to try. Especially with those vegetables neither she nor Cook had ever encountered before.

Emboldened by optimism, Prim purchased several large bunches of very green things, which no doubt would give Cook hysterics but might prove tasty with the application of Italians. They made it back to the ship in very good time and without being abandoned.

Percy was wandering around the main deck looking stuck-up and arrogant — more so than usual, which was a sure sign of worry. They were headed out over the open ocean of the South Pacific next. It was a rarely travelled route. He'd found only two recorded currents, and both would require multiple jumps through the Charybdis. That was assuming no major shifting had occurred since last they were charted. It was going to be a dangerous journey.

The Spotted Custard was not a long-haul airship. She was designed for world travel, but only in short stints. This particular route would put them almost ten days in the grey, divided into two legs. Primrose herself wasn't comfortable with that from the supply side of the equation. Ten days of travel without a wheystation pushed their reserves. Fresh water would have to be restricted to drinking and cooking only. If her brother was off at all in any of his calculations, they'd have to ration. And they would be using Swiss milk for tea, which Rue loathed more than anything. Swiss milk would make their captain even more grumpy than usual.

Prim worried about Tasherit too. Almost a fortnight without food or drink? Even deep in dreamland, would she survive undamaged?

Back aboard and decoupling from the station for float-off, Primrose touched the lioness's hand, hesitantly.

"Ten days asleep, you'll be all right, won't you?"

"You worry, little one?"

"Of course I do. You're part of the crew, it's my job to worry."

"Your job. Only that?" The werecat looked wistful.

"So you won't starve?"

"I am an immortal."

"You can't starve?" Prim fiddled with one glove, missing the bump of the engagement ring beneath it. She found the times when the werecat focused solely on her rather unsettling. Tasherit's brown eyes were painfully direct.

"I can, yes, but not to death. And ten days is nothing compared to..."

"Compared to what?"

Tasherit reached forward, slowly, as though Primrose would leap away, and pressed the frown wrinkle in Prim's forehead with one soft thumb. "None of that, memories is all. I will be fine. And this is a good thing. I shall sleep through full moon."

Prim considered the lunar calendar. "Oh, yes you will. That's fine then. Replacing your scratching mats is getting a little expensive."

"Always so sensible, my little one."

The possessive made Primrose uncomfortable, even though she knew it was only a cat's way. So she tried to change the subject.

"Before you sleep, before we make the grey again, you should eat a full meal."

"A good idea. You'll join me?"

Prim said quickly, "I'll call the others. We'll make a formal gathering of it."

"Of course, the others." Tasherit's tone was disappointed.

Primrose hurried on. "In fifteen minutes or so – let me just tell Rue."

Rue was amenable to a slight pause for a formal meal before they took to the aetherosphere. So Prim arranged for an early supper and a quiet gathering without too much pressure on Cook to formally provide.

"Cold pies and cut fruit and cheese is sufficient," she assured the red-faced man. He snorted at her and made certain there was pudding, because that's all Rue would really remember anyway.

Prim attempted to be relentlessly cheerful as she presided over the meal. Rue, although captain and technically in charge, always let Prim take head of table and lead the discussion. Primrose enjoyed social niceties and the etiquette of address, and she was good at it. She was also good at passing around corner dishes and pouring the tea without trailing her sleeves in either. Tasherit sat to her right, as she often did, in defiance of precedence. *Well, I suppose we are all friends here.* The werecat ate mostly meat and cheese and drank mostly cream or milk. Rue sat to Prim's left, and then Quesnel. Percy slunk in late and slumped next to Tash, with Anitra on his other side.

Prim asked everyone how their day had been, and whether they felt their stations and crew were prepared for the longer float. She wished, privately, that Mr Tarabotti were available for meals – he might better balance their numbers and conversation. The higher ranks of *The Spotted Custard* leaned in favour of women. However, the very notion was ridiculous: one couldn't simply have an Italian murderer at table, no matter whose cousin he may be.

Formerly Floote was there, but he disliked actually sitting with them. He preferred to hover off to one side, perhaps in memory of his years as a butler. Or perhaps so he might observe without interruption. It was not as if he could partake.

Everything seemed to be going as well as might be expected. Until Percy looked up, turned slightly, and said to Anitra, "Miss Anitra, what exactly does *aravani* mean?"

Anitra dropped her fork with a clatter and her dark eyes went very big. "Sir! How did you hear such a word?"

Percy, ignoring (or unaware of) her distress, popped a cherry-like fruit into his mouth and said, "Mr Tarabotti used it to describe you. He called you a *lovely aravani*. I tried to look the word up, but it seems neither Latin nor Greek nor Italian nor anything else I could find."

Anitra flinched and looked down at her hands where they rested near the dropped fork. They were strong and covered with pretty gold rings and bracelets. She had a certain style to her dress that Primrose very much admired. Of course, it was not proper British attire, but Anitra was a Drifter, not an Englishwoman. Tonight she wore a long tunic of deep blue over multiple flowing skirts. Her head was draped in a black veil held in place with a bloodred diadem embroidered in gold thread. Her hair showed from under the veil as two long braids – very long, for they fell well past her waist and had red tassels at the ends.

Anitra said, awkwardly trying to deflect Percy's probing question, "It is not a word my people would use."

"Oh," said Percy, "then it is not Arabic nor Amharic nor..."

"No, it's not." Anitra had stopped examining her hands and was staring down at her food, fiercely. "It is something from India or perhaps one of the nomadic peoples nearby. Drifter cousins, if you would."

"Then why should our Italian friend use such a word?" Percy was only getting more curious, and he had no empathy at all. Primrose would have kicked him under the table except that he always sat out of reach of her boot.

"He is a well-travelled man, Mr Tarabotti. It is likely the only word he knows to use." Anitra stood at that. "If you will excuse me, I am feeling a little unwell." And then she rushed from the room.

Primrose glared at her brother. "Oh, Percy!"

Percy looked with great surprise after the departing lady and then turned back to those left around the table. "What? What did I say?"

Quesnel pointed a small gherkin at him with his knife. "You, my fine young friend, are an absolute imbecile."

Percy did not dignify that with an answer, turning his gaze on Primrose. "What have I done now?"

Prim fell back into her customary role of trying to explain things to her clueless brother. "That word clearly makes her uncomfortable. It's possible that it means something quite rude."

Rue now glared at Percy with mild annoyance. Although she never found him as annoying as Primrose did.

"Surely not." Percy returned to his meal.

"Why not?" Primrose asked him, grinding her teeth.

"Well," said Percy, "it's a very pretty word and Rodrigo said it in such a very nice way."

"Rodrigo, is it?" Primrose narrowed her eyes at her twin. "Just how chummy are you getting with that horrid man?"

"Oh, he's a decent sort."

"Percival Tunstell." Prim tried to keep her tone under control. They were, after all, still at table. "That man is many things, but *decent* is not one of them. You go after Anitra and apologise to her this instant!"

"Oh, but Tiddles, I haven't finished my – "

Primrose brought her wineglass – empty, thank heavens – down heavily on the tabletop. "Now!"

Percy grabbed an apple-looking thing from the centrepiece arrangement and stood, leaving the room as ordered.

Prim could only hope he caught Anitra before she locked herself in her private quarters. And that he not ask the girl any more personal questions.

"Well done, Miss Tunstell," said Formerly Floote's quiet voice.

"Thank you, sir. I do apologise for losing my temper. My brother would try the patience of a saint. That poor girl. *Aravani* probably means something horrible and crass."

Formerly Floote did not offer to explain. Which Prim felt was a good thing, or her ears might burn with mortification.

"Well," said Quesnel, looking smug, "that was dramatic."

Prim sighed and reached for the decanter to refill her wineglass.

Next to her, Tasherit went suddenly quite still.

"Miss Primrose," said the werecat, more formal than usual.

Pleased with the correct address, Prim turned a radiant smile on her dining companion. "Yes, Miss Sekhmet?"

The werecat's eyes, liquid and luminous, were fierce and concentrated on Prim's bare fingers. "You are not wearing your ring." Prim drew her hand back quickly, nervous and self-conscious. "No. No, I am not."

Across the table and down, Rue sat back in her chair, crossed her arms, and looked very interested in whatever was going to happen next.

Quesnel glanced at the hand in question. "Oh dear, Miss Prim, have you had a falling-out with Lieutenant Plonks? I thought you were quite fond of his – "

He was abruptly cut off when Rue, obviously and with no attempt to hide the gesture, elbowed him in the side.

Quesnel pressed on, grinning, his remarkable violet eyes twinkling in delight. "Quite fond of his legs."

Primrose narrowed her eyes. At table, no less! Really, the officers aboard this ship were barely civilised. "Yes, indeed I was."

Tasherit let out a slight hissing noise, like air escaping a ballast balloon.

Prim refused to look at her. "But he, as it turns out, was not so very fond of me."

Quesnel looked at Rue in shock, then back at Primrose. "*He* broke it off?"

Prim inclined her head, haughty. "He did."

"He is a fool," said Tasherit fervently.

Primrose felt herself go hot. It was humiliating to have her private affairs aired like this, over supper. Without her ring, they were bound to figure it out eventually, but to say something about it, to her face and across the dinner table, was really taking things too far.

It ate at her. The embarrassment at being discarded. The guilt of having engaged herself to someone on the basis of his legs, although she could not, for the life of her, think of a better reason. After all, she had liked *something* about him. Prim's embarrassment had another component. Something sank at the pit of her stomach, where it curled, making her nauseous.

Something that had to do with Tasherit noticing that Prim was found wanting by others.

Suddenly Primrose felt that she'd sampled a little too much of the excellent wine. Her head ached. She stood up.

"Well, on that note, I believe I, too, shall retire. I think Percy said we would hit the grey in two hours and then puff up twice to catch the correct current. I recommend we all strap down our breakables and prepare for a bumpy float."

Tasherit stood when she did and put out a hand.

Primrose pretended not to notice and fled the room feeling just this side of humiliated.

Percy tried to apologise to Anitra, but by the time he caught up to her, she'd already closeted herself inside her room. He was no cad to attempt to follow a lady into her private quarters. Besides, he wasn't entirely sure what he was apologising for. He'd only asked for a word to be defined, nothing salacious. Purely academic enquiry.

As long as I live, thought Percy, *I shall never understand the nuances of dinnertime conversation.* He sighed and turned back down the hallway. Wondering if it was safe to return to supper or if he was better off retreating to his own quarters, waiting out the general discomfort, and begging something more to eat from Virgil later.

Then he heard voices.

His sister and Tasherit stood in front of Prim's door a short way away, engaged in a fiercely combative discussion in low voices.

He didn't mean to pry, of course. But they were right there in the hallway and didn't seem to notice him closing in on them. He froze, unsure of what he should do in these circumstances.

"You didn't think it necessary to tell me?" the werecat hissed.

Prim threw her head back in that maddening way of hers that

said she was better than you and that the conversation you were forcing her to have was beneath her. "Why should I single you out for a private confidence of such delicacy?"

"You were free. You *are* free. And you said nothing!" Tasherit twitched. Percy fancied he could see her metaphorical tail lashing.

"It's embarrassing!" Primrose's tone was the height of frustrated.

"It's important. You are free. You can be mine now." Tasherit sidled in closer, in a way Percy wouldn't have dared when his sister was in such a temper.

"I am not a kipper for you to claim!" Prim's voice turned high and strident and breathy. Percy had never heard his sister like that before, not even at her most volatile.

Tasherit leaned forward. "Please be mine now."

Percy thought how much it must pain a cat to beg.

She tapped at Prim's shoulders, petted, tentative and hopeful, but also a hunter stalking her prey. When his sister did not flinch away, Tasherit tugged her in, pressing against her in an ardent manner.

Percy felt the blush stain his cheek. He really did not want to be here, and yet he dared not move or breathe for fear of notice.

It was no kiss, not as Percy had experienced or witnessed before, that's certain. No, it was more of a hug, except that Tasherit crushed her cheek to Prim's. Rubbed softly. A melting of bodies and need. Catlike.

Prim relaxed in the werecat's embrace for a long moment, as if she were letting herself breathe freely for the first time in her life. She lost, for one precious moment, all that stiff propriety that Percy had watched her don over the years like armour. Armour no doubt she needed to cope with their mother, to cope with Rue, and to cope with the world and its demands on her, and to cope with him.

Prim's eyes closed. She rested her temple on Tasherit's shoulder, her face turned towards Percy. He grimaced. There was such serene joy there, it embarrassed him more than anything else ever had. A brother ought not to see his sister so incandescent, it wasn't decent.

Then Primrose pulled back and dodged out of reach. Her relaxed posture turned into a slump of misery that Percy would not have thought possible while wearing a corset.

"It's no good."

Tasherit's eyes were flashing and fierce. "Little one, it's not only one direction. I am yours too."

"You shouldn't say such things." Prim turned to face her door and fumbled with the knob.

Percy felt his own hand press against his throat, his eyes drawn wide and tight.

"But why?" The werelioness was clearly in pain. "Is it because I have no pride to help provide for you? I assure you, I am an excellent hunter."

Prim looked wholly unhappy. "What? No. Nothing like that. It's that, well, you are, well, female . . . as such."

Tasherit cast her hands up to the heavens. "Of course, and this signifies how?"

Prim looked to her hand, still on the doorknob. "It's not *natural*. I have to go, there are things for me to do before the grey. Please excuse me."

She opened the door to her room and disappeared within, the sound of the bolt on the other side audible even to Percy where he still stood, frozen and ashamed to have witnessed such a profoundly private moment.

Tasherit leaned forward to thump her head on the wall next to the door.

She turned to look at Percy. No doubt she had been aware of him all along. She was, after all, a werecreature with a highly developed olfactory sense. "Of course it's not *natural*! I'm a *supernatural* being. How could anything I feel be less than that?"

Percy only blinked at her.

The werecat stalked towards him. "Explain your sister!"

"Umm," said Percy.

"Why is she so stubborn? I am not alone in this. I *know* I am not. I see her watch me. I sense her lean towards my warmth. I can smell . . . She is braver than this."

"Uh," said Percy, shifting from foot to foot. He had never been more uncomfortable in his life. Not even that time in front of the fourth form class after that ill-advised experiment involving a model hot-air balloon filled with gravy. *Well, maybe then, but still!*

"Explain!" Tasherit hissed at him. Even her anger was beautiful. Fierce, but beautiful.

"I don't . . . That is, I can't . . . That is . . ." Percy let out a puff of air he didn't realise he'd been holding. Then he glared at the stunning creature pacing before him. *How dare she put me in this kind of position? The very last thing I should ever want is to be at all involved in my sister's love life, let alone tangentially.* "She is difficult."

"So I gathered. Have you anything more useful to offer?"

Percy shook his head. "Do excuse me. I have, uh, New World vampires to investigate."

"A pleasure, as always, Professor Tunstell." Tasherit stalked away to her own room, closing the door with a decided click. Although not, Percy noted, sliding home the dead bolt.

Really, emotions are running awfully high all of a sudden on this ship. Percy retreated to his library, where Footnote bunted at his ankles and Aquinas proved modestly distracting. At least the epistemologist was a great deal more sensible than anyone else aboard *The Spotted Custard* at the moment.

Primrose did not make an appearance abovedecks for their puff up into the aetherosphere. Percy wasn't surprised. No doubt she was busy sulking in her room. And Formerly Floote and Tasherit were down for the duration. Thus it was a smaller audience than normal as he took the helm back from Virgil and piloted them into the grey.

Percy had the calculations noted, the level dialled in to the Mandenall Pudding Probe, and the charts to hand, but there was no denying his nervousness. These currents were very little used, and he'd found only two references to the first one. He had to hope it would carry them in the correct direction, or they'd be in a tumbled teakettle situation. If this current had drifted, or been noted down incorrectly, they'd come down out of the grey over open ocean with no recourse and not enough fuel to get them safely to land. They might be thousands of miles offshore. Even the nicest of dirigibles was good transport only with known currents to hand. This leg had them using two underutilised eastward currents. *I must be right about this. If my calculations are off...*

He corrected himself. *My calculations are never off! Buck up, Percy old chap. And let's float this beauty.*

He narrowed his eyes, flipped on the propeller, and gripped the helm sure and firm, using muscles he'd only recently developed helming. He pushed until they pointed in the correct direction.

He picked up the speaking tube to engineering.

"Yes?" Aggie's curt voice at the other end.

"Approaching the aetherosphere. Is engineering ready for multiple puffs?"

"Of course. You gave us the timetable."

Percy bristled. "Ship's protocol demands that I get a verbal affirmation."

"Consider it affirmed then, Freckles. Now get off the blowhorn, some of us have real work to do." A decided click from the other end.

"Really." Percy shook his head and looked at Rue, who was hovering nervously nearby. "I don't know why Quesnel allows her to converse with others. There's no excuse for that level of rudeness."

Rue laughed heartily. "Says Percival Tunstell."

Percy had no idea what was so funny. Really, one would think after twenty years of association he would understand Prudence Akeldama more. And yet she only became more confusing.

Fortunately, it was time to catch their first current.

He puffed them up.

The grey surrounded them completely. Close, still silence was everywhere.

Rue grimaced but Percy felt no change in emotional sensation at all. He never did. It was only that things were a little muffled and curiously absent of sound and smell and taste. One was suffused with an eerie sensation of knowing that the Earth must still be there, far below them, but no longer visible. Percy rather liked the aetherosphere, a restful sort of place, like taking a deep breath and sinking down into the murk at the bottom of a lake. Only substantially less slimy.

He checked his notes and did two full puffs up in quick succession. They shifted through the Charybdis currents, those tiny useless directionless flows that hindered travel for years until the first explorers determined that there were other more useful currents in between them.

The *Custard* caught one Charybdis and swirled into a lazy waltz-like spin. It wasn't bumpy per se, but the ship listed a little, a hint at the possibility of danger. If one current caught and twisted the balloon section while another caught at the gondola, then they were in real trouble.

Percy puffed them again. So many puffs put them fully within the known levels of the grey. There were an unknown number of levels: no one had managed to get to the top as of yet, because the higher one puffed, the less breathable the air became and the stronger the Charybdis currents. So far, twelve puffs was the highest anyone had ever gone. Percy fancied a diver's rig, with breathing tube trailing down, might do the trick for puffing even higher. But he would rather someone else tried it out. He wasn't the adventurous sort at all, not with his own safety. Well, not unless his sister and her best friend forced him into it. He would have been happy at home in London with his library and his academic arguments and his mother's meddling. *Fine. Well. Perhaps not happy, but content enough. Instead here I am, navigating an unstable aetherosphere.*

Below him, the Mandenall Probe spat out its viscous fluid near one of Percy's shoes, confirming his supposition. Pulling himself back to the serious business of navigation, Percy puffed them up one more full depression. This *should* be the correct current.

He relaxed slightly but then they listed badly to one side. The balloon above him began to cave.

"Percy!" yelled Rue as if he hadn't noticed.

"Yes, Captain, I see it." It was a switchback current, dragging the airship in two different directions. *We aren't fully nested in the charted one, and a different current, one that isn't supposed to be there, is hitting us broadside.*

Percy checked his calculations against the puffer dial, to make absolutely certain he'd entered everything into the probe correctly. Fortunately for his ego, everything matched up perfectly. *Because I don't make silly mistakes.*

Unfortunately, that meant they had a different problem. Either the current had shifted vertically or it no longer existed and the charts lied. There was no way to know which of these options was the reality.

"Captain, charted current not as charted. Orders?" This was, after all, Rue's job.

Rue frowned. "Assessment of most likely scenario given what you know of the previous navigation jaunts?"

Percy frowned. The record of this current was over five years old. That meant the ship which had puffed before them was of a vastly inferior technology. Calculations on puffing were likely to have been less precise, based on instrumentation alone, regardless of whether the navigator was as good as he was. (Which was unlikely, of course.) An older ship was also less accurate on height per puff. But what model of ship had it been?

Percy thought over what he knew of the records. *Chinese. Junk with a softwood hull for the gondola, like the* Custard. *Smaller two-balloon structure. Puff would need to be timed for both balloons and would let off excess air unmonitored.* Percy rapidly did the mathematical adjustments in his head.

"Percy! We're listing!"

"Sorry, Captain. I'm attempting to calculate the differential in puff quality between us and an older-model Limber Junk Mark Eight."

"Well, calculate faster."

Percy huffed out in annoyance. He was loath to do it but he simply didn't know enough about older dirigible construction. He picked up the tube to engineering.

"Yes?"

"Miss Phinkerlington, put Mr Lefoux on the tube."

"He's busy."

"Now, Miss Phinkerlington."

"But – "

"NOW!" Percy never raised his voice. Around him the decklings stilled in shock. Even Rue paused her customary frenetic pacing.

Aggie grumbled but he heard her yell for her supervisor. Moments later Quesnel Lefoux's cheerful voice said, "This had better be important, Professor." Things must be tense in the boiler room, as the man's French accent was showing.

Percy didn't bother to explain. "Tell me the puff differential between our ship and an older-model junk."

"How much older?"

"Five years at least, possibly more. I simply need to know if a Junk Mark Eight would likely put out more or less air for an upward puff."

"Percy, this had better be important."

Percy looked up to see Rue red-faced and sweating, the balloon above her caving even more. The whole ship was now tilted to the left at a twenty-degree angle – things, people were beginning to slide. They had to be feeling this in engineering. Soon the boilers would cease to function. *Or, of course, explode.*

"I suspect our lives may depend upon it, Mr Lefoux."

"More than us. *More!*" gasped out Quesnel, and then, "I must go, second kettle isn't looking healthy."

Percy hung up without bothering to sign off. Letting out more air meant the older ship would take each puff higher. Assuming the charted current was still there, this meant *The Spotted Custard* needed to drop down slightly.

Percy took on half a quantity of air and depuffed them a half mark. He looked up.

This was the main issue when floating: everything was slower to act and react than with other forms of transport. This was usually a good thing. But in this instance, he couldn't tell if the cave-in was getting worse or better.

"Rue, I need an assessment, ask your high eyes."

"Nips!" Rue hollered up to their deckling in the crow's nest. "That better or worse?"

"Hold a moment, Lady Captain!"

A tiny figure far above them leaned out from one arm and one leg and swung himself in a wide and hazardous arc.

"Don't kill yourself, you nubbin!" yelled Rue, her face now quite pale.

"It's looking better, Lady Captain. But I'm thinking top point is still in that twister."

Percy depuffed them again, this time only a quarter.

The balloon began to re-form into its nice chubby shape once more, a big spotted ladybug.

Rue let out a long breath. "Good job, Percy."

The speaker tube squawked at him. Percy picked it up.

"What the hell was that!" Quesnel Lefoux's voice was all irritation, but smoothly English once again. No hint of the French. All was now well with the boilers.

Percy glared at the tube. "Not my fault. Original charting was off due to an older-technology bias."

"So the probe coordinates were off?"

"Yes. And before you ask, yes, I'll make a note to take into account this bias for the next jump and any further charts originating with airships of this class. Yes, we're going off the same charts for the next leg. Looks like each charted puff was about an eighth of a point higher than modern measures."

"You'll report it back to the nearest chartographer of record when we reach the next aetherographic transmitter?"

"Have to. Anything less than a ship of our calibre would never have survived that kind of twist. And it was purely a lucky guess I made, that we needed to depuff. Others might not make that same choice."

"You're sure depuffing put us in the correct current?" Of course, Quesnel asked the question that Percy really didn't want to ask himself.

Percy didn't want to admit it, especially not to an academic Frenchman, but if anything happened to him it was better if this man knew. Quesnel was the only other person aboard capable of making the calculations needed.

"No. But it's my best guess based on what we know of old junks and these currents. Compass says we are heading east, so that's something. How fast is another question, but we're nested in it now."

The Frenchman on the other end let out a sigh. "So you say."

He then hung up the tube without further discussion. Percy glared at it. Then he glared at Rue.

"It really wasn't my fault!"

"Of course it wasn't," she said, condescending.

"My calculations were based on faulty data."

"Of course they were."

Simply because she couldn't understand what he did to get them where they were going!

"*Ex nihilo nihil fit.* I am surrounded by inferior intellects," Percy told Footnote, who had appeared at some point in the preceding chaos and was now sharing the navigation pit with him. When Sekhmet took to her bed, Footnote considered the entire ship his personal domain, and preferred to be wherever Percy was.

Rue didn't listen and Footnote only gave him a wide-eyed look of terror. The cat did not approve of his ship suddenly tilting wildly to one side.

"How long are we floating inside this one?" Rue asked.

"I gave you the details, Captain!" And he had. He'd pulled all the charts and notations together for her to look over hours ago.

"Yes, well, I missed that part."

Percy sighed. "We're four days in this one before we drop down to atmosphere over the South Pacific Ocean. Once we are out of the grey there are no landmarks to let us know if we are on course. So the next leg is even more dicey. We'll be out for a few hours while we wait for the next current to shift over us. Then we do this again, hopefully without the balloon collapsing. As I told Quesnel, I'll have to correct my calculations based on our newly assessed floatation errors. Calculations were off by – "

Rue held up a hand before he could explain further. "I don't need the details, Percy. Will four days be long enough for you to do what needs to be done?"

Percy looked at her in disgust. "Four hours is more than enough time. Didn't you listen, Rue? I only need to adjust the puffs by an eighth and then – "

"Yes, yes, Percy, I'm certain you will do an excellent job."

I hate it when she gets like this. And she does seem to be worse than usual. I wonder if there is something seriously wrong with her? No, only Rue being Rue. Percy sniffed. Loudly. "I'm going to get started right away. This is supposed to be a quiet current, now that we're in it. Unless, of course, we are in the wrong one, or a new one. Virgil can take over for me for the time being."

And I need to be where other people are not for a while. Percy knew himself well enough for that. Especially as everyone clearly blamed him for the rather exciting puff they'd just endured. And absolutely no one was smart enough for him to explain how it wasn't his fault.

He glared at everyone, and everyone – decklings, deckhands,

Spoo, Virgil, Rue, and Anitra, who were all on deck for the hop – looked away from him.

Percy stormed off to his quarters, grumbling about inferior intellects and clutching the offending charts to his breast.

At some point over the last few hours he seemed to have misplaced his hat. He was perversely smug about the fact that no one, not even Virgil, dared to tell him so.

CHAPTER
SIX

In Which Thomas Aquinas Is an Absolute Corker

Primrose caught her brother hurrying to his library. He was gripping charts and looking fit to be tied.

"Percy, what was that? I've never felt such a rough puff from you, not unless we were under attack."

"Oh, don't you start!"

"We tilted, we positively *tilted*." Prim was feeling rather overwhelmed by the way her day was going thus far. Then to have all one's possessions suddenly go sliding across the room for no good reason. Well! That on top of a highly sentimental encounter with an eager werecat? It was too much. *Really, quite, too much.*

"It happens sometimes when a chap's starting data is flawed. I'm fixing it for the next one. But it wasn't my fault!" Percy waved the chart at her. As if she could even read one of those mysterious things.

"I never said it was, brother dear. Do you think Tash...uh, Miss Sekhmet is well? I worry she may have fallen off her bed all unawares with this kind of rough activity."

Percy glared at her. "Really, Tiddles, that's most unfair. If you genuinely don't want her, you must stop leading her on."

Primrose felt herself heat with agitation. "Leading her on? *Leading her on!* What nonsense you talk."

Percy snorted and scrunched his charts in clear annoyance.

"Either she is yours to worry about or she is not. It's no good get-ting all concerned and aflutter when she's fast asleep and can't see it, only to ignore her when she is awake. It's like how you are gen-tle and petting when she is a lioness and aloof when she is not."

"I've no idea what you're talking about, Percival, really!" Percy really did come up with the most extraordinary statements on occasion. *My brother is a loon. I'm not aloof! I'm polite and friendly and a good-natured wholesome young lady of quality.*

Percy was obviously still grumpy about the bad float. He was also frustrated at having to talk to her when he would rather be alone recalculating his charts or what have you. Prim recognised the signs. *I only want to know what happened. Trust my brother to turn it into a ridiculous argument about his ego and my actions.*

Percy let out a noise like an aggrieved bagpipe. "Primrose Tunstell! Even I have noticed your bad behaviour. Me! And I rarely notice anything about people – or so everyone implies. Especially not people *with* other people. You are being cruel to that woman. And a hardened flirt. I thought my sister was better than that."

Prim felt her eyes fill with tears. Yes, Percy could be cruel himself when he deemed it warranted, especially regarding her intelligence and lack of advanced education, but he wasn't often cutting about her behaviour. Mostly because, to be fair, she never gave him reason. "I have been perfectly proper in all things. As I *always* am."

"Exactly!" said Percy, as if this explained his annoyance per-fectly. At which juncture he slammed into his library, leaving Prim alone in the hallway.

Primrose gritted her teeth and tried not to cry at the unfair-ness of his accusations. *Stupid brother.*

Thomas Aquinas was an absolute corker. And Percy was toler-ably certain no one had ever thought to link those particular words together before in the history of mankind. But there was no denying his popularity with the newly formed *Spotted Custard* philosophy-club-meets-book-group. Aquinas caused a sensation. Percy had selected *Summa Theologica* (of course). It was a most agreeable collective that gathered in Mr Tarabotti's cell to mull over the implications of human law versus natural law versus supernatural law and the relative merits of each when applied to preternaturals. Rue insisted that despite the fact that there was only one of her, and more metanaturals were unlikely ever to occur, she was *almost* comparable to a preternatural and ought to be included in the discussion. Which devolved them quickly into a debate on the nature of personhood and the rights of those with only partial souls. Even Spoo got in on it. Spoo had only recently learned to read but she was a crack at it. After discovering Percy's library was on hand to loan books, Spoo was making quite a nuisance of herself. Percy didn't mind overmuch, so long as she returned the books unsmudged.

Since Spoo was mildly terrified of Percy, the books always came back in pristine condition. Then she would hesitantly ask him about something else that interested her and he would consult his cloud about it and find her some tangential work and send her on her way. Percy wasn't a hoarder, he liked to share his knowledge.

Anyway, when Spoo discovered that he and Rue – whom she practically worshipped – were reading philosophy together, she asked if she could as well. Which brought Virgil into the mix, because they were chums. Rue brought along Anitra and glared at him about it. Which Percy suspected had something to do with his lack of apology about the *aravani* question. Fortunately, the Drifter woman didn't seem to be holding a grudge against him.

All this meant that Rodrigo Tarabotti's quarters were overflowing with ship's navigator, ship's captain, head deckling, valet, lead interpreter, Footnote (of course), and, last but not least, ship's prisoner.

Spoo and Virgil were rather endearing in their enthusiasm, even if Aquinas was a little much for such young souls. If Percy was being honest with himself, which he did try to be within the confines of his own head, Aquinas was a little much for him too.

With nothing better to do, trapped for several days in the grey, they agreed to move on to the next book and pass it around quickly, so they might discuss again sooner rather than later.

The discussion having come to its natural conclusion – Aquinas will do that to a crowd – they all turned to Percy expectantly.

Percy frowned at Rodrigo. "Do you feel improved, Mr Tarabotti?"

"What?" The Italian looked confused.

"Well, isn't this a course of improvement?" Percy looked to Rue for help. *Do I have this wrong?*

"That's what I thought," said his captain, grinning at her cousin. Something about Percy's question seemed to amuse her greatly.

Percy slumped. *I must have said something wrong again.* He wracked his brain, which squelched at him, exhausted by charts and philosophy. *Did Rodrigo not know our intent?*

Anitra said, "Are we supposed to tell him that outright? Doesn't it defeat the purpose, him knowing we are after improving him?" She darted quick, hesitant, dark-eyed glances at the Italian man.

"Know what?" wondered Rodrigo.

"That we are trying to save you." Rue didn't stop grinning.

Rodrigo frowned darkly, reminding them all of the murdering scoundrel who had first come aboard *The Spotted Custard.* "*Basta.* There's nothing to save. I have no soul."

Anitra gasped in a small hurt way.

Spoo and Virgil looked at each other, surprised not by the statement but by the vehemence.

Percy felt a little like a hero who had somehow fallen. He struggled to make the man understand. "That is the point of our whole discussion. We aim to see if we can reform you with reason, as we cannot save you with theology."

Rodrigo Tarabotti sat back, long fingers steepled like the churches he would never have been allowed to enter. "You can reform a daemon?"

"That's the point," said Rue. "We don't think you *are* a daemon. The argument being that soullessness doesn't necessarily make you evil. Just soulless. Evil is what you do with that absence."

Percy tapped his cheek with a stylus he'd picked up at some point for some reason he could no longer remember. "Personally, I don't even believe *soulless* is the correct way of thinking about a preternatural, nor for a metanatural. I think it's simply scientists using religion to explain away a thing they do not understand." Percy tried not to sound as annoyed as he felt. *Really, it's lazy science to go about anything that way.*

Virgil tutted at him and took the stylus away. No doubt he was marking up his face with carbon smudges something fierce.

Rodrigo looked disbelieving, and then humbled. "Thus making my whole past a lie."

"Not to mention the attitudes of various churches for generations. But that's Percy for you." Rue had no sense of propriety.

Percy shrugged. "Worse things have happened."

"Not to me. You are cruel, professor." Rodrigo's dark eyes were introspective. His shoulders curved downwards. He looked... *What is that? Shaken?*

Percy would have none of it. This was self-pity disguised as an attack. "No. Your past was cruel to you. I am honest. Now, let me see, what was I saying? Oh yes. If the premise of the theory is at root faulty, to wit, that you are soulless and Rue here has only half of a soul some of the time" – Rue inclined her head and Percy continued – "then we must, perforce, formulate a new supposition."

"Sì? Big words, but I think I am with you."

"And what supposition is that, Percy?" Rue played right into his hands. Percy thought, not for the first time, she might have made a decent stage actress had she not been born, well, quite rich.

Percy gestured at Rodrigo with the flat of his hand. "That you, my good man, are capable of basic human decency."

"Oh. Now. Professor! Too far." The Italian looked legitimately appalled at this accusation.

Spoo giggled.

Virgil glared at them all. Percy ignored his valet. What did a valet know of logical suppositions?

He hastened to make himself clear. "I'm certainly not accusing you of *possessing* basic human decency, or practicing it, Mr Tarabotti. I'm merely intimating that you likely possess the capacity for such."

Mr Tarabotti tugged at his ear in a pained way. "You say there was..." He faltered on his phrasing, he was never very good with past tense. The rest of the book group held their collective breath. "I had a choice?"

Percy nodded curtly.

"Oh." He looked... Percy could not quite figure the man's face. Crestfallen perhaps. Something more.

They left him then. Best let a man reshape his view of the world on his lonesome.

Rue, who had no tact, commented on the man's expression once they were outside in the hallway. Fortunately, she waited until Virgil and Spoo skipped off, leaving only her and Anitra behind with Percy to mull over what had so recently occurred.

"He looked shattered," said Rue, and she looked sad. She had been hiding it before. Hiding it well. *Is it part of being metanatural?* Percy wondered. *To take on other moods and other modes with such ease? Just like she takes on shapes.* He never could. Too blunt, old Percy. Too honest. Lost his friendships because of it, not that he ever had that many.

Percy nodded. *Shattered* was a good way of putting it.

"Will this break him?" Anitra's voice was low and soft, with a tremble to the question.

Percy was surprised at the very idea. *Thought, of course, is powerful. But how can the study and discussion of philosophy destroy a man as tough as Rodrigo Tarabotti?*

Rue was practical and overly honest. "He's broken already."

Percy nodded again. *True enough.*

"You are harsh, Miss Prudence." Anitra's big brown eyes were filled with sympathetic pain. Percy wondered that anyone could be so compassionate. But then she was Formerly Floote's adopted granddaughter. The ghost had quite revered his former master. Alessandro Tarabotti, Rue's grandfather, was (so far as Percy could gather) not unlike Rodrigo. No doubt Anitra had learned compassion for deadly preternaturals at the feet of one who understood them best.

Rue defended herself. "Acknowledging the break gives us an opportunity to fix it."

"I think we should invite Formerly Floote to join our group – once we are out of the grey again, of course." Percy said it in that way he knew drove everyone around him spare, because he had followed his own train of thought, and they had not. Thus it seemed as if he wasn't paying attention to their conversation and was starting a new one without cause. When, of course, it was all connected.

Anitra and Rue rounded on him. Anitra looked confused, but Rue asked, "Why?"

"Because he was Alessandro Tarabotti's valet. I think he may understand our troubled Italian friend better than most." *Better than anyone else aboard this ship.*

"Because he once lived with his own version?" Rue's tawny eyes were squinted in understanding.

"Exactly. And loved him."

Rue started. "You think Floote was in love with my grandfather?"

Percy gave her a funny look. *I thought everyone knew that.* "Love of a kind. In love? I cannot say, but loved, certainly. How else do you explain his excessive loyalty?"

Rue and Anitra exchanged startled looks.

"Percy." Rue tilted her head at him. "Sometimes you are so perceptive it's uncanny, and the rest of the time you're a ninnyhammer."

Percy nodded. "You are not the first to notice this. Of course, I think I'm perceptive all the time, and it's simply that the rest of the time you can't follow my superior intellect."

Rue said to Anitra, "And there he goes, off bobbing for arrogance at the bottom of the pickle barrel."

Anitra gave a small smile. "Sometimes I wonder if he's worse than Mr Tarabotti."

Rue laughed. "He does come off as awfully soulless, doesn't he?"

Percy did not rise to the bait. Which only proved their point, of course, but he would not be mismanaged. "Ladies, do pay attention. Our objective, as I understand it, is to make our charming friend there think critically about his past actions and realise that how he was raised was a manipulation that worked against his best interests. Not to mention the best interests of the world around him. Am I right?"

Rue nodded.

Anitra said, "I believe that has already begun."

"And with this philosophy club we are giving him a new foundation, a way forward into feelings of benevolence towards his fellow man, as well as a means for him to believe in his own capacity for objective critical choice. I'm merely pointing out, ladies, that by doing this we also give him the capacity to eventually question *us* about *our* agenda."

"Percy, sometimes you are as bad as Aquinas." Rue was clearly getting annoyed.

Percy glared at his captain. "My point is merely this: we *do have* an agenda. And the very manner by which we are encouraging him to become less a killer and more a civilised gentleman will also provide him the means to question our own motives."

"Oh," said Rue. Understanding creased her smooth forehead.

"Oh dear," added Anitra, following Percy's reasoning as well.

"Independent thought," emphasised Percy, "is *independent* thought. We cannot control the outcome. And if we try, we risk becoming the very thing we fear and are persuading him against. Evil." He was blunt in order to drive his point home. He hoped both of them fully understood the implications of a proper philosophy club.

"So? What do we do then? I would rather turn him than see him hung for treason, be it in my country or his. He is, after all, my only cousin."

Percy shrugged. "The only one you know of."

Rue blanched at that.

"So what more can we do?" Anitra wrung her hands together, the bangles on her wrist flashing occasionally in the dim gas lighting of the hallway.

"What is it, in the end, that turns a man to the path of righteousness?" asked Percy, genuinely interested. Women, after all, were supposed to understand such things.

"Tea?" suggested Primrose, popping out of her own room to join them at that exact moment. She grinned. Apparently, all her worry over Miss Sekhmet had passed for the time being.

Percy glared. "Be serious, Tiddles."

"Well, at the risk of idiocy, having only just joined the conversation, may I remind you of that old saying?" His sister closed her eyes to think. " 'To render a man's soul without religion requires logic, love, loyalty, or legal tender.' "

Percy nodded. Pleased. "Exactly, sister. So we are assuming Mr Tarabotti does in fact have some kind of salvageable consciousness or functioning emotions. Right now we are collectively trying *logic*. I recommend we attempt the other three as well: love, loyalty, and legal tender."

Rue put a hand to her throat. "Percival Tunstell, how Machiavellian. I should never have thought it. You. Devious."

Percy tilted his head back. "Don't push me, Rue, I'm unwilling to sacrifice myself. I'm not that noble."

"I say, Percy! What on earth do you mean?" All three ladies looked at him in utter surprise, but it was Prim who asked the question.

Really, thought Percy, *am I the only one who pays attention to what is actually going on aboard this ship? And I don't even like people.* "I mean to say, I'm not willing to play the part of a seducer in order to try and render him in *love*."

Primrose sputtered. Rue laughed. Anitra looked upset and thoughtful.

Silence descended.

Finally Anitra said, tentatively, "He gave you an opening?"

Percy shrugged. "So to speak."

Primrose gasped. "Percy! Never say you...!"

Percy glared at her. "What's so wrong with it? No, don't answer. Simply because you are all caught up in society's standards, never think I share your weak-willed pandering to the expectations of aristocratic snobs. You know me better than that. You all do. I don't care what people think."

Rue took a swallow and stepped forward. "You aren't of the Dama persuasion, are you?"

Percy sniffed. "No, I'm not. Which is why you can't use me on Rodrigo."

"Oh," said Rue, then, "Oh! But you think he might be?"

Anitra gave a pained little gasp.

Percy frowned at himself. *Clearly I am doing this very badly indeed. Ah well, I've messed everything up, I might as well be straight with them.* The thing is, Percy being direct with women had never done him any favours.

"Ladies. I am afraid I must be blunt, prepare yourselves."

"Percy, are you trying to be...nice?" Rue grinned.

Percy glanced at Anitra, who was still looking upset. Poor

thing, she seemed to be having a rough time of it of late. He took a breath. "It is my understanding that Mr Tarabotti favours both females and males. A varied diet, if you would."

His sister looked, if possible, even more shocked, which didn't really matter to Percy. She would pull herself forth from her ridiculousness or she would remain forever unhappy. *There is nothing I can do to help her in the matter of her own heart when she wilfully persists in ignoring it.*

Rue, on the other hand, looked intrigued.

Percy risked another glance at Anitra. The sweet little interpreter had brightened up, even relaxed slightly at his crass statement. *Good.* Percy nodded to himself, gave a curt little bow to the ladies, and made for the safety of his library as quickly as possible.

Behind him he heard Primrose say, in a hissed voice, "Is that possible? I mean, to like both?"

"Anitra, are *you* interested in our handsome criminal?" That was from Rue.

Percy did not hear what Anitra said to that, if anything.

He turned back to remind them, "Four ways, remember, ladies: *logic, love, loyalty, or legal tender.* You are, so far, thinking on only the first two."

He was rather proud of that for an exit line.

So far as Primrose Tunstell was concerned, this was not a particularly pleasant journey thus far. First there was the disastrous confrontation in the hallway with the werecat-who-shall-remain-snubbed, then her brother was an utter bother, then everyone got all excited about philosophy, and then they became disgustingly direct about perverted Italians.

I am prone to thinking of my brother as bumbling through life in that obtuse manner of his, and then he surprises me by noticing the oddest things. Prim tried to flinch away from what Percy had intimated in the hallway. She could not quite countenance it. She had accepted, as one must after continued exposure to Lord Akeldama, that there were men who preferred the company of, and presumably some form of physical intimacy with, other men. Primrose shuddered to contemplate how that might even work. She did not like to think on, at all, the fact that logic then dictated that there be *women* who felt the same about *other women*. Because contemplating how that might function was shudder-inducing as well, although not in quite the same sort of way.

There were the practical dictates of the marriage bed to consider, of course, of which her own understanding was limited. No doubt Rue would be happy to elucidate in detail if her relations with Quesnel were proceeding apace. Not that Prim wanted to know, but at least she had that resource. Rue and Quesnel remained rather disgustingly happily unmarried, but they were as good as – if one took matters of the carnal into account.

And now. Well, and now it seemed there might be those who enjoy the intimacy of both. And Percy, of all people, seemed utterly unperturbed about this. Primrose herself had little exposure to Rodrigo Tarabotti, and now she thought she would limit it even further. She wasn't certain how she felt about this revelation regarding his character, that character already being besmirched, not to say tarnished.

It did not occur to Prim to doubt Percy's accusation. She thought, in the end, that Mr Tarabotti might be perceived as gluttonous, or at least indulging in a significant lack of circumspection. But then, he did not seem the type of man to deny himself anything. He had been raised to believe he was evil, after all.

Prim's aether float from that point forward was spent in rather a tizzy of distressed finer feelings. She did not like it when the world, or the people in it, behaved beyond the bounds of polite expectations. Not that she was entirely fixed in her opinions.

Prim had enlarged her views in order to accept Rue's outrageousness with regard to keeping and maintaining a French lover, in the manner of some sordid opera singer. She had accepted this because she had learned to expect the outrageous from Rue. She filed Rue under the auspices of being perhaps overly fast. Although Prim would never say this to Rue's face. But at least her friend was engaging in horizontal exertions with a *man*.

Beyond that, Prim became flushed and distressed. She did not wish to know the preferences of imprisoned Italians. She did not like how accepting her brother was of such things.

Imagine, said Italian flirting with Percy! And Percy, no doubt in his brusque and uncaring way, simply brushing these advances off like specks of dust from a shirtsleeve.

How could Percy be so untroubled by such a thing when every time Miss Sekhmet comes near me I come over all faint and angry and rush for escape in either mind or body? It isn't fair. I'm supposed to be the composed twin.

This line of thought proving fruitless and vexatious, Prim spent the lion's share of her time – *oh dear, there it is again,* lion's *share* – investigating reports on the high mountains of South America and any possible vampire presence therein. She brushed up on her Spanish, which never would be as good as her French or Arabic. *Well, who would have thought one would need Spanish in one's life?* And generally spent more time in Percy's library than he did, for a change.

Footnote was delighted. They had always gotten along quite well. Primrose had an affinity for cats. He was happy to occupy her lap the moment she sat down. He performed his ritual of kneading imaginary bread and circling three times before the flop and purr with about as much seriousness as a cleric about his Sunday sermon.

And then, well, *and then* it came time for the next hop.

Primrose went up on deck, more for a chance at sunlight and fresh air while they dropped out of the aetherosphere than out of interest about the depuff and current transition.

Everyone was tense.

It was no secret Percy anticipated this hop would be as bad as, if not worse than, the last. He made noises about the unreliability of the charts they were using. The only charts they had. This was likely a way of blaming someone else for any prospective mistakes. She knew this was a pattern to Percy's behaviour in the past, but it had been years since he'd emphasised so vehemently the flaws in his tools rather than himself. Over the years, Percy had grown into his confidence as well as his arrogance. It was more like him to admit to no possible mistakes at all. Which made Prim think that perhaps there really was something wrong with their charts.

The fact that Quesnel Lefoux was equally nervous did not help. Rue's paramour was, in general, such a relaxed individual that to see him concerned at all was a profound shock to the system. To see him pacing about and barking orders in a decidedly French accent put everyone on edge.

The depuff was easy enough and *The Spotted Custard* popped out into the atmosphere without fanfare or flourish.

It was nighttime over the South Pacific, the skies around them free of clouds. This was both a delight and a relief, since they might easily have hit a tropical storm on a blind depuff like that.

The stars were vast and twinkling with savage cheer above them, and the sea was a vast and satin-rich bed of cruelty below. Primrose shivered at her own fancy, but there was something about the wide emptiness that terrorised. *I suppose I am nothing if not a creature of cities with bustling streets and cosy hearths. This vastness is not for me. And I am not for it.*

Prim tried to recall a time when she had floated so far offshore that land was no longer visible. She could remember none. Here, for all its rotund spotted majesty, their dirigible felt desolate. Abandoned. As a child Prim had crossed to Egypt by steamer, but she was too young to remember that journey. Since her mother became a vampire and settled in Wimbledon shortly thereafter, Primrose rarely left London (except to shop in Paris, of course). But crossing the Channel was nothing like this.

Steaming to Paris was a rough-and-ready passage, well used and crammed with other boats and fellow travellers.

Here Primrose looked down to the ocean and saw nothing: no one else, no longships, no gallant naval vessels. Nothing.

"Isn't it glorious?" A warm, mellow, slightly accented voice broke her loneliness. Primrose didn't need to turn to know who spoke.

She shivered. "No. It's too much." *Just like you.*

There was a rustle at the railing next to her and Tasherit appeared, leaning out over the abyss, perfect in profile. Tempting, utterly off-limits, vast in her possibilities. As terrifying as the ocean below.

Ordinarily Prim would have been on guard, and annoyed, and secretly pleased. Tasherit always awoke and sought her first. It was clear she'd recently emerged from her bed, for the werecat wore only a long flowing robe and her hair was loose and unbound.

Primrose shook off her sentimental mood and her terror, chiding herself for behaving like her mother – lowest of the low in Prim's opinion. She tried to simply be happy to have the company, as the crew went about their business in a tense silence. The decklings were usually prone to chatter and songs, but the vastness affected even them.

Primrose managed a calm, pleasant demeanour, angling politely towards the werecat.

Tasherit spoke to her but continued to face outwards. "There are places in the deep desert as still and abandoned as this, but there is something more lonely about the open water than the rolling sands."

"I've never been this far from land before."

"Nor have I. It is strange to have a new experience when one is as old as I."

Primrose wondered, because she was warped and perverse, if Tasherit had ever been with a man. Was she like Rodrigo Tarabotti, ambitious in her wanting, or was she one as marked in her preference for women as Lord Akeldama was in his preference for men? Was there something about being supernatural or preternatural that made one more flexible in one's desires? Or was it simply that having lived in and through multiple histories and times, one's judgement was less confined by the culture of the day? Had there been a time, once, when it was more common for a woman to be coupled to a woman than a man? *Surely not.*

Primrose shook her head at her own warped ideas. *Where is my mind wandering this evening? It's as off course as Percy's damnable charts.*

"How was the first leg?" asked the werecat.

At last, normal conversation. "Not so bad, really. Rough passage into the right current. But smooth once we hooked in. That's why everyone is so tense right now. Percy is worried about his calculations for this next hop."

"And it's the longer one."

It was not a question but Primrose answered it as if it were. "Yes. And if he has miscalculated, there is a chance we could go far off course. You'll be asleep throughout regardless. Speaking of, should we get you fed before we pop back into the grey?"

Tasherit looked at her, then nodded. "Who am I to turn away food? Will it be only us?"

Prim tried not to flinch. "Yes, the others are occupied and we only have a short window. I'll let them know there's tea in the stateroom should they need it, but nothing formal. They can stop in when they have the chance. Let me alert Cook. I'll meet you there in twenty minutes?"

The lioness inclined her head.

Twenty minutes later, they managed to be civilised about it. Prim felt the burn of the werecat's chocolate gaze on her at odd moments, but Tasherit did not press the advantage afforded by a mostly private tea. Her questions remained broad. She concerned herself with the state of the crew and ship.

She was mildly interested in Percy's book group. But frankly she was overburdened with soul and did not need ethics to fill a moral vacuum. Prim said she thought there were enough members already. She did not say that she did not like the idea of Tasherit sitting so close to a preternatural killer. He was, after all, trained first and foremost to assassinate supernatural creatures. Prim didn't think it a good idea to throw Tasherit into the mix. Might be too much of a temptation. Knowing that Rue attended the meetings was bad enough.

The rage Prim's missing engagement ring had engendered before seemed to have dissipated while Tasherit slept. Or perhaps the werecat merely stifled it. She looked at Prim with more concern than desire. Prim wasn't certain how to take that. So she drank her tea and made polite talk. Her stomach being strangely uneasy, Prim ate little, pressing meat pies and cups of cream upon her dining companion instead, worried that on this next leg Tasherit would be asleep for six days straight. How might this detrimentally affect her health?

Formerly Floote joined them briefly, materialising through the wall as he made his rounds. He did it most evenings first thing and always after any length of aetheric travel, drifting about through the public areas of *The Spotted Custard* as if running a check on staff and crew, assuring ship's safety and ascertaining that all was up to his ghostly standards.

Primrose decided she might ask him a delicate question, given the privacy of the tea. Ordinarily she would not interfere but there was no proper chaperone aboard the *Custard* so she felt it her duty. "Formerly Floote, may I have a word, please?"

The ghost paused and rotated in the air, settling across the table from her. Tasherit watched them both with interest.

"Certainly, Miss Tunstell. How may I be of service?"

"It is a delicate matter, a question about your granddaughter." "Yes?"

"When she first boarded, she said something about not being available for courting. Or she said it to Rue and Rue told me about it. I can't quite recall. It was something to do with coins or bells being absent from her veil."

"Yes?" Formerly Floote was not the most loquacious of ghosts. "Is this something chosen by her or by her family? If a gentleman were interested, how might he change her mind or advance his prospects?"

The ghost looked thoughtful, and then intrigued. "Is your brother . . . ?"

Primrose blushed. "Oh, no, forgive me. I am not asking for Percy. Another has expressed interest. I am concerned for her respectability and safety."

Formerly Floote smiled. "Anitra can take care of herself, I assure you."

Primrose wanted to tell him about Rodrigo Tarabotti's interest. That she suspected the girl was not as repulsed as she ought to be. But somehow she felt this would be betraying a confidence. She would not meddle if it was unwanted.

So she only inclined her head. "If you trust her judgement, so do I."

"Very good, ma'am," said the ghost, before floating on his way.

Tasherit shifted in her seat and put down her cup of cream. "What was that about, little one?"

Primrose shook her head. "Anitra's choices may not be so good as her grandfather believes, but it is not for me to expose them to others without grounds."

"Quite right. Who are you to call into question the viability of anyone else's relationships?"

Was that a cut? It certainly felt that way. Primrose hung her head. "It is true. I have been engaged more often than not. I am fickle."

"Is that what you think I mean?"

"It is all this travel I do. In very short order, any decent gentleman will want nothing to do with me. I shall be too worldly."

"Then perhaps you should stop looking in that particular direction."

Primrose put down the teapot. She shut her eyes and took a small breath. "Miss Sekhmet, I mean to marry."

"Yes, so I gathered."

"I wish to keep my own house. I want children. Family. Stability."

"Ah. So." The werecat flinched and took a gulp of her cream. Then she stood. "I should head to bed. We are almost to the puffing hour."

Prim watched her go. Then, very slowly, she listed forward and thumped her forehead on a spot of the table that was empty of dishware and available for such a necessary thing as knocking sense into young ladies of quality.

SEVEN

A Very Warm Welcome

The puffing went much more smoothly than Percy had expected. This meant he felt foolish for his concern, and angry with everyone else for doubting him. Even after having doubted himself. He solved this contrary sensation by ignoring all humanity for about twenty-four hours. Only Footnote was deemed acceptable society, and because Tasherit was once more abed, Footnote was off courting Prim. This only served to irritate Percy further. Why his cat so vastly enjoyed the society of his irritating sister was a complete mystery of unfair proportions.

However, Percy attended the next philosophy club meeting as if nothing had happened. Everyone followed his lead in this, because, frankly, nothing had happened. This time the group discussed the first half of *The Higher Common Sense*. Percy felt that if Fausse-Maigre couldn't cure Rodrigo Tarabotti of what ailed him – whatever that was – nothing could.

They traded around the book. Fortunately, Percy had two copies, as everyone should. *Higher Common Sense* was a masterpiece of modern thought, even if he hadn't written it. The book discussion was animated and persisted over the next few days while they floated in the grey. Even the aetherosphere couldn't subdue *Higher Common Sense*.

It was a lazy float, in the end. With nothing better to do, the sooties and decklings played cards, Primrose and Rue did each other's hair, Anitra quietly flirted with Rodrigo, and Percy read a great deal. Any reports on vampires in the mountains of South America were maddeningly elusive or mainly oral in nature. (It was not, certainly not, that his library was subpar.)

Percy should have known, of course. Such peace never lasts.

The Spotted Custard depuffed off the coast of South America to find, spread out below them, a massive vivid emerald lushness. This was marred only by a spine of brown, which represented the high-peaked mountains, and a ribbon of butter-coloured sandy beach before the rich teal of the ocean. It was so lovely that Primrose considered having a dress designed in that exact colour palette.

It was a bright sunny day, the kind of day one expects from the tropics. Too much for an immortal. Thus, Primrose doubted Tasherit would be joining them for float-down, to lean over the rails and make euphemistic commentary. That Prim missed the werecat was no excuse to go back below to ascertain if said werecat was awake. More than likely, Miss Sekhmet would sleep solid through until nightfall.

Prim did not like how long she took to convince herself of this fact. *Really*, she thought, *self-delusion is extremely hard work.*

Percy depuffed them several times, dropping the *Custard* by stages down through the atmosphere towards the city of Lima, which proved to be a white smudge of civilisation nested near the shore at the base of one of the many mountains.

Once the buildings became moderately distinct, he fired up the propeller to steer them in properly.

Rue, assured that everything was sufficiently under control, came over for a chat.

"What do we know about Lima, Prim dear?"

Primrose shrugged. "You realise that I haven't any guide-books for South America?"

"You must know something."

Prim scrunched up her nose. "It's Spanish speaking. Adobe houses. Good seafood. It is the source of alpaca, or this part of the world is the source at any rate."

"Alpaca?"

"A kind of cute, furry, goaty creature with very big eyes, makes wonderful wool. You know that afternoon dress I have with the skirt and sleeves of mignonette green? That's alpaca."

"Oh!" Rue remembered. "The one with the white silk bodice and the velvet neckband? That's alpaca? Soft."

"Yes, so you always say when I wear it. Then you pet me."

Rue tilted her head. "I'm irresistibly tempted by soft fabric. Oh, stop looking frowny, you *adore* me. So, what else do we know about Lima or its highlands? Or hinterlands?"

Prim considered. "Republic of Peru. You'd be better off asking Percy about local politics."

"But then I'd have to listen to him talk."

Primrose gave her friend a *look*.

Rue rolled her tawny eyes. "Percy doesn't have the same kind of insight as you. And I know you must have been reading up on the place. You like to pretend all you care about is hats and shopping, but I know better. Spill!"

Prim spilled. "Catholic, although I think I heard somewhere that they had trouble converting the highland tribes."

Rue grinned. "Recommendations?"

"Approach the lowland city for refuelling. Send Percy and anyone else who speaks Spanish out to listen in taverns or pubs or whatever the equivalent is in Lima. You're truly planning on vampire hunting or rescuing, or hunting to the rescue, as it were?"

"As instructed. Could be fun."

Primrose felt, as always, that Rue's idea of fun was warped at best. Still, it was her duty to be the prepared one in their relationship, always had been. "Any local supernatural element will be entirely in hiding. The conquistadors would have seen to that hundreds of years ago, and the church would have instituted an ongoing Inquisition ever since. So don't you or Miss Sekhmet dare change forms unless you absolutely must. They behead in this country. Keep a tight guard on Mr Tarabotti too. He could disappear easily here, and I doubt preternaturals are known or understood."

Rue looked pensive. Danger always made her at least a little bit thoughtful. "We have to go in, we need to restock."

Primrose took a breath and delivered the bad news. "This is not a land that drinks tea."

"What?!"

"They drink a beverage brewed from a leaflike stimulant. I can't remember what it's called."

Rue perked up. "So, a *kind* of tea?"

"Not exactly. Not even slightly." Prim dismissed the very idea that any other leaf beyond the sacred black could be of any interest whatsoever. "One Irish explorer wrote, and I quote, that it *tasted like fish scales mixed with rabbit droppings*."

Rue nodded. "So, worth trying then?"

"Oh Rue, you're so very droll." Primrose patted her friend's shoulder and wandered away. Rue's adventurous spirit translated to an exploratory palate that Prim neither envied nor admired.

It seemed, however, that fish-scale-flavoured beverages were not in Rue's future. Because when they were about a mile up off the coast of Lima, Lima started shooting at them.

Percy was not at all happy when the gunfire commenced. But then again, who is? Except maybe Rue. Percy had come to suspect, at a very young age, that Prudence Akeldama enjoyed being shot at overmuch. Perhaps that's why she became captain of a dirigible.

"Nothing in anything I've read on this part of the world led me to expect an attack!" objected Percy, to no one in particular.

Rue was already swinging into motion. "Willard, man the Gatling gun. Spoo, into the crow's nest, I need to know where that volley is coming from. I don't see anything. Doesn't *anyone* see anything?"

Rue began dashing about the main deck, going from one side to the other, looking for the source of the gunfire.

They had all heard it clearly but they didn't seem to have been hit and they couldn't see a thing.

Percy, who had a decent vantage from navigation, as he should, also couldn't see the enemy. On a hunch, he puffed them up. He theorised that higher was better, and if all else failed they could pop back into the grey and seek refuge there.

"Percy?" Rue leapt up to the poop deck to glare at him.

"Taking us up, Captain."

"Why? We need to refuel."

"It is the customary approach, when someone is shooting at you, to attempt to get away."

"Well, fiddlesticks!"

"Captain. Do you have a better idea?"

Rue whirled away. Then she paused and picked up the speaking tube.

"Quesnel?"

Percy could just make out a grumpy feminine voice from the other end.

"Miss Phinkerlington, put Mr Lefoux on the tube right away...please. Yes, I know. Yes...No...No! Yes...*Miss Phinkerlington*, this is rather urgent. Well, if you have concerns of that nature, you should bring them up at the next crew meeting like everyone else. Yes, I *know* you never attend those meetings...Mmm-hmm."

Rue took the tube off her ear and stared up at the heavens. Or more precisely, she stared up at the underside of the big red-spotted balloon above them.

"Remind me, Percy, why I haven't thrown that woman overboard?"

"She's good at her job."

"Yes, but is that enough?"

"You keep me around."

"Excellent point."

Another spate of gunfire reverberated through the air. Fortunately, it seemed farther away now. Unfortunately, it was still clearly audible and easy to distinguish as gunfire.

Aggie Phinkerlington's tone turned more annoyed and she became even louder. Still not loud enough for Percy to distinguish her words, but he got the gist.

"Yes!" Rue's tolerant tone was rapidly becoming pure impatience. "I *know* that sounds like gunfire! Well, because it *is* gunfire. Why do you think I wish to talk to Quesnel?" She covered the mouthpiece and looked at Percy. "And *now* she summons him."

Percy only shrugged.

The slippery tones of a French boffin could be heard after that. Now Percy really couldn't understand anything that was said. Quesnel was soft-voiced and melodic at the best of times; under stress he became more so. Frankly, Percy was pretty darn certain that he didn't want to understand, for Rue was blushing.

"No, darling." Unfortunately, he was still exposed to one end of the flirtation. "I simply wished to warn you, we are in a spot of bother up here. Well, not to put too fine a point on it, but we appear to be under fire...No, I don't know who...No, you shouldn't come up. You *know* what happened last time. Well, yes, but more importantly, you got shot!...Yes, that *is* the point. Stay below, there's a good fellow...I'm not being condescending. I simply want you safe. You still aren't healed up properly. *Of course* I'm being safe. I'm always safe...Now, now, that's plain old rude." She paused and looked around. "Yes, Primrose is abovedecks. No, I don't know if she has a gun. And I resent that you think she is more capable than me in a fight...Well, yes, I know the twins rather saved my life last time, but...Oh, very well, I'll ask him."

Rue looked over at Percy, her cheeks flaming. Percy didn't realise she could blush like that. He'd assumed that was mostly his job, being the redhead of the group.

"Percy?"

"Yes, Lady Captain?" He did like teasing her with that ridiculous moniker.

"Do you have a gun on you?"

"No. It's not something I regularly carry about my person." He patted his waistcoat pockets to make certain. Virgil sometimes snuck the odd useful item in there – a pocket watch, a pork rind, a bit of string. A gun might be considered a smidgen above a pork rind in the usefulness category. No such luck this time.

Rue continued. "Quesnel would like to suggest that you begin doing so, forthwith, considering what happened only a few months ago, and you having returned his dart emitter to him, and all."

Percy gave the matter some thought. "I shall go shopping when we return to London and look for something with an ivory handle. Not too big."

Rue nodded, eyes wide.

"I shall need some sort of holster. Otherwise it'll dirty my waistcoat with gun oil and burn marks. Virgil would never forgive me. And without a holster, I'll leave it behind places, like I do my hat."

"Agreed." Rue looked as if she were trying not to laugh. Really, what had he said that was so funny?

"I want it to be pretty."

"Pretty?" Rue sputtered.

"Yes," said Percy firmly, "*Pretty*. I don't like how angry and utilitarian most guns look."

"Very well." Rue sounded faint, or possibly she was repressing an inclination to laugh, which made no sense. "*Pretty*." She returned her attention to the tube. "Quesnel? He said he'd get one . . . No, he doesn't have one with him now . . . Yes, fine, send

Aggie up with her crossbow if it will make you feel better. Just you stay in engineering."

Rue hung up the tube and puffed out her cheeks, then she left navigation without further instruction.

Percy held them steady, floating higher than anyone liked and battling the breezes with a fast-whirring propeller and too much fuel use.

"Spoo!" yelled Rue. "Report!"

Spoo dropped down from the rigging and came running over. "Can't see anything anywhere, Lady Captain. No idea where those shots came from. We're all confused and everything's gone pie shaped."

"Unhelpful, Spoo."

"I know, Lady Captain, I'm mad too!"

"Aggie's coming up top."

"Must she?"

"Extra firepower."

"She *is* handy with her bow." Spoo's compliment was given in tones of great disgust.

Rue glared at her head deckling. "Only if we have something to aim her at. Gatling gun too. We need a target, Spoo. Who the hell is trying to kill us?"

Spoo shrugged. "On the bright side, Lady Captain, nothing seems to have actually hit so far. And the last volley was further away. So taking us up was the right choice."

Percy grinned at his own genius.

Spoo continued. "What if we dropped back down, set a watch all around at all possible angles, and waited to see what happened?"

Rue frowned. "Try to lure them out of hiding by moving within range? It's a grave risk."

Percy finally decided to stick his oar in. "Well, we can't stay up here. No charted current from this spot except what we rode in on, and this is the end point for that flow. We can't simply do nothing either. We'll run out of fuel floating about like this forever."

Rue nodded.

Primrose came over. "You're contemplating dropping back down to lure them out, aren't you, Captain?"

Prim was good like that: under official actions Percy's sister always remembered to call her old friend by her shipboard title. Rue was not so cultured. "How did you know that, Prim, my dove?"

"Because that's who you are, Captain. Reckless."

"Oh, now, Prim, you wound me."

Primrose shook her head and pressed on. "Should we wait until nightfall?"

"So we have Tasherit?"

"She is better at battle tactics than all the rest of us combined. Decades of experience." Primrose did have a very good point.

It never hurt to have an immortal werelioness on one's side. If only because Rue could use Tasherit's immortality to heal herself, if necessary.

"Yes, but sunset is eons away." Rue almost pouted.

"Would it kill you to be patient once in a while?" Primrose had her hands on her hips.

Uh-oh. Percy knew that look all too well.

Virgil appeared at that juncture.

Percy ignored Rue and his sister's bickering, and looked at his valet, aggrieved. "Virgil, there's been gunfire."

"And you here, sir, without your hat."

"Yes, well, apologies for that. Do you think you might go below, just, you know, until we've dealt with whatever it is that's shooting at us?"

"No, sir, I could be more useful up here."

Percy tried again. "You could get me a hat?"

"I brought you one, sir."

Virgil produced a blue velvet Turkish lounging cap with silver embroidery and a long rather ostentatious tassel. *An unfortunate gift from my mother,* Percy remembered. *I thought I left that abomination in London. In fact, I'm positive I did.*

"Virgil, that's hardly the thing to wear right now. A fez is for after dinner and preferably behind closed doors. That particular fez should have been drowned at birth."

"It's the last hat you have, sir. You've lost all your others."

There was a distinctly vindictive glint in his valet's eye.

Percy turned away, askance. *Hats like that were meant for nefarious purposes and fraternising with ladies of ill breeding and poor eyesight.*

"Absolutely not." *I will not be moved.*

"Sir!" His valet could get very ominous for such a small cherub-faced lad. "You will put it on this instant."

"Why? In case I die in battle?"

"Exactly, sir. At least you'll have your head covered like a proper gentleman."

"I shall make for a most amusing corpse. That is a particularly ridiculous tassel."

Virgil looked at the hat quizzically. "I think it's very fine, sir."

Another spate of gunfire stopped all conversation and caused most of the crew to start running around again.

"If I put it on, will you go below?"

"I'll think about it, sir."

Percy put on the fez with a wince.

Primrose was never very comfortable in battle. It simply wasn't in her particular sphere of expertise. *Perhaps if I had been trained as a soldier?* She had been trained in household management and personal defence – but not to scale. Which, fortunately, translated to shipboard stewardship and purser's duties admirably, but did not benefit her when an invisible enemy was hurling bullets in their general direction.

To be fair, Rue also hadn't been trained for battle. Or perhaps she had. Lord Akeldama had peculiar ideas about rearing a girl child. When one was a centuries-old vampire, one got eccentric

about advanced education. Primrose supposed that Rue's life was
always going to be in danger. After all, there had been kidnapping and death threats when she was still in nappies. Primrose
did not want to acknowledge that perhaps her dearest friend was
skilled in a manner not entirely respectable, but when under fire
it was difficult to believe otherwise.

Bullets whizzed and Rue came over calm as the proverbial
cucumber. Her pretty face took on a deadly serious guise. Her
yellow eyes narrowed and her mind became a thing of rapid-fire
crisp beauty. She issued orders fast as a Gatling gun. She was
like a tugboat, capable of pulling many times her own weight
in responsibility.

In a very short space of time the decklings were spread about
the ship, each eyeing some part of the apparently empty skies.
Willard manned the Gatling gun with a sootie to assist, sent up
from engineering to help.

Aggie Phinkerlington was sitting aft near Percy in the poop
deck, crossbow at the ready. Primrose herself was at the front of
the forecastle, armed with a pistol rather larger than she liked,
but deadly enough, and pulled from goodness knows where.

Primrose had never tried to be a good shot, she'd never want
to be thought sporty. Despite her mother's token protestations,
one of the Wimbledon Hive, a vampire by the name of Gahiji,
had taken Prim and Percy aside at a very young age. They were
just old enough to grip a pistol properly when he gave them their
first lesson. "The human children of a vampire queen are a great
vulnerability to the hive as a whole. I go against my mistress's
wishes in this matter, but as her *praetoriani*, I must insist you
learn to shoot."

So they had learned and both become proficient. At the time, it
was as an act of defiance against their mother. Gahiji had known
full well what he did when he encouraged the twins to defy
royal notice. Percy might think guns crass, and Primrose might
consider them quite rude, but if their mother didn't want them
shooting anything, by golly they would learn to shoot everything.

And now I'm lodged in the prow of an airship with a pistol. Funny old thing, life. Primrose adjusted her hat and reached for her special armed parasol. Once she ran out of bullets she'd switch to the darts secreted in its shaft.

"Is everyone ready?" called out Rue. "Eyes to the sky, report in!"

One by one, each of the decklings called out their place on the ship and their viewing area.

Rue corrected two of them. "Nips, you're looking port and down, much as possible, not up. We've got up covered already."

"Aye, aye, Lady Captain."

Prim checked her gun and made certain that her reticule full of bullets was securely attached to her pretty filigree belt.

There was a quiet stirring of air and no other warning, and then a warm presence settled next to her.

Prim started.

Tasherit flashed her a quick, breathtaking smile.

Cats. Always so silent on their feet.

"What are you doing awake?" Prim's tone was harsh with irritation, because she felt a spike of giddy joy so profound it hurt.

"Gunfire." The werecat gave her a chocolate-eyed appraisal as if searching for injury.

"Don't be ridiculous, you've slept through louder. It is the middle of the day. It's not healthy for you to be out here."

"Little one, you care." Tasherit was shrouded in long silky robes. A big wide straw hat of a potlike nature squatted atop her head. She was so amazingly beautiful, the hat was an insult to the world at large and Prim in particular.

Prim glared at both Tasherit and her hat. "You're in real danger. You won't heal properly! Go back inside. Do."

"We're about to go to battle, it seems. I'm the first mate aboard this ship. I'm needed here. And you are mortal, the danger is greater for you."

"Disastrous hat," said Prim, for lack of any other insult.

"It keeps the sun off." Tasherit looked tired, she always did during daylight. It wasn't healthy for any supernatural creature to be up with the sun, let alone awake and floating high in the air close to the aether. The werecat's eyes were shadow-dark and red-spiked.

Rue appeared at that juncture on the forecastle near them. "Prim, report! Are you ready? Oh, Tasherit, what are you doing up?"

"Situation, Captain?"

"Gunfire from a mysterious and possibly invisible source. We're trying to lure them out of hiding, see what we're up against."

Tasherit nodded. "Orders, Captain?"

"You're good where you are, for now. Nice rifle."

Only then did Prim notice that Tasherit was leaning heavily on a long, rather elegant-looking Swedish Mauser. She used it as if it were a cane.

"Where'd *that* come from?" Primrose asked, glaring at the blond rifle like a jealous lover. Her only excuse being she was still tetchy and it was a very pretty firearm.

"Oh, I just picked it up."

"Found it arbitrarily lying about somewhere, did you?"

Tash stroked the barrel in a highly suggestive manner. "Not really my style, of course. But we seem to get ourselves into messes on this ship, and if I have to shoot, I wanted something bigger than average and threateningly loud."

There was absolutely nothing Prim could say to that, so she didn't.

Rue said, "Sounds like my Paw, only in gun form." She, of course, either didn't notice or didn't care about the innuendo.

Rue left the forecastle then, yelling out once more, "All right, crew, tell me now if you aren't ready."

Nothing but tense silence met that.

"Percy," Rue barked as she moved to take up her position in the exact middle of the main deck. "Depuff on my mark. Three, two, one, puff!"

They sank downwards.

The *rat-tat-tat* of gunfire sang out a few minutes later.

And then... *There!* Primrose spotted their enemy, dead ahead and down slightly to the left. It was a warship of some ilk, unlike anything Primrose had ever seen before. It bore absolutely no resemblance to the standard Gifford-model dirigible that had started the mad craze to float some fifty years ago.

At the same time, the deckling above her, hanging out over the bowsprit so she could see as much downwards as possible, shouted out, "Spotted!"

"Rue, over here!" called Prim.

Tasherit swung her rifle about and rested the barrel on the railing, standing up to sight down it. Prim tried not to worry that a woman with supernatural strength needed help holding up her weapon.

The Spotted Custard was relatively small for a dirigible, sleek and fashion-forward but at root a pleasure craft, made for tourism, not war or commerce. Prim had seen members of Her Majesty's Airborne Floatillah. They were truly massive airships, impressive and mean looking, but still essentially an almond-shaped balloon – or two, or three stacked atop one another – with a boatlike gondola suspended beneath. They usually had an aetheric sail fore or aft and a propeller or two down below. Postal craft were similar.

The *thing* in front of them right now had no more in common with a standard dirigible than a muffin did with a kipper. An odd analogy, Prim knew, especially as her favourite food was the muffin and Tasherit's was the kipper.

This *thing* had three tall teardrop-shaped balloons, two higher than the third. Prim assumed the higher ones held helium and the middle lower one was air ballast. They gave the distinct impression of bubbles in a glass of champagne. Except they were painted grey. The whole ship was painted grey.

The gondola looked like nothing so much as a massive soup ladle, with a propeller off the front of the bowl, another propeller sticking directly down off the bottom, and a third about halfway down the long handle, which Prim supposed was an extraordinarily long and misshapen bowsprit. It was the oddest bowsprit she'd ever seen – twice as long as the ship itself, sticking far out in a hazardous and precarious manner. The bowsprit supported part of a sail, which was open and up, even though they were in atmosphere not aether. There was a gun at the very tip. The ship was ugly, and incongruous, and made no aeronautic sense whatsoever.

And it had – Prim would swear to it – simply popped into existence in front of them out of thin air.

"Where the hell did that come from?" Tasherit asked, finger on the trigger of her rifle.

"I don't know. It simply appeared there."

"The laws of physics and nature would make that impossible, little one."

Prim agreed. "It's like it emerged from the grey, only we aren't close enough to the aetherosphere for that to be possible."

"Add to that the fact that they are below us and the aetherosphere is above us."

"I can't explain it any more than you can." Prim tried not to sound annoyed.

"Well, little one, let us hope we survive long enough to find out what the hell is going on."

God, she looks so tired and fragile. Primrose suppressed the urge to reach out and stroke Tasherit's perfect face.

"It wouldn't hurt anyone," said the werecat.

"What wouldn't?"

"You kissing me."

"I...I..." Prim scrabbled for something, anything, to say.

"You?" Chocolate eyes could be so warm.

"Percy!" Rue's shout cut through the moment. "Take us down to their level. Get us up close and intimate. I want to know what's going on."

Prim felt relief and disappointment in equal measure.

"You were saying?" Tasherit pressed.

"Nothing. I was saying nothing. It is of no consequence."

Tasherit shook her head. "What hundreds of years haven't wrought, you will manage in the space of mere months."

"I beg your pardon?" Prim glared at the werecat, convinced she was being insulted – being irritated was so much easier than any other feeling.

"You will be the death of me. But such a lovely way to go."

"I quite dislike you sometimes," said Prim, a touch unguarded.

"I know," said the werecat, cheerfully. Then she bumped her shoulder. "Gives me hope."

Prim enjoyed the nudge more than she ought.

Percy depuffed them so that they were practically prow-to-prow with the enemy ship. A chubby ladybug dirigible facing up against a sublimely odd-looking midair soup ladle.

Rue rejoined them on the forecastle deck. "That is the ugliest floating utensil I've ever seen."

A blast of gunfire. They were still not quite in range. Which is why Rue hadn't swung them broadside to return fire with the Gatling gun yet.

"They keep wasting bullets. If we know that we are out of range, they must know that too. Do you think they really have evil intent, or are they simply trying to scare us off?" Tasherit asked this, but did not leave off sighting down her rifle.

Rue frowned. "Or they don't know their own equipment."

"Stolen ship?" suggested Prim, thinking hard. It *was* odd behaviour.

"Or they have better guns than we do and are terrible shots." Rue shrugged, dismissing the discussion. In typical Rue fashion she was more concerned with the immediate crisis than the reasons behind it.

"Any idea where they came from?" asked Tash.

"None whatsoever." Rue wandered back towards navigation and leapt down to the main deck to yell up at Prim's brother. "Percy, ramp up the propeller and ease us towards them. Slowly now, bring us around at the same time, show them the starboard side. Willard, man your gun and prepare to fire, we're almost in range!"

Prim was briefly distracted by a press of sweet dry lips against her own. Yes, they were exactly as soft as she remembered from their encounter in the hallway. Only a brief kiss this time, though. Tasherit had nothing to prove.

"What?" Prim blinked, surprised.

"You weren't paying attention to me. I don't like it when you aren't paying attention." The werecat looked smug.

Prim opened her mouth, could think of nothing snappy to say, sputtered slightly, and suspected she looked rather more like a fish than a cultivated young lady of superior understanding. So she shut her mouth and glared.

"Ready to fire on my mark!" sang out Rue, her voice rather too full of delight for Prim's comfort. *My dearest friend is a bloodthirsty little creature. Or maybe she simply enjoys the power.* Prim considered, *Which would be worse?*

"Three, two, one, God's teeth! What the hell?"

Prim blinked.

Everything around them vanished.

They were surrounded by grey – closing in, muting, shrouding. The aetherosphere. *But how?*

The enemy ladle ship, which had, mere moments before, been right there in front of them, had completely vanished.

Prim turned to see Tasherit's reaction.

Only to find that the werecat was crumpled and insensate on the deck next to her.

CHAPTER
EIGHT

A Mystery, a Fez, and an Italian Mathematician

Too many mysteries. Percy did not like mysteries. Far too many unexpected, unexplainable, and frankly unscientific things had just happened, and Percy felt stretched by improbability. He was a rubber band that had suddenly become less like rubber and more like a wet sock. His intellect was challenged. And Percy's intellect hadn't been challenged in years. It was a novel experience.

An airship appeared from nothing. Then disappeared into nothing. And what a ship! I have never seen its like before – ridiculous. Why build a dirigible that looks like a large soup spoon? Everything must be interconnected. The ship, its appearance, our current plight. And... now I'm distracted.

What the hell is that ghastly noise?

Percy blinked and stood up on his toes to discern what was occurring at the very front of the forecastle deck, at the opposite end of the airship.

That would appear to be my sister. Screaming. Screaming her nonsensical head off. Why is it my destiny to be chronically plagued by lesser intellects and hysterical females?

Percy couldn't quite tell, but it looked as though Primrose was bent over someone's crumpled body.

Oh, really! A death right now would be most incommodious.

Primrose usually kept a calm and practical head in a crisis. It was one of his sister's few admirable qualities. Very little caused his unflappable sister to start flapping her lungs in such a fashion. His own death, of course, might engender such hysteria. *Yet I'm not dead. At least, I don't believe I am. Does one know when one is dead? I must ask Formerly Floote.*

Rue's death, most likely, would also cause Prim to squeal. *But she is also not dead.*

And – he frowned – *the death of Tasherit Sekhmet.*

So it's the werecat who is collapsed. Not unlikely if we are in the grey. I shall take my sister's histrionics as confirmation that, against all odds, we are, in fact, somehow back inside the aetherosphere.

"Don't be a ninnyhammer, Tiddles! She's not dead, she's only sleeping," Percy yelled across the ship, without concerning himself further, knowing his theory was sound.

It seemed this fact had been simultaneously ascertained up front, because Primrose abruptly stopped screaming. It could not be his yelling at her, because if history proved anything it was that Percy had little to no effect on his sister's behaviour. Particularly when he yelled at her.

In the blessed silence that followed, Percy turned his attention to the manifold mysteries at hand.

Come on, Percy, you old chump, put it together. He cast his mind back over theories of aetheric conversion, Charybdis current formation, aetherosphere balance. Nothing he'd read or heard accounted for what they had just experienced.

How could we end up back in the grey? How did we rise so far so suddenly? He checked his instruments. According to the Mandenall Pudding Probe, they were still well below aetheric levels.

And then, to make matters worse, there stood Rue, in front of him, glaring.

"Percy! Explain!" She made a wide expansive gesture.

Percy growled, more frustrated than she could ever imagine. "I can't!"

"But Percy!"

"It doesn't make sense, Rue! There's no theory to explain this. We can't be in the aetherosphere. We simply can't. The world simply doesn't work like that. Even gravity is against us in this matter. I don't know what to say or do. Dash it all, I've completely run out of science!"

"Don't you dare have an existential crisis on me right now, Percival Tunstell. Do you need help? Should I get Quesnel to figure this out for you? I'll chivvy him up, shall I?" Rue reached for the speaking tube.

Rue always knew exactly what to say to offend Percy the most. Well, to be fair, Primrose was slightly better at it than Rue, but only slightly.

"How is my sister?"

"What? Oh. She's fine. A little perturbed to find Tash suddenly all floppy."

"Sounded worse than that."

"She's stopped screaming, hasn't she?" Rue was always more concerned with results than deductive reasoning.

But Percy was, if nothing else, a man of reason. "I can't understand this, Rue. I simply can't. It doesn't make a lick of sense. Nothing makes sense right now." He knew it was as close as he would come in his lifetime to the pained cry of the truly heartbroken.

"Yes it does, she was screaming because she's in love with – "

Percy held up a hand. "It's not my sister I cannot understand. She's regrettably simple."

"Oh. But – "

"Rue. Captain. Please, give me a moment?"

Rue opened her mouth.

"A *quiet* moment."

Rue stood there, staring at him and twitching, but blessedly silent.

Percy thought hard for a long minute and then he spoke the only possible conclusion out loud. "Very well. If we did not go up into the aetherosphere, then the aetherosphere must have come down to us."

"Is that not equally impossible?" Rue ground out. She couldn't help herself.

"No, just extremely implausible. Wait a moment . . ." Percy began to mentally tally up what he did know to be true, given that reality seemed to be squiffy right now. First, the aetherosphere was still up there, above the atmosphere, tight and confined. It didn't move up or down and it didn't leak. It just *was*. Second, the aether currents within it moved around, sometimes predictably, sometimes erratically. But to fall all the way down here, into the middle of the atmosphere . . . ?

Percy's brain hurt.

He searched back over his studies, over papers he'd read in university. Desperate for anything, anything at all, no matter how wild the hypothesis, no matter how disregarded the scientist, that explained what they'd just experienced . . .

"Cappiocra!"

"What?" Rue reared away from him as if she'd been slapped.

Percy reached over and grabbed the speaking tube.

"What?" said an aggrieved female voice at the other end.

"Miss Phinkerlington, if you don't want to talk to any of us up here, why do you keep picking up the tube that end?"

"Because someone has got to. Himself is off shovelling coal like a peon, and him with a bum arm and all kinds of issues."

"I'll thank you not to go into Mr Lefoux's issues, we'll be here all day."

A grunt met that statement of truth.

"Miss Phinkerlington." Percy made certain to sound as dry and acerbic as he knew how. "Unless you know anything about the Italian mathematician Cappiocra, I suggest you get Mr Lefoux to converse with me forthwith."

"Well, there's no need to throw Italian mathematicians at me."

Mere moments later, Quesnel's mellow voice said, "You summoned, Professor?"

Percy didn't bother with a greeting. "Cappiocra? Did you ever study him in school?"

"Wasn't he laughed out of Europe and roundly discredited for some silly unsubstantiated theory about the properties of aether? Didn't he die in poverty and obscurity?"

"I'm not interested in the man himself, only his theories."

"Well, we do have an Italian on board. Why don't you go ask him, you wiffin?"

Percy returned the tube to its cradle. "I must go speak with Rodrigo Tarabotti immediately."

"Right now?" Rue glared. "Percy, this is not the time for moral philosophy."

"No, as I just intimated, this is the time for obscure Italian mathematicians. Please excuse me." Percy climbed out of the navigation pit intent on this new line of possibilities.

Rue grabbed his sleeve. "Percy, really, must you?"

"Prudence Akeldama, if you wish to know what is going on, I need an Italian and I need one now. Let me go to him."

"You get more peculiar by the hour."

Percy did not dignify that with an answer. She let go and he was already jumping down to the main deck so he could climb below and beard the Italian in his lair.

Rodrigo was waiting for him, or waiting for someone, looking concerned and curious and a little shaken. Anitra was with him, and he held her hand in a white-knuckled grip as though to reassure her, or himself, or possibly both. Percy supposed it was scary to be trapped belowdecks during an air battle with no idea as to whether one was being shot out of the sky or not. He spared a brief moment of sympathy for Quesnel and his staff, perennially stuck in the boiler room. But only a brief moment.

As to hand-holding intimacy between ship's interpreter and prisoner? Percy did not find this as odd as others might. They suited one another admirably. He approved. Anitra was a *good person*, for all she was Lord Akeldama's spy. Percy fancied that she'd be good for Rodrigo. In fact, seldom had Percy approved a match as much as this one. Assuming they made a match of it.

Difficult to tell with foreigners. Not quite the same perspective on marriage as the home battlegrounds, so to speak.

Percy greeted them both as warmly as he was able under the circumstances. Which was, he had no doubt, one degree off from an icicle at the best of times. "Miss Anitra, Mr Tarabotti, good afternoon."

The Italian did not care for niceties. Percy respected that. "Professor, why is it people are always throwing the gun at this ship?"

"Throwing guns? Oh, you mean shooting. Why are they always shooting at us?"

Anitra explained, "We heard the uproar abovedecks."

Percy shrugged. A bad habit that he refused to admit he'd picked up from Quesnel Lefoux. "I believe we chronically irritate people."

"Sì. So now we are in grey? Hiding?"

"Yes, but by accident. I didn't take us up into it. It sort of *happened* around us, while we were down floating inside the atmosphere."

"How?" Rodrigo looked fierce. Well, fiercer than normal.

Anitra frowned as well. "It is not possible."

"Precisely. Yet it has happened. You see my current predicament? Mr Tarabotti, did the Templars ever teach you about Cappiocra?"

"*Matematico?* Sì. He had the idea of, how you say, *tasca* with aether."

"*Tasca?*" Not a word Percy knew.

"Sì. *Tasca.*" Rodrigo reached forward and touched the pocket of Percy's waistcoat. Tugging at the top, opening it slightly. Percy was suddenly very glad he did not, in fact, have a gun stashed there. He liked Rodrigo, but he still didn't trust the man.

Anitra said, "Open? No, that's *aperto.*"

"No, noun," insisted Rodrigo.

"Pocket? *Tasca* means *pocket*? Oh? Oh! Now I remember. His was the theory of spontaneous aetheric pocket phenomena!"

"Sì."

"Of course! Thank you."

"But Professor, what – " It was unpardonably rude to interrupt a lady, but Percy did not let Anitra finish.

He left the room. He had to get back on deck. He remembered most of the theory now, at least he thought he did. And what he could remember entirely explained the odd shape of their enemy's ship *perfectly*. In fact, it explained everything!

Primrose left off screaming and cradling Tasherit's head (like some sort of gothic heroine over a corpse) as soon as she realised that the werecat was not, in fact, a corpse at all. *Sleeping. Only sleeping.*

She dragged herself away, even though tiny needles around her eyes tried to persuade her to stay. It really was simply the shock of it. A flaw inherent in loving an immortal, Prim supposed. One assumed they would always be there. The idea that they might die first was beyond comprehension. To be confronted brutally by such a possibility explained her laboured breathing and heart palpitations. Of course, she was only hypothesising. This was all idle speculation.

Desperate for some kind of distraction, she wandered over to navigation, where Quesnel had defied orders and come up top to find out what had just happened.

Rather daring, that Frenchman, because he'd dropped down into the navigation pit, which was most assuredly and distinctly Percy's domain. As a rule, only Virgil and Footnote were allowed down there. Even Rue feared to tread into Percy's sanctified territory, and she owned the ship.

"Uh, Quesnel, is that wise?" Prim asked, looking down at his blond head. He was poking about in Percy's stuff.

"Miss Tunstell, to be wise one would never float at all."

Rue got tetchy with her paramour. "Get out of there. I won't defend you, you realise?"

At which exact juncture Percy reappeared up top, looking like the cat who got the proverbial cream. Until he saw Quesnel in his lair, of course.

Percy lost his temper in a stereotypically redheaded manner. (Which is an unfair way of putting things, as he was ordinarily admirably stoic.) "Get out of my pit!"

"What did you learn?" the Frenchman demanded back.

Percy only glared at him. "Did you touch anything? Please tell me you didn't touch anything."

Primrose couldn't help herself, her eyes were drawn to the top of her brother's head. A sort of blue velvet and silver-embroidered flowerpot perched there. It sported a long silken tassel out the top which trailed down one side to tickle his temple.

"Percy, what *are* you wearing? Is that a Turkish lounging cap? It's midday! We're outside. There are so many things wrong with that right now, and I can't even begin – "

Percy swung around to glare at her instead of Quesnel. "Well, you clearly *have* begun! And it's not my fault, Virgil made me wear it."

"It's truly appalling."

"Listen to the lady, Professor, my eyes, they bleed." Quesnel added his voice of support. It was most welcome, the French were to be trusted on such matters.

"It's a gift from Mother." Percy attempted to either defend or excuse himself, probably both.

Prim nodded her complete and total understanding. The world being what it was, someday odes would be written to their mother's abysmal taste in hats. "But, Percy, she isn't here. You don't *have* to actually wear the Turkish lounging cap. Not in public. People can see!"

Rue moved beyond frustration and into anger. "Oh my goodness! You three will be the death of me. We have work to do. Did you forget? You are officers aboard my ship." She reacted, predictably, by ordering everyone about. "Quesnel, get out of Percy's pit. Percy, get inside your pit where you belong. Primrose, stop prattling on about Turks. No one cares about Percy's apparel. Could we get to the business at hand?"

Quesnel flashed that charming dimpled grin of his, the one that made him look about twelve years of age, and climbed out of navigation.

Percy slithered back in and glanced around, presumably to ensure that nothing had been touched by greasy engineer fingers.

"Did you adjust anything? It's absolutely vital that we not alter any part of our current course."

"I didn't touch a thing, you conker. We're adrift in the aetherosphere, exactly as you left us."

"That's the point, we aren't, not exactly."

"We aren't *what*? You do realise being intentionally obtuse doesn't make you smarter than the rest of us, it simply means you're more of an ars – "

Rue put a hand up to stop Quesnel from proceeding any further. "Percival Tunstell, explain to me right this minute, and in terms we all can understand, what is going on here."

"Cappiocra," said Percy, as if this one word should satisfy everyone.

"Cappiocra? Which is what, a kind of pasta?" Rue's mind ever turned towards comestibles.

Italians again? was all Prim could think. *Why is it we are always plagued by Italians? Really, Rue's ancestry has a lot to answer for.* But Primrose knew better than to interrupt her brother when he looked to actually be getting to the point at long last. It always took Percy forever to address matters of import; best not to detour him with questions about vermicelli.

"No. It's a kind of mathematician. A rather discredited one, I'm afraid." He whirled on Quesnel. "I want it established up front that this time I get first placement on the byline for the resulting article. This must be settled now or I'm not saying anything further."

Quesnel shrugged. "That's fair, as I still don't know what you're on about." His violet eyes crinkled. "Oh. Cappiocra. Wait a moment. You think that insane theory of his might be true. *Zut!* What was it called?"

Percy gave his most annoying small smug smile. When they were children, Prim would bop him on the head with her reticule when she saw that smile, on principle.

"It's called *spontaneous aetheric pocket phenomena*. And yes, I believe it is the best explanation we have. The only one, if I'm honest. It fits all current unexplained occurrences."

"There is an easy way to check and confirm," said Quesnel with a thoughtful narrowing of violet eyes.

Percy looked, if possible, even more smug than ever. "Yes, of course there is." He raised his eyebrows at Rue. "Should the good captain wish to check, we could depuff, and then we would pop out and be entirely visible to our enemy, who is, no doubt, still waiting for us inside the atmosphere, guns blazing."

"Ah," said Quesnel, looking a little abashed, "I forgot that part."

"Engineers," spat out Percy.

"Percival." Rue drew his name out into a long growl. She sounded very like her werewolf father in that moment. "Explain!"

Percy explained. "Cappiocra's theory of aetheric pocket phenomena was developed in the late 1860s. Given how little we know about the original formation of the aetherosphere, he deemed it likely, if not inevitable, that a combination of specific atmospheric conditions and low-hanging Charybdis currents would cause parts of the lower aetherosphere to break off. These would drift, like weighted bubbles, or pockets of aether, down into the atmosphere. He was laughed out of scientific circles and blacklisted for bubble extremism."

Rue frowned. "So we are trapped inside a bubble of aether?"

"No, not trapped. We can get out at any time. But we are inside one. A prevalence of aether pockets in this area would explain the strange shape of that airship."

Quesnel perked up. He was, after all, a master builder. "What? What shape?"

Rue was frowning. "That incredibly long bowsprit?"

Percy nodded.

"With the gun at the end!" said Primrose.

"Exactly."

"What shape!" Quesnel yelled.

Rue took pity on her Frenchman. "The one that attacked us was shaped very like a soup ladle. So that most of the airship might be inside one of these aether pockets with just the end of the handle part sticking out into normal atmosphere. Mount a gun, and put a gunner and a lookout with a speaking tube on the end, and you have what amounts to an invisible ship. So long as you can mostly stay inside the aether bubble."

Percy was frowning. "I don't think it'd be too difficult to rig up a Mandenall Probe for that. I mean, the aether pockets would simply float inside whatever breeze they're caught in at the time. Like a hot-air balloon. Or a cloud."

Quesnel looked amused. "So you're saying the enemy ship was inside one of these bubbles or pockets when they fired on us. And somehow they popped out of it and we got inside instead?"

Percy nodded. "That's the gist of my hypothesis."

Primrose let out a little gust of a breath that she didn't even realise she'd been holding. "And since we are, essentially, surrounded by aether, Tasherit – I mean to say, Miss Sekhmet – fell asleep without warning."

Rue put a comforting hand on her shoulder. "Exactly. Percy, how common are these bubbles likely to be in this area? Are we going to be hitting them all willy-nilly as we float through the atmosphere in this part of the world?"

Percy nodded. "Very likely. And difficult to avoid. It's not like we can see them. It's like the northern lights – mix the right conditions and they occur, but they are hard to predict, chart, or fully understand. At least, that was Cappiocra's theory. They happen when they happen, and then they go away again."

Quesnel was shaking his head. "Then why go to the trouble of building a ship exactly to take advantage of the pockets? No,

I think there Cappiocra must be wrong. We must have a predictable, even chartable, series of these bubbles which the locals take advantage of. Otherwise why evolve the technology?"

Percy looked like he agreed but didn't want to say anything to that effect. Because he hated it when Quesnel was right.

Rue brought them back around to practicalities. "So, why hasn't the enemy ship come in after us?"

Percy and Quesnel looked at each other. "Can't," they said at the same time.

"Why not?"

"Even if this pocket were big enough, one can't fire explosives in aether," Percy explained.

"No?" Rue blinked.

"No," corroborated Quesnel.

"Whyever not?"

Percy frowned and Quesnel bit his lip.

Finally, Quesnel said, "Aether is charged, or experts think that it is. Like light or sound."

Percy added, "One theory claims it has its own vital humour."

"Guns don't work in aether." Quesnel put it bluntly.

"They don't?"

"And that's a very, very good thing," insisted Quesnel.

Rue still looked confused. "It is?"

Frankly, Primrose was confused too, but she didn't say anything. Let Rue ask the questions.

"Why?" Rue asked obligingly.

Quesnel flinched and looked to Percy for help.

Percy, uncharacteristically, stepped into the breach. "Because, my witless friend, it might start a chain reaction."

"Oh," said Rue, and then, "Oh!"

Primrose did so hate being the only one not following. "What? What does *that* mean?"

Rue was nodding. "The whole aetherosphere could explode."

Prim blinked. "Oh, that's not good."

"No, it isn't."

"Except, didn't Percy just say that we aren't in the actual aetherosphere? We are in a pocket of it."

"Guns still won't work, we don't think. And I wouldn't want to test it out. Would you?" Percy said.

"But..." Prim was still trying to understand. "Wouldn't it also work in reverse? I mean, couldn't they stick the end of their ladle handle with their gun into our bubble and fire away at us?"

Quesnel nodded. "They'd risk losing their gunner and a piece of their ship if the chain reaction is fast enough, but nothing else. A desperate but still possible tactic. They'd have to really want us dead."

"And they'd also lose one of their pockets of aether," added Percy.

"But we would explode?" Rue wanted to be certain.

Percy nodded. "Why yes, Captain, yes we would."

Rue blanched. "Percy darling, I think it is a very good idea at this juncture to get us out of this bubble. I'll take regular gunfire over a possible massive explosion, if it's all the same to you."

"Agreed, *chérie*," said Quesnel, breaking for the ladder to return to the boiler room.

"Agreed," said Percy, who probably would love to debate the whole thing further and maybe do a few calculations and take some measurements. Fortunately, Prim's brother was smart enough to respond to urgency in others when absolutely necessary.

"Agreed," said Prim. Although they didn't really need her agreement.

It'll be nice to have Tasherit awake and alert once more.

The Honourable Percival Tunstell was rather pleased with himself as he depuffed the *Custard*. Despite all efforts to the contrary – as the fez was a clear attempt to undermine his authority, not to mention the gravity of their situation – he'd deduced exactly what was occurring. He was the hero of the hour. And there was a good chance, if only Rue would let him take measurements before they left the area, that he'd get a bally good scientific paper out of it.

Of course, they had to survive battle first. But that was a minor concern in the grand scheme of things. Percy contemplated handing over the helm to Virgil. He should jot his conclusions down now, for posterity. If they were about to be shot out of the skies, there ought to be notes with his name on them detailing the existence of pocketed aether, so future scientists understood his genius.

Percy, after all, had priorities.

Rue, unfortunately, had different priorities. Like survival. *Silly girl.*

"Percy, bring us about broadside. Willard, prepare to fire."

At which juncture, Percy realised that they were being shot at. Again. Enemy fire seemed to have resumed the moment they returned to normal air, it had just taken Percy a moment to notice it. Well, he had his legacy to consider.

He also had an airship to steer. Percy toggled the propeller knob and they swung around. This is where *The Spotted Custard* had the advantage. Their dirigible design made them more manoeuvrable in atmosphere, and their guns were mounted on *both* sides of their airship. This gave *The Spotted Custard* a much wider field of fire than their enemy, who had only the one gun sticking off the end of a long handle.

Primrose was standing on the poop deck near Percy. She had her deadly parasol in one hand and a small pistol in the other. *When did my sister acquire a pistol? And how does she reconcile herself to its ownership? Really, it is quite out of character.*

He was about to ask, when Tasherit stumbled over. "What happened?"

The werecat looked decidedly ill. Well, it was broad daylight and she'd recently been knocked out.

Primrose said, "It seems there are these bubbles of aether

in this part of the world. We hit one. You collapsed." His sister's tone intimated quite clearly that she found this kind of behaviour unacceptable in werecats.

"Little one, were you worried about me?"

"I was *not* worried!"

Primrose was a horrible liar. Percy had no idea why she bothered.

His twin stuck her turned-up nose into the air. "I was maybe a little *concerned*. But only because it was a highly confusing situation."

Tasherit nudged up against his sister and put an arm about her waist. "I love that you care."

Sometimes that werecat reminds me so much of Footnote. Percy shook his head. Primrose looked like she wanted, more than anything, to lean into the embrace. Instead she glanced around, panicked – even though no one was looking except Percy – and broke away.

Percy glared at her. *Silly bint.* He rather liked the idea of having a werelioness as part of the family. *Of course, Mother will be appalled if word gets back to her, but Mother is always appalled at everything. Prim ought to simply be happy and stop trying to make everyone else happy. Besides, I'm fond of cats. She ought to take my wishes into account too. I am her brother.*

Another volley of gunfire passed over them. They were being shot at, but not very efficiently.

"Nordenfelt," said Tasherit. "Terribly old-fashioned, and that's saying something, coming from me." The werecat grinned.

Percy looked up at her. "You believe so?" She should know. Tasherit favoured a rifle so new and fancy it technically wasn't yet in production. Percy may turn up the proverbial lip at those who insisted on solving everything with bullets, but he still knew his guns. Not well enough to distinguish them by noise alone, however. Still, if the werecat had access to brand-new firearms, she must know something out of the ordinary about them.

Tasherit nodded. "Sounds very like. Formerly Floote could confirm, of course, but it's daylight so he's not up."

Percy said, "Interesting that you are."

Tasherit made a dismissive gesture. "It's not pleasant or comfortable, I'll tell you that much."

"You can identify the type of gun by the noise of it shooting alone?" Primrose was impressed despite herself.

Tasherit smiled. "I have excellent hearing and rather too much familiarity with Nordenfelts."

Percy nodded. That made sense. He didn't know all of the werecat's history but if she spent the lion's share of it in North Africa and Arab nations, well... "Germans?"

"All too often, yes."

Which means she knows how often a Nordenfelt needs to be rearmed.

"Have you been keeping track of the volleys?" Percy asked.

"How long was I asleep?"

"Long enough for them to change the feeder."

"In that case, we have two more passes to go."

"Tell the captain, do." Percy put one hand to the helm, using his other to speed up and adjust the angle of their propeller. "I'll bring us in close enough so we have a clean line of fire once they stop shooting to reload."

Tasherit strode away to find Rue.

Primrose stayed behind. "You did well, Percy. Remembering about the bubbles and the Italian mathematician and such. It was a bad situation and you got us out of it."

"Pockets, not bubbles," Percy corrected her, and tried not to glow at the praise. It was rare for his sister to say anything nice to him. He hadn't realised how rare until that moment. "*Bubbles* is Rue's word."

He couldn't help but gush. "The very idea that Cappiocra pockets are real! That they exist. And that *we* were inside one! Tiddles, it's amazing."

"Yes, Percy dear, amazing." His sister was scanning the skies, her own small pistol at the ready. They'd been boarded midair by Rodrigo and his people, so now they knew it was possible. Primrose must be thinking of that. She'd had to shoot a person then. They both had. It was a little embarrassing to remember, and no doubt she did not wish for a repeat performance. Percy felt the need to revel further in his scientific breakthrough. "I'll be welcomed back to the Royal Society with open arms."

"Aren't you already their dearest darling? After you betrayed Tasherit and exposed the existence of werecats?"

Ah well, thought Percy, *that didn't last long.* She was back to criticising him. "I apologised for that."

"Did you, Percy? Did you really?" He forgot how fierce his sister could get when protecting the people she loved. She'd been a hellion when they were little. He was skinny, sickly, awkward, and always saying the wrong thing. It was Prim who'd defended him. A tiny perfect champion in plaits and lace, using vicious cutting words and a well-wielded fan, even at age eight.

Now she more often used her words against him rather than in his defence. *Is that because I have changed, or because she has changed?*

Percy couldn't stop himself, even knowing she'd react badly. "Bah! In the end who really cares if there are yet more shape-shifters in the world? This! This proof that aether pockets exist. This isn't simply *a discovery*, sister. This is *the discovery of the ages.* This is real science. I shall be famous."

"Oh." Primrose looked him up and down, disappointed rather than angry. "Is that all you want? Fame?" Disappointment, as it turned out, was worse than anger.

Percy glared. To be revered and praised for his mind was all he'd ever wanted. He thought she understood that. "Of course!"

"Fine, then will you stop after?"

"Stop what, exactly?"

"Being a total prat."

Rue interrupted them with a look that suggested she was doing it on purpose. "Percy, bring us in. Prim, deploy your battle parasol. Willard, fire when ready."

Percy went back to his job of navigation and ignored Primrose. She wasn't making any sense anyway.

Primrose jumped down and went over to stand near the Gatling, ready to fire when they were in range of her small pistol. She pushed open her parasol. Quesnel's mother had armoured it somehow. Prim arranged it so that she was partly protected by one side, and Willard by the other. *Of course, she'd do it like that.* She was fearless, sometimes, his sister. Usually when she was most annoyed with him, or felt her family was threatened. And *The Spotted Custard* was her family now. His too, if he let himself love them even a little.

Percy shook his head at his own whimsy. He was horrible at loving. Better to write papers on aether pockets and have done with it.

Prim took to the main deck in the hopes of an opportunity to shoot something. Ordinarily she wasn't bloodthirsty but her nerves were frayed by too much worry in too short a time, and she thought, if pressed, she might shoot her brother. Better to give herself an opportunity to shoot the enemy instead.

Sadly this was unnecessary, as Willard took a clean pass with the gun and disabled the ladle with no spill, no fuss, and no loss of life.

Perhaps the pocket people weren't accustomed to dirigibles with *The Spotted Custard*'s level of nimbleness. Or perhaps it was the superior technology and reach of the Gatling gun that got to them. Regardless, Willard's first volley hit the enemy craft amidships and did a tremendous amount of damage.

By rights it should have been a great deal more dramatic. Prim was disappointed and kept her weaponised parasol open and raised against the sun, just in case. And to ward off freckles, of course.

With his second volley, Willard took out their bottom propeller and then the lower section of the bowl of the ship. It was his best guess as to where their boilers were located. It was pretty common to put engineering in the base of any ship.

The enemy airship was such a strange design, one might expect boilers to be located abovedecks or somewhere equally incongruous, but this time the airship was per international standards.

A massive chunk of the ladle's grey hull fell away, and steam burst forth from the gaping hole left behind. Apparently Willard had hit their main boiler. The hull must be made of some very flimsy material indeed, paper thin, as the escaping steam continued to tear away at it, peeling it back until nearly half the side of the ship was gone, exposing the crude structure within.

Prim was no builder and certainly no engineer, but even she could see that just as the enemy's Nordenfelt was an older gun, their steam technology was old-fashioned as well. Perhaps a decade out of date.

The airship itself may have been unique and new to them, but what drove it wasn't new at all.

Since all the ladle's balloons were still whole, the ship remained floating, but she had no manoeuvrability and was adrift on the breezes – no longer a threat to *The Spotted Custard*.

Rue barked out orders and Percy propelled them out of range, but then he maintained a steady drift so that they paced the lame craft.

"Percy, hold us on their broadside."

"That's what I'm doing, Captain."

Something has my brother's britches in a bunch.

Rue ignored Percy's snappy reply and continued barking out orders. "Willard, keep them in your sights. I don't want them boarding us. Fire on anything that leaves that ship and heads in our direction."

"Aye, aye, Captain."

"Primrose?"

"Yes, Rue?"

"Call up Quesnel and see if you can find Anitra, please. I'd like a quick meeting on the poop deck in half an hour with all officers."

"Aye, aye," said Prim, trying it on for size. It was kind of fun to say.

She climbed down to engineering first. She might have used Percy's speaking tube, but she'd rather not be close to her brother at the moment. She was disturbed by how far he'd skewed his priorities. She'd thought that his overt concern with facts and academic standing was a mere front to hide a sweet and squishy soul. Now she wasn't so certain.

Did I lose my twin when I wasn't looking? Did I let him get broken into nothing but sharp and cutting parts? Was it my job to remind him there's more than ambition to this life? Or are we both lost? Oh heavens, have I too turned cold? Is my need for a husband just my version of Percy's need for approval, in another guise?

Surely not? It can't be that. I want a marriage of convenience because I hope it might be easy. Simple. And I would make an excellent wife. But do I want it because I don't think myself capable of more? Does Percy prioritise scientific discovery because he believes it the only thing he is good for? Are we both limiting ourselves in the guise of ambition?

She stuck her head into engineering. "Mr Lefoux?"

"Miss Tunstell?"

"The captain would like a word up top when you have a moment to spare."

"I take it we are out of danger?"

Prim smiled. "The enemy has been neutralized for the moment."

"Topping. I'll be right up."

"Do you know where Miss Anitra has gone? She's not in her quarters. I knocked."

"Check the prisoner's cell."

"Like that, is it?"

"More than. Ask the professor. He spends considerable time with them both."

"You think that's something Percy would notice?"

The Frenchman gave a funny kind of a half smile. "I think your brother is more observant of people than anyone gives him credit for."

"That was always my role."

"You are twins. More alike than either of you think. You saw his hat."

"What's a fez got to do with it?"

"To be truly insensitive to the feelings of others, Professor Tunstell would have removed that hat or refused to wear it. Consider why he did not."

"Only a Frenchman would place so much import on the presence or absence of a chapeau."

"My mother did once own a hat shop."

"So she did. If you'll excuse me."

Quesnel nodded.

Prim caught sight of Aggie Phinkerlington, just beyond him, issuing instructions to her team of sooties. Everything looked good in the boiler room, but the sooties scuttled quickly at her command, as if they were still in grave danger.

Primrose admired her efficiency. She gave Aggie a nod of approval.

The woman's gaze was startled, but she nodded back.

Prim went to check their imprisoned Italian's cell, thinking about why her brother would wear a hat he loathed. Because he didn't want to offend Virgil? Because it was a gift from their disastrous mother? Perhaps he was not so hardened as she had previously thought.

She nodded to the sootie on guard detail and knocked loudly before entering the locked room.

Rodrigo Tarabotti was, without question, the handsomest man Primrose had ever met. His eyes were deep and dark and bubbling with barely suppressed passion. His lips were well formed, his cheekbones high, his brow fierce. He had thick hair and a compelling voice, with that Italian accent women customarily swooned over. There were, no doubt, statues in vampire houses all over the world depicting men much like him – only naked.

And she cared not one jot for any of it.

Primrose hadn't had much contact with the man. She'd shot at him once, of course. But that was standard practice these days. She thought that, in his presence, she *ought* to feel palpitations. Ladies of her age and breeding were known to faint upon encountering such a magnetic specimen of manhood. He might be paraded through the finest drawing rooms in London as a Byronic ideal of masculine beauty.

But she felt nothing.

Anitra, clearly, was not so immune.

Primrose gave their interpreter an assessing look.

Mr Tarabotti was reclining, Roman feast–like, upon his bed in an attitude of performed casualness. Anitra stood a discreet distance away but she looked mussed. Her lips were a little swollen, and her veil was askew. The tassel at the end of one braid was wrinkled.

Primrose suddenly felt as if she had failed in her duties as chaperone. *First I lose Rue to a Frenchman, and now I lose Anitra to an Italian. There has been a Continental invasion into my domicile and I didn't even realise I needed to mount a defence of the fortress of womanhood. Now it is too late.*

Anitra's eyes fairly shone when she looked on their prisoner. Primrose had little hope of rectifying the situation. Although she would surely try to put a dampener on proceedings come nightfall.

She looked back and forth between them, pointedly. "I shall have to talk with your grandfather about this, Miss Anitra."

A mostly idle threat, the man was dead after all. But not powerless. Formerly Floote was many things, but powerless wasn't one of them. He had knowledge.

Anitra hid her face briefly behind her veil. "He's not really my grandfather."

"And how would your *father* feel about this? You said you were not available for courting, if I recall."

Anitra hissed, "Not here!"

But Mr Tarabotti sat up at that. "You're not?" He looked truly injured by this revelation.

Uh-oh, thought Prim. *Have I got this wrong too? Is it Anitra who is taking advantage of Rodrigo? Could he genuinely wish to marry her?*

Anitra ducked her head. "You know why."

Rodrigo stood up from his bed, no longer relaxed. He clasped Anitra's hand in both his own. "As if that should matter to me of all people! You know what happens with preternaturals and children. We cannot even be in the same room with our progeny."

Prim felt extremely uncomfortable; this was a private matter and absolutely none of her business. It seemed Mr Tarabotti was implying that Anitra was barren. A confidence most intimate indeed! Was that why she'd no interest in marriage? Poor thing. And how had she possibly found this out?

It's all none of your concern, Primrose Tunstell! she told herself firmly. "Perhaps this matter might be addressed later, with the supervision of Formerly Floote? As it stands, the captain has requested Anitra's presence up top. If you wouldn't mind, my dear?" Prim looked pointedly at the Drifter girl, ignoring the impassioned Italian.

Anitra nodded, her dark eyes full of profound sadness. She gently withdrew her hand.

The two ladies made their way out into the hall.

Compelled to offer some form of consolation, for Anitra really looked most unhappy, Prim stopped her with a touch. "I did not mean to intrude."

Anitra wobbled out a smile. "He is most persuasive."

"I can see how he might be."

"I have never attracted the interest of such a man before. I always believed this, what I am, was all I would ever have. We don't – " She paused, struggling for words. "We don't get offers very often, women like me. Usually they come from an older man, widowers with children already, looking for a servant rather than a wife. A companion in old age."

Primrose could understand that. Men married because they wished for a mother to their children. *What would I do if I were unable to have children?* A tingle went up and down her spine. *I'd be free to choose whatever I wanted.* She was immediately horrified that this was her first thought. Her stomach churned.

"And do you want more than that?" Prim asked the young lady.

"I never thought to *want* at all." Anitra dimpled in a smile, sudden and sweet. "This, being here on this ship, is so much more than I hoped for in life. To have love as well? It is too much. Overwhelming."

Primrose cocked her head. "Do you trust him? He seems awfully flirtatious."

"That is a concern. But still, the fact that he is interested at all. In me. Even knowing what I am."

She spoke about being barren as though it were a curse. As though she were a pariah or an outcast. In her culture, perhaps she was. Perhaps Drifters threw barren women overboard.

Primrose knew exactly what to say to that kind of diminished self-worth brought on by others. "If he does not care," she said, staunch and confident, "then neither should you."

Anitra bowed her head again, as if, again, she was trying not to cry. "I don't think you quite understand."

Primrose narrowed her eyes. "We are worth more than our capacity to produce children!"

"Oh, you think...? Oh no, that's not..." Anitra bit her lip. "I mean, that is true, I can't give him babies. But I'm" – she gestured to herself – "this."

Primrose was confused.

Anitra winced. "*Aravani.*"

"Is that like being outcast? Untouchable?"

Anitra looked down at her feet. Smoothed out her braid tassel.

Prim patted the other woman's arm, tentatively. "Let's talk about this more later? Rue needs you now."

Anitra straightened and nodded. "Yes, of course. My duties." And there was a tone to her voice, a tone Prim well knew from herself – relief and comfort found in responsibility. As if by organising the outside world, she might ignore the confusion in her heart.

NINE

Soup Ladle of Death

Percy leaned against the helm and contemplated the last few highly successful hours of his existence. Aside from Prim's obvious disappointment in his life goals, he considered it a most productive day.

When Virgil appeared, delighted to find Percy had survived the battle with his hat still firmly affixed to his head, Percy sent the valet down to his quarters to bring up a notepad and stylus. He must make notations on these Cappiocra pockets posthaste. He rather liked Rue's preference for thinking of them as bubbles. Or had he started that codswallop? He might have to rename them such. Although *Tunstell Bubbles* didn't sound quite right. He speculated on how they kept cohesion without dispersing into air, as aether ordinarily did. *Ambient magnetic charge, perhaps? Some kind of particulated friction indicative of the air over South America?* He ran calculations in his head. It was a most enjoyable half hour.

He'd no idea what was taking his sister so long but he wished her to perdition. Or at the very least away from him for another twenty minutes of uninterrupted bubble contemplation.

It was not to be, however, because someone else disturbed his mental wanderings.

Tasherit Sekhmet came to sit on the edge of his pit – half in and half out. It was much in the manner of Footnote, always lurking at the threshold of doorways, unwilling to commit to staying in or heading out. Cats liked to occupy liminal spaces: both inside and outside, both tame and wild, both yawn and meow.

Percy gave Tasherit an appraising look. One that he hoped also said, *Enter at your own peril, this is my territory.* The werecat would likely only understand that if he urinated in the corners of the navigation pit. He grinned at himself.

"Miss Sekhmet, what can I do for you today?" He cocked his head at her. Remembering his stupid fez at the last minute, he put a hand up to hold it in place. Virgil had been so pleased to see it still perched atop his noggin, he hadn't the heart to remove it just yet. Perhaps after the lad went to bed.

Tasherit's gaze was instantly drawn to it. "That's a wonderful thing, isn't it? So shiny." Her dark eyes went wide and covetous. "I do love a nice tassel." She looked like she really wanted to bat at it.

Percy wondered how Virgil would feel if Percy gifted the hat to her. He couldn't be faulted for being generous, could he? *Perhaps I'll wait until my valet is present to witness the act. Then he can see her genuine affection for the ghastly thing.*

In fact, the gleam in her eyes suggested something on the order of adoration.

"Is that Turkish?" she asked, licking her lips.

"It is."

"The Ottoman Empire was a glorious time for tassels." Her eyes went misty with memory.

Percy nodded. "Now mostly confined to carpets and pillows, I'm afraid. Tassels, I mean, not the Ottoman Empire."

Tasherit nodded sadly. "Although, that too. Once tassels were all over everything – parasols and belts, sleeves and the tops of slippers. It was magical. I do think of tassels as the height of civilisation, don't you?"

"Anitra has them at the ends of her braids." It occurred to

Percy that this was a rather bizarre conversation to be having with an immortal. But clearly Tasherit was particularly fond of a good tassel.

The werecat nodded. "She does. She lets me wiggle them sometimes." A quick glance up at that, and a flush of shock on her gorgeous face. "Not in a courting sort of way, mind you," she hastened to add. "My preference is for genitalia on the inside, you understand."

That was not only embarrassing but a highly confusing statement to make.

"Uh?" said Percy.

"I mean to say, my intentions towards your sister are entirely honourable."

Percy flapped his mouth a bit, wondering what *honourable* meant, exactly, to a werelioness hundreds of years old. Finally he said, "I never thought that they weren't."

The werecat let out a breath of air. "Oh, good. Rue tells me it is the custom in England to ask a male family member for permission to court his female relation? Yours is an extremely odd culture."

"Is it?" Percy squeaked.

"Once, for us werelions, the queen had to be asked for permission to court the male breeder of a pride. But that was many decades ago. There are so few of us left, the tradition has long since been abandoned."

"Has it?" Percy really had no idea where this conversation was going.

"So, may I please have your permission?"

Percy baulked. "You wish to *breed with me?*"

"No!" Tasherit practically shouted.

"Oh, good. I don't think Prim would like that at all. And she *is* my sister. I wouldn't want to upset her quite that much. And as you are an immortal, it wouldn't work anyway. You know, the breeding." He was babbling and he knew it. But in Percy's defence, this was a most uncomfortable conversation.

Tasherit frowned at him. "I see what your sister means when she says talking with you is like dancing with jellied eel."

"She says that?"

"Yes." She looked around. "Now quickly, please, before she returns – may I court her, by your leave?"

"Aren't you already?"

"Well, yes. But I should still like to have your permission to do so."

"I hardly think it makes a difference. You're in for a slog either way."

"Nothing worth having is easy to acquire. Except cheese, of course, and even that took hundreds of years to reach my part of the globe. You see my point about the tassels?"

"No longer popular? What has that to do with my sister... or cheese?"

"I should have kept more around. Tassels, not cheese. Cheese doesn't keep, tassels do." Then, obviously to herself, "Why is this so difficult?"

"Do you love her?" Hard to get a cat to be direct, but Percy would not budge on this one point. He may have resigned himself to lonely scholarly pursuits, but Primrose deserved affection. Also needed it, he suspected.

Tasherit fidgeted under his direct gaze. Percy tried for a fierce glower in the manner of protective brothers the world over.

"Well, Miss Sekhmet?"

"Yes."

Simple, and, Percy thought, *genuine.* "Elucidate further, if you would." It was not his role to make this easy for her.

The werecat twitched and fidgeted in obvious discomfort. "Look, Professor Tunstell... Percy... I wish to keep your sister around. Or she can keep me. Or we can keep each other. Please let me?"

I just got a cat to beg. This really is a most excellent day. Percy decided to stop while he was ahead. Although it was unexpectedly enjoyable to torture an immortal. "You may proceed. However, it's possible she's more stubborn than you. One might say that your time with tassels may have entirely ended."

The werecat looked determined. "Ever been stalked by a cat on the hunt?"

"I do live with Footnote."

"We don't give up easily."

"Well, fine then, hunt on. And if you're successful I'll give you this fez of mine as an engagement present." He considered, *Could one use the word* engagement? "So to speak."

A stunning smile split across Tasherit's already stunning face. "Thank you."

Percy quirked a brow. "I didn't say I thought you'd succeed. Simply elected to sweeten the pot."

Tasherit reached forward, lightning quick, and batted at the tassel dangling over the side of his face. Percy was rather pleased with himself for not flinching.

"I think I shall like having you as a brother-in-law."

Which might, just possibly, have been the nicest thing anyone had ever said to Percy. So, of course, he blushed beet red and turned away to pretend he had something very important to do down low, under the Mandenall Probe.

They had ended their chat none too soon, because Primrose reappeared with Anitra in tow. Rue and Quesnel joined them on the poop deck for a consultation. Since Percy was the only one who couldn't leave his station, they all came to him.

As it should be.

Although, because Tasherit was still sitting on the edge of the navigation pit, legs dangling, the others all did the same. Percy wasn't entirely convinced he approved the precedent this set. Seemed awfully casual and possibly disrespectful. Still, he was having such a pleasant day, he decided not to make a fuss.

Percy was looking awfully red in the face when Primrose arrived back at the poop deck, but that could be for any number of reasons. What worried Prim more was how incredibly pleased her brother looked. Almost – *Dare I think it?* – happy. Probably something to do with that academic paper on bubbles that he intended to write. The one that will change the world. *Or what have you.*

Rue got straight to the point. "Ladies and gentlemen, we essentially have our ladle enemy trapped. The question is, What to do with them? Do we destroy them utterly and shoot them out of the sky? Do we board and attack hand-to-hand at great risk to ourselves? If we board, do we take prisoners or simply try for the airship alone? We already have enough trouble with the one prisoner we've got – where would we put more? Yet I'm not entirely comfortable simply killing everyone aboard. That seems wasteful. Your thoughts?"

Primrose felt it incumbent upon her to add, "We are strangers, new to this area. Locals might look at such behaviour askance."

Percy said, "I'd really like to take a closer look at that ladle, Captain. Take a few measurements, make more calculations based on closer inspection."

Quesnel said, "I concur. We already know most of their technology is older than our own, but it would be good to know how much older."

Primrose blinked. *Did Quesnel just . . . ? Yes, he did. He sided with my brother. Amazing.*

Tasherit shook her head. "Not a good idea. Boarding is always a logistical challenge even if we could deploy highly trained warriors. The enemy knows their ship much better than we ever could. It's too easy for them to hide and to ambush us. In addition, we've got no one trained in the correct combat techniques. That includes me. Even the best of our deckhands is a mere amateur."

Prim knew Tasherit was referring to Bork, a former boxer and very handy at fisticuffs if it came to it. *If Tasherit thinks of him as an amateur, she must really be embarrassed by the rest of us.*

Rue sighed. "I see your point. Still, it would be nice to find out why we were attacked. I mean to say, they don't *know* us. We don't *know* them. Was it mistaken identity? Or do they treat all strangers like that here?"

Primrose spoke again, taking it as her duty to find a balance. Everyone was making good points. The scientists wanted to know *how*, Rue wanted to know *why*, but they were ill equipped to discern either without considerable physical risk. "How about we approach them and get close enough to simply ask, without boarding?" she suggested.

Everyone stared at her.

Prim soldiered on. "That way we might see what they have to say. Take a closer look at their ship without risk of combat. Keep our guns trained, knowing they'd have rearmed by then themselves. Percy, you could make some estimated guesses, and Quesnel, you could see most everything with advanced-focus opera glasses. After all, we did open up a massive hole in their hull right into engineering."

Rue was nodding. "That seems an acceptable compromise."

Percy looked like he didn't agree at all, he'd never settle for less than actual measurements. But, for a change, he didn't say anything. Instead he gave a curt nod. "I'll start now, then. If it's all the same to you, Captain? Virgil can take over navigation. I've got a set of very high-powered lenses and we'll be losing light soon. It is getting on to sunset."

Oh dear, thought Primrose, *we missed luncheon. Everyone must be starving. I shall go get Cook to rustle up a picnic.*

Quesnel nodded as well. "I'll go get my opera glasses and some sketch pads." He disappeared below. Percy followed after.

Primrose asked, "When the time comes to approach them, what should I do?"

Rue smiled. "Nothing, dear, stand there looking useless and pretty with your parasol ever at the ready. We may still need an element of surprise."

Prim nodded. "Done. Meanwhile, should we eat?"

"Yes, very fine notion, just one moment more." Rue's sharp

tawny gaze fell on their Drifter. "Anitra, how good is your Spanish?"

"I've been making a study of it with Professor Tunstell, but neither of us are fluent. We'll do our best."

"If Percy is busy examining their ship, conversation will naturally fall upon you, I'm afraid."

Anitra straightened her spine. "May I make a recommendation then, Captain?"

"Please do." Rue smiled encouragingly, clearly attempting not to railroad the girl.

Aw, thought Prim, *she's trying to be kind! How sweet.* She gave her friend a nod of approval.

"If we waited until sunset, my grandfather could join us. His Spanish is excellent."

Rue shook her head. "I think not. This is anti-supernatural territory, remember?"

"If he were to stay hidden? Floating with only his head above the floorboards, for example, near my feet where he can't be seen from overboard. He could help me to understand."

"Perhaps. But that still is quite risky." Rue nibbled on her lip.

Anitra nodded. "There is another option." She paused and grimaced. "Rodrigo Tarabotti. He's fluent. He's been helping me learn the language."

"He could betray us." Rue's tone was more hopeful than suspicious.

"Have both my grandfather and Rodrigo join us, then? The one could keep an ear to the other." Anitra was standing her ground. A good thing, Primrose felt, as she had a predilection for timidity which would do her no favours aboard *The Spotted Custard*.

Rue frowned. "Waiting until nightfall gives us one other advantage." She looked to Tasherit.

The werecat tapped her cheek with her fingers, thinking. "You want me in lioness form?"

Rue nodded. "You can leap further than any of us can jump, and if we do end up having to board them . . ."

Tasherit finished the thought. "Far better to have an immortal shifter fighting on your side."

"Your lioness is *very* impressive." Rue grinned.

Primrose felt a strange touch of jealousy at that. Not that she thought Rue was flirting with Tasherit, but that she, Primrose, could not be the one to deliver such a compliment. *Praise comes so easy to me with everyone else. Why not with Tasherit? She deserves it too.*

Tasherit continued. "It'd be better if we were lower down. I'm stronger the further we get from the grey."

Rue nodded. "If we are waiting for sunset we have some time. If we gunned down one of their helium balloons, they'd likely drop twelve puffs or so. Horrible waste, of course, but it'd sink them."

Tasherit nodded.

Primrose interrupted. "Meanwhile you should take a nap, Miss Sekhmet, you look peaky. I'll organise food for everyone, the gentlemen will make notes and draw sketches and argue about calculations."

Rue was nodding her agreement. "And I'll let Spoo shoot that balloon. She needs the practice."

Primrose laughed. "She'll love you forever."

Virgil appeared at that juncture. "Can I help with the shooting of balloons?"

Rue shook her head. "You're needed here in navigation. Sorry, my lad."

"Spoo always has all the fun."

"You're a valet, not a deckling." Primrose felt firmly that everyone and everything belonged in its place and that a place should be found or built for everyone and everything. It might even be her philosophy on life. Poor Virgil kept drifting.

Virgil looked resigned. "I suppose I do get to wear much nicer britches."

"That's the spirit!" Rue stood and patted him on the shoulder. "Your pit, Mr Virgil."

"Yes, Lady Captain." Virgil hopped down.

They dispersed about their separate duties.

Rue and Anitra went to consult with Bork, Willard, and Spoo.

A moment later the Gatling rat-tat-tatted out. There were shouts from their enemy and one of their balloons began the death wiggle. They sank, rather faster than anyone thought they would. That ship was definitely older and out of date.

Virgil depuffed *The Spotted Custard*, pacing them down through the air. They came to a stop riding a new breeze, one that was carrying them gently inland.

Prim's ears popped.

Tasherit gave a little sigh of relief and some of the tension, which was likely part of what made her so twitchy, left her shoulders.

"Better?" Primrose asked, concerned.

"Much."

"Nap now?" Prim pushed her friend in concern.

"Yes, and you're visiting the galley. Shall we?"

Primrose found herself accompanying the werecat below-decks. They paused, uncomfortably, in the hallway outside Tasherit's room.

"I like your brother," said the werecat.

Prim pursed her lips in surprise. "You'd be the first."

"I thought the ladies went mad for him."

"They do, but I don't think they ever actually like him. He's more like something they want to collect and put on the mantelpiece."

"Look at the pretty smart man in my drawing room?"

"Exactly."

"Poor Percy."

"I wouldn't go that far." She paused. "Percy? You call him *Percy* now?"

"We've reached an understanding."

"You have? What kind of understanding?"

"It involves tassels." Tasherit grinned wide and self-satisfied. Prim's knees wobbled slightly. She wasn't sure if it was fear or the opposite of fear that caused her stomach to clench. *I'm simply hungry.*

"Tassels?" she asked, seeking clarification.

"Tassels." Tasherit leaned in, no doubt waiting for Prim to bolt.

Primrose straightened her spine and stood her ground.

The werecat smelled of hot sands and whipped cream, warm salt and mellow sweet. As she had once before, Tasherit pressed close, rubbing Primrose's cheek with her own. This was not a kiss of the lips but of the flesh, satin smooth – an affection and a claiming in one. Then she nuzzled in against Prim's neck, under the high lace collar of her day dress.

It made Primrose feel languid and cherished and fluttery and flushed all at once.

Tasherit scraped her teeth lightly across the spot directly under Prim's ear. No bite, just the smallest of nibbles.

Prim's whole body tingled.

The werecat drew back. "You taste divine. And you smell like amber and honey and milk."

Primrose swallowed, and Tasherit watched the movement of her neck muscles with avid chocolate eyes. Possessive. Dangerous.

Prim searched desperately for a safe topic. "Should I bring you something to eat, before you sleep?" Her voice had gone overly husky, but strangely enough, she wasn't embarrassed by that.

"No, I'll bother Cook when I wake up at sundown. But thank you for the thought."

I'm always thinking of you. "You're welcome. I'll instruct Cook to put something nice and bloody aside for you."

The werecat gave her a tiny genuine smile.

Primrose backed away, frightened of how utterly she needed to lean in. She wanted more of cheek against cheek, lips against skin, teeth against neck.

"You say the nicest things, little one."
"Sleep well." Primrose fled.

Just before sunset, Primrose took up position next to Bork, who was manning the Gatling gun. She'd changed into evening attire for the negotiations, as was right and proper. Her dress was a midnight-blue velvet affair trimmed in delicate black lace and a tasteful sprinkling of crystal. She chose it because on a dark evening like this one, it was good camouflage. Plus it matched the night sky, the crystals like tiny stars scattered across the bodice. Primrose liked things to match. It also had gargantuan puffed sleeves, so big she needed her shoulder crinolines to support them. As the saying went: *the bigger one's sleeves, the more angelic one's appearance.* Primrose rather thought that massive sleeves would make her look intimidating to an enemy unfamiliar with current fashions.

However, the gown, while stunning, did not have any pockets. After much consideration, and with no little embarrassment, because if it became necessary she'd have to pull it back out again – in public! – Prim wedged her pistol down the front of her bodice into her corset. It fitted there well enough. She may not be as generously endowed as Rue, but her pistol was also only a .22.

Primrose did pause to consider the fact that she could stash any number of pistols inside her sleeves, and perhaps she should devise a means to do so in future, but for now, having one down her décolletage would have to suffice. In the end, she had to carry her battle parasol anyway, at night, so she was doomed to make a fool of herself over weaponry no matter what.

She put on a floating hat with a long veil, to protect her neck, to ward off the evening's chill, and for fear of bugs. This was, after all, unknown country.

She made her way back up top in time to watch the sun set in a glorious riot of colour and majesty over the vast dark ocean.

Rue had all the sooties and deckhands hidden out of view for their safety, except Bork of course. He nodded at Primrose politely as she took position next to him, prepared to pop open her parasol at the slightest provocation. She didn't know if he was familiar with the scope of its protective powers. She hoped neither of them would have to find out who would win in a pitched fight, her parasol or a Nordenfelt.

Tasherit bounded up shortly after dark, looking stronger and healthier for her rest. Or perhaps it was because she was in lioness form. She bunted Prim's hip affectionately. Primrose could not resist a few ear and chin scratches. The werecat's fur was thick and coarse and strangely beautiful. As ever, Primrose found Tash much easier to accommodate with equanimity when the werelioness was physically a cat – as opposed to only mentally.

Anitra arrived next. Rodrigo trailed after her. Rue had allowed him to leave his cell before, of course. Even a dog, she said, was allowed perambulations and fresh air. She could do no less for her cousin, even if he was an ass. She wasn't an utter monster. Nevertheless, the Italian looked both thrilled and nervous to be suddenly free, involved in their affairs, and on the side of good. Or perhaps he understood that this was a test. Or perhaps he planned to try and escape. He was difficult to predict, their Italian.

Formerly Floote was there as well, hovering, as requested, with only his head above the deck boards. This was nothing if not bizarre looking, but he was hidden from enemy view by the *Custard*'s lower railing. At least they hoped he was.

It must be very odd to encounter the bottom half of his non-corporeal body hanging from the ceiling of whatever room was directly beneath him. *Very odd.* Prim considered the layout of the *Custard. That's the galley, most likely. Poor Cook.*

Percy, of course, was secreted in navigation, his upper body a blurry shadow behind the helm up on the poop deck at the opposite end of the dirigible. This encounter was dependent on close manoeuvring. Percy was better utilised steering the ship than as an interpreter.

"Where's Quesnel?" Prim asked.

Rue rolled her eyes. "He and Percy would not stop arguing about the efficaciousness of the ladle design, now that they have notes and sketches and numbers to argue about. I had to separate them."

"Oh?"

Rue gave a wicked smile and turned to Rodrigo, whom she'd positioned at the very far end of the line. The order they now stood in, facing the main deck rail, was: Tasherit, Bork and the Gatling, Primrose, Rue, Anitra, Floote's head, and Rodrigo on the far end. This put the preternatural Italian away from Rue – because he had once tried to kill her. This also put him very far away from the gun and the werecat, which were their two best and most vulnerable weapons. No one ever forgot that Rodrigo was a preternatural. He could turn Tasherit into a naked mortal human with a single touch. Uncomfortable for everyone, and hazardous to Tasherit's health and well-being.

Rodrigo nodded to Rue. "Little Cousin."

"Mr Tarabotti," said Rue, formally. "Nice weather for it."

"Sì. That it is." He was holding Anitra's hand.

Rue must have noticed, but she managed to restrain herself from making comment.

Without looking away from Rodrigo, Rue said, "To answer your question, Prim, I have Quesnel stashed safely away behind that barrel there, with his dart emitter focused on my dear cousin here. An extra precaution, if you would."

Primrose nodded her approval. "Admirable forethought, my dear."

"Thank you, I do try."

"Shall we get on then?" suggested Prim, indicating with her head the waiting enemy airship.

"Percy, are you ready to move us in closer?" Rue's yell cut through the still night air.

"Yes, Captain," came Percy's voice out of the darkness behind them.

"Bork, take aim."

The deckhand settled his grip on the gun and shifted it to aim at the main deck of the ladle, where they could safely assume any people would appear. Firing the Gatling was usually a two-man job, but it could be manned solo if the gunner was long-limbed and dexterous enough to crank it with one hand while he fed in the belt with the other. Bork was one of the few aboard more than strong enough. Prim would hazard a guess that his biceps alone were as wide around as her waist. And while she kept her figure trim, she was corseted for comfort, not training. *I ought to find much to admire in such a very masculine physique*, Prim berated herself. She thought of Tasherit's long golden limbs. Just as strong as Bork, and also able to shoot a Gatling alone and without aid. Which thought made Prim's mouth a little dry, and her heart beat hot in her ears. *I am entirely unnatural in my tastes. Well, at least I am in good company.* She thought of Lord Akeldama and her mother's hats. She forced herself to reconsider Bork's biceps. That's why he'd been chosen, muscles enough to fire without assistance. That way there was one less crewman exposed and at risk.

Rue barked out an order. "Percy, bring us into range of their aft balloon."

Percy ramped up the *Custard*'s propeller. Prim could feel the *whump-whump* beneath the leather soles of her dancing slippers. *We've been running it without break for a while now.* Prim frowned in concern. An active propeller required a great deal of boiler power. *Goodness, I hope this works. Quesnel is probably desperate for coal.*

Primrose raised her parasol. To the tip and base of the ferrule she'd tied a corner each of her best white handkerchief. She waved it, like a small white flag, back and forth.

Generally speaking, people the whole world over regarded this as a symbol of peace, or at least a request to parlay, but that was by European tradition; they'd no idea if it would work here in South America. After all, they were in the land of soup ladle dirigibles – anything was possible.

Anitra stepped forward and hailed the crippled airship in halting Spanish. Even Prim could tell that her accent was abysmal and her understanding crude. But her voice was strong and clear, carrying across the intervening distance between airships with ease.

They were now about two stories apart, not yet close enough for Tasherit to safely make the jump, if needed. But getting ever closer. *God, I hope she isn't needed. I want her here and safe.*

Silence greeted Anitra's words.

Primrose waved her parasol harder, white flag fluttering.

Anitra tried again.

Then Rue nodded to her cousin and the Italian spoke. His accent was different but he said exactly the same phrase as Anitra. They were keeping him close and tame as possible.

Rue said, "Tell them we are still armed and can shoot them out of the sky if necessary. They only have one helium balloon remaining. We only wish to talk, but we don't have to be nice."

Anitra rattled off a string of staccato Spanish.

Primrose saw movement on the main deck of the other ship. The only deck, really, it didn't have a forecastle, quarterdeck, or poop deck. It wasn't modelled on a galleon like most English-made dirigibles.

A figure resolved itself out of the shadows on the ship and said something back to Anitra.

Primrose realised, now that she had some sense of scale, that the ladle was less than a quarter the size of *The Spotted Custard*. Voice and stance, what little she could see of it silhouetted against the night sky, indicated their enemy was male. He was wearing, so far as Prim could make out, rather old-fashioned attire. He looked somewhat like the flywaymen of fifty years ago who used to plague the southern reaches of England. He even had a tricorn atop his head, with an impressively large feather. Rue, no doubt, would be quite envious.

Rue said, voice curdled with amused disgust, possibly at her own expense, "Is that a *pirate hat*? Is someone throwing a masquerade? Are we invited? And me without my shepherdess costume."

Primrose was willing to play along. "Well, you do have the ghastly cocked sugarloaf. And I've a sort of a medieval-style jester cap you could borrow, if you want to one-up the man. And there's Percy's Turkish cap."

"Perhaps later. Anitra, what did he say?"

"He was *very* rude, Captain." Anitra's tone was more than disgusted.

Rodrigo laughed. "He called us all the bad things. This is fun, little cousin."

"Hush now, no one asked you. Anitra, please ask him why he fired on us without warning or provocation."

Anitra rattled off the question. A long response was yelled back almost immediately.

Anitra interpreted it for them. "I think he said they don't like visitors. But I suspect it's more that they are interested in our ship. He's very curious about the Gatling gun. Keeps calling it *pretty*."

"So it's possible they are simply pirates or opportunistic scavengers, and not representative of local government attitudes?" Rue asked.

Primrose said, "In that outfit? I've never seen a statesman in a tricorn, except in paintings of questionable American presidents, of course."

"Good point."

Quesnel's voice emanated from somewhere behind them, speaking French. Rue, Prim, and Percy all spoke decent French and it was a pretty safe bet that their enemy did not. No doubt that was why Quesnel did it now, to keep the enemy confused. "It would further explain the construction of their ship if they used it mainly for stealthy attacks."

"Privateer is also a possibility, then." Rue was thinking out loud, she did that in times of stress. "Anything else? Rodrigo, Floote, did Anitra miss anything?"

"No," said both man and ghost at the same time.

"Very well, Anitra, please ask him if he knows anything about vampires." Rue did, after all, have a mission to pursue. They were supposed to be tracking down local vampires, so it made sense to ask the local pirates for details.

Anitra tried.

No response came to her question at all.

Rodrigo tried.

Still nothing.

Floote made a few quiet suggestions on syntax and word choice.

Anitra tried again.

Finally Anitra said, "Sorry, Captain, but we don't know what the right word is for *vampire* in Spanish. I tried *vampiro*, and *blood-eating* and *flesh-eating old man*, but as you can tell, he either doesn't realise what I'm after or he doesn't care to give us an answer."

Rue was having none of that. "Bork, fire a few shots under their bowsprit. Wake him up a bit."

Bork did as ordered.

A yell of rapid Spanish followed that.

Anitra tried to follow it. "He says they acknowledge our superior firepower. He doesn't understand what we are asking about."

Rue sniffed. "Tell them we are hunters. And we are hunting monsters."

Anitra gave it her best effort. Formerly Floote had to supply the word for *monster.*

More Spanish came back in response to that.

Anitra responded in kind, without translating.

Again, their erstwhile enemy replied.

"What?" demanded Rue. "What are you two saying?"

Anitra sighed. "I asked about monsters, and he said that there are no monsters in the skies except him. I would suspect from the tone that there are more of these ladle ships around these airways. Probably all independent agents. I doubt he will tell us how many. I said that we were looking for *real monsters*, those that are on land and only come out at night."

Rodrigo added, "*Immortal and supernatural*, she said. Or tried to."

"They know those words. They said they are from Lima. No *pishtacos* there." Anitra exchanged a look with Rodrigo. "We think *pishtaco* may be their word for *vampire*. Or it may be a kind of shifter. Or it may be something else."

"So," demanded Rue, "where do we find these *pishtacos*, then?"

Anitra asked their now chatty pirate friend.

A long silence, and then a single short sentence.

Anitra turned to Rue without bothering to consult with Rodrigo or Formerly Floote. "In the mountains."

Without them asking an additional follow-up question, more Spanish flowed over the intervening gap.

"He says that they live with – or is that on? – the Quechua. What's Quechua?"

Rodrigo corrected her. "No. He say *depredare*. Bah, how to put in the English?"

Formerly Floote said, "Prey. He's saying these pishtaco creatures *prey on* the Quechua. Whatever they are."

Rue threw her head back and yelled, "Percy, know anything about Quechua?"

Percy's voice came back, acerbic as ever. "Of course. They're mountain tribespeople indigenous to the high Andes mountain range of South America. Formerly known as the Inca. Perhaps you've heard of them? Gave the conquistadors a bit of a bother back in the 1500s or so." Sarcasm fairly dripped from his voice.

"No need to be rude, Percy."

"Well, really, Captain, you might have read *something* about the place we're visiting."

Rue raised a hand up, sharp and curt. "Percy! Anything else that might be *useful*?"

Percy yelled back, "You're asking the questions. How do I know what's useful?"

Primrose tried not to think too hard about murdering her brother.

"Ask him how many Cappiocra pockets there are here," suggested Percy.

"Oh my God!" Prim could not help herself. "Why are you so annoying?"

Quesnel said, still hidden, "Actually that would be very useful to know."

"Thank you, Mr Lefoux," said Percy, smug wiffin.

"But impossible to ask," shot back Prim. "We don't know what they call the aether bubbles here."

Rue threw her hands in the air. "Besides which, he's hardly going to tell us their atmospheric secrets, even if he is outgunned!"

"He did just say much on the local catching-taco people," Prim protested.

Rue rounded on her. "*Pishtacos*. That's because they fear them and we have made clear our intent is to hunt them. It's no risk to tell us about a danger to us. Ask about their ship, or their tactics, or their aether bubbles, and we put *them* in danger."

"Very strategic, little cousin." That was Rodrigo.

Anitra said, tentatively, "Anything else you wish me to say to him while we have his attention?"

Prim turned back to the enemy and away from her annoying brother. The tricorned silhouette was pacing about, impatient.

Clearly frustrated by the situation, Quesnel popped out from behind his barrel and dashed up to join the crowd at the railing. He kept his wrist pointed at Rodrigo, but said to Rue, "Ask them what they call the shape of their ship at the very least. Please, *chérie*? We can't keep going around referring to it as a ladle, it's undignified."

Across the gap, loud screaming suddenly commenced. And someone started firing at them.

TEN

Cats Can't Be Trusted

Primrose immediately pushed open her parasol and lowered it down to protect Bork. Fortunately, it seemed to be simply a personal pistol or rifle or two firing at them, not the Nordenfelt. She wondered if they were out of repeat fire, or if this was an unauthorised and uncoordinated attack.

Rue and the others ducked down, including Quesnel, who hit the deck hard. Unfortunately, they didn't have Prim and Bork's level of parasol protection.

Tasherit belly-slunk over to Prim and screamed out a roar of anger, her tail lashing. This only seemed to panic the crew opposite them further. More yells and more gunfire resulted.

Rue panicked, dropped her captain's persona, and said, "Quesnel, are you all right?"

"Yes, *chérie*, only surprised."

Rue glanced at the others. "Anyone wounded?"

Negative headshakes all around.

Quesnel's eyes were wide and scared. "What did we do? Why did they suddenly start firing at us? Was it me? Was it something I said?"

"Perhaps they object to the French tongue?" suggested Rodrigo pertly.

"Don't be silly, they probably don't even know it to identify it." Rue dismissed her cousin as an imbecile. "Bork, return fire. Clear their deck."

Bork did so, firing a volley across the main section of the ladle. They could still only really see the man in the tricorn. At the sound of their Gatling, he dropped out of sight. There must be others, of course, because someone was shooting at them, but they couldn't see anyone at all now.

Rue was quite annoyed at this turn of events. "For goodness' sake, what spooked them?"

Primrose looked about for some kind of indication or sign. The only thing new to the mix had been Quesnel and his French. To be quite honest, there was nothing remotely fearsome about either. Quesnel had likely engendered many sensations during his lifetime – love, annoyance, affection, amusement – but never terror. A medium-sized slender gentleman of erudite manner-isms and easy smile with blond hair, violet eyes, and dimples simply was not scary.

Rodrigo crouched next to Anitra with one arm over her back in a protective manner. He looked rather more thrilled than concerned. His expression in that moment was so like Rue's, Primrose began to suspect that a reckless love of danger was inherent in the Tarabotti line.

The gunfire stopped and they began to discern words mixed into the shouting cries on the ship opposite.

"Pishtaco! Pishtaco!"

Well, we can discern one word.

Anitra said, "I believe that they think we have one of their much-feared vampire monsters aboard our ship."

Rue frowned. "What did you say to make them think that?"

Rodrigo positively glared at Rue. *"Basta!* She say nothing wrong."

Percy waved him off. "Oh, stop, don't get all passionate on us now. No call for strong emotions, not even from you."

Anitra's big eyes looked wounded. "I didn't. That is, I don't think I implied anything of the kind. Did I, grandfather?"

Formerly Floote's ghostly head shook a negative.

Rue grumbled. "This is ridiculous. We aren't going to get anything more out of them now. Percy," she yelled, "prepare to pull us back." Quietly, to the others, she added, "At least now we have an idea where to start looking for my mother's vampires. The Andean highlands."

Then, without acknowledgement or permission, Tasherit slithered back halfway across the width of the deck, stood fully to her four paws, and charged the railing. She got up a decent amount of speed and, muscles bunching, leapt the gap between the airships in a remarkably stunning display of physical prowess.

Primrose squeaked in horror.

Tasherit landed safely on the ladle.

Rue yelled, "What in hell? Miss Sekhmet. I say! Get back here this instant!" Had she been standing, Rue might very well have stomped her foot. "Oh my God, why can't cats *ever* do what they're told?"

She twisted where she crouched. "Percy, belay that order. Take us in even closer. Primrose and Bork, fire when you've a clean line of sight, prepare to cover her return. What on earth did she go over for? What's she after?"

Rue glared at Primrose.

As if I know anything about the workings of Tasherit Sekhmet's mind.

"Don't look at me," Prim defended herself. "She's not my responsibility."

"Oh, you say not?"

Graced with the presence of a werecat, the other ship descended into utter chaos. The main deck, which had appeared empty mere moments before, was now swarming with figures. A half dozen at least, and it was *not* a big deck.

There was a great deal of yelling. It was a kind of horrific shadow puppet display, complete with flailing arms and flying hats, possibly a limb or two, although Prim tried not to notice.

There were screams and crunching noises and people leaping

and falling and crashing about. Occasionally, they caught sight of a cat tail or a cat head as Tasherit wreaked absolute havoc. She was doing a decent amount of damage. Well, she was a supernatural creature. Prim and Bork were too afraid of hitting her to fire their guns. Fortunately, their enemy seemed too afraid of hitting each other to fire either. Tasherit was a blur. This chaos persisted a goodly while, while everyone on board *The Spotted Custard* held their collective breath.

Finally Rue said, "Percy, bring us in closer. If she's gone to fetch something, she won't be able to make the leap back as easily with the extra weight." Rue seemed to have resigned herself to their current predicament.

Primrose breathed out a sigh of relief. She didn't know what she'd do if her friend insisted on abandoning the werecat for insubordination and reckless behaviour. Probably become insubordinate and reckless herself. *I'd hate to have to choose between my best friend and my...*

Tasherit gave another of her loud roaring screech noises. Primrose felt she could make a good case for that sound being equally as frightening as a werewolf's howl, if not more so. It was, after all, less common.

Then the cries of fear across the way evolved to keening wails of distress. Tasherit's big cat form leapt back towards them. She carried in her mouth and slung partly over her back the limp body of a man. Primrose guessed it was the no-longer-tricorn-wearing captain of the enemy airship.

The lioness landed with a tremendous thump, skidded a bit across the deck, and then spat out the torn and bloodied body of the ladle pirate.

"Marvelous," said Rue. "I thought I made it entirely clear that I did *not* want another prisoner. And this one's been savaged to perdition. What possible good can he do us? Prim, run and get the bandages, will you?" She yelled back to navigation, "Percy, get us out of here! Make for the Andes Mountains behind Lima."

"But Captain, I don't think we have enough – "

"Now, Percy!"

"Yes, Captain."

"Bugger it," said Rue, much to Prim's shock – *such language!*
"Where are we going to put him?"

"He can have my room," replied Rodrigo, rather too cheerfully.
Rue glared at him. "Speaking of, we'd better lock you back
up again."

"So soon? I was just starting to like you." The Italian pouted.
"Was I not useful?"

Rue sucked her teeth. "Fine, you can stay. But don't touch
anything. And don't kill anyone."

"Not even him?" Rodrigo indicated their new prisoner, who
was in rather worse condition than their old one.

We traded down, thought Prim, slightly hysterically. She was
well aware that she had been given orders to collect bandages.
Nevertheless, she made her way over to the lioness first.

Tasherit was giving herself a post-battle wash, long pink
tongue diligently at work.

"How could you?" Prim hissed, finding herself a great deal
more angry than the situation really warranted. "You defied
orders. You put yourself at grave risk. You could have been
killed! The leap alone – even an immortal can't survive a fall
like that."

The massive raspy tongue licked over the finger Prim was
waving in Tasherit's furry face.

"Yech! Your mouth's all bloody. That's disgusting." Primrose
retracted her hand and flapped it to dry it off, she didn't want
to wipe it on her very nice evening gown. Then she remembered
her handkerchief was still tied to the tip of her parasol, a parasol
that was still open in defensive position. She made a show of
closing the deadly accessory, removing the handkerchief, and
wiping her hand off on it.

Tasherit emitted an affectionate chuffing noise at her and
flopped over, exposing her belly.

Frustrated to near tears, or perhaps it was some form of relief at seeing the werecat unharmed, Primrose whirled away and went to find the bandages.

She returned ten minutes later, composed and with good clean linen wraps, poor man's brandy, and iodine.

The situation was well under control.

Rodrigo, of all people, took the brandy and began cleaning the injured man's wounds where he could. One of the decklings brought over a good gas lantern with a steady flame, so Prim could sew up one particularly deep claw slash on his thigh. The pirate remained insensate, which was better for all concerned.

"You're very good at that," she told the Italian, as he efficiently wrapped the man's forearm. *Defensive wounds.*

"Practice," he said succinctly.

Primrose supposed Templar training would include field dressing. After all, they sent their soulless out into the world expressly to hunt and kill supernaturals. The man had to have had his fair share of injuries over the years. Even if he could touch supernatural creatures and make them mortal, he was mortal himself and susceptible to serious damage.

But his fingers were nimble about the dressings and his touch was sure and gentle.

Prim finished her stitching, glad she didn't have to play nurse further. It usually fell to her, and frankly, it was her least favourite duty. She hadn't signed up for that one at all.

Anitra and Floote stood a little way away watching the proceedings.

Rue, having ensured they were well out of firing range and conferred with Percy about making for the Andes, came to check on them. "Is he awake yet?"

"No," replied Prim.

"You're sure he's not shamming?"

Rodrigo hauled off and slapped the man's face, hard. Certainly harder than was necessary.

I take back my thoughts on his being gentle.

No response.

"You are a bastard, aren't you?" said Rue to her cousin, but with very little irritation. "Well, we can't keep him forever. Knowing we will let him go – "

Tasherit hissed.

Rue rolled her eyes and corrected herself. "Eventually. We'd better not let him know we've a supernatural advantage aboard. He'd go off and tell his friends. Formerly Floote and Miss Sekhmet, if you would make yourselves scarce? Prim, go ready our improvised cell, we'll put him there."

The Italian looked hopeful.

Rue noticed. "Yes, cousin, you can take one of the guest quarters."

Prim said, as the man stood, "I'll see your belongings are moved, such as they are. And ask one of the staff if they could change the linens."

Without any pretence, she then turned and said to Rue, "I don't think this is a good idea."

"Trusting Mr Dark and Smarmy?"

"Yes."

Rodrigo gave Primrose a big-eyed pleading sort of look that suited him ill, like a shark attempting puppy eyes.

Primrose rolled her own eyes at him and continued talking to her friend and captain. "He's still, you know, *him*."

"What's he going to do?" Rue looked unconcerned.

"We are in a foreign land and among possible enemies. He's incredibly dangerous. He could turn us in to the local authorities. He could murder us all while we sleep. He could try to steal the *Custard* and take us to parts unknown. He could escape. I don't know. He could generally behave in accordance with his training and nature."

Rodrigo Tarabotti said, "Never!"

Rue gave a dismissive downward wave at her cousin. "Hush, you. Your opinion is neither required nor helpful. Primrose, for now we'll give him enough rope to hang himself. I'll be careful, I promise. Please go see to the room arrangements."

Primrose nodded reluctantly. Rue was in charge, after all. Before attending to her duties, Prim visited her own room and dropped off her parasol. She left her gun tucked into her bodice, having decided that she'd better keep it there while Mr Tarabotti was loose.

Percy was concerned about the state of their fuel. Or perhaps, not so much the state as the absence of any state. It wasn't really his job to worry about such things, it was Quesnel Lefoux's, but at the moment that didn't stop him.

This was out of character. Percy mistrusted the Frenchman in many ways, of course. Not the least of which being that he was, in fact, French. But he trusted Mr Lefoux to do his job as ship's engineer with aplomb.

Yet the worry persisted. *The Spotted Custard* had spent a great deal of time in atmosphere, working the propeller enough to put them dangerously low on coal. Everything Percy had read suggested Lima would have supplies, but now Rue was insisting on making for the smaller, more mysterious city of Cusco. And he worried that they simply couldn't do it. Even Rue couldn't out-stubborn coal.

He and Quesnel had not discussed the matter, yet he knew this was a shared concern. There was no need to talk about it. There'd been an exchanged look when Rue insisted on heading onwards without stopping.

Are we becoming kindred spirits? Do we have a mutual understanding and respect? Percy shuddered. *Are we friendly? How ghastly.*

On top of that, Cusco was a difficult location to navigate into. The city nestled between high peaks in a high mountain valley. Percy wasn't even certain it boasted a wheystation, let alone a coal supply. He'd certainly read no indication that there might be one. They might very well be limping into Cusco only to get flat-out stuck there.

He'd tried to tell Rue all this but she was insistent they press on. Now that they had taken a local man prisoner, they were at risk and unable to make nice with the government. She wanted them in and out quick, not *dabbling about like ducks in the wind*. Whatever that meant.

"I believe that I can get us in fast, Captain," he said, hedging. "It's the getting us back out again I gravely doubt."

In typical fashion, Rue only replied with, "Let's worry about that when the time comes."

"Rue, that's my point, the time has come."

"How long until we get within depuffing distance?"

Percy shrugged. "Several hours, maybe more, maybe less. I'm floating mostly blind here, especially at night. Not much to go on. Have you looked down? The country has no gas. I mean I know, loosely, where Cusco ought to be located, and there are some roads, but they aren't cobbled, and nothing else indicates the direction of civilisation."

Rue nodded. "Get Virgil up here to sit the helm then, so long as a course is basically set in."

"It is. But why?"

"I want your opinion on this new prisoner of ours."

"I don't have opinions on prisoners."

"You have opinions on everything. Now, see here. I'm letting Mr Tarabotti out on a longer lead and locking this one up in his place."

"Greedy."

"Percy, are you trying to be funny? I didn't know you could."

Percy ignored this. "How does Mr Tarabotti feel about his newfound liberty?" Percy was genuinely curious.

"Cheeky," said Rue. "You aren't mad at me about it? Primrose is."

"Primrose is usually mad about something. Nice to have it be you instead of me, for a change. I think that it is premature and thus risky. We haven't finished reading *Higher Common Sense* yet. But you always were a risk taker who ignored common sense."

"Do you believe my cousin really is now considered a traitor by the Templars? Might he be friendly to our cause?" Rue clearly wanted to believe it.

"It seems not unlikely." Percy was cautious. He wasn't the best at reading people, never had been. Maps he could read. And aetheric current charts. Even cats used their tails to indicate feelings in a predictable manner. But people? Especially personable secretive people like Rodrigo Tarabotti? It'd be easier on Percy if they, too, had tails.

"But?" Rue pressed.

"Rue, why are you interrogating me on this subject? Ask my sister, she's much better at judging the accountability of a man's character."

"Yes, but you're Mr Tarabotti's friend."

"Friend? Am I indeed?" First Percy had heard of it.

Rue shook her head. "Just summon Virgil and come over with me, please."

Percy waved a hand about, attempting to summon his valet out of thin air. Virgil was no doubt hidden somewhere on deck. There was no way he would hide below for a second time, not if Spoo got to stay up top and watch the excitement.

When no valet materialised, Percy took off his fez and waved it about. Then he threatened to toss it.

Virgil appeared.

"Take over for a bit here, would you please, Virgil? The captain wants me as a character reference."

Virgil gave him a very confused look.

"Exactly how I feel." Percy levered himself out of the navigation pit and followed his captain.

He joined the group around the injured prisoner. Their new man was not very prepossessing. He was on the shorter squarer side of humanity and dressed in unequivocally piratical-looking apparel of dark material and ill fit. He wore a loose shirt belted at the waist and loose trousers that could only be drawstring, like a potato sack. *No boots, though. To be a true pirate there would be boots.* Instead he had on rope sandals of some ilk. Against his dark complexion the many bandages were startlingly white and expertly applied. *Probably Prim's doing.* Someone's jacket was balled up, propping up his head.

Quesnel stood on the opposite side of the man's chest from Percy, looking down. Rue went and stood near the man's head. Rodrigo and Anitra were at his feet, with Bork standing beyond, brawny arms crossed.

So it was that when their prisoner blinked awake at last, he was staring first at Rodrigo and Anitra.

Rue said, "Ask him how he feels, please. And welcome him aboard."

The man looked up at Rue's voice. Then tilted his head slightly to catch sight of Quesnel.

At which juncture he screamed in unmitigated terror and tried to scoot away from the Frenchman.

Percy could understand that kind of reaction to Quesnel's personality, of course, but not to his appearance. Percy didn't like the man, but that didn't stop him from acknowledging the fact that Mr Lefoux was easy on the eyes. It was a *fact*, after all. Percy was always careful with his facts.

The man's eyes widened in horror. They were riveted on Quesnel. He tried crab crawling backwards on the deck. It was more flop than crawl, as he had been recently savaged by a lioness (such things detrimentally affect mobility something fierce). His efforts to escape caused him, eventually, to bump up against Percy's feet and ankles.

The prisoner started and jerked his gaze from Quesnel to Percy.

At this he screamed even louder, eyes fairly bugging out of his head, mouth gasping and panting between cries.

Percy, startled to engender that kind of reaction in anyone, put both his hands up instinctively in a warding gesture and then bent over to touch the man in an attempt to calm him.

Much to everyone's horrified embarrassment – except the man himself, who was too far gone into terror to feel anything but pure fear – the prisoner then wet himself and fainted.

"Well. I say. I mean, really," was all Percy could sputter.

Everyone was staring at him as if it was all his fault.

He flushed. "Do I have something on my face? Or... is it the fez?"

Rue ignored his weak attempt at humour. "It's not your fault, Percy. He reacted badly to Quesnel too."

Percy exchanged glances with his fellow boffin. What was so scary about them to the exclusion of the others? Could their prisoner somehow sense a scientist? Was this academiphobia? They were not the only men, so it wasn't their trousers. After all, the man had seen Rodrigo first. He and Quesnel were no taller and no more fearsome looking than the Italian. In fact, if it came to masculinity, Rodrigo had them both by a mile and a glower.

"Why us?" wondered Quesnel. "What's so different about us?"

It was Rodrigo who figured it out. "You are the *bianchi*."

Anitra grinned. "Oh, yes, I see. The skin. You boys are white. Pale." She made a motion around her own brown face.

Percy nodded. It was true. He'd a few freckles but he was about as white as one could get. His sister had insisted that even abovedecks the navigation pit be protected by a wide shade parasol, and the rest of Percy's life was spent in libraries. And Quesnel was a blond, prone to working inside boiler rooms and laboratories. They were, not to put too fine a point on it, as near to white as pink humans could get. Especially if compared to the others currently present.

Rodrigo had lost some of his colour during his imprisonment, but he still had an olive complexion by birth. Rue was nut-brown as a result of her heritage and her disinterest in maintaining any kind of complexion. She tended to run about abovedecks without a parasol or broad-brimmed hat. Anitra, being of Drifter blood, was darker still. Bork, while standing in the shadows, had African ancestry. Percy and Quesnel were positively ghostly by comparison to the others assembled around them.

"Oh." Percy understood Rodrigo's line of thought. "Vampires. He thinks we're vampires."

Rue let out a surprised laugh.

Percy nodded at Rodrigo. "You're assuming, of course, they're just as pale in this part of the world as they are back home."

"It does make sense." Quesnel raised his hands at the revelation. "They started panicking the moment I appeared on deck, remember?"

"But Prim's pale. She was there all along." Rue was confused.

"My sister was wearing her floating hat and veil." Percy wondered at himself for having noticed such a thing. But he had.

Anitra added, "And she spent most of her time shielded behind a parasol."

"Then you appeared, my love, all blond and angelic."

Quesnel side-eyed Rue. "Angelic, is it?"

Anitra continued. "That's why they started screaming about pishtacos. They thought you were one, Mr Lefoux."

Rue was grinning. "Well, I did ask Anitra to explain that we were hunting vampires."

Anitra frowned. "It is possible I got the word wrong and said *catching* instead of *hunting*. In which case . . ."

Quesnel smiled. "And Percy is even whiter than me. Plus if they don't get many blonds in these parts, they surely have even fewer redheads."

Percy nodded. "Well, that's a relief. I mean to say, I know I'm no Byron, but my face has never before engendered *that* kind of reaction."

They all looked back down on their prisoner, still insensate.

"So much for trying to hide the fact that we have supernaturals aboard." Quesnel looked thoughtful. "Not sure how I feel about being mistaken for a vampire. Should I be insulted?"

"I'd take it as a compliment, if I were you, dear." Rue's tone said he'd better. Rue's much-beloved adoptive father was a decidedly handsome and charming blond vampire, and she would never allow a word said against him. *Wait a moment*, thought Percy. *Charming. Blond. No wonder she likes Quesnel.*

"I suppose Mr Lefoux and I should make ourselves scarce

and warn Prim. Best not to torture the man at the get-go. I don't think he'll be useful when we're around. You can use us to frighten him later, of course." Percy found himself oddly untroubled by the idea of being an instrument of torture.

Quesnel nodded. "Agreed. I find it funny that he won't be scared of Miss Sekhmet in her human form. And she's the only real supernatural we've got."

Rue was considering the whole situation. "Very well. Bork, come give us a hand with the prisoner, please? Rodrigo, if you would take his legs and Bork his shoulders? Let's get him below-decks. Anitra, Rodrigo, you're with me in case he wakes up. Quesnel, if you would please run on ahead and warn Primrose about this reaction of his? I mean to say, if he screams when he sees her face she could burst into tears. Could do irreparable damage to Prim's emotional stability."

Percy wholeheartedly agreed. His sister was thoroughly invested in how others perceived her.

Rue continued. "Oh, and please ask her if she can look through ship's stores and find him some spare trousers. We must have something that will fit."

Since the smell of the man's emission had hit them all now, Percy felt Rue was on a roll with intelligent orders.

"Percy" – Rue looked at him – "you have the deck. Don't crash us into anything." *And then she goes and ruins it like that.*

Percy did not dignify that with an answer.

It didn't take all that long to turn over Rodrigo's former cell. Prim found one of the maids huddled in the dining mess and corralled her into helping. The girl had been with them from the start and still found gunfire daunting. *I may have to let her go. It's not like the gunfire is going to stop anytime soon, not with Rue for a captain.* The application of instructions and familiar duties, however, effectively brought the young woman out of her shock.

There wasn't much to do. Mr Tarabotti had no luggage with him when he boarded the *Custard*, of course, and had had no opportunity to acquire any during his confinement. He had only a few books borrowed from Percy and some personal effects that Prim had supplied as a matter of basic human decency out of stores. These included a change of clothing, a bottle of pomade, and a shaving kit. These were easily moved to the guest quarters down the hall, directly opposite Anitra.

Primrose chose that particular room because she was still uncomfortable with the decision to allow Mr Tarabotti his liberty. She could have put him up front in their spare officer room, now that Quesnel had essentially taken up residence in the captain's quarters. But that would place a preternatural right below Tasherit, and *that* made Primrose awfully uncomfortable. She could move Anitra, of course, but the girl preferred to be near Floote's tank, so she could visit with her grandfather's ghost. The officers' quarters were beyond Formerly Floote's tether reach. Besides, a ghost was a pretty good chaperone. She hoped.

"We're done here, Jane, thank you," she informed the little maid. Jane bobbed a curtsey and made herself scarce, taking with her the dirty linens.

In taking on another prisoner we also have another mouth to feed. And I had to dip into my medical cabinet again. Goodness, I do hope Rue lets me shop at our next stop. We need supplies badly. Primrose went to retrieve her ledger, intent on making a list to that effect. *I should check with Cook. I'm sure we're running low on everything, but I'd like to know what we're in dire need of, what we can substitute, and what can wait.* Things like puff pastry and milk kept their captain in good spirits, but lemon and vinegar and brandy alike were medical necessities as well as vital to the cuisine and palate.

Primrose was so very intent on her list that she might be excused on the grounds of distraction for bumping full tilt into Tasherit as the werecat emerged from her room. She was back in human form and swathed in her customary colourful silken robes.

"Oh! I do beg your pardon," said Prim, stumbling into the wall.

"All right there, little one? What's the rush?"

"Must jot down some thoughts on our next supply run while they're fresh in my head."

"Always so busy."

"Keeping a ship of this size sufficiently supplied is no mean feat. I mean, I'm aware you must know something about such things. You are, after all, in charge of our security."

Tasherit inclined her head, eyes as always intent and wholly focused on Prim. "You're angry with me."

It was not a question.

Primrose was, of course, but she wasn't going to say anything. However, if the werecat opened herself up like that, well then . . .

"You just *leapt* over there, under enemy fire. Did you know you could make such a distance safely? Was it worth it simply to bring back a prisoner, when that was expressly forbidden?"

"We need answers. Hunting is what I do. It is what I'm good at."

"That's all? Like a dog? Nothing but instinct? No self-control, no class?" Primrose spat.

That got Tasherit angry. Her chocolate eyes flashed and narrowed. She pressed Primrose back against the hallway wall.

Prim refused to be bullied. "You are hundreds of years old, don't excuse a premeditated action with animal drive. That's cheap and shoddy and beneath you. You're better than that. I know it. You may have Rue convinced you're some half-wild foreign creature. She knows what it's like to be in animal form, so she thinks she knows what it's like to be you. But she's wrong. You're stronger and much older. And you knew *exactly* what you were doing just now, and what you did was *wrong!*" Primrose didn't even realise she was now the one pushing Tasherit back. She had two fingers out and was prodding the woman in her sternum and walking her backwards down the hallway towards her own quarters.

"Fierce little one," breathed out Tasherit, eyes still hot but not at all angry anymore.

"Why? Why would you *really* do that?"

"The captain's order was wrong and lacked forethought. We need insider information. We know nothing about this place, these people. I brought us leverage."

"You can't defy orders like that."

Tasherit shrugged. "This is not a military operation. Besides, I was in lioness form. I couldn't very well ask permission."

"Better to beg forgiveness?"

The werecat hissed. "I *never* beg. Although you, of course, are welcome to try to get me to."

"I cannot believe I am attempting to argue with a cat."

"Neither can I. You should kiss me instead."

"I should...what!"

"You want to, little one."

What Primrose wanted was to scream. She wanted to keep yelling at Tasherit, no matter how ineffectual, because it was the only way she could manage the roaring in her ears and the vibrating in her body. On deck she had wanted to lunge after the leaping lioness. To catch her by the tail and yank her back or to follow her into the abyss, Prim wasn't sure which. It terrified her, and now that fear had become rage.

I'm a tangled mess of needs I never thought to have and cannot seem to control. Tasherit pretended to be this wild untamed creature and she seemed to engender in Primrose something equally wild and untamed. Prim had never felt such sensations in her life. No book of etiquette addressed this mad desire to touch or to strike. No dancing lesson had ever taught her how to waltz this fast. She had no means but anger, even knowing anger was a childish recourse.

She deflated on that thought. *I am behaving like an infant.* She pulled herself in and up, dropping her hand, humiliated by her own fierceness. Ashamed at her loss of control. And yet still yearning.

Primrose knew the moment that her own face crashed into misery. She could feel it sink, cool prickling over her flushed cheeks. She saw it register in Tasherit's eyes – always so intent, always so focused on her, always so filled with yearning. But Primrose could no more control Tasherit's wanting than she could her own.

"Help me," she pleaded with her torturer. "Please." She was only human, and she allowed herself to beg.

"I like it when you let go." There was sympathy but no compromise in the werecat's soft words. Did Tasherit think Prim's turmoil a petty thing or simply mortal and, by extension, childish?

"That's the problem, isn't it?" *I build fortifications of what* should *be and she pushes, and pushes, and pushes at me with the possibility of what* could *be. And I want it so very badly and am so very afraid.*

Tasherit tugged. At some point the werecat had taken Prim's hand in her own – cool and soft and sure. Primrose followed the unspoken request.

Tasherit's lips were cool and soft and sure too. She murmured into Prim's mouth, before switching to tiny lapping licks that Primrose found less shocking than she should. It was as if Prim were spilled cream from a broken jug and Tasherit was tasting her – tentative, wary of sharp pieces, yet deeply taken by the flavour and the risk.

Tasherit was pressed against her a full body length now. Everything about it felt perfect. One golden hand pressed the back of Prim's neck, more for reassurance than insistence, fingers nestled into her hair, testing the softness, thumb curved about her throat, testing the pulse of blood beneath. Primrose had been kissed and held by a few of her many fiancés. Society allowed some canoodling, up to a point and within reason, of course. Primrose had allowed it precisely because she felt nothing and thus it was easy to stop. It never felt *right*.

She fit against Tasherit *right*. The werecat's other hand was exactly right against the small of her back, fine boned and very strong, warm sandstone and satin. The fingers pressed a pattern of *right, mine, right*, over and over into Prim's flesh.

Because of that, Primrose regretted her favourite evening dress, velvet was too thick a fabric. She regretted her stays, solid reinforcement though they may be. She wished only for Tasherit's hand as her support.

Tasherit's fingers at Prim's throat slid around, exploring, down to her collarbone.

"I've known vampires whose skin was not so fine. Like warm alabaster." Tasherit silenced herself, pressing her lips to the spot where her thumb had recently been. She tested Prim's pulse points with tiny nips and licks, almost worshipful.

Her hand kept petting down from collar to chest, and Primrose knew she should stop it. She'd never allowed a man such liberties, and she was tolerably certain she should not like anything as much as she liked this.

Then Tasherit encountered the hard ivory handle of the pistol down Prim's cleavage. Primrose noticed for the first time that it was pressing most uncomfortably against her sternum.

The werecat drew back with a startled laugh.

"Surprised?" said Primrose, knowing she was flushed and mussed.

Not for long. Soon Tasherit would return to kissing her, her eyes promised it. And Primrose was going to let her, because she wanted it more than was proper. And Primrose had never wanted *anything* more than was proper.

A polite cough emanated from down the hallway.

We are in a hallway. A public hallway. And someone has seen us. Prim's whole body froze up. Where seconds before she had been flushed, she turned clammy and cold.

CHAPTER

ELEVEN

Our Lord and Saviour *The Spotted Custard*

Tasherit said something, no doubt quite foul, in some long-dead language of the deserts, raspy with hunger and disuse. She dropped her hands from Prim's waist and chest. This left Primrose shivering and incomplete.

The werecat backed slowly away. But her eyes, while human for the moment, said *mine, mine, mine* in gleams of pure feline possession.

Primrose jerked, ashamed and intent on running into her room. Not sure she even wanted to know who had caught them *in flagrante delicto*.

But she had to look.

Formerly Floote hovered a ways down the hall at the point where the ladder led down to the stateroom, with crew quarters beyond.

The fact that it was the ghost who'd seen her in a compromising position was a relief. No doubt he would tell Rue if she asked, but she would have to know to ask. He was the least forthcoming human Primrose had ever met in life, and was even more taciturn in death.

There was no censure on his noncorporeal visage. There might even have been a gleam of understanding or sympathy.

"Apologies. But you are not alone, ladies," he said.

Tasherit glared at him.

So Primrose responded with a polite, "Thank you."

"Ah yes, well…" The ghost slid aside, to reveal the fact that Quesnel was almost to the bottom of the ladder, climbing down from the deck. He had paused there, dangling slightly from his one good arm, and was staring down at them, mouth agape, big purple eyes blinking in utter confusion.

Primrose knew she must have turned absolutely scarlet in humiliation. Quesnel's shock was genuine. Rue had never told him. She trusted Rue, of course, knowing that her friend would never betray her struggles, not even to a lover. Yet now, through her own indiscretion, he knew it all. He knew more than Rue did. More than Percy implied he'd guessed.

Since Primrose had no other way to manage the situation, she ignored it.

"Formerly Floote, the captain has decided to put the new prisoner in the old prisoner's cell. Or what amounts to his cell. Which means I am putting Mr Tarabotti in the guest quarters across from your granddaughter. I realise this is not ideal, but I won't have him any closer to Rue or Miss Sekhmet."

The ghost nodded. "I understand."

"I don't think it is a wise decision to allow Mr Tarabotti his freedom, but it is not my place to question Rue's assessment of her cousin's character."

"You don't trust him?" That came from Quesnel, who'd recovered from his surprise, climbed the rest of the way down, and was now on a level with them.

Tasherit crossed her arms and glared at both ghost and man. Prim found herself unexpectedly attuned to the werecat's movements. As if they were tethered in time as well as in space.

Prim said, "No, I don't trust Mr Tarabotti. And as it's your granddaughter, Formerly Floote, I thought you might be persuaded to keep an eye on him as much as possible."

"Agreed," said the ghost. He did not seem as concerned for Anitra's reputation as Primrose would have anticipated. After all, he must have seen them holding hands during the battle earlier. But she supposed, on a purely practical level, if Anitra was indeed barren, ruination via illegitimate children was impossible.

Quesnel seemed to remember he had something official to report. "They're bringing the new prisoner down now. Is the room ready, Miss Tunstell?"

"It is, Mr Lefoux," replied Prim, falling back on formality and official duties with no little relief.

"You and I, Percy, and Formerly Floote here are all to avoid contact with him," Quesnel said.

"Why is that?"

"We think that this prisoner believes that those of us with very pale skin are vampires, or *pishtacos*, as he says. He awoke to find Professor Tunstell and myself bending over him and went insane with panic. Rue does not wish to provoke him further."

Prim frowned. "That will make maid and footman service quite difficult. They are all near as fair a complexion as you."

Quesnel, and by extension Rue, had clearly not thought of this issue.

"For now, don't extend him the courtesy of staff visitation. One of the others will take him his meals." A wicked grin split the man's face. "We could make Mr Tarabotti tend to him. With supervision, of course. If that Italian is going to be loose about our ship, he should earn his weight."

Prim's smile was equally evil. "Very good point, Mr Lefoux. By all means, let's keep Mr Tarabotti occupied. Could you use some help in engineering as well – coal scuttling, perhaps?"

Quesnel laughed. "I shall put Aggie in charge of him."

"Poor fellow. That's going too far."

Quesnel gestured at his injured arm and shoulder, still supported by a sling. A serious gunshot wound – he'd nearly died at the hands of that Italian.

Primrose was pleased to know that someone else aboard mistrusted Rodrigo Tarabotti as much as she did.

Tasherit hissed, "I'll watch him for you."

Without looking at her, Primrose said, "No, you will not. You're the most vulnerable of any of us. He's trained his whole life to kill your kind."

"He's trained to kill werewolves."

Primrose raised a hand. "A trifling difference."

"I *beg* your pardon!"

"And vampires," Quesnel added.

Tasherit curled her lip back at him.

Primrose sniffed. "Yes, yes, you're special, better and more powerful than werewolves, a superior hunter in all things."

Tasherit preened under the praise, oblivious to, or uncaring of, the sarcasm. "Thank you."

"He can still kill you."

"He can't! I can take him down, you see if I can't."

That finally forced Primrose to glare directly at her. "How long has it been since you faced off against a Templar-trained preternatural?"

Tasherit looked disgruntled. "About a hundred years or so." She pouted. "But I am still *better*. I would show you." Her tone said this bragging was all for Primrose's benefit.

Oh dear. This is about her being good enough to provide for me. This is about her worthiness as a mate. Prim had read something on lion society when Tasherit first joined the crew. Also, they had spoken at length over the dinner table on the subject of werecat dynamics. Everyone found it fascinating, it being the opposite of everything they knew about the supernatural.

Europe's vampires and werewolves skewed almost entirely male, no one knew why. When women did survive the bite, they were automatically in the superior social position of vampire queen or Alpha werewolf. Scientists had believed this connected to the general inclination for muscle mass in the male physique. Although if one took into account some vampires – Lord Akeldama for example – the point about muscle mass would seem to be moot. Regardless, when Tasherit revealed the fact that werecats were predominantly female, and that males were the ones less likely to survive metamorphosis, the scientific community had been thrown into a tizzy. (Percy had added this to his paper.) Some found this fact even more shocking than the revealing of their existence in the first place. After all, the existence of new shape-shifters in other parts of the world had been hypothesised, but the idea that females might dominate was tantamount to social upheaval. The suffragists were ecstatic about the whole thing, and had seized upon the lioness as a symbol for their movement. Tasherit had even been invited to speak when next in London. Lord knows what she would say. Primrose counted it fortunate they rarely visited the capital.

What Primrose had learned and would have told said scientists if asked (which she would never be, because she was, after all, only a woman – and wasn't *that* ironic?) was that a female social structure for lions was mirrored in nature. Why be surprised? Prides were made up of sister lionesses and their young, as a rule, with only one male. Why should the supernatural be any different? The lionesses did the bulk of the hunting. They were, in effect, the family providers.

And Primrose was learning by the moment that Tasherit hated it more than anything when Prim questioned her ability to provide. Whether that be affection or protection.

So Prim hastened to smooth over the situation. "Miss Sekhmet, I'm certain you could protect us all from Mr Tarabotti. And I promise to call upon you if necessary. But please stay away from him if your intent is merely to test his mettle? No one requires that you prove yourself capable." *Least of all me.* She did not say it out loud, but she hoped Tasherit understood that it was implied. "We all know you are a fierce warrior."

Just then they heard a commotion at the top of the ladder. Quesnel made an *erp* noise and rushed past them towards the captain's ladder, which would take him safely up to his and Rue's quarters. Formerly Floote sank down through the floor, leaving Prim and Tasherit alone once more.

Mindful that she had been instructed to avoid the prisoner, and not knowing if he was awake, Prim pushed passed Tasherit, avoiding the werecat's questing hand, and retreated to the safety of her own room.

Behind her she heard Tasherit hiss in frustration. But Prim wasn't sure if that was because she had so carefully avoided contact, or because of the lack of an immediate fight with Rodrigo Tarabotti, or both.

There was a tentative knock on her door just prior to sunrise. Primrose supposed she ought to have expected it. She was preparing for bed, and some small part of her hoped that it might be Tasherit knocking. A larger part of her was terrified that it actually was.

She put on her ugliest robe. Prim had, most of the time, most excellent taste. This robe was a quite flattering teal colour, but it was not well cut. She didn't want to display her figure to Tasherit. That was a very bad idea.

Fortunately, or unfortunately, it was not Tasherit at her door. It was Prudence.

"Rue? Aren't you exhausted? Shouldn't you be abed?"

"Prim dear, we need to talk." Rue looked stubborn. Well, more stubborn than usual.

Uh-oh.

"Come in. I was just completing my ablutions." Primrose gestured with her tortoiseshell hairbrush.

Rue marched in and grabbed the brush from her hand. Then she guided Prim to sit at the small vanity.

It was a soothing thing to have one's hair brushed by another. They'd done this for each other many times over the years — fashioned braids and coils, woven in flowers and ribbons. All this to the manifest horror of Rue's mother, the amusement of Rue's fathers, and the delight of everyone else. It was Uncle Biffy who eventually took them under his wing and showed them how to really arrange hair properly.

These days Rue barely bothered with her coiffure. Even Primrose resorted to a simplistic if stylish arrangement, which she tried to improve upon with sophisticated hats.

But Prim still loved it when Rue brushed her hair. It reminded her of her youth, easy innocence and lost silliness.

"Quesnel told me what he saw," Rue said after a few strokes in silence.

"Of course he did." Primrose was no fool. She'd always known she could rely upon Rue to keep her secrets from Quesnel. However, she could not rely upon Quesnel to keep *anything* from Rue. He adored her, and for him adoration turned into verbal incontinence.

"What's going on, Prim dear, really?" Rue's brushstrokes did not pause.

Primrose hedged. "How can I be certain that he was honest in his description of the physical transaction, as it were?"

"He said he saw Tasherit Sekhmet kissing Primrose Tunstell in the hallway." Rue could be blunter than the tag end of a rutabaga when it suited her. "Well? Was she kissing you?"

"She was."

"And were you kissing her back?"

"I was." Primrose may do many dishonest things in the pursuit of perfection, but she never lied to her best friend. To herself, assuredly, but not to Rue. Well, not unless it was for Rue's own good.

Rue and Prim always joked that when they handed out *shame*, Rue got confused and took a double helping of *daring* instead. It was never more obvious than at times like this – Prim's best friend had no shame whatsoever. "Do you want her?"

"I don't know *what* I want."

"You know what you think you should want, and that clearly hasn't worked, has it? How many failed engagements is it now, Primrose?"

Prim hung her head and tried to work a defensive statement around the lump in her throat.

Rue continued brushing her hair. "And you know I don't mean *that* kind of want. I mean the kind where you want to push her down on your bed and pounce, or let her pounce on you."

"Prudence Akeldama!"

"Yes, me. Remember? The one you used to trust."

That hurt. "I like affections with her more than I ever liked affections with any of the fiancés."

"Oh, *stuff affections*, is it? And you've done more affectionate activities with her than with any of them, haven't you?"

Primrose could feel herself blushing. "How on earth do you know *that*?"

Rue gave her an eye roll via the vanity mirror. Quesnel must have seen a great deal more in that hallway than Primrose realised.

She whimpered in humiliation. Then she whispered, "Rue, I genuinely don't even know what she wants me to do... with regards to said stuff." She waved a limp hand at her own body. "I mean to say, what do two women even do together?"

"*Affections* apparently."

Prim groaned and sagged forward to rest her forehead on the vanity.

"My Primrose, always wanting to plan and be prepared for everything. That's not something I can answer for you, darling. But I will say with confidence that I'm certain Tasherit has more than enough experience for the both of you. Centuries of experience. And no doubt a willingness to teach you everything."

"Oh God." Prim thumped her head against the lacquered surface.

Rue tried to hide a smile and failed. "Leaving aside your objections over the social acceptability of such a relationship –"

"Yes, about that..."

Rue forestalled her. "Oh, can we not leave it aside? Very well. Primrose Tunstell, *I don't care*. No one on my ship will *ever* care, or they won't remain on my ship. You can hide it if you like when we go home. Tash won't mind hiding. She's a werecat, stealth is part of her nature. You are creating obstacles for yourself because of your own rigid expectations, and none of us can help you overcome those."

Rue put down the brush and petted Prim's hair, soothing her, as if she were the lioness, not Tasherit. "I know it's difficult for you to give up the ideal of home and marriage and children." She hugged Prim's shoulders gently. "But what is *The Spotted Custard* if not your home? What is the crew if not your children? You spend your days mothering us all. And we love it. You must merely change the way you look at the world. And I *know* that's hard for you. If not impossible."

Primrose gave a most unladylike gulp noise and unexpectedly started to cry. And not in the pretty way, but with those stupid fat tears that made her skin go all blotchy.

"None of that, now." Rue rubbed little circles on Prim's back. "You're strong, you'll figure it out." *You'll come around* was what she was really saying.

Rue kept rubbing in silence for a few minutes. "I actually didn't come here to upset you. I've a present."

Primrose managed to stop crying at that. She loved presents.

"Quesnel gave me something to pass along. We thought, you know, if you were scared of the unknown, these might help."

Rue reached into the pocket of her dressing gown and pulled out a stack of postcards.

Curiosity won over misery. Primrose dried her eyes and blew her nose on a silk handkerchief and then reached for the cards.

They were *French* postcards.

Oh my, thought Prim. *I knew they existed, of course. Like French letters. One hears of such things. But I didn't know they came in such numbers and with this particular variant.*

They were all quite lewd, and most upsetting, and absolutely fascinating. She didn't want to touch them, and she wanted to keep flipping through them as fast as she could. It was humiliating, because these had clearly been selected with her in mind. The very idea of Quesnel and Rue discussing such a thing! And why did Quesnel have this variant in the first place? The images were tasteful...to a point. The ladies in them were all wearing lovely underpinnings – lace abounded and the corsets were very well fitted. Until they were not wearing anything at all. Or one of them wasn't and the other one was only in stockings. That being the nature of this particular stack of cards, all the images were of ladies *with* other ladies.

Primrose found herself tilting her head to one side, as if she might see a different angle. "You can do that?"

"I suppose you can and they do." Rue looked slightly uncomfortable. Which, frankly, Primrose didn't think was possible with her friend.

Prim flipped to the next one. The one girl had her mouth... Well, she had her mouth going where Primrose was tolerably certain that no mouth ought to go. Really, it was *too much*.

"Now *that* I know you can do." Rue was grinning.

Prim swallowed, eyes wide. "Does Quesnel...?"

"Oh yes."

"How extraordinarily...French."

"Oh, but I do it too. So it must also be English."

"What!" Prim wrinkled her nose in disgust. Somehow *that* seemed like a horrible idea. *Male parts were so dangly. Wouldn't that be a little like bobbing for apples? Or bobbing for sausages?* "Yech."

She flipped to the next card. It was quite sensual. The two women were kissing, nothing more, but enjoying it. *I like this one.*

"Aren't you jealous that Quesnel has these?" she asked Rue, fanning out the collection of French postcards full of pretty women.

Rue laughed. "No, silly. Look at the ladies."

Primrose was looking. But then she kind of understood what Rue was getting at. Quesnel clearly had a *type of lady* that interested him, and that type looked exactly like Rue. Generously curved, cheerful, dark haired. "Oh, they all look like you, or one of them does in each scene."

"Exactly."

Rue's grin broadened as Prim's discomfort increased. "Not to your taste, is she?"

Primrose thought of Tasherit's long lean golden limbs. She blushed. "Probably not. Um, no offence?" The very notion that she might find Rue attractive was incestuous. Not only were they essentially sisters, they also looked alike. They'd successfully pretended to be siblings on more than one occasion.

Rue actually giggled at Prim's horrified expression. "No offence taken. Now, I'll leave these with you, shall I? It'll give you an idea on concept and possible acrobatics, you know, for you and Tash's *stuff.*"

Primrose put the cards down and put a hand to her throat. "Oh dear."

Rue stood and made to leave. "You'll be fine." Then she had the temerity to wink. "Have fun."

Primrose wouldn't have called it that, but she certainly had an educational hour or so after Rue left. After all, Rue was right, she did like to be prepared for every eventuality. The French postcards gave her much to think about, and at least some preparation.

It took Percy less time than it ought to recover from the fact that he'd been mistaken for a monster of some bloodsucking and ill-named sort. *Pishtaco, indeed!*

He puffed the *Custard* through the rest of the night's float without incident. With Rue and the others asleep – even Virgil needed his rest, he was a growing boy – Percy sat skipper through to luncheon the next day. By which time he was almost the monster their new prisoner feared him to be. He was accustomed to long nights without sleep from his time at university, but he was beginning to think he was too old for such carrying on now.

He used the propeller to guide them in over the last mountain towards a point where all the roads below them seemed to be leading. From what he'd read, that point should be the city of Cusco. He was, it must be admitted, a mite worried. If the locals reacted universally in such a virulent manner to these pishtacos, there must be a serious extermination mandate in place. These Andean vampires were in grave danger. Humans were, of course, food to vampires, but they also always outnumbered them. If the Dark Ages proved anything, it was that no matter how strong the supernatural creature, enough determined mortals could kill them to near extinction if given the right motivation. And fear was the best motivator of all.

It was puff and go, as he had no map, so he kept having to run to the rail of the poop deck and look over, see where they were, run back, and make the adjustment accordingly. In this, he kept being thwarted by scraggly white low-floating clouds obscuring his view.

Nevertheless, *The Spotted Custard* cleared what he hoped was the final mountain peak and sank down through the clouds to find a city spread out below.

It was a tidy-looking thing from up high, all muted browns, greys, and whites, gridded out with clear main avenues and smaller streets. It reminded him of those European cities that were based on Roman fortifications – well planned and militarily severe. A warlike race preferred organised civilisation, Percy recalled from his old history professor. The Incan policy on construction seemed not dissimilar to that of the Romans.

I wonder if they too wore big bottlebrush rooster combs out the tops of their helmets?

Percy twirled his own tassel thoughtfully.

He toggled the propeller over a nudge to guide them in, and the thing simply ground to a halt. The *whump-whump* noise beneath his feet, the one that permeated the ship like a heartbeat whenever the propeller was active, stopped whump-whumping.

Percy didn't want to talk to anyone about this problem. He

really didn't, because Percy knew Quesnel was asleep. That meant Aggie Phinkerlington had taken on the dusk shift. But this was a serious problem. Without a propeller, *The Spotted Custard* had no manoeuvrability.

He picked up the speaking tube. "Miss Phinkerlington?"

"Mr Tunstell."

"Professor, please. Or *Navigator*, if you must."

She did not acknowledge his request for proper address. "We are out."

"What?"

"That's what you called about, isn't it?"

"The propeller has stopped propelling."

"We're out of coal. Both kettles are dry. And it makes not a jot of difference if you ask me to lift coal reserves from the maintenance burner, or take the last of Cook's stock, we're done here. We've no water either. We are dry in all ways."

"I've lost steering?"

"You've lost steering." Aggie's tone said a million things. That this was not her fault. That this was most likely Rue's fault for pushing the *Custard* too hard. That she would yell this into Rue's face when she saw her next.

"You can't give me anything at all?"

"Not a single steamed sausage, sweetheart."

"Charming, Miss Phinkerlington. A ten-minute warning would have been common courtesy."

The impossible woman clicked off the tube at her end without bothering to reply. *Common courtesy* was not in her vocabulary. Percy sighed. He'd never thought to meet anyone more rude than he was. *I should try to be nicer to people if this is what it feels like on the receiving end. Except being nice is so very exhausting.*

Percy considered *The Spotted Custard*'s next move. They couldn't stay hovering: there was a distinct breeze running through the valley, it was already carrying them southwards over the city, without the propeller to fight it. There was no wheystation anywhere in sight and no obelisk for a tie-down.

So far as Percy could tell, that left him with only one option. Fortunately, a Catholic country like this one boasted said option in abundance. All he really needed was a nice tall church steeple.

Percy depuffed them quickly. No doubt everyone's ears were popping, but this was an emergency.

He scanned the terrain. There appeared to be a massive church in the centre of the city, just south of them now, and if he was quick he could ride the valley breeze and get them down in time to drag anchor for it.

He had a skeleton crew of only a few decklings, with Willard as sole deckhand in charge.

Lacking any other resources, Percy yelled over to him. "Willard. Emergency depuffing with the intent of tying down immediately. I'm making for that church, just there, to the southwest of that assembly square. Do you see it?"

"That's no church, sir, that's a cathedral."

"Yes, I do believe you're right. Oh well."

"Locals might take that amiss, sir."

"I'm sure they will."

"Do we anticipate hostiles?"

"Is anyone *ever* happy to see us?"

"Sir, we really need the captain for this kind of thing."

"And we need more than a skeletal crew, I couldn't agree more. But I can't spare a single one of you at the moment to go fetch her. Have all your decklings prepare ropes to lasso anchor on that steeple. Let's hope it's a sturdy one. I picked the biggest I could find."

"Yes, sir. I could run below and get – "

Percy shook his head, which made his temples ache with exhaustion. "No. You need to take the Gatling. Like I said, no one ever seems happy to see us. If anything goes wrong, like – oh, I don't know – we crash into their favourite cathedral, we might want to be able to defend ourselves."

"Understood, sir." Willard began yelling instructions to the decklings as he took up position behind the Gatling gun.

The Spotted Custard dropped steadily downwards and drifted steadily southwards.

The city was more chaotic and less formal close up. It was rough-hewn from mountain rock, with dirt packed in between. It had an old-fashioned feel to it, with no pillars of industry belching black smoke into the clean mountain air. The roads were unsullied by monowheels or coccinellidae steamers. There weren't even omnibuses or carriages crowding the streets. Percy blinked in surprise. They didn't appear to have horses at all in this part of the world. A strange place indeed. Perhaps horses didn't do well in the high mountains? There did seem to be some form of extremely hairy long-necked beast of burden, but that was it. No one was riding anything. People actually seemed to simply walk everywhere. *How novel.*

It was also rather colourful. Not dark and gloomy with soot and fog. The locals were dressed in bright primary colours, and so were the long-necked not-horses. There were flags and ribbons flying here and there of a similar garish cheerfulness.

The square around the cathedral they were aiming for was packed with humanity. A market or a parade or an assembly of some kind was occurring. Percy wondered if it was a saint's day, this being a Catholic country.

The Spotted Custard continued her inexorable sink and drift. Percy kept one hand to the helm, using sail and rudder to give them some kind of guidance, but it was pure hope. Both systems were meant for sailing the aetherosphere, not the atmosphere. The *Custard* was, at this moment, nothing more than a glorified hot-air balloon. They were at the mercy of the elements. Percy could puff them up, or depuff them down, through the manipulation of helium and air ballast, but that was the sum total of their manoeuvrability.

They didn't actually *hit* the church steeple, but it was a very near thing. Tiles might have been lost. The decklings proved their mettle with a concerted swarm of small bodies to the starboard side, where they threw out the linking net, the one the

Drifters had once used to keep balloons connected midair. The net was a good choice, it gave them a bigger margin for error. Percy was pleased, *Spotted Custard* decklings were smarter than the average deckling.

The net fell in a cascade of brown, and some part of the centre caught and held right over the steeple. The decklings having lashed it all along the starboard side, the *Custard* jerked and then listed to starboard. It wasn't bad enough to cause a dangerous tilt, but Percy suspected everyone but Tasherit would be awake now.

Percy puffed them ever so slightly to counter the sideways strain. The *Custard* righted herself. He locked down the balloon flaps to keep them at this height and let out a relieved breath.

The sooties let forth a huge cheer. Well, huge considering there were only four of them.

Percy almost wanted to cry. He was so tired. But they'd done it: they were down and they were moored, against all odds.

And so far, no one is shooting at us. I'll take that as a win all round, he thought.

Then Percy heard the cheering, huge and loud and rolling and not coming from his sooties. Oh no, this was coming from the city beneath them.

Primrose awoke to a strange roaring rushing sound. It came in waves like the ocean but was not so soothing. There seemed to be music involved as well. It took her a long lazy moment to realise what it reminded her of – the crowds at the opera or in Vauxhall Gardens.

Someone is cheering. Many, many someones are cheering.

She yawned and thought about tea. The light was slashing fully through the porthole and her stomach was growling away. *Must be just past noon, or so,* she surmised.

She tumbled out of bed and went to the porthole to look.

They were down close over a city, only a few stories up. She'd no idea what they were lashed to, but something held them steady. There was that little bobbing sensation that came when the airship was tied down rather than holding steady under her own steam with the propeller. She thought it might have been the jerk of rope attaching to its mooring that woke her.

They were over one part of an assembly square, cobbled and built of grey mountain rock, military in design and precision. The three sides she could see were made up of buildings of the barracks variety, but more likely to be government and religious in nature, she suspected. They were universally three stories high, except for the occasional church, with the second level cantilevered out over the first, providing for long interconnected balconies above and shaded colonnades below. The balconies were decorated with extremely colourful draped woven fabrics, and people stood on them wearing extremely colourful draped woven outfits. The locals had dark complexions with soulful eyes and ready smiles. Prim remembered Rue's instructions that she and Percy and Quesnel stay indoors and out of sight because they were scarily pale.

She hoped Percy, the only one on deck, had remembered this and remained safely crouched in his navigation pit, mostly out of view.

She looked down into the square. They'd obviously arrived during a celebration of some iteration. Lots of peaked hats were involved. She could see nuns and other religious representatives gathered in flocks of black or white among all the colour. People seemed to be waving about an inordinate number of wooden crosses, a few gold statues were raised up on platforms, and everyone would occasionally break into song. Well, not the statues. The melodies were faintly familiar, although the singing was in Spanish.

"Is it...?" Primrose frowned. Surely they would not have forgotten. Not the whole crew. Although they had been very busy recently. "I think it might be."

Throwing a wrap about herself, Primrose ran to the hallway and yelled up at the captain's quarters.

"Rue!"

Rue's head appeared, looking down the ladder. "I was just going up top, you're to stay down here, remember?"

"Rue, it's Christmas!"

"Well, I never. Surely not."

"Oh yes it is, they're singing about the three kings out there and holding up statues of the saviour and all sorts. Timing works out if you think about it. I mean, you must at least acknowledge we're nearing the end of December. We simply got distracted by the grey and air-pirate soup ladles."

"I don't have gifts for anyone."

"That's the least of your problems. Percy seems to have set us down right over the main assembly square in Cusco. Knowing my brother, he's likely lashed us to their central cathedral. This is a Catholic country, remember."

"Bloody hell," said Rue, shockingly profane given the current circumstances. Her head disappeared.

Quesnel's head appeared in her place. "What's going on?"

"It is Christmas."

"Oh, is that all?"

Primrose remembered last night and the French postcards and blushed beet red. She pulled her wrap close about her. "I'll just go get dressed."

"Breakfast?" The Frenchman tried one of his dimpled smiles. "I'm not allowed to go up top either, remember?"

"Luncheon, I should think, now. I'll go check with Cook after I'm decent. Give me a half hour?"

"Excellent."

"Christ almighty," said Primrose, giving herself licence to swear under the circumstances. "I need tea immediately."

TWELVE

Rumours of Pishtacos

Percy!"

Percy awoke with a jerk to find he'd dozed off at his station, slumped over the helm and drooling slightly.

"I wasn't sleeping!"

"You were snoring. I didn't realise that the roar of an angry mob could be so soothing." Rue was standing over him. She was backlit, so he couldn't tell if she was really angry at him or not.

He scrubbed at his face. "It's likely some form of reaction to my relief. Not that I was worried, I don't doubt my own abilities, but it was a humdinger of a landing."

"You've lashed us down to a *cathedral*."

"Yes, I have. We needed something tall and pointy. No whey-stations or obelisks in this part of the world."

"I understand your reasoning, Percy, and I appreciate your getting us depuffed in one piece given the circumstances. But a religious icon is, perhaps, a problematic choice."

"I didn't choose it. There was no choosing. It simply happened."

"Whatever you say. Also, not to put too fine a point on it, so to speak, it's also Christmas Day."

"What? Is it indeed? How perspicacious." Percy could see how the cathedral might be an issue under these particular circumstances. "Would it help if I said oops? Or apologised to the crowd?"

"You know I don't want you seen. Go below and go to bed, would you please? I'll take care of the cathedral."

That was an oddly ominous way of putting it. "I wasn't *really* asleep at my post."

"Of course you weren't. That line across your face is merely from hugging the helm out of affection, I'm sure."

Percy climbed out of navigation with as much dignity as he could muster. "Very well, but if the angry mob attacks, please don't bother to wake me. I always said I wanted to go in my sleep."

"Done," said Rue.

Percy was to learn later that several things happened after he left the poop deck to seek his well-deserved rest. Firstly, the mob turned out to be no mob at all and not even slightly angry. In fact it was simply a celebratory crowd, and they were cheering the arrival of a great big red-spotted airship. They'd never seen its like. To have one float in on Christmas Day was perceived as some sort of representative of the Star of David. (Albeit a rather chubby version.) They weren't considering the appearance of *The Spotted Custard* exactly a miracle, but they did think it a very nice sign of the Almighty.

Rue met with the local bishop shortly after Percy went to bed. Said bishop was absolutely delighted that they'd moored to his cathedral.

"Apparently they don't often get visitors," she told everyone over tea later that afternoon.

"I believe he thinks we're representatives of the Inquisition branch of the Vatican on a supernatural extermination mission. Straight from Rome or what have you. It helps that I took Rodrigo and Anitra with me to meet him. Anitra's veil threw him into a tizzy, he thinks she's some kind of specialist assassin nun. And because it's easier all round, we were all speaking Latin. Rodrigo's presence didn't help. Or it did. He used to be an agent of the church, of course, or the Templar offshoot of it, so he knows exactly what to say and how to say it. The bishop was awfully impressed."

Rodrigo Tarabotti was with them at the tea. Rue's praise seemed to have the same sort of effect on him as it did on everyone else. He almost glowed with the pleasure of it.

"Thank you, little cousin. It is fun to play with empathy."

"I think you mean play on his sympathies, dear, but we take your meaning," corrected Anitra delicately.

Rue added, in that open self-effacing way of hers, "Well, you know, none of us have much exposure to the Catholic Church. You're very good with the ritual of it all."

Rodrigo nodded. "I have never been in a church, *ovviamente*. I am the soulless. But I know the basics."

"You watched and observed hierarchy and practices when they were off holy ground. They trained you for that." Anitra placed a comforting hand over his on the table. Percy wondered if she'd seen hurt in his face that the rest of them did not.

The Italian inclined his head. "It is no fun to grow up soulless in the Catholic places."

"It's very colourful here," observed Rue. "Is that a Catholic thing too?"

Rodrigo looked confused. "I don't think so."

Anitra asked, "What is this *nun* word they kept using on me?"

Percy explained, "Nuns are committed female practitioners who give up their mortal lives to essentially marry the church. Take a vow of chastity and so forth."

"They marry God," corrected Rodrigo.

Percy sneered. "For Catholics how much difference is there between the two?" He held up a hand. "That was a rhetorical question. Now, where was I? Oh yes, nuns. The ritual clothing is called a *habit*, it customarily involves flowing black robes and a veil."

Rodrigo was looking at Percy askance. Percy refused to be deterred from his dismissive tone. He found religion nothing less than illogical and he would not be moved to respect Catholicism merely on the basis of longevity. What's next? Running around worshipping vampires?

"What do these nuns do?" Anitra asked, touching her own veil thoughtfully.

"Charitable works mostly. Feeding the poor, knitting hats, delivering baskets, kite flying, that kind of thing." Percy admitted this part grudgingly. "You are dressed similarly but not to standards, I'm sure. I suspect this bishop has not been visited by the Vatican for many years, that he believes you to be a special Inquisition nun."

Anitra looked shocked. "They think I have taken a *vow of chastity?*"

Rodrigo chuckled at her offended expression.

Primrose spoke at this juncture, driven by desperate sanctimony most likely. "More tea, anyone?"

Rue brought them to order. "We must consider how to tackle this situation. It's good that the bishop speaks Latin and has welcomed us so openly. I will continue to converse with him. Rodrigo, you had better stick with me. You and I pass for Italian without incident."

"I *am* Italian," Mr Tarabotti reminded her.

"Yes, yes. Plus I can keep an eye on you this way. And the bishop seems to wish to deal with a man." She continued on. "We still need to acquire large amounts of both coal and water."

Quesnel said, "You still believe the twins and I should remain unseen? Aggie too, I assume."

"It seems most wise. Right now the locals are welcoming us, wouldn't want to sully that with accusations of vampiredom. Rodrigo and I will see what the bishop can do for us in the matter of fuel."

"Mostly coal. If we can get enough water to get us an hour of propulsion, I spotted a stream south of the city," said Percy. "We can pull the rest from there."

"What about me?" Anitra asked.

"You'll have to go into market for Prim's supplies. It's not ideal, but Primrose will give you the list."

Primrose pursed her lips. "You know I like to do the shopping in person, especially in a foreign country. Consider this, Rue – I have my floating ensemble. It has a veil and it's a nice dark brown material. There are ways it might be misconstrued as a habit. The full veil is not very much used nowadays, as I understand it, but we *are* the exotic visitors from Italy. Perhaps they might overlook eccentricity? If I entirely covered my face and wore gloves, it would prevent Anitra from having to go in alone."

Quesnel said, "Is it safe for the ladies to go into market without escort?"

"Nuns are forever safe," interjected Rodrigo.

He did not seem perturbed by the idea of Anitra alone in a foreign city. Percy felt he was the type of man to be protective, if it was warranted. And if his affection was genuine, of course.

Rue nodded. "Very well. But take Spoo and Bork with you, Prim. If you like, you could even dress Spoo as a girl for a change and make her wear a veil too. What are the baby nuns called?"

Everyone looked around at each other. Percy wished he'd brushed up on religious studies before their trip.

Rodrigo said, "I know not the English. *Neofita.*"

"Neophyte," said Quesnel.

Rue pursed her lips. "And Bork will act the part of manservant."

"What should I do?" wondered Percy, hoping they wouldn't suggest he too dress up as a nun and go shopping. That seemed some sort of purgatorial punishment. Navigation had no resources to stock, and very little to do once they were safely in a port.

"Go back to bed?" suggested his captain.

Percy was relieved. "Keep an eye on Virgil for me? He's pretty pale too. I'd rather my valet weren't lynched, or staked through the heart, or burned. Or whatever it is they do to vampires in these parts."

Rue considered. "Good point. Thank heavens all the decklings

are so tan. I'll make certain he stays hidden along with the rest
of the household staff."

"What about Footnote?" Percy asked. The tuxedo tomcat
was currently occupying his lap. Footnote would have preferred
Prim's lap, but at meals she was always too busy – leaning over
to pour tea, or passing the potatoes, or what have you.

As Tasherit slept most days, Footnote felt the entire ship
was his rightful domain during daylight. It was difficult, if not
impossible, to keep the cat confined to quarters. Better to confine
him to a picnic basket if they *had* to keep him safe.

Rue looked at Rodrigo. "How do Catholics feel about cats?"

Rodrigo shrugged and made a *comme ci, comme ça* gesture with
his hands.

Quesnel grinned. "I don't believe there is a particular religious
inclination either in favour or against."

Considering both Footnote and Tasherit half expected to be
worshipped at all times, this was oddly hilarious. Percy hid a
chuckle and sipped his tea, mildly saddened by the lack of milk
but hopeful for a restock in their near future. Not that he cared
as much about such things as his sister did.

Percy wondered if he had any books on the politics of the
Catholic Church in his library, and thought he might take a
little light reading to bed with him.

Primrose donned her floating ensemble with full veil. She didn't
think of it as particularly nunlike, but she was sure she could
modify it to appear more so.

It was quite modern. Her mother would have been appalled –
but then one's mother was never meant to see one's driving
ensemble. Prim's was composed of a long skirt and duster coat
in chocolate brown over a high-necked cream muslin blouse.
Chocolate had recently become one of Prim's favourite colours.
A fact that had everything to do with how well it flattered

her complexion, and nothing to do with Tasherit's eye colour. Nothing at all.

The outfit also included matched goggles, a wide straw hat with cream-coloured veil, a pretty velvet belt, leather gloves, and a reticule.

Thinking of nuns, Primrose left off the goggles, belt, and hat and buttoned the duster closed so it looked more robelike. It was meant to be left open except when floating, so she felt a little silly. She kept the gloves, of course, and Anitra helped her to arrange and pin the veil over her face in such a way that only her eyes were visible.

She hoped it was enough to disguise her white skin.

In deference to their collective limited information on nuns, Anitra coiled back her customary braids and wore all black in layers. Black was a very popular colour among lady Drifters but rarely worn head-to-toe. White, however, was the provenance of men, so she borrowed a cream scarf from Primrose and used that for her veil.

Spoo agreed to dress as a girl because it meant she got to explore the city. She was a small wiry thing, so she didn't fit Anitra's or Prim's clothing. They borrowed a long dark blue nightshirt from Percy, and improvised with various blue scarves for everything else. She looked slightly more like a pint-sized disenfranchised washerwoman than a religious neophyte, but it was close enough.

She also kept grinning. Primrose had to repeatedly remind her that nuns were *serious*.

Leaving the ship was an exercise in comedy regardless. It was remarkably hard to negotiate a dangling rope ladder in a veil, not to mention skirts.

Bork went first, bless the man, carrying a large bucket-shaped basket across his back for immediate purchases. Prim intended to have most of their supplies delivered, or they'd have a lot of walking back and forth to do. Spoo also carried a few empty flour sacks to fill.

It was rather cold for such a sunny day. This being the southern hemisphere at Christmastime, it was meant to be midsummer as well. Primrose supposed it had something to do with being up high in the mountains. She was very glad for her duster. They found the market simply by following other people with baskets. The fact that it was Christmas Day seemed more an excuse for shopping than a reason to close the stalls. As in other foreign lands they'd visited, custom leaned in favour of a vast open-air market.

Cusco boasted a series of small mobile stalls, each specialising in only one or two products, like costermongers. Primrose half anticipated a hawker roasting chestnuts at every corner. Certainly there was a great deal of roasted meat, although there were only two kinds of meat: a cubed gamey-looking red meat, like mutton, and a very chubby rodent on a stick, roasted whole. The first proved, after inquiry, to be alpaca, the goatlike creature that supplied that soft wool. The second was something called *cuy*, and Primrose had to admit the look of it quite horrified her. Spoo, being Spoo, wanted instantly to eat one.

"Simply think what the other decklings will say if I told them I ate something ratlike!"

Because she was titillated by the horror of it, Prim purchased rodent-on-a-stick for Spoo. Copper coin seemed acceptable legal tender, regardless of what was stamped on it.

Spoo crunched away happily and proclaimed it to taste like a cross between rabbit and pork. Primrose refused to try it on grounds of appearance alone, appearances being very important, after all, regardless of the very idea of walking *and* eating at the same time! Appalling. What she said to Spoo was that she couldn't eat anything because of the veil.

Anitra and Spoo had arranged their veils with face showing, given they were both so tan. Anitra tried a nibble and seemed fine with the taste. Bork held himself back with a shocked expression.

Primrose purchased him some of the cubed alpaca instead.

He pronounced it tasty but, being a taciturn individual, said nothing further on the subject.

"Good," said Prim. "If we find a butcher we can buy that for Cook. He won't be too upset by it if we simply call it goat."

They were treated with universal deference, which was nice. People kept making the sign of the cross around them, with particular reverence to Prim – something about the full veil unnerved them. Prim developed a beneficent nod which sent them on their way starry-eyed and grateful.

Anitra's limited Spanish was sufficient to most of their shopping transaction needs, although some of the stall owners spoke a mountain tribal dialect that Anitra couldn't understand at all. These mountain folk wore hats that bore a remarkable resemblance to a gentleman's bowler of the kind preferred by Scotland Yard. It was disconcerting.

Anitra asked one of the Spanish speakers what the language was called and got the response of *Quechuan*.

"Perhaps," said Prim, "we should ask them about the vampires. Wasn't it the Quechua who were supposed to know where they are located?"

Anitra said, "Is that wise? It seems whenever we bring up the pishtacos, a negative reaction is engendered."

The stall owner, with whom they were bartering for potatoes, baulked at the word *pishtaco*, proving her point.

He rattled off something at Anitra. She turned to Prim. "He wants to know if we are nuns of the Inquisition. Sisters of Mercy."

Primrose gave one of her holier-than-thou regal nods.

The man instantly turned to his bowler-hat-wearing neighbour and began conversing with her at a rate of knots. He spoke Quechuan, too, as it turned out.

The lady came out from behind her stall and clasped Anitra's hand, babbling at her.

Anitra asked the man to explain. Then she translated for Prim.

"Apparently they have been begging the papacy for hunters

for decades. They have a pishtaco problem. Or are having problems getting the last of them. I think by *hunters* they mean someone like Rodrigo. They do not know quite what a preternatural can do, but they have an inkling. They seem to think we are his support staff."

Primrose blinked. Never in her life had she been taken for *staff*! "I suppose it's no surprise that the preternatural are conflated with the Inquisition here, unless there is a Templar branch in South America that Mr Tarabotti neglected to tell us about."

Anitra leapt to the defence of her Italian. "He may not know the answer to that, even if there were. It's not like they told him much. Just used him as a weapon."

Primrose didn't want to argue about it. "Please ask them if they know where the pishtacos are. Hive location, or the vicinity? Even a feeding ground. Are they here, inside the city?"

Anitra asked and they got more than Prim expected. Apparently, being a nun loosened tongues. It seemed the locals genuinely believed *The Spotted Custard* had come expressly to exterminate monsters.

The pishtacos were reputed to be south of the city in a rural part of the valley.

For the rest of their market jaunt, Anitra freely asked questions about the pishtaco threat. By degrees they gathered more information on the location of the hive. That it was near a lake and on a hillside. There were Inca ruins and something called a *hacienda* involved.

On a more practical level, the ladies also managed to convince those from whom they purchased in bulk to wheel their carts back to the ship and deliver the goods. It was easy to relay the address, given *The Spotted Custard* was tied to the city's central cathedral. This fact only lent credence to their status as nuns and vampire hunters.

By the end of their trek, Primrose had sent a veritable parade of costermongers back towards *The Spotted Custard*. These individuals pushed carts laden down with meat, fruit, grain, and vegetables. Still, her options were severely limited. Prim ended up settling on a great deal of corn and potatoes. Potatoes in the Andes came in a startlingly large variety, including a brown fleshed one that was highly prized. She'd sampled a bit and found it to be the consistency of a turnip but sweet. There was also freshwater trout. Prim figured they would have to salt the fish for preservation themselves. Curing, smoking, potting, and canning seemed entirely absent from local cuisine. Fortunately for Cook's sanity, there were eggs. He was as reliant on eggs as any other chef under Victoria's rule. Unfortunately, there was no flour, sugar, or dairy to be found. Rue would be without her maintenance puff pastry. And worse, they would all have to continue with milkless tea. Poor Tasherit would not have her beloved cheese or cream.

Anitra asked for alpaca milk. But apparently alpacas, and their cousins the longer-necked and bigger-eyed llamas, were not so goatlike as Primrose hoped. No milk.

There was a small seedlike grain, various nuts, and some leafy greens that looked akin to cauliflower leaves. Prim purchased samples of each. There was also, it being high summer, fruit from the lowlands. Primrose purchased every pineapple she could find. They were ridiculously inexpensive, and she knew quite as acidic as oranges or lemons. They could have pineapple with their tea, to aid with digestion and prevent scurvy.

Primrose also acquired a few more exotic fruits in which the market vendors took communal pride – a black bevel-skinned almond-shaped thing that proved to have green flesh, a single large pit, and a savoury buttery texture that was not unpleasant if one thought about it as a spread for toast rather than an actual fruit. There was a similarly shaped yellow creature with orange flesh and many tiny black seeds in a hollow centre that looked exactly like caviar. That one was very sweet, with a burnt perfume flavour, which Primrose found off-putting but she thought Rue might enjoy. Prim's favourite was a small spherical fruit with a very thick purple skin, like bark, which opened to reveal yet more caviar-like seeds encased in an orange and green jelly. In this case one ate the seed jelly, which tasted quite tangy and only a little flowery. She thought with such a thick hard shell they would likely keep well, so she bought almost as many of those as she did pineapples.

They walked back to the ship, triumphant. Primrose always found shopping local the most exciting aspect of being the airship's purser. Determining what they might stock of the native produce, trying to balance supplies against health and taste. She was charged with managing personalities via comestibles by a captain who had strong opinions on *eating* food and a cook who had strong opinions about *preparing* food. It was a lovely challenge.

This moment, walking home (before either personality weighed in on Prim's choices and found them wanting), was suffused with a sense of profound accomplishment. She basked in the glow of it. Of course, she was doomed to disappoint, as both her friend and her subordinate would rail against her selections, but for now all was glory and success. She was the heroic conqueror of the marketplace dragon.

Thus, Primrose could not be faulted for wishing to delay matters. After having been trapped aboard for almost two weeks, she took her time strolling back. She and Anitra examined the colourful woven cloth, Bork looked at tools and weapons, and Spoo investigated the various trinkets that made up life's joys rather than its necessities.

Primrose found a shawl of knitted alpaca wool that was so soft and warm it was practically cashmere, and she simply *had* to buy it. The next stall over displayed little baby booties of the same material.

That gave her the opening she'd been looking for. "Anitra, forgive me if this is intrusive." She thought better of it. "Of course, we are in public, although speaking English..."

"You wish to ask me something personal?" Anitra's bright dark eyes were welcoming.

"Yes."

"About Rodrigo?" guessed the interpreter.

"In a way."

Anitra seemed to wish to encourage the confidence. "I never thought to earn such a man's attention. I understand if you... that is, if you are offended that he chose me instead of..."

"Oh, goodness no. How, um, *kind*, but I believe he is, and prefer that he be, most firmly attached to you."

"Yes." Anitra blinked and she looked more amazed than happy. "It is a surprise."

"Because of your troubles?" Primrose felt saying the word *barren* out loud was too harsh.

Anitra dipped her head. "Yes."

"That is rather what I thought to ask about."

Anitra winced.

"Oh, not the details, I shouldn't intrude. It's more, how do you reconcile yourself to it? To not having children?"

"Oh, I've always known that if I did, they would not be mine."

"I don't understand."

"A woman like me, she marries a widower and raises his children by a previous wife. If she marries at all. It is not the same as Ay."

"Ay?"

"You remember from the meeting in the skies with my people, where Footnote saved the barter and Ay tried to buy you for a wife?"

Primrose did remember. She'd not been part of the negotiations, but she had made an appearance, and one of the Drifters had tried to bid for her hand in marriage as part of the trade.

"Ay was the man who wished to marry me?"

"Yes. He surprised Rue with this request. And Rue was wearing the wrong colour."

"I'm sorry, Anitra, I don't understand. What has this to do with children?"

Anitra puffed out her cheeks. "Ay would marry widows, much

as I would marry a widower – those who already have children – because that is the only choice."

Primrose thought she followed. There were rumours of male impotence, of course, but male doctors always denied it was possible, blaming barrenness on the wife. It was very forward thinking of Drifter culture to realise the flaw might lie with either party.

Anitra continued. "Ay is a male in the eyes of my people. Powerful. Head of his household. I am not. Mr Tarabotti does me great honour."

Primrose remembered then what Rue had said about Ay. Prim had dismissed it at the time as one of Rue's more eccentric moments. But had Rue been telling the truth? Primrose had thought Ay a dandy, clean shaven and a touch effeminate. But a man. Rue had said Ay was actually a woman, breasts and everything. That she had taken on the role of a man, and fellow Drifters simply accepted this.

"Anitra, are you . . . ? That is, do you have . . ." Primrose could not believe she was about to ask, but it was too amazing. "Do you have *gentleman parts?*" She waved an expressive hand down low.

Anitra nodded. "Of course."

Well, that would explain why she can't have children, Prim's brain supplied. "I never would have known."

Anitra grinned, clearly taking that as a compliment. "I am a woman in truth, if not in body."

Primrose nodded. Anitra certainly looked and behaved as a woman. It was difficult to think on the details of her genitalia, but Primrose preferred not to think on male genitalia if at all possible anyway. She found that she could, therefore, understand why someone who had them wouldn't want to either.

She tried to say the polite thing. "I have occasionally thought how nice it would be to be a man."

"Of course you have," said Anitra. "Your preference in lovers is for women."

Primrose winced. Did everyone aboard the ship know her shameful secrets?

"But that is not quite the same thing. Your world doesn't understand *who you love*, but it really doesn't understand *who I am*. Drifters have found a means to accept my kind, but not yours. In my culture your inclination would dictate you *be* male, and I don't think you want that."

"So, had I expressed my inclinations at an early age, I should have been raised a man?" This was very odd to think on. Primrose rather enjoyed being female. Besides, she was tolerably certain that Tasherit liked her being female too. It was very confusing to think on sexual preferences, and physical appearances, and biological structures as independent entities.

"The captain has told me of her father, the vampire. His preference, like mine, is for men, but his soul is, and always was, male." Anitra tilted her head. "Would you say your soul is male?"

"No." Primrose frowned at the girl. "So for you it is something more than taste in lovers?" Primrose tried hard to understand. "Your soul is female. Is that how it works?"

"Exactly."

"Does Mr Tarabotti know?"

Anitra smiled. "That is what surprises me so. I think it is the basis of my appeal. Drifters accept women like me, but because we cannot have children we are not often the first choice as wife. Rodrigo seems to want me because of who I am, rather than despite it." She blushed and dipped her head and made a small downward gesture with her chin. "He likes *every* part of me."

Primrose considered Rue's mother, Lady Maccon, and her endlessly bizarre way of looking at the world. All practical and assessing, oddly lacking in judgement. "Preternaturals are like that. Is that what *aravani* means?"

"Yes, but it is not a Drifter word. It is from the northeast, and not exactly kind."

"So what do Drifters call people like you?"

"Women."

Primrose nodded. "It all comes down to semantics in the end, doesn't it?"

Anitra laughed. "Why do you think I am so drawn to interpretation, translation, and languages?"

Primrose wondered if Anitra had ever dressed as a man for her espionage work, but felt it might be rude to ask.

Unfortunately, while all this was utterly fascinating, it meant that Prim's real question – how she might reconcile herself to a life without children – was to remain unanswered. Anitra would have always known she could not give birth. Primrose was facing barrenness by choice. Even if Tasherit were a human, they could never have children together.

Wincing away from that thought, Primrose contemplated Anitra's revelation about the malleability of the soul as separate from physical form and sexual inclination. She liked the idea. It was comforting to think that it was her very soul that had chosen to love women. That she was born this way. Perhaps it had hurt so hard resisting Tasherit's easy affection because it was natural to love where one would and not as society dictated.

"Are Mr Tarabotti's intentions honourable?"

Anitra smiled wide and happy. "He has asked to marry me."

Primrose nodded. "Good. Do you know Rue, as captain of the ship, is able to perform the ceremony? Or we could do it here, I suppose. We are moored to a cathedral at the moment." Trust was all very well and good, but if a thing was to be done, it ought to be done properly.

Anitra laughed. "I think the bishop would look askance if asked. I'm dressed as a *nun*, remember."

"Oh dear, I forgot. Well, next time we're in a float, Rue would do it, I'm sure. If you wanted."

Anitra nodded. "I'd like that very much."

Primrose thought, but did not say, that would provide one more tether keeping Rodrigo from drifting back into evil. *To render a man's soul without religion requires logic, love, loyalty, or legal tender.* Percy thought epistemology would do the trick. No doubt Rue was already working on loyalty – since Prim sensed camaraderie and respect was developing between the cousins. But looking at Anitra's happy face, Primrose rather felt love stood the best chance of them all.

Percy attended dinner reluctantly. He'd been nose deep in an absolutely fascinating book on the ancestral relationship between the alpaca, the llama, the white-tailed deer, and something called a jackalope. Quite, quite fascinating.

Some delicious scent disturbed his studies and drove Footnote into fits of meows and scratching at the door. It smelled like proper roasted meat – *venison perhaps?*

Percy shut his book, remembering that his sister would have gone to market that afternoon, which meant fresh produce at last. After so long in the grey, the very idea was mouthwatering.

He chivvied up to the mess hall. Footnote, tail high, led the way in that manner of cats which is one part banner-waving herald and one part attempted murder by tripping. Cats in hallways – escort meets assassination attempt.

They found everyone else already at supper. Percy apologised for his tardiness and took his customary seat. Footnote made no excuses and went to beg at Anitra's feet. Being Drifter born, Anitra categorically adored cats in general and Footnote in particular. Which meant Footnote, most of the time, could take her or leave her, but he knew a sucker when meat was on the table.

"Is that venison, sister?" Percy asked.

"No, alpaca. A sort of hairy goat with big eyes and a long neck."

Percy sniffed cautiously, then helped himself to the cubed meat. "I know what an alpaca is, I was just reading about the species. They aren't goats but more likely some offshoot of deer."

"Doesn't look at all like a deer," objected Primrose.

"You know nothing on ancestral cross-procreation, Tiddles. Does it *taste* like deer?"

"No, it *tastes* like pork."

Percy snorted and took a bite. Unfortunately, she was right, it did taste like pork.

"Now, as I was saying before my brother so rudely interrupted" – Primrose turned to Rue and Quesnel – "you'll never guess what Anitra and I learned about the local vampires while we were at the market."

"I very much doubt I could guess, so please don't be coy about it." Rue leaned forward, eager.

"Well, wait till you hear!" Primrose spoke in exaggerated fashion for dramatic effect, being, in fact, quite coy.

Percy chewed his alpaca loudly in annoyance.

Prim ignored him. "We got our friend the potato man to ask his Quechua neighbour at the marketplace about pishtacos. She said that they aren't inside the city at all, but are south of here down the valley. We kept asking everywhere we went, since, being nuns, it seems no topic is off-limits. Apparently pishtacos occupy an Incan ruin a half day's trek away. Or they live near to one. Distances are hard to convert in the highlands, but we got a description of the ruins, and it shouldn't be too difficult to spot from the air. It sounds pretty isolated. There's also something called a *hacienda*, which we think is a sort of a house or maybe a very big tree. According to market rumour, pishtacos feed off the villagers nearby. From what I could gather, it is not a symbiotic relationship, they don't take drones or anything. It's more like the old-fashioned feudal system of Eastern Europe. The pishtacos are lords of the manor, preying upon the local daylight folk."

"Primrose! That is all excellent information. Really, very good." Rue pointed her fork at Percy's sister in excitement.

"Well, thank you for my part, no need to wave cutlery at me. And besides, Anitra did most of the talking."

Rue shifted her fork and beamed at the Drifter girl. "Thank you so much!"

Anitra ducked her head and glowed with delight.

Percy sometimes – not often, mind you, but *sometimes* – wished he had Rue's capacity for openhearted generosity and charismatic leadership. It was most annoying to see in action, even knowing that if that fork headed in his direction he would succumb himself. It was just so very nice when she noticed his hard work and thanked him for it.

Primrose laughed. "Never underestimate the power of market gossip."

Rue put down her fork and rubbed her hands together. "Well, Rodrigo and I learned from the bishop what pishtacos look like. He seemed happy to explain once he truly believed we were sent by the Vatican to exterminate them. He said he was planning on tracking them down and seeing to their demise himself soon. If we go after them, as he put it, he promises to send a cleanup and extermination team to follow." Rue's lip curled in disgust. "As suspected, they are all quite pale in complexion, which as you may have noticed is a great deal less common in this country. They are also quite thin. Apparently a lady of endowments is much admired in Cusco." Rue indicated her own rounded figure with no embarrassment. "The bishop was most complimentary, I must say. *Most* complimentary."

Quesnel looked up. "Oh *was* he, indeed?"

Percy frowned. "Well, to be fair, that's not illogical in the high country. After all, it is cold enough now during their high summer. It must get very cold indeed during the wintertime, with crops lean and hunger common. The more fat you have, the more likely you are to survive a harsh winter."

Rue glared at him. "Oh, thank you very much, Percy."

What? thought Percy. *What did I say?* "I'm only trying to imply that thinness might be perceived as disfiguring in this part of the world." He warmed to his topic. "This would make the skinniness of most vampires an additional aspect of their perceived monstrosity. London is, in effect, dominated by the vampire aesthetic of pale skin and slender limbs. My sister's waist and complexion are envied *because* they are near to the vampiric ideal. But as such, she would be thought quite ugly here."

Now Primrose was glaring at him. "Thank you, Percy, that is more than enough."

Oh, for goodness' sake, thought Percy, *why is truth so often taken as rudeness?* He decided to stop talking and keep eating instead.

"And on that note," grumbled Rue, "let me tell what else the bishop said. According to local legend, the *only* way pishtacos can be killed is by sunlight. I've no idea if the garlic allergy, or a sundowner bullet, is as effective. But I'm tempted to say that a good beheading works on everyone."

Rodrigo seemed to be following the conversation well enough to nod fervently at that. "Are we here to kill them?" he asked, hopefully.

"No."

Rodrigo looked disappointed. Percy supposed he hadn't taken much exercise in the last few months, he probably wanted to stretch his legs and arms a bit. What better way for a preternatural than killing vampires?

Rue continued, looking hard at her cousin. "Mother only wanted us to *save* them, they seem to be the last of their kind. But we have to assume they will be hostile. They are, after all, under constant threat and duress. This country is obviously against supernaturals. Also, let us not forget the Rakshasas. They could be quite nasty to us regardless of our intentions. Ideally, we get on their good side and come up with a plan to protect them permanently."

Percy shuddered. The vampires of India had been quite the most unpleasant of creatures. Rakshasas were carrion eaters rather than bloodsuckers, so they had smelled to high heaven and boasted the most ridiculously enormous teeth. The fact that they were also the local tax collectors had merely added insult to injury.

That reminded him. "What about shifters? Did you ask his holiness if they have werewolves or werelions or weremonkeys in the area?"

"I didn't ask. The bishop assumed we were here to hunt pishtacos. I didn't think it wise to divert him off that subject since it pleased him so much to instruct us on the matter. Plus us going hunting hopefully keeps him from doing it and making a mess." Rue looked thoughtfully down the table at her cousin. "Rodrigo was most helpful, of course, being trained as a vampire hunter and all. He asked all the right questions."

Rodrigo gave a tiny bow. "Your servant, cousin. It was a, as you say, delightful conversation."

Primrose said, "Not to shift the topic off of killing things, which I know you both enjoy, but could we please discuss logistics? We've now acquired sufficient supplies for another two weeks of travel. How did the refuelling go, Mr Lefoux?"

Quesnel gave one of his annoyingly charming smiles. "The cathedral was most accommodating. They have a great deal of coal in this area, which they use mainly in their local limekilns, if you can believe such a waste. Anyway, we've entirely restocked and at a fraction of the normal expense. We've more than enough water to make that stream the professor spotted south of town."

Rue said, "Given that fact and that we now know the general location of this hive is in a similar direction, I suggest we float off within the next hour. That way we can make it to water and still have enough daylight to search for these Inca ruins we're after. Percy, are you up for it?"

Percy looked up from his meal. *Oh, now they want me to talk?* "I'm well rested, thank you, Captain. I don't suppose anyone thought to ask after a map from the bishop or the market?"

Rue and Primrose looked acceptably guilty.

Percy smiled. "I guess I shall have to prove my mettle taking us south by skill alone. I'll need a deckling to play lookout for me. Quesnel, whenever engineering is ready, so am I."

Quesnel give Rue a small smile. "Just one more cup of tea first, my love?"

"Always," said Rue.

CHAPTER

THIRTEEN

On Hives, Haciendas, and Hijinks

The Spotted Custard puffed away from Cusco's cathedral square to companion cheering, flag-waving, and fanfare. The bishop stood out on his balcony for all to see and blessed them with Latin recitation and dramatic arm flails. It was all very theatrical.

Primrose in her full veil stood on the port side of the main deck and raised her own arms in kind. Anitra did the same on the other. The crowd seemed to find this very rewarding. Flowers were thrown.

Primrose enjoyed herself more than she ought. She'd always felt a kinship to actresses. Her mother had once trod the boards, and her father had died tragically, stage left, during a hugely well-regarded soliloquy. She felt them with her there, on the Cusco stage. She had played her role well. *Daddy would be proud.*

They left the city behind, floating on the ever-present southward breeze. It had kicked up at the approach of nightfall into a veritable wind.

Percy explained that this was common in high mountain valleys like this one.

Southeast of the city, it became clear that the terrain below was tilting downhill, for they were following a stream in the direction of flow. It was little more than a thin trickle this time of year, but the pishtaco hive was situated near a lake, and they hoped that it might be deep enough for the *Custard* to take on water.

One of the most confusing things about their journey was the number of ruins. From marketplace conversation, Prim thought they were looking for just the one. Unfortunately, the valley seemed to have once held several Inca villages and cities and such. Each hill they floated over boasted a ruin of some kind. They were easy to spot, being stone, where the living used mudbrick and built lower down, near the water.

However, these ruins were little more than one or two walls, no roof. Supernatural creatures, be they pishtacos or anything else, always had a means to create darkness during daylight. Their immortality depended upon it. So none of these could be the ruins Rue was after.

So instead the *Custard* looked for the lake.

By the time it became visible ahead, the sun had retreated behind the first of the mountaintops. It hadn't set yet, however, so Tasherit had not appeared on deck. But the world around them was descending into long shadows, and it was getting ever colder.

Primrose leaned over the prow. Their lake, when they finally found it, turned out to be a big wide brown thing, still and low in its banks. The water was muddy. They'd have to drink what they'd got from the bishop and use this stuff for their boilers.

"I suppose we'll have to make do with sponge baths for the foreseeable future," she lamented to Anitra.

The Drifter patted her arm. "Even those are a luxury to me."

"What a nice thing to say." Primrose wondered how people bathed in the desert. Then, figuring she and Anitra had crossed a point in their relationship where such a question might not be deemed intrusive, "How do you bathe in the desert?"

Anitra laughed. "There is the occasional oasis. But mostly we rub down with sand."

"And that works?"

"It does."

"Remarkable."

Rue came up and joined them.

"Ladies, what do you think?"

"It won't be good to drink or wash, but it'll do for the boilers," said Prim. "Probably smelly."

"Probably. Keep an eye out for those ruins we're after. I'll tell Percy to take us down and Quesnel to get the sipper tube ready."

She wandered back towards navigation.

Primrose pulled out a pair of opera glasses and began scanning the hills all around. Anitra did the same with a pair of glassicals that looked suspiciously like they had once belonged to, and been modified by, Rodrigo Tarabotti.

"Where's Mr Tarabotti?" Primrose asked.

"Collecting things that can kill vampires."

"Is that allowed?"

Anitra gave a small smile. "It's not like he wants a gun. Only sharp pointed objects. I think the captain might be persuaded. It is, after all, his nature. And hers."

Primrose gave her an arch look. "I shall be interested in seeing the pointed objects fly, should it come to that." *And hope they do not fly towards us.* She went back to scanning their surroundings with her glasses.

"Look, over there, see that long adobe structure? Very Spanish looking and a great deal larger than any of the village houses we've seen in ages."

Anitra followed Prim's pointed finger and trained her glassicals on the area. "Hacienda? Didn't they say something about the pishtacos living on or near a hacienda as well as ruins? Is that a hacienda?"

"Your guess is as good as mine," said Primrose. But she was thinking that it was the most likely structure to hold a hive they'd found so far. It was large and seemed to be in good condition, it had a fully tiled roof and very few windows.

"We'll have to circle over and see if there are guards. No vampire would ever sleep without guards during daylight."

Anitra nodded. "And do you see there, above them on the hill?"

Primrose shifted her opera glasses. "Oh yes, those appear to be ruins. Goodness, there are a lot of them. Yes, I think we've found it."

She turned to look for Rue. The captain was leaning over the side of the main deck to observe the sooties and their sipper take on water.

"Captain?"

Rue turned and wandered over, looking up at them on the forecastle deck. "Yes?"

"We think we've spotted the hive house."

"Really? That's excellent news. Can I see?" Primrose tossed her the opera glasses. Rue plucked them deftly out of the air.

"Over there, see? At the edge of the lake, about halfway up that hill, is a large single-storey structure. We think that's the hacienda, our vampires are most likely inside. There are Inca ruins above, but like the others they're mostly remnant walls and fortifications. Unless our pishtacos dug caves, I wager on the hacienda."

Rue nodded agreement. She tossed the opera glasses back. "I concur. Let me just tell Percy. It'll be another hour before we're done with the sipper, so we have time. I wish we had sundowner bullets for our Gatling. Then again, I hope, even if we did, that we wouldn't have to use them. I'm imagining we can have a civilised conversation with these folk, but they have been living in contested territory since the conquistadors, if not before. So I think we have to assume they're hostile."

It seemed the sun had set at last, because Tasherit came wandering up onto deck as they were retracting the sipper tube and preparing to make for the hacienda.

She settled into her customary position leaning on the railing next to Prim.

"You are well, little one?"

"I am."

"And where are we now?"

"Still in the Andes, south of Cusco, over a lake near some Inca ruins and a Spanish hacienda, and possibly a hive full of pishtacos."

"So the usual for us, then?"

Primrose laughed. "Yes, the usual. You wanted excitement in your old age, did you not?"

"That too, yes." The werecat's eyes took on the intense focus they always did when she was flirting.

For a change, Primrose didn't let herself flinch away from her own wanting. She stared back, seeing beyond the chocolate warmth to the weariness of centuries, stretched vast as the desert sands. Immortality meant loneliness.

Primrose tore her gaze away and looked over the ship. Decklings and deckhands were scattered about, diligent at their duties. Rue was striding here and there, barking orders. Percy was at the helm, Virgil hovering nearby. *My family.*

Primrose considered. She had accepted into her life so many people not approved of by society. Her best friend stole bits of souls and made them her own. Rodrigo Tarabotti had no soul at all. She was now friendly with a Drifter who had a woman's soul trapped in a man's body. And her own brother was apparently soulless by acerbic personality choice if not birth. Frankly, to be right and proper she should reject them all. *I live on a ship full of outcasts, populated by society's unacceptable. And yet, here I stand, happy. And I love them all.*

It is time, Primrose thought, *to tender myself the same level of courtesy. Or perhaps it is time that I simply accepted that I too am one of the strange and abandoned. Appearances be damned.*

Turning back, she found Tasherit still looking at her, no doubt watching the series of emotions play over Prim's face.

Primrose Tunstell was a consummate actress, for all she never trod the boards. She was practised in keeping her expression still and polite. But Tasherit would see beyond appearances, she always had. Primrose relaxed and allowed her to do so.

"Something's changed," said the werecat. "You've changed." The desert in her eyes was back, stretching into infinity. "You're going to keep me," she breathed, long and soft and almost too quiet to hear.

Primrose found herself suddenly crowded back against the railing, a long-limbed immortal pressing her close – smelling of sun-warmed sands and feeling like silk. Tasherit pressed her face against Prim's neck. Primrose felt a wetness but it wasn't the expected licks or nibbles. A surge of pride and responsibility met the realisation that she, plain old Primrose Tunstell, could make such a powerful being cry in relief. Or joy. Or both.

Tasherit drew away, framed Prim's face with both hands, brushed the tops of her cheeks with rough thumbs, as if Prim were the one crying. "Now?"

Primrose laughed, feeling light as aether and yet anchored firm and sure by that one caress. "We have pishtacos and a hacienda, remember?"

Tasherit nodded. "I can wait a little longer."

Primrose wondered if she herself could wait. Now that she had decided to let go, she *wanted*.

"Tash! You're with me!" Rue's yell came from below.

Tasherit drew away reluctantly. Primrose watched her retreating back, before she turned to look over the railing and find they were floating low over a hillside, apparently above the backyard of the hacienda.

The decklings had tied down to a large tree in the yard, and gathered below them, looking up, were a half dozen creatures straight out of nightmares, who could only be immortals.

And me without my parasol.

Percy was pleased to find that, given all accounts and data, the pishtacos were exactly as he would have hypothesised, had anyone bothered to ask. There were six of them below, and assorted mortals who were either drones or slaves or mercenaries. The mortals looked like the other locals, dark and stocky, only a great deal slimmer. *Interesting*, thought Percy.

The pishtacos themselves were thin to the point of emaciation – practically skeletal. Their flesh was so white it was almost transparent, hugging bone and tendon. They were mainly quite tall as well, with white hair, red eyes, and long silvery fingernails. Instead of pointed fangs they boasted a kind of columnar tooth. Percy suspected it was hollow to better assist with sucking at higher viscosity levels.

Rue pulled her team together quickly. She chose Tasherit, Rodrigo, and Anitra to go down with her.

Formerly Floote appeared next to Percy and glanced down at the pishtacos with that remote fascination the already-dead have for the still-mostly-living. "*Those* are the local vampires?"

"Pishtacos, yes. Creepy-looking chaps, aren't they?"

The ghost inclined his head.

"Ever met their like?" Percy asked. Formerly Floote had once travelled widely as valet to Alessandro Tarabotti. *Much as Virgil travels the globe with me.*

"No," replied the ghost.

Formerly Floote accompanied Percy back to navigation. They both watched from there as Rue issued instructions to her team. Rodrigo stood very close to Anitra.

"She likes him," Percy observed, interested in the opinion of a ghostly grandfather.

"Unfortunately."

"Why unfortunately?"

"She wishes to save him."

"Is that wise?" A question Percy found himself asking pretty regularly concerning the actions of others.

"Wisdom is not in play."

"Is it possible?"

"Perhaps."

"You warned her of the risks?" Formerly Floote knew more than most about what it meant to live with a preternatural.

"Of course."

Percy shrugged and turned back to the pishtacos. He was already making mental notes for his report to the Royal Society. He continued talking to the ghost. "What more can you do than that? You're dead."

"Exactly so."

Of all people, Quesnel Lefoux appeared next to them at that juncture.

"What are you doing up here?" Percy wasn't going to have him interfere with navigation again.

"There's nothing to do in engineering, we're anchored."

"Yes, but you know she doesn't like you up top."

"Why do you think I'm skulking over here with you charmers?"

Percy ignored the insult. "What if we have to retreat and puff up quickly?"

"Aggie can handle a rapid boil without me."

Percy glared at the Frenchman. "Rue needs you safe!" How could Lefoux not understand, he was supposed to be in love with the chit. Percy explained, as if to a child, "She can't concentrate when you aren't safe."

Quesnel flashed him a very annoyed look. "And I need to watch over *her* too! It's not fair she keeps me confined to engineering every time there's the possibility of battle."

"You did nearly die in a fight recently."

"But I didn't *actually* die."

Percy tried a different tactic. "You are *The Spotted Custard's* chief engineer, therefore meant to be *in engineering*. Look at me, ship's navigator. Where am I located? Why, I'm here in the navigation pit, because that is the place where I can do the most good."

Quesnel glared. "Yes, but you don't actually want to leave your station, ever. Except to go to your library. You hate adventure."

"True, but beside the point." Percy reached out to grab at Quesnel's arm. Rue was leading the others over the edge of the main deck and down the rope ladder. Quesnel clearly intended to follow.

"Let go!" hissed the Frenchman.

"She has Tasherit with her."

"It should be me!" Rue disappeared from sight.

"Oh yes, because *that's* logical. She can borrow Tasherit's immortality and heal herself in a heartbeat, not to mention become a lioness. What can you do for her?"

"I hate you sometimes, Percy."

Oh ho, that warranted my given name, did it? "And yet you came to me because you knew I'd hold you back from doing something stupid."

Quesnel lost his impassioned panic in a flash of amusement. "Well, Professor Tunstell, you *are* the smartest man on this ship. Besides me, of course."

Primrose climbed up to the poop deck and came marching over. "What are you two malcontents up to? Virgil, would you be a dear and fetch me my battle parasol? It's the really ugly one leaning right next to the door in my room."

Virgil crossed his arms. "Well, all right, but don't say anything exciting, and don't let them do anything interesting groundside until I get back. Please?" He gestured behind him to Anitra's disappearing head. The Drifter was the last one to climb down off the airship.

He scampered off, fast as he could.

Primrose had her parasol in hand mere moments later. Percy was impressed, his valet never moved that fast for him. Nevertheless, by the time Virgil returned, all three of them and Formerly Floote were back leaning over the railing, watching the encounter below.

Percy thought, for the sake of mathematics, Rue ought to have taken two more with her. Preferably heavily armed. But perhaps she didn't want to appear threatening. After all, Tasherit was still in human form.

Rue stood at the front with Anitra to one side and Tasherit to the other. Anitra for interpretation and Tasherit for immortality and protection, no doubt. Rodrigo was on the other side of Anitra. Farthest away from their immortal, and in a position to defend his lady-love. Percy approved, it was all very strategic. It was a chance for Rodrigo to prove himself to them.

Even though they were floating above, the night was quiet enough for conversation to travel up to them. Percy's Spanish wasn't great, but he loosely translated for his sister, and Quesnel helped with some of the vocabulary when it was similar enough to French. Formerly Floote helped the rest of the time.

Primrose had her parasol out and at the ready. It was pointed down with darts dialled in. Percy didn't know if numbing darts would work on the pishtaco type of vampire, but that wouldn't matter to Primrose. The two greatest loves of her life were down there confronting the local bogeyman. His sister was tense and needed to do something.

"They are exchanging formal greetings and introducing themselves. Rue has taken charge," Percy interpreted.

Quesnel glared. "I don't like the way they are all looking at her, do you? It's awfully covetous."

"Hungry," said Prim, who was good at reading people. "They look hungry."

Percy shrugged. "Well, Rue is chubby, I wager she seems the tastiest."

"Percy! You can't say things like that!" His sister, without taking her eyes off the group below, boxed his ear.

"Ow! Stop it, Tiddles, I'm not ten."

"Then stop acting like it."

Percy's attention was drawn back to her deadly parasol. "You should prepare to cover any retreat with your lapis solaris."

"What? Why? Aren't we trying to be friends with them?"

"Did we not just establish that they look more hungry than friendly? Look here, sister, I'm not convinced the numbing darts will work." He exchanged a look with Quesnel, who inclined his head. The darts were Lefoux manufacture, so he should know.

The Frenchman said, "They're made with humans in mind and only work in a limited manner on immortals. And, of course, we've never tested them on pishtacos."

Primrose narrowed her eyes. "Well, it's the best I've got for now. Won't the same standards apply to all the parasol's armament?"

Percy glared at her. "No, the acid is based on the principles of distilled sunlight."

Quesnel tried to be nicer. "He means to say that lapis solaris is meant specifically for vampires, which we are assuming these pishtacos are, and so – wait, what's that?"

He leaned forward to see what was going on.

The vampire who'd taken primary negotiator position was edging towards Rue.

Rodrigo stepped forward and twirled some kind of wooden stake casually in one hand.

The pishtaco laughed.

"Bet he wishes he had a sword right now," said Percy. "Beheadings *always* work."

Primrose scoffed. "Like any of us would give Mr Tarabotti a sword."

"We might want to rethink that particular policy in future." Percy was thinking that Rodrigo Tarabotti's stance was as near to fighter's perfection as he had ever seen down at White's.

Percy himself was no Corinthian, but he understood the basic principles of hand-to-hand combat, had read a great deal on the subject.

Their former prisoner stood perfectly balanced, sure and easy on his feet, and he held the stake like it was an extension of his arm. Percy would eat his velvet fez if that man couldn't handle a sword with consummate aplomb.

"I wish *I* had a sword."

"Percy, you wouldn't know which end of a sword to draw."

"True, but I could throw it down to him."

Below them Anitra moved, hands placating, clearly trying to soothe matters. She kept urging Rue to back away.

But Rue was too stubborn and she knew vampires. She refused to give quarter or appear in any way like prey.

Suddenly the lead pishtaco lunged for her.

Quesnel shouted. Primrose shot one of her numbing darts, narrowly missing the vampire.

Rue turned into a pishtaco.

"That went well," said Percy, to no one in particular.

They'd all lived with Rue's metanatural abilities their whole lives. But it was strangely easy to forget exactly how they worked. Partly because when Percy and Primrose were children, Rue always chose to be a wolf, and now aboard the *Custard* her only choice was lioness.

They tended to forget she could also be a vampire. Or in this case, a pishtaco.

Rue utterly changed in appearance at the contact. She grew taller and very thin, her hair bled out to white, and her eyes went fully red. Her gown hung loose and short on her newly emaciated frame. But her face still looked like Rue's face in shape and expression. That expression was one of annoyance. Even Percy could follow what Rue was feeling.

The pishtacos froze, totally and utterly surprised by Rue's transformation.

The former pishtaco leader was now a short, chubby, dark-skinned gentleman wearing a shocked expression and overly tight clothing.

Capitalising on their shock, Rue and her team flew into action.

Rue, now vampire strong and swift, turned and made for the ship, running to stretch the tether so it would snap and return the pishtaco to his immortal state, and her to her mortal one.

Tasherit shifted into lioness, screaming out a cat's challenge. This also startled the pishtacos. Either there were no animal shifters in the Andes, or there hadn't been in generations.

The werecat charged, and the pishtacos recovered from their shock and scattered. All except for the one who was now mortal. He sort of folded up where he stood, collapsing into a heap. One of the drones dove for him and began tugging him to safety.

Rodrigo swung in front of Anitra and flicked out his wooden stake with a twist of a wrist. It hit a pishtaco in the throat, but the creature merely snarled and pulled it out. No blood dripped out, not even the slow black blood one expected from a vampire.

In the blink of an eye, a new weapon appeared in Rodrigo's hand. This one looked to be a bread knife, long and serrated. That, at least, gave the pishtacos pause.

Rodrigo and the werecat exchanged a look.

"Anitra," came Rue's yell, "back to the ship."

Rue was still a pishtaco, as evidenced by the spiderlike efficiency with which she was climbing up the *Custard*'s rope ladder.

Anitra turned and sprinted towards the *Custard*.

One of the pishtacos went after her.

Rodrigo snarled, leapt, and slashed out with the bread knife.

"See," said Percy, "I was right. He needs a sword."

As usual, no one was listening to him.

Quesnel had out his dart emitter and was firing at the pishtacos below. They were too far away to hit, regardless of whether or not the darts were effective.

"Oh, stop wasting darts," said Percy to him. "You aren't doing any good. Might as well use a gun. At least that has the off chance of slowing them down a bit."

Quesnel glared at him. "Do *you* have a gun?"

Virgil appeared at Percy's side, as if by magic, and handed him his pistol. "Sir?"

"Oh, Virgil, how did you know?"

"Such a thoughtful young man," said Primrose warmly.

Virgil blushed. "I fetched it when I got Miss Tunstell her parasol."

"Very perceptive of you, Virgil." Percy took the pistol and checked it for rounds.

"Percy!" yelled Quesnel, gesturing for the gun.

Percy snorted. "Don't be ridiculous, man. I'm a much better shot."

Quesnel sputtered. "Give it to me!"

Percy avoided him and made his way to the other side of Primrose. She had fired all her darts, to little effect. She now had her parasol swung about and was holding it by the finial, dialling in for lapis solaris acid emission.

She'd have to wait, however, until Rodrigo and Tasherit were back aboard – acid was an indiscriminate weapon and would damage everything in its path.

"Primrose, please!" begged Quesnel, clearly in distress, as he was resorting to the first name of a female. Percy supposed he should be more sympathetic to the man, but Rue was fine. Still climbing.

"Primrose, please make your brother give me the gun."

Primrose did not look up from fiddling with her parasol. "Don't be ridiculous, Mr Lefoux," she said, sounding exactly like Percy. "He's a much better shot."

"I forget you're twins until something like this happens." Quesnel slumped. "So what am I supposed to do?"

Primrose glared at him, then quickly returned to looking down at the scene below. "Prepare for float-off, you dolt. Look, over there? Rue's fine. Rue is *always* fine."

Rue had, indeed, attained the main deck. She was also still a pishtaco. The decklings seemed to find this hilarious. Rue grumbled at them to stop laughing and man their crossbows.

As Percy watched, Anitra climbed over the railing as well, and sank down to her knees, shaking slightly.

Percy turned back to the fight. Tasherit and Rodrigo were

holding their own. Better than Percy would have predicted. Had that been five British vampires against a preternatural and a werewolf, he wouldn't have given his two crewmates more than five minutes.

But these pishtacos didn't know what to do about their opponents.

The werecat was fast, not as fast as a vampire but stronger, and her claws were very sharp. Understanding why Rodrigo had brought a bread knife, she was concentrating on taking out throats. A cat's attempt at decapitation.

But Percy's attention was drawn to Rodrigo. The Italian was fascinating to watch fight. Near to ambidextrous, he'd reach out with his free hand to touch his opponent, seeking bare skin and a solid grip. And then, as the pishtaco lost his immortal pallor at preternatural touch, Rodrigo would strike with his knife. A new pishtaco would attack, so Rodrigo would have to let go the first and repeat the procedure. He wasn't killing them, but he was slowing them down. Each pishtaco would have to pause to heal a near mortal blow and then return, slowly, to vampire state.

Pishtacos took longer to shift back from preternatural touch than British vampires did. The flickering between mortal and immortal merely added to the surreal melee surrounding Rodrigo.

Percy was making mental notes on all the various differences between pishtacos and vampires, even as he also noted the preternatural's fighting technique. The style was designed entirely around taking advantage of preternatural touch. No wonder Templar-trained soulless were so feared. Rodrigo may be a mortal, with only a mortal's speed and strength, but his very skin was a weapon against his opponents.

Percy was almost distracted enough not to shoot. Then he remembered he was one-upping Quesnel and took careful aim at the recovering pishtacos as each withdrew to heal from either Rodrigo's bread knife or Tasherit's claws.

The drones had pulled away. Interesting that the pishtacos did not consider them expendable.

As they fought, Tasherit and Rodrigo were backing towards the dirigible. Eventually, Rodrigo's head bumped the hull.

Tasherit roared at him.

The Italian turned and leapt to grab the rope ladder, swinging himself easily up. He had a manic grin on his handsome face. He boasted a few injuries here and there, and he looked as if breathing pained him. *Blow to the ribs perhaps?* But otherwise he seemed quite pleased with life.

Percy shot the pishtaco that tried to climb after him. The bullet struck the creature midchest and propelled him away from the airship, but the immortal recovered quickly. If anything, bullets seemed less effective on pishtacos than on other immortals. *Another point of interest for my prospective treatise on the subject.*

Bork was ready with the Gatling. Once Tasherit was out of the way, Rue would give the order, and he would see if a full spray of bullets was any more effective.

Next to Percy, Primrose started whimpering. Tasherit was the only one left fighting, and she was up against five at once. Also, she wasn't made to climb a rope ladder, not in lioness form.

Rue's voice called out, "Primrose, ready with that acid."

"She's too close," yelled Prim back, voice shaky and pained. "She'll catch part of the spray."

"Better a little burned than a lot dead. Wait for my mark." Rue kept a cool head in battle – her fathers' training, both of them.

Percy said, trying to soothe his sister with factual information, "It's not as bad on werewolves as it is on vampires. Not that parasol's variant. Even if she gets a few drops, it will hurt but not kill or maim her. At least, I don't think it will kill her. Werecat physiography isn't as well understood."

"Thank you, Percy, that's very comforting."

Well, no need for sarcasm, I was trying to be nice.

Tasherit let out one final screaming hiss and then turned and leapt up against the ship, claws out to catch purchase. Lions weren't really climbing cats, but she did her best, hauling herself up.

Then, with a remarkable display of bunched muscles and supernatural strength, she jumped and twisted, changing form midair, to land as a naked woman, hands sure and tight about the rope ladder.

Percy turned to his sister. "Good luck with your acid." Then he dove for navigation, reaching for the speaking tube even before he was fully inside the pit.

He shouted into it, "Now! Now! Now!"

Without waiting for an answer, Percy reached forward from his sprawled position and pressed the puffer.

He heard Rue yell for the decklings to cut the anchor ropes.

The Spotted Custard jerked once and then rose majestically upwards. The puffer let out its customary aggressive flatulent noise, but to Percy's ear it sounded especially fierce this evening.

He engaged the propeller for good measure. Anything to get them out of there.

They were moving away at last.

Primrose shifted slightly, leaned out as far as she could over the railing, holding her parasol firmly.

She tore her eyes away from Tasherit's naked form. The werecat was scrambling up the rope ladder, slow but steady. She was bleeding in places but it didn't look too bad.

The pishtacos were leaping after them. After her. They clung to the hull with weird spiderlike supernatural strength, digging their silver claws into the soft wood.

Primrose firmed her resolve, braced herself against the railing, and twisted the emissions dial on her parasol, hoping the wind was in her favour, hoping like hell that she missed Tasherit with the spray. Knowing in her heart that this was gravitationally impossible.

Acid rained down from the parasol's ribs.

At first the pishtacos below continued leaping up at the ship, climbing after Tasherit. They did not react to the wetness raining down on them.

Then the acid began to burn. The pishtacos started screaming, a horrible wounded howl noise. Clawing at their own eyes and faces in agony, they fell back.

Primrose felt sick to her stomach that she had done such a thing to another creature. She turned the dial and stopped spraying.

Tasherit was up and over the railing, collapsed and panting but safe. The decklings rushed to pull up the ladder. Percy puffed them up again, the *Custard* tooted rudely, and they were high enough now to see the whole of the hacienda set out below them. The angry whiteness of the pishtacos still gathered in the yard, but they either could not jump high enough to reach *The Spotted Custard* or they were not willing to risk acid again.

Primrose rushed to Tasherit's side. She dropped next to her gracelessly, parasol still clutched backwards and open in one hand.

"Did I get you?"

Tasherit turned her face towards her. A few red speckles marred one cheek and one side of her back and leg.

"Oh no." Primrose put a hand to her mouth. She tried to recall what salves she had on hand for burns and if they would work on immortals. Tasherit had cuts, too, from pishtaco claws and teeth. She held one foot funny and wasn't standing up. "You're injured."

Tasherit only tugged Prim in and kissed her softly. "I heal, remember? It'll all be gone come morning."

Prim settled down to sit on the deck next to her. She curled her legs under and, greatly daring, she pulled Tasherit's willing head to lie in her lap. She started petting the long dark tangled locks. Tasherit's hair was thicker and coarser than her own.

"Everyone returned safely?" Tasherit asked, nuzzling into Prim's skirts and closing her eyes in pleasure.

"They have." Primrose looked around.

Rodrigo and Anitra stood close; the Drifter girl had her head on his shoulder.

Rue had returned to her normal plump self. She looked none the worse for having recently been an emaciated blonde.

Quesnel appeared abovedecks and rushed to Rue. Rue, who was no romantic, batted him off with annoyance. The Frenchman demanded a kiss and then, apparently satisfied that she was unhurt, returned below.

Rue went over to Percy, who was busy floating them further up out of harm's way.

"Suggested course, Captain?" Primrose heard her brother ask.

"Hold the retreat, Mr Tunstell." Rue's tone brooked no argument.

"We're staying *here*?" Percy's voice was incredulous.

"Percy, what was it you said to me about being chubby?"

Percy's voice didn't sound at all shamefaced. "I've been led to believe that that's not something I ought to bring up to your face, not even in the interest of science."

"They went after *me* for a reason, and not only because I appeared to be in charge."

"I would concur, Captain." Percy was being judicious. Percy! Judicious. Of course, he'd picked the most inopportune time to develop circumspection.

Right now, circumspection only served to make him all the more frustrating.

"And you know what that reason is, don't you, Percy?"

"I have a hypothesis," Percy said, carefully. Only Percy could turn tactful when it was least required of him.

"Which you chose not to share with the rest of us!" Oh dear, Rue was not happy. Not happy at all.

Percy defended himself. "It's unsubstantiated. And you and Prim kept getting mad at me whenever I tried to explain anything. Now that you've been one of them" – Percy's voice turned covetous – "will you tell me if it's true?"

Primrose glared at him through narrowed eyes. "What's your hypothesis, Percy?"

Percy looked nervous. "You're not going to get mad again, are you?"

Rue grunted at him.

Percy said, because he couldn't help himself, he loved explaining things *so much*, "It's because of *where* we are. And how scared the locals are of pishtacos. And how the latter have clearly been hunted to near extinction."

"*What* is because of this?" asked Tasherit, not opening her eyes. Primrose kept running her fingers through the werecat's hair, disinclined to stop. She watched Tash's face closely, hoping to see the burn marks heal before her very eyes.

Percy pressed on. "Well, I figured, what's most valued for survival in high altitude and low temperature? No offence but, well, *fat*. So I thought, you know, they'd be after that, not blood."

Primrose goggled at her brother. "You're saying pishtacos are *fat-sucking* vampires?"

Rue nodded. "Absolutely. When I was one of them, the urge to feed was not blood related, it was definitely fat I craved. Don't worry, I can resist the craving. It's not the same for metanaturals."

Percy glowed with success. "There, you see? Rue, may I quote you in my paper on the subject? This is another one for the Royal Society. Fat-sucking vampires! Everyone will be most interested."

Primrose said, "So they went after you, Rue, because..."

Rue nodded. "I looked the most delicious."

Percy was scribbling notes but then seemed to remember his responsibilities. "So what now, Captain? Back to Cusco?"

"No. We're going back down. We aren't done with them yet."

"But they attacked us!" said Primrose. "And I don't have any more acid."

Rue shook her head. "We handled this ill. I handled this ill. We went straight into their territory without invitation. It was unpardonably rude. I should have thought of that. It's as though Dama taught me nothing. They're still vampires, or enough like vampires that I should have realised a direct approach would be seen as a threat to their hive. I'm an idiot. I want to try again."

"Why?" Primrose could feel her skin prick with horror at the very idea.

"You know what they told me, before, you know, the whole attack?" Rue asked, not expecting an answer.

Anitra and Rodrigo came over to join the conversation.

Anitra said, looking sad, "The pishtaco said that they are the very last of their kind."

Primrose now understood Rue's reluctance to simply leave the pishtacos to their own devices. Rue was the *only* one of her kind. And she was the daughter of a vampire. Of course she would be sympathetic to the pishtacos' plight.

"And they're trapped in a country that hates them," Rue said, looking sad herself.

Primrose considered the matter. True, the pishtacos had attacked them, but if it was all a matter of mistaken communication or breach of etiquette...?

"You want to save them, Rue, don't you?" Her friend had a good heart under all her madcap scheming.

Rue nodded.

Primrose smiled at an idea. "They would do very well with the matrons of London high society. Imagine setting them up in Bath? Ladies could go take the cure, then go in for a quick fat-sucking treatment. It would be all the rage inside a season."

Rue laughed. "Unfortunately, I don't think it's possible to relocate them back to England. Certainly not by air, not even if we arranged for a swarm."

"Is that what you want to do, arrange a swarm? Move them somewhere where they'll be appreciated?"

Rue nodded. "It's only the beginning of an idea. I'll need Percy to research where and how."

Percy's eyes gleamed. Primrose knew Rue had just made his day.

CHAPTER

FOURTEEN

The Etiquette of Proper Introductions

Percy retreated to his library. He wasn't accustomed to thinking about ground-based transport but if they had a swarm to relocate, it had to be done by train. Did trains even exist in this part of the world?

He had his work cut out for him and, knowing their glorious captain, very little time in which to conduct it.

Primrose, Anitra, Tasherit, and Rue discussed the proper etiquette for a second approach to the pishtacos over tea.

After no little back-and-forthing, Primrose advocated strongly in favour of good old-fashioned traditional *visit of introduction*.

"Send around my calling card." She set her teacup down firmly, indicating her resolve.

"What?" Tasherit didn't like that idea.

"It has to be me," insisted Prim. "They never noticed me during the tussle. Thus I carry no ill favour for having maimed someone important. Also, I'm the best officer aboard ship at social interactions, you know I am."

"You are good at soothing troubled waters, or should I say

troubled butter in the case of pishtacos?" Rue thought she was so droll.

Anitra laughed obligingly.

"I don't like this idea," objected Tasherit, glaring possessively at Primrose.

Primrose ignored her but freshened the pot and continued. "If they allow me to call, we could include a present for the hive queen as a show of goodwill. Percy can accompany me as escort, or Quesnel if you prefer. Someone else who wasn't in the battle. Someone unthreatening." She stirred in the fresh leaf gently.

Anitra was on board with the scheme. "Professor Tunstell speaks more Spanish than Mr Lefoux. He's a better option."

"He's also less threatening," added Rue. "Not that Quesnel is particularly fearsome with those adorable dimples of his."

"Percy is also my brother," Primrose added.

Rue frowned. "How is that useful?"

"We are the children of a vampire queen, remember? We can play this all off as a kind of long-lost familial reunion." Prim topped up her cup and added a dollop of pineapple juice in lieu of milk.

Rue blanched. "Only if Aunt Ivy never hears of it."

"How would she?" Primrose was warming to her topic. "Drop my calling card now, as soon as possible. That way they can accept tonight, on their terms. If we leave it too late, they are faced with the choice of having to wait until tomorrow night, which puts them asleep and vulnerable with us still lurking nearby. They won't like that."

Rue sucked her teeth and looked at Tasherit, whose invisible tail was clearly twitching.

"No, I can't allow it," Rue said finally in her captain's voice. "I'm not comfortable sending you and Percy into a hive of fat-sucking vampires without protection!"

"Neither am I!" added the werecat, throwing an arm about Prim and dragging her close.

Primrose set down her teacup hurriedly before she spilled due to the violence of Tasherit's affection. Prim liked the gesture, for all it interrupted her tea and came under the guise of thwarting her will. Although public affection was a bit embarrassing. "See here, we think rationally. We start with the classic calling card. We arrive punctually, in style, and appropriately attired. We observe all the proper forms of address and etiquette as established by vampires. Percy and I were raised with that, raised with the ancient Egyptian version, no less. Very old and well-established traditions and patterns of behaviour. I know these aren't the same *kind* of vampire, but this is the best approach we have."

"But Prim, you're food!" Rue could never be prey, since contact would always give her the advantage, so she'd never had to think of herself that way.

Primrose straightened her spine. "Physically, not as much as you, apparently. I'll barter a nibble or two if necessary."

"Oh no, you will not!" Tasherit did not like that idea *at all*. The arm about her tightened into an iron band.

Primrose shrugged. "I've given blood before. Fat can't be that bad. A little off the waist or a little off the hips, perhaps."

"No one," Tasherit hissed, "is doing anything with your waist or hips. Unless it's me, of course." Her hand stroked the threatened parts of Prim's anatomy.

Primrose blushed heartily and batted her off. She was not to be detoured. "Can you think of a better way to handle this situation? Presuming the initial social gaffe was ours in approaching them without invite, then this is a vampire problem. Sending the children of vampires to fix it seems an elegant solution." Carefully she poured Rue a bit more tea, soothing her with ritual.

Rue considered Primrose, carefully tending to all their teatime needs despite the werecat's hold, tidy in her dress and careful in her manner. She capitulated, as Prim knew she would. "Oh, very well."

"What? No!" Tasherit stood and pressed her hands to the table to steady herself.

"So long as Percy agrees," added Rue.

"You're leaving it up to *Percy*?" Tasherit hissed.

Rue's eyes gleamed. "I'll go ask him and then send Prim's calling card if he agrees. Prim, have you any on you?"

Primrose took out her ledger and extracted two of her better calling cards. They were full-sized, gilt embossed, and very elegant. These were the ones she used when she needed to *impress*.

The Honourable Miss Primrose Tunstell, daughter of Baroness Ivy Tunstell, vampire queen, Wimbledon Hive, London, England.

On the back of the card, Prim wrote carefully, mindful of preventing any further cultural confusion:

Respectfully requests to call. The Honourable Professor Percival Tunstell as escort. She acts as hive representative and hopes to rekindle global relations between our queen and yours.

She handed that and the blank one to Rue. "Have Percy translate my words to the blank one *exactly* as written, placement and everything."

Rue nodded, taking the two cards. "He's going to need a bit more time to do his research. Shall we reconvene in an hour?" She looked pointedly back and forth between Tasherit and Primrose. "You're welcome to try to persuade Prim to your way of thinking, Miss Sekhmet." Rue's grin was wicked.

Anitra giggled.

Rue's tawny eyes focused on Anitra. "As for you, young lady..." Anitra was older than Rue, so this was a slight insult. "My cousin? Are you certain?"

Anitra looked perturbed. "That's hardly fair. You're gallivanting illicitly about with Mr Lefoux. And Miss Tunstell is now gallivanting about with Miss Sekhmet, but my Rodrigo is not worthy of gallivanting?"

Primrose objected mildly, as she wasn't sure she qualified as a gallivanter yet, but nevertheless grinned at her friend. "That does seem particularly unfair, Rue."

"You're defending this assignation? You, Prim?"

Primrose only inclined her head. "Did you see him with that bread knife? He's an asset."

Tasherit nodded. "Can we keep him?"

Primrose turned to glare at the werecat. "What's with you and the keeping?"

"Oh, not in the way I want to keep you, little one." The chocolate eyes were warm and she raised a hand as if to pet Prim's hair. Prim shook her head slightly and the werecat's hand fell back to her side, reluctantly.

Rue said to Anitra, "He's likely still evil. I mean to say, we are doing our best, but ethical clarity doesn't come easily to any of us. You marrying would be beneficial, I believe."

Anitra looked cheeky. "Yet you haven't married Mr Lefoux."

Rue rolled her eyes. "He is not likely to murder us all in our beds. Quesnel has exemplary moral fibre and clear indications of soul. Rodrigo Tarabotti, on the other hand, needs mending. Marriage would do him good. Primrose? Tasherit?"

Primrose nodded. "Yes, Anitra would set him a good example. Keep him tethered."

Tash shrugged. "I've never been married. But love is ever a stabilising influence on preternaturals. Or so my various encounters with the soulless would lead me to suspect."

Anitra clearly had objected only in order to make a point. Under the combined regard of all three ladies her token resistance crumbled. "We have discussed it." She crossed her hands in her lap and lowered her gaze, hiding a small smile.

"Oh, have you?" Rue didn't like to be the last to know things aboard her ship.

"Primrose said you were qualified to perform the ceremony. So I asked Rodrigo, and he found the idea hilarious."

"He thinks marrying you is amusing?" Rue was not pleased with that.

"No, he thinks you officiating is."

Rue cast her hands up to heaven. "Fine, we will arrange a wedding, then. Perhaps *after* we settle the matter of annoyed fat-sucking vampires? Now, go on with the lot of you. I must go pacify Quesnel, he's annoyed with me for some reason."

"You left him aboard ship and dashed into danger, as you do.

He doesn't like to be left behind," Prim explained as she stood in response to Tasherit's insistent tugging.

"And yet I will continue to do so for the rest of our lives, I expect. Poor boy. Don't worry, I've ways of making him forgive me." Rue's smile was wicked. "I'll see you all in the stateroom in an hour. Use your time wisely."

Tasherit immediately dragged Primrose out the door and down the hallway.

The werecat's room was closest. Tasherit pushed her inside.

"Wait, my tea!"

Tasherit slammed the door, pushed Primrose up against the wall. She nudged in against her, rubbing their cheeks together, inhaling her scent.

"I love the chase, little one, and you have led me a merry one, but I caught you fairly now."

"You have," capitulated Prim, not caring anymore. It was too difficult to care. "So what will you do with me?"

Tasherit leaned even further into her, as if she were trying to shift into Primrose, inhabit her skin. Prim felt warm and flushed and itchy with want. Not knowing what to do, she made a small helpless whimper at her own inexperience.

The noise seemed to spark something in the werecat. Tash took it as surrender. And perhaps it was.

Tash lifted her easily (supernatural strength and all) and tossed her to the bed. Prim had hardly a moment to realise she was sprawled back before the werecat pounced down atop her.

Tash kissed her then, licking into her mouth with hungry murmurs. Prim thought it was like being loved by a sunbeam — a damp sunbeam, but still. She thrilled under the attention, her skin drawn and hungry although Tash was the one nibbling. Tiny bites, small hints of teeth along neck and sides.

The werecat's response to Prim's underthings was priceless.

"Why so many ruffles?"

Her frustration with the stays nearly resulted in her rending the laces asunder.

"I must have a knife here somewhere."

Prim glared and laughed at the same time.

"Don't you dare, it's my best corset!" Prim showed her how to unlace the back and then pop open the front.

Tash stripped her of the last of her undergarments and frowned over the wrinkled fabric impressions the tight restriction had left on Prim's ribs and stomach.

"They go away in a short while."

Tasherit rubbed Primrose then, elegant golden hands on Prim's pale flesh. Primrose thought she had never seen anything more arousing in her life. It was as if Tash thought she could stroke away the remnants of Prim's self-inflicted confinement.

"Tash," Prim whispered, arching into the touch. Reminding her there was no injury here, there was something else that needed attention. Something Prim could not name and did not understand.

But Tasherit did. Decades on this earth, and she understood it very well indeed. She was a patient tutor and a delighted guide, and a single point of joy both in finding Prim's pleasure and in taking her own.

For the first time in her life, Primrose forgot entirely about her tea.

An hour later, after retreating to his library, Percy reluctantly left it once more and joined the rest of the officers, and Rodrigo, in the stateroom.

Primrose had laid out a nice little spread of snacks, but the tea was cold and overbrewed. It had been left sitting out. There was no other explanation. He was aghast.

Percy glanced around suspiciously. Everyone looked awfully relaxed: Quesnel and Rue shared that secret smile of theirs, Anitra and Rodrigo were billing and cooing as if they were, in fact, doves, Tasherit looked even smugger than usual, and Primrose was positively dishevelled.

Percy was tolerably certain that his sister had never in her life left out the tea things. And was she wearing one of Tasherit's robes? In public?

Tasherit nuzzled – really, actually nuzzled! – his sister's ear. Primrose giggled – positively giggled – like a schoolgirl. Percy suppressed an inclination to shudder.

I mean to say! It's all very well for things to have finally settled in that regard, but to nuzzle and giggle? Percy glared. *Puts a man off his feed, that kind of behaviour with sisters.* He pushed away his plate of food petulantly.

"Percy, what have you got for us?" Thank heavens Rue decided to get on to official business. All these happy satisfied couples were quite messing with Percy's peace of mind.

Percy cleared his throat. "If we can get them to swarm – and no, I've no idea how that might work exactly – but if we *can* get them into motion, then our only option is to send them north."

He brought out a map. "Central America, here, and the Mexican territory above that, here, are both also Catholic countries. So we must get the pishtacos through those fast. I recommend we put them on a sleeper train out of Lima. If we rent the whole first-class carriage, board over the windows, and hire guards, it is two weeks' journey into that new state that just got approved, here. California." He traced the route with his fingertip.

Rue frowned. "But isn't North America just as bad about vampires as the church?"

"No, they aren't *just* as bad. They're *differently* bad. California is a mere infant, but still vested in the United States and that silly constitution of theirs."

"What's that got to do with anything?" Rue wanted to know.

Percy felt this should be perfectly obvious so he glared around the table, waiting for someone else to know the answer.

"Separation of church and state?" suggested Quesnel.

"Exactly, Mr Lefoux. No Inquisition is permitted within the United States."

"But don't they still hate vampires?" Rue was like a dog with a nice juicy bone, or a vampire with a nice juicy neck: she would not let it go.

Percy could only explain what he'd read. "California doesn't have any vampires of record, never has. There are no vampire hives west of the Rocky Mountains. Settlers' records suggest this had something to do with coyotes. I'm not clear on the particulars. Regardless, if we can get these pishtacos up there, and convince the locals that these aren't *real* vampires, we might have an in."

"Why?"

"Americans," said Percy succinctly, "like to be skinny."

Primrose brightened up. "Oh, Percy, very nicely done. Prey on their vanity? I applaud this idea."

Percy gave her an assessing look. "With you for a sister I could hardly discount the importance of appearances."

"I don't know whether to be insulted or not."

Percy rolled his eyes. "Appearances kept you from doing what was needed for near on your whole life. If you can't resist, neither can all of North America."

"He's right, you know," said Quesnel. "Morality has a way of folding under the pressure of vanity."

Prim frowned. "Hey now – "

Percy cut her off. They hadn't time for her to get huffy. "We simply must convince them that pishtacos are the latest and greatest diet scheme *ever*, and the local Californians will welcome them with open arms."

"Percy – and you know I don't say this lightly, because I hate to have to do it . . ."

Percy looked at his captain with expectant dread. "Yes, Rue?"

"You're a genius."

Percy let out a long breath. "Oh, good. Yes, well. I know that. Nice of you to say, though."

Primrose put down her fork and grinned at him then, in a way he found most suspicious. "So, brother darling, are you ready to go try to persuade them of your *genius* plan?"

Percy nodded. He hated the idea, of course he did, but he could see why Prim had suggested the approach. They had been raised in a hive, and as a rule, people that his sister couldn't convince with charm, he could persuade with facts. It'd worked before.

Primrose sipped her tea and looked pleased with herself. No one would dare tell either of them how much she looked like him in that moment. But Percy knew it to be true.

"They shot a message dart up with an affirmative acceptance of our call. We are to be welcomed to supper."

Percy suddenly wished he'd put on a great deal more weight, just in case he and Primrose *were* the supper in question.

"I don't think this your best idea, Tiddles, in terms of our safety."

"But you do think we can do it, right? Persuade them."

Percy gave her his best supportive look. "Don't be silly. *Of course* we can do it."

Primrose did not put on her best visiting dress. Instead she opted for her *minty disguise,* as she called it, because it was one of the few gowns she owned that made her look slender. There was something about the very simplicity of cut and colour that turned her curves into planes. Ordinarily, this was to be avoided, but occasionally some role or another drove her to present as a stylish maiden aunt or severe chaperone or young-but-strict governess, rather than the coquette. This dress was a very pale sateen with a reverse scalloped edge worn over cream watered silk.

The *minty disguise* was all over pale mint in colour, with nothing to disturb its refreshing qualities. It had a tiny bit of cream lace in a military detail about the shoulders and a very high collar, but otherwise nothing but mint. It was severe rather than flattering, and had such long tight sleeves no part of it might be thought of as an invitation. With the addition of cream gloves, every part of Prim's skin was covered except her face. She wore a pearl brooch that she could afford to lose, and silk flowers in her hair.

Despite the fact that it clashed most awfully and was low on darts and acid, Primrose took her battle parasol along. She had great faith in her own abilities, but it was always best to have a parasol in reserve.

Then she went to retrieve her final accessory – Percy.

She found him mostly dressed in a very dark green evening suit that emphasised his lanky form. But he was only *mostly* dressed. He was facing up against his valet, who was practically in tears, on the subject of headgear.

Virgil was wringing his hands. "But sir, you can't go calling on vampires without a hat!"

"I refuse to wear that bally fez any longer!" The fez in question had been cast in disgust upon the bed, where Footnote was pacifying it into submission through the simple expedient of wrapping his teeth about the edge to hold it steady and attempting to eviscerate it with his back legs.

Primrose felt that both Footnote and her brother were correct in their fez offensive. The royal blue velvet clashed with his green suit, the silver embroidery was garish to say the least. And frankly, one couldn't go calling on pishtacos in a Turkish lounging cap, that absolutely wasn't *the done thing*. But Virgil was a sensitive lad and Prim didn't wish to hurt his feelings unduly.

"Gentlemen, what seems to be the issue?" She pushed her way into Percy's room.

"Oh, Miss Tunstell!" Virgil turned wet pleading eyes on Primrose. She suspected some of those tears were from frustration, and the rest from the idea of Percy heading into grave danger, with or without a hat. Virgil was oddly fond of her brother.

The little valet wrung his hands together. "He hasn't any top hats left, and he can't just go visiting immortals *hatless*. What will he take off at the front door? It's not dignified."

"Your valet has a valid point, Percy. Virgil, run and ask

Quesnel if we can borrow one of his top hats for the evening. This is an important visit and a formal matter of ship's business, I'm sure he'll be accommodating."

"Oh, thank you, Miss Tunstell!" Virgil scampered off.

"I agree about the fez, brother dear." Primrose decided to try and get on Percy's good side. The last thing she needed was a hostile sibling while headed into hostile territory. "It's perfectly horrid."

"Oh dear," said Percy, sounding disturbingly cheerful. "Pity you feel that way. I'm about to gift it to your lioness." He extracted it from Footnote's abrasive affection and placed it safely in a drawer.

"What?"

"Miss Sekhmet is a great admirer of my Turkish lounging cap. Something about the tassel, I believe."

"Oh my heavens."

"Speaking of which, you know I don't follow women's fashions, but I think you should commission a gown with fringe, or tassels, or both. Then that woman would never let you out of her sight."

Primrose blushed beet red. "You don't mind?"

"Fringe? Not on principle, no."

"Not fringe, Tasherit..."

"Mind that you've taken up with a werecat? Why should I? I'm not a species snob, you know that. We were raised in a vampire hive."

"Not her undead state, her unmale state."

"I prefer women myself, who am I to criticise? Does she make you happy?"

"Ridiculously."

"So, there it is. Think no more upon it. Sorry to have to burst your bubble with the fez, but I made a promise on the strength of her commitment to you. If that ridiculous smile you're trying to hide is anything to go by, she's proved herself worthy of being fezzed."

Primrose waved a hand in the air. It was of no matter. Percy may look a right chump in that fez, but Tasherit would look positively *adorable*. "You really don't mind about us, do you?"

"Oh, Tiddles, no one minded except you."

They looked at each other and said simultaneously, "Mother will mind."

Percy added, "Mother always minds. Just don't tell her. Or if you insist on honesty, I'll back you up, and we can both be disowned together."

"I love you, Percy," said Primrose, meaning it. Her brother was endlessly frustrating, but he had his good days. Never did she think she would like the part of him that didn't give a fig what anyone else thought. Except now it meant that he didn't give a fig what anyone else thought of her either. Turns out she needed that.

"I know you do," said Percy, immeasurably smug.

And there he went, right back to being a premier pompous prat.

Virgil returned at that juncture with a perfectly serviceable top hat. He popped it onto Percy's head. It was a little big but would have to do.

Prim looked over her brother critically.

Virgil had made him wear collar points, and thus Percy's gold cravat was nice and high, completely covering his neck. Of course, there was no way to know if pishtacos went for the neck. Not a particularly fatty area, so Prim thought it unlikely. Still, it was best they observe the dress forms of their vampire training. Percy's suit was cut tight and worn over a velvet waistcoat of gold and cream. He had enamel cuff links depicting gold birds.

Primrose considered. "Gloves, I think, Percy."

"Must I?"

"Yes, everything but the face ought to be covered. We don't want to give them any ideas or unwitting offers."

"I see your point. Virgil, I have a pair somewhere, don't I?"

Virgil rummaged about and produced some leather drivers for

the park-side dirigible roaming about town. They didn't quite work with the outfit but were good enough. And since they had him dressed in record time, Prim didn't want to press her luck.

"You look thin and inedible," she complimented with a nod.

"As do you, dear sister." Percy offered her his arm, quite like he was actually a proper gentleman. "Shall we show them how it's done?"

"By all means, let's go pacify some pishtacos with courtesy."

"I am in your very capable hands, Tiddles." Percy smiled at her. And it actually seemed to be genuine.

Primrose found, for once, she didn't mind the childhood nickname.

Percy hadn't lied. If anyone was going to lead him into a hive of alien creatures with only manners to save them, he'd place all his chips on Primrose Tunstell.

"You greased the squeaky beasts?" he asked. "To ensure our welcome?"

"Of course. I had Spoo drop the initial calling card along with a Christmas pudding. Thank goodness, Cook made one several months ago and then we all forgot our dates. Apparently, Cook was the only one aboard who accounted for Christmas."

"What has pudding to do with it?"

"Cook crams his pud full of fruit and brandy and, of course, a great deal of only the very best *lard*."

"Oh, a commendably fatty choice, sister. But how did he feel about losing his pud in the interest of diplomacy?"

Primrose chuckled. "Cook was both offended by its loss and thrilled to see it utilised as an ambassador of good taste and goodwill."

"A Christmas pudding olive branch." Percy nodded. He had no firm feeling on Christmas pudding himself, but it seemed to generate great affection in others.

Primrose raised up a bulging reticule. "Two bricks of sweet butter – the very last of our reserves – a tin of my best face cream made with rose water and lanolin, and a gold filigree cuff bracelet."

Percy frowned. "The bracelet isn't made of fat, is it?"

"I am of the opinion that every woman likes pretty things, even pishtaco queens."

Percy let this go. The only thing his sister knew more about than he did was women. Clearly more than ever these days, if her general aura of relaxed smugness was anything to go by.

By this point they'd made it up on deck, where the decklings were doing over the *Porcini* as a visiting conveyance. There was no way for Primrose to climb down a rope ladder in that dress, and arriving by float simply felt more formal, even if they had to do it in an improvised sling suspended from a stolen mushroom-shaped dropsy.

"It seems like a *slightly* more dignified and regal means of paying a call," Primrose said, sounding only a little nervous about the lack of gondola.

Mushroom filled with helium and air, Percy took a cautious seat in the sling and then tried to assist his sister. She tipped backwards and somersaulted out of it on the first try, losing her hat and squeaking like an excited chipmunk. On the second go they managed it, and after much shifting and squirming, and then a sort of synchronised hopping, they scooted together over the deck and then sort of flopped over the railing.

Percy used basic balloon technology via cords and flaps to depuff them, pulling in air to sink them rather than letting any helium out – this so that they might get back up, of course, later. They also kept a long rope lead between the *Porcini* and *The Spotted Custard*. Rue had the larger dirigible in position above the hacienda, well out of firing distance for either party, for the sake of diplomacy.

Percy and Primrose slid out of the sling once they reached the ground. Fortunately, his sister was better on the dismount.

Percy took on more air to compensate for the loss of body weight, leaving the mushroom to bob gently only a foot above the path to the front door.

Leaving the dropsy behind felt rather more isolating than it ought. The *Porcini* was their only connection to their airship, a tenuous thing indeed to be entirely reliant on a mushroom for one's escape.

He tilted his head at his sister. "This had better work."

"Yes, it had." Primrose managed to look confident, nervous, and annoyed all at the same time. But her jaw was firm and her face was carefully blank in that way that meant she was about to resort to *the height of propriety*. Lives might be lost with the mere twitch of a disapproving eyebrow.

"Right, my dearest brother, just be polite and let me lead. This is what I'm best at."

Primrose hoped that by separating all their current actions as much as possible from the previous more violent approach, they might appear more aristocratic and diplomatic by comparison. Certainly less interested in fighting or killing anyone.

Something seemed to have worked – the card, or the mushroom, or the pudding – because no mass of enemy pishtacos met the twins with angry red eyes and silver claws.

Instead, a slender dark-eyed maid opened the hacienda door for them, and with trembling voice invited them to enter. In Spanish, of course.

Primrose hoped Percy's linguistic skills were up to the task before them.

As per a lifetime of training, Percy actually removed his hat upon entering the pishtaco domicile.

All six of the pishtacos who had attacked earlier that evening were waiting in the main room. The room appeared to serve as a sitting room meets parlour, only bigger. It was whitewashed and plaster walled and bare of hangings or decoration, totally uncluttered as if it were a hospital or a tomb. The chairs and furniture all boasted those colourful patterned weavings in the form of cushions, blankets, runners, and throws. There was a fire in the hearth, which Primrose found most cheerful, but there was a definite air of musty damp shabbiness despite the crackling flames. Quite unfortunately, the mantel above the nice fire was decorated with a row of human skulls, each trepanated in the same place.

Interesting choice of mantel adornment.

The pishtacos were all seated, but they rose upon the Tunstells' arrival and made bows of greeting in an old-fashioned but polite way.

Primrose was careful to keep her back straight and her chin up as she dropped an equally old-fashioned curtsey. Percy was Percy about the whole thing. He never considered posture important and his bow was barely sufficient.

After a long awkward moment, everyone straightened and cleared throats and shuffled about, attempting to determine what precedent dictated under such circumstances.

Primrose took a quick assessment of the situation. There were drones lurking in the shadows, still and observant. Or she assumed they were drones. She decided they seemed to be undertaking the role of staff and should, therefore, not be directly acknowledged.

In an attempt to get them off on the correct footing, she fell back on the protocols she'd always used when visiting Countess Nadasdy's hive on her mother's behalf.

Primrose spoke first, and Percy translated. "Good evening. Thank you for accepting our call. Especially after such an unfortunate misunderstanding. I tender you the greetings of our mother, Vampire Queen Ivy Tunstell of Wimbledon Hive in England."

One of the pishtacos interrupted at that. So Percy interrupted her to translate. "But you are human."

Primrose inclined her head. "Yes. My brother and I are both mortal, born to her before her immortality took effect."

"That is permitted in your country?"

"No, but there were extenuating circumstances around her metamorphosis."

"So you act as her ambassadors? Mortal children to move around the globe when she cannot?" The pishtaco swirled his hands, a confused gesture made menacing by those silver claws, which were, Primrose realised, actually long silvery nails. Primrose ruthlessly suppressed the inclination to shudder.

"In a way." She inclined her head.

"We are honoured to meet cousins from the far reaches. It has been centuries since word was brought to us of the *sanguinus*."

Percy interrupted his own translation to say, "I'm thinking that's from the Latin for *blood*, so *sanguinus* would be *blood people*. Probably the pishtacos' word for our kind of vampires."

Primrose nodded and continued with the formalities. She concentrated mainly on the male who had interrupted them. He seemed to be in charge, or at least the spokesman for the group.

"We apologise for any inadvertent neglect. I'm ashamed to report that our vampires had no record of your existence. Although my mother is a young queen, perhaps another..." She purposely let the thought trail off. She did not want them to think pishtacos had been wholly forgotten.

The man shrugged. "We did not anticipate even this much. You have your own problems, or so we must surmise. The Inquisition is everywhere."

Primrose nodded, face sympathetic. Although, to be fair, in Europe the Inquisition had died down to a shadow of its former self – the Templars being that shadow. "In our country, Britain, vampires live openly and are accepted. But it is true that in the rest of Europe they continue to be persecuted."

"Your mother is safe?"

"She is."

"A queen without danger, what joy is yours."

There was real envy in his voice, and an awkward silence descended.

Finally, Primrose said, "Permit me to introduce myself. I am Miss Primrose Tunstell, and this is my brother, Professor Percival Tunstell. May we know your names, or the correct form of address?"

The one who had been talking said, "It is most generous of you to ask and to offer. I am Cauac, the guardian of this nest. And these are Paucar, Yurac, Suhay, Mullu, and Auqui. We all take for our second name that of our queen, as we are sons of her making: Acebo."

Primrose said, attempting a compliment, "You have a large hive, your queen must be strong."

Cauac looked sad rather than flattered. "We did not all start out as Acebo."

Percy added, "I think he means they were metamorphosed by different queens but have all ended up together now."

Cauac added, "We have collected from all over because we are the last pishtacos."

Primrose was genuinely shocked. "Oh, how sad! The last pishtacos here in the Andes?"

"The last pishtacos anywhere," said Cauac.

Primrose allowed her pity to show. She did not find them appealing to look upon, nor were their dietary habits pleasant to contemplate. Where, for example, did they suck fat from? The thigh? The fundament? She flinched inwardly. But no species deserved to utterly die out.

"I understand then, how you might fight first and talk later. We must apologise for our clumsy initial approach. Our captain is enthusiastic by nature and was eager to meet you, directly and without warning. To us you are amazing, a new species, a discovery. We are honoured merely to make your acquaintance."

"Your captain is the delicious one? The one who walked away in my skin when I touched her?" Cauac looked less upset than intrigued. Rue had that effect on people.

"Yes, Lady Prudence Akeldama. She meant no offence. Her father is a vampire, so she should know better. She forgot her manners." Primrose decided not to go into details on Prudence's birth.

"And her mother?"

Percy did not know the word for *soulless*. He explained that Rue's mother was like Rodrigo, whom they had also fought earlier. The man who took away immortality with his touch.

Cauac nodded. "History would call him Pachacutec, he who changes the world. We have records of such hunters from before the Wari claimed these mountains, but we have never met one before. And the captain, what is she?"

Percy struggled again, finally resorting to a clumsy string of words. He explained what he'd said to Primrose. "I told him she was a borrower of the soul and skin. *Metanatural* doesn't translate."

Cauac's long white face frowned. "Puric, perhaps, a walker? We have no records of her kind at all, but there was once a legend."

"Nor do we. There are only one or two rumours of them throughout history. They are scary," said Prim with a smile. "But ours is friendly. Well, she is if you do not try to bite her."

At this Cauac hung his head. "That was my fault, I thought she was an offering from your ship. Or that she herself was offering to join us as a companion."

Percy interrupted his translation to say, "I would think *compañero* is their word for *drone*. It would appear they use *nest* instead of *hive*, and my temptation is to say that is an allusion to a wasp's nest, not a bird's, because they do still have a queen."

"Percy, you're getting distracted by details again."

"Oh, yes, well I do like details. Where was I?"

"Companions."

"Righto. So it seems they misunderstood and thought Rue was a gift of food or a petition to join the hive. He was going to have a taste as a kind of test of acceptability, and then we attacked."

Primrose said, "Then please explain that this was not our intention. That we came to talk, only to talk, and not to feed or be food."

Percy did so.

Cauac's response was a frantic nod. "We understand that now, for you have sent us the gift of food as a separate item, and a formal written request for a meeting."

Primrose said, "Our cultures are different. We did not know the right approach."

Cauac gestured, silver nails flashing. "This is better."

The other five pishtacos nodded as well. They had remained silent throughout, but closely observing both Primrose and Percy. It was difficult to tell the difference between the six. They all looked so similar with their white skin, white hair, and long sharp features. Primrose wished the others would speak, perhaps their voices might help her to distinguish between them.

Primrose wondered if one of them spoke English and was keeping tabs on Percy's translations. That's what she would do if she could, given their circumstances were reversed. Also, they could then track if she and her brother were communicating elsewise. Prim decided to act at all times as though one of them might understand her, just in case.

Cauac continued. "You brought a *nahual* too. We had thought that they, like us, were exterminated by the Inquisition. Although we have never seen one quite that shape or golden colour."

Percy frowned. "I apologise, Tiddles, but I don't know what *nahual* means."

"Well, Anitra is mortal, and he likely knew that, we've already addressed Rue and Rodrigo, so process of elimination would suggest that *nahual* refers to Tasherit. Perhaps that is their word for shifters."

"Nahual?" Percy asked. Cauac said something quickly and Percy nodded. "Yes, cat shifters. Although he says *jaguar* or *puma*. I am assuming there are no lionesses in this part of the world."

"Explain that she is a cat from Africa, or Egypt. Would they have heard of those places?"

Apparently yes, because Cauac nodded his understanding. "An ancient one. We are honoured."

Primrose relaxed a fraction. Things seemed to be going well so far. No one had charged for their necks, or bottoms, or whatever it was that pishtacos charged for when they were hungry. Remembering her stuffed reticule, Primrose held it up. "I have brought offerings of amnesty."

At the pishtaco's nod, she reached inside and produced the butter. "For you." And then the face cream and the bracelet. "For your queen."

"The children of the *sanguinus* are most kind."

"The butter is merely a token, for we suspect you cannot eat it, much as my mother could not drink the blood of an animal. But we wished you to understand that we know who you are. And we thought your companions might enjoy the treat."

"They will indeed, thank you. Would you offer of yourselves?"

He and the other pishtacos made a show of examining both Percy and Primrose from head to toe. It was odd to be so viewed, as if they were a juicy chop on display at the butcher's, but there was no menace to it. It was almost like a form of flirtation, only without fans or flowers.

Primrose said, voice gone a little lower to prevent it from shaking, "If it is necessary to engender trust I would offer a very small amount, but, you understand, I would prefer not." Percy gave her a startled and slightly disgusted look but spoke her words faithfully. His gesture indicated he was making it very clear that she was the only one on the table, as it were.

"We understand. And without contract, it is merely a remnant of very old traditions. Not necessary given your own birth mother's immortality."

Prim let out a relieved sigh.

"However, if you wish to meet our queen, you must offer her something more of yourself than jewellery." Cauac's tone suggested there could be no other reason for their visiting.

Primrose pursed her lips. "It is a delicate matter, which has been stymied by an unfortunate initial foray." She straightened her spine, put on her best autocratic air and her most serious expression. "We are on a rescue mission."

The pishtacos all looked around after Percy translated this, taking in their shabby surroundings and their timid companion drones. Everything about them was slender and transient, as if they were wraiths from a forgotten time.

"Our companions are all volunteers, children of the *sanguinus*. We see to their care as much as we are able. It is a consequence of who we are that they appear so thin. We do feed them well and often. They are offered the bite by our queen when the time is right so that they might become one of us. We observe the correct protocols of transition."

Primrose shook her head. "No, no, you misconstrue. It is *you* we wish to save." Primrose thought of Tasherit and her werelions. They too had been the last of their kind. She couldn't bear the idea that these ancient people would be eliminated forever, wraiths or no.

The pishtacos didn't seem to know whether to be pleased or insulted by this statement. The idea that they could not take care of themselves would, of course, take its toll on any immortals. But manifest to all was the fact that there were only seven of them left in the world. They clearly needed someone's help. And any race to have lived so long also knew when to ask for help. "Pride," Lord Akeldama always said, "only lasts a century or two. It is the first sin to go. Deadly sins don't last long if you're already dead."

Primrose also suspected the pishtacos might be motivated by a profound need not to be forgotten. They were now, quite unexpectedly, known to the vampires from overseas. They were different, but they were no longer so very alone.

A voice spoke from the shadows of a hallway to one side of the fireplace. "I will speak with her, Cauac."

And into the light of the fire walked the snowy perfection of the pishtaco queen.

FIFTEEN

Weddings and Their Consequences

U nlike the vampire queens of Prim's experience, which admittedly was confined to her mother and Countess Nadasdy, the pishtaco queen had not waited in an inner sanctum for others to come to her.

Instead, like any friendly society hostess, she came forth towards them, both hands held out in true welcome. Her fingernails were silvery too, but much longer, almost as long as her fingers themselves, and they had been pierced and decorated with silver rings.

"You are strong and brave, children of my fellow queen." Her voice was low and musical, lilting and siren-like. The pishtaco queen resembled her male counterparts but skewed slightly. Like them, she was thin and very white from head to toe. But she also wore white, where the males were dressed in the colourful woven cloth of local manufacture. Her eyes were more pink than red, magenta in tone. This made them look less tired and less angry. She was very tall, much taller than any of her menfolk. There was something unnaturally beautiful about her in ways they lacked, powerful ways.

Primrose was reminded, inexplicably, of stories told to her by an Irish nanny, of the people of the mounds. Percy, as a child, had become obsessed with researching them for a time. She looked to her brother. "Does she remind you of the *daoine sídhe?*"

The queen said in English barely accented but somehow old-fashioned in tone and cadence, "*Daoine sídhe*, what means this?"

Primrose blushed, she had forgotten to be careful that someone might know her native tongue. "Your pardon, great lady. It is a word from Gaelic times, before our recorded history. The Fair Folk they were also called. You look much as they were described: terribly beautiful."

A flash of a smile exposed the queen's fangs, columnar like the other pishtacos', yet unlike them she had two sets. *Maker fangs*, thought Primrose. *So pishtaco queens are much like vampire queens, in this at least.*

The queen's thin face brightened with real pleasure. "You think me beautiful?"

Primrose nodded. "I do." *Like an ice goddess.*

"You have surprised me, little mortal. And it has been many years since I have been surprised. I will listen to what you have to say." She turned to one of her drones. "*Mate de coca*," she said, and he scuttled away.

She gestured. "Please sit. I am Queen Madera Acebo, welcome to my nest."

Things proceeded remarkably smoothly from that point on. The queen greatly admired both the face cream and the bracelet Prim offered up. She did not try to bite either of them. The tea, when brought in, was as Primrose feared, that of local extraction, which tasted one note shy of horse dung. *Or should I say, alpaca dung?* But she managed to drink it without even a nose wrinkle of disgust. For all its flavour it was most invigorating.

Primrose and Percy shared stories of their childhood growing up in a hive, and much of what they knew of vampires. Queen Madera was fascinated. They even discussed excess soul. It seemed the pishtacos had no better way of knowing if a mortal might survive their metamorphosis bite.

"Our preference is to feed off the truly dramatic – singers, actors, and so forth. Like you two."

"You believe Percy and I are actors?"

"You aren't? What a waste. You perform beautifully."

Primrose had no idea whether to be flattered by this or not, so she carefully moved them on to the concept of relocation. She explained that their visit may have encouraged the bishop to pursue an extermination mandate. Even if they left the pishtacos untouched, others were coming.

The queen only sighed. "We have never been safe here since the *conquistadores* came, and before them we were barely tolerated. We do not have your history of occasional acceptance of the supernatural. Fat, in the mountains, is highly prized and jealously guarded. We have ever been a threat rather than an asset to our country."

"See," said Percy proudly, "I told you it was an environmentally deterministic stance."

"Yes, Percy, you were right." Primrose rolled her eyes.

"Go on," said Percy, crossing his arms. He glared at his sister.

The pishtacos were clearly trying not to be amused. Primrose allowed Percy's sibling antics because they were, at least, relaxing in their familiarity.

"You're *always* right, Percy. O brilliant brother of mine. Now explain to the nice lady your scheme."

Percy outlined his plan of putting her nest on a private train north into California. "The North Americans are rather obsessed with a slender physique, even if they generally do not welcome the supernatural. It is my opinion that fashion may override sense in this matter. No offence."

Primrose quickly jumped in. "What my brother is trying to say is that a moral objection to something, like ladies in trousers, may be overcome by something perceived as more immediately valuable, like bicycle riding."

"You think we may be overlooked for being devils under religious law because we can make people thin? Thin is..."

desirable?" The queen looked doubtful but did not outright refuse. "What is the name of this town in California, this one you think might welcome us?"

Percy said, "It's rather small but very up-and-coming." He scrabbled for something nice to say about the place. "Has a large theatre district. It is called Los Angeles. Still predominantly Spanish speaking. You might set up there, buy a music hall or something similar. Encourage performances of willowy blondes."

The queen smiled, taking that, too, as a compliment. Which Primrose supposed it might be. She had no idea into what arena her brother's tastes ran. She hoped he had not developed a tendre for the pishtaco queen.

The queen looked cautiously interested – difficult to tell with magenta eyes. "There is nothing to keep us here. We have no particular ties or love for this place. I should enjoy going somewhere warmer, near the sea."

Primrose frowned. "It is not difficult for you to leave? You are not tethered to this house? Our vampire queens cannot move home without great trauma."

Queen Madera frowned. "We must stay together, close, the seven of us. If too many of them weaken or depart, I would die, but we can relocate together."

Primrose nodded and side-eyed Percy. "So, more like werewolves in that, then?"

"I have only heard of your werewolves, never seen one. Are they like your vampires, survivors?"

Primrose nodded.

"We should like to be survivors too. I am not so old and not so tired that I have given up the fight."

Primrose said, "How can you trust us?"

The queen shrugged. "You bring me gifts of fat. You come into my nest with no weapons and no fear. You bring us hope when we had none. You talk of trains and places far away. If you are spinning lies they are great ones, but I think perhaps too complicated to be anything but truth."

"How are you on floating?" Primrose asked, intrigued.

"To fly, above the ground and close to the aether? It would likely not be healthy for any of us. We could try, of course, but we must stay together. How do your vampires react?"

"They go mad," said Primrose, not attempting to hide the horror of it. "Werewolves get very ill. But our werecat, our *nahual* as you call her, she is fine. She falls into deep sleep. It seems all immortals react differently."

Percy was frowning. "We could use the *Porcini*. Keep it low and near the ground whenever possible, and drag them behind us over the mountain tomorrow night and into Lima to catch the morning train."

Primrose hesitated and then asked, "I know they pose more danger than Percy and myself, and I know we all started off on the wrong foot, but might my captain and her officers come to speak with you as well? It would be good to have her confidence."

The queen considered a moment and then agreed.

And so Rue joined them, bringing with her food and tea. She was accompanied by Quesnel (who clearly was not letting her out of his sight again) and Tasherit (who clearly wanted to make certain Primrose was not sucked to a skeletal state). Which meant Anitra was in charge of the ship, with Rodrigo. Which made Primrose less nervous than it should. Which she assumed meant she trusted the Italian.

So it was that they used the *Porcini* and an improvised sling to transport seven pishtacos into Lima. Percy said it took more mathematics than was healthy in an eight-hour period to keep them from dragging, and everyone ought to be very grateful to his old trigonometry professor, and, of course, Percy's innate genius. Tasherit said they looked like nothing so much as a fishing net full of large sardines, although pishtacos did not smell as good as sardines would. Then she licked her lips in such a way that meant Primrose had to kiss her, right there on the main deck. No one minded.

Those companions who wished to immigrate with their pishtacos travelled to Lima in great comfort aboard *The Spotted Custard*, where Cook went to every effort to fatten them up. Cook was thrilled by the challenge, a true test of his genius. There was a lot of pudding.

After some consultation several of the crew and staff came forward and offered themselves for feeding before the pishtacos departed for points north. Including, much to Prim's surprise, Aggie Phinkerlington. She was a very solid lady, all things considered, but it had never occurred to Prim that Aggie was self-conscious about anything, least of all her weight.

Rue was not surprised. "I would have offered myself, despite Quesnel's griping, except, of course, it won't work."

Prim gave her a shocked look.

"Oh no, not for *that* reason. I've never minded how I looked. It's simply that we live aboard a dirigible, weight is a concern." Rue frowned then. "Pity we can't keep them with us, it would make restock calculations so much easier if we could simply take a little off the crew now and then."

Primrose blinked at that. "I think I find that mildly upsetting, Rue dear."

"Do you? Is it? Well, it's not possible either way."

Once in Lima, Rue spared no expense in seeing to the pishtacos' comfort. She drew extensively upon her vampire father's resources, which, fortunately, stretched even to Lima. Apparently, Lord Akeldama had investments in local lime quarries, which meant he kept money in a local bank, which meant Rue could access it. Good thing, too, for Rue ended up having to purchase the pishtacos' whole train car. She ordained them Akeldama's Travelling Circus on all customs forms, and apparently thought it hilarious that there was no elephant. (When Prim asked, Rue muttered something about Gaugamela.) Quesnel and his team boarded over the windows as much as possible (on account of sensitive circus animals, they claimed), and outfitted the interior with every luxury they could find.

The pishtacos were gratifyingly grateful. They acknowledged that, should they survive the journey, they would owe Lord Akeldama a huge debt. Rue was pleased, no doubt her Dama would be as well. Vampires have long memories, and even cross-continental agreements are no bad thing.

Primrose ensured that Queen Madera had her personal forwarding address. It was Prim's mother's hive but Primrose very much wished to keep up relations. "Once you're settled, please do write. I may take some time to answer – heaven knows where we are headed next – but I should love to stay in touch."

"I shall send you news when we are safely settled," the pishtaco queen assured her with a companionable hand squeeze despite the deadly nails.

Then the train was tooting, and Primrose left the dark carriage, shutting the door and joining her friends on the station platform.

Rue said, "Is it a good thing we do here?"

Primrose tucked her arm into her captain's. "It was our best option. And it is done now. What next?"

Rue sighed. "Anitra and Rodrigo. I rather fear we have a wedding to plan. Would you be interested . . . ?"

Primrose knew that pained expression well. Rue was all enthusiasm and excitement for adventure and intrigue and floating and even fighting, but attempt to organise a social event and she promptly fell apart.

"I should be delighted to coordinate the festivities," Primrose said, because it was her duty and because she was indeed delighted.

In the skies over the Pacific Ocean near Lima, Anitra Floote married Rodrigo Tarabotti on a clear New Year's evening. *The Spotted Custard* rang in 1896 with cognac and smoked trout, which oddly pleased all parties concerned. Except, of course, for the sooties and the decklings, who, being still young, were allowed only the trout.

The stars twinkled, as stars are wont to do. The air was crisp and tinged only slightly with the scent of smoked fish. Cook's attempted preservation techniques earlier that afternoon had met with only limited success, hence the need to eat most of the trout at the wedding.

Lady Prudence Akeldama, captain of *The Spotted Custard*, presided over the ceremony. The Honourable Professor Percival Tunstell, in a borrowed top hat, stood as best man, with his sister, the Honourable Primrose Tunstell, as maid of honour. Tasherit Sekhmet made a very nice speech on the enduring nature of love, while wearing a Turkish lounging cap of dubious taste and questionable length of tassel.

No official announcement was sent to the London *Times*. It was too far away and anyone who cared already knew anyway.

Percy withstood both the ceremony and the following feast and musical celebration with great dignity. Until someone brought out a pennywhistle and someone else the bagpipes, and really, it had all gone too far.

He escaped to the forecastle prow with a glass of cognac and a long-suffering expression. He wanted his library, but he thought Primrose would yell if he left too soon.

He found Formerly Floote already floating there, looking away from the celebration and out at the vast ocean.

"You all right there, Formerly Floote?" he asked, because it was the polite thing to do. And the ghost wasn't half bad, he never got chatty.

Formerly Floote nodded.

Percy sipped and frowned. "You aren't displeased with the match?"

The ghost wafted in distress. "Not at all. What would give you that impression?"

"You're here, apart, and not there enjoying the festivities."

"Ah, no. It is simply disconcerting to be attending a celebration with nothing to do. I am accustomed to being behind the magic, as it were."

It was Percy's turn to nod. "Then you approve a love match?"

Formerly Floote cocked his noncorporeal head. "I recommend it. It saved his grandfather, did you know? Love. Not for very long, of course. But long enough for him to know happiness. And what else is there to life than that?"

Percy would like to say that facts were also good, but it was so rare for the ghost to really talk and he didn't want to disturb such an unexpected confidence. Facts, Percy had come to realise, generally disturbed people. Besides, Percy had something he'd always wanted to ask the ghost and enough cognac already inside him to be forward about it.

"Did you know Rue's grandfather had a son as well as a daughter?"

"Of course."

"Did he know?"

"If he did, he never shared it with me. I found out after he died."

"Is that why you played both sides? To keep them both safe?" Percy had heard the stories from Rue's mother about Floote's betrayal. Floote had been so loyal for so long, yet apparently was always plotting behind the scenes with a preternatural agenda and devious schemes, one of which ended in murder.

Formerly Floote looked sad. "I had to keep the Templars happy, you see? They had Alessandro's son."

"And then his grandson."

The ghost inclined his head.

Percy twirled his glass. "And then you were stuck once again with the guardianship of two children raised in opposite cultures with conflicting agendas."

They looked at Rue and Rodrigo. The cousins were laughing together about something, tipsy with liquor or giddy with happiness. Rue was gesticulating wildly, regaling Rodrigo with some story at length. Quesnel was leaning against her side, grin wide and dimpled. Rodrigo had his arm about Anitra's waist, and her veiled head was rested on his broad shoulder.

Formerly Floote said, "You see what I have wrought?"

Percy nodded. "I do see. Is this what Alessandro Tarabotti asked of you, all those years ago?"

"He only had it for such a short time, you see. And he never knew he needed it until then," the ghost tried to explain.

"Love?"

"Yes."

Percy nodded, thinking of his sister. "He wanted his daughter to have it longer than he did. And you took that to mean his son as well. And then his granddaughter. And then his grandson. He charged you with a very grave burden, Mr Floote. Very grave." *Matchmaking the generations. Even I know you can neither guide nor govern the emotions of others.*

The ghost gave a sad little smile. "And I took it to my grave."

Percy winced at the pun and then looked once again at the last of the Tarabotti line. "Don't you think it's done now?" he asked. "They both look very happy. And they are together, almost like family."

"Not . . . quite . . ." said the ghost mysteriously, before slipping away, down through the deck and back to his tank.

The sun was near to rising. Percy downed the last of his drink and pondered the nature of love and manipulation and ghosts and souls, confident in his own superiority in needing none of these things to be content with his life.

Although he would never admit it, when his sister tracked him down to chastise him gently and drag him back to the fray, there was a strange pleasure in being wanted too.

All in all, Primrose felt, it was a most excellent wedding. Everything went swimmingly, bagpipes notwithstanding. Willard did so love to play, and Rue always claimed it was in her heritage so let him trot them out in defiance of all taste and logic. *After all*, Prim thought, *pipes have nothing to do with Drifter or Italian culture. They might have been left out, just this once.*

She and Tasherit made themselves scarce upon the appearance of the dreaded bladder shrieker (as Tash called bagpipes). Dawn was only a little ways off, and Prim was in accordance with Tasherit on the subject of bagpipes.

Tash muttered something about cats in heat and bygone days in tones that suggested these were bad memories, then she grabbed Primrose by the hand and insisted a private pouncing was not only imminent but, with Prim flaunting such a very flattering gown, mandatory.

She also came up with an extremely pleasant way to block out the sound abovedecks. It transpires that when blood rushes through one's ears and mind at the height of the most decadent of pleasure, even bagpipes may be ignored.

Tasherit's tongue was likely the most talented thing Primrose had ever encountered. As she told Tasherit, it was a genuine pity it was a skill that could not be shared with others. Or a pity for others – good for Primrose.

Tasherit was pleased with this possessive compliment and made her feelings clear with a similarly decided statement of ownership. "I know we cannot marry, not by your people's laws, but you are mine and I am yours and that is that."

Primrose had agreed. It was all she could do at the time. Tasherit's tongue was involved in this statement, and Primrose was learning she could not resist that tongue.

Just prior to sunrise the werecat curled against her back, leaving little licks and nibbles to the nape of Prim's neck, and despite a near soporific relaxation – the result of exquisite application of the same only moments before – Primrose was beginning to feel restless for more. Again. She wondered if she might pretend to hear the bagpipes again. And she wondered if they had time before sunrise.

Tasherit paused her ministrations to say, "It was well done, your ceremony for Anitra and her soulless man."

Primrose nodded, stroking Tasherit's arm where it draped over her waist. "Yes, yes it was. Oddly perfect in its way."

Tasherit nuzzled in. "Yet you are sad, I think, little one."

"Like us, they will have no children."

"Ah, we return to this?"

Primrose nodded. "It may take me some time to reconcile. I had always imagined a big family."

A sharp nip kept her from becoming maudlin.

"You want children? I will catch some for you. Can't be too difficult."

Prim didn't even know where to start with that statement.

The werecat continued. "There are plenty of unwanted children. What kind would you like?"

As if there were a buffet of babies on offer. But Primrose supposed the werecat was right. There were many workhouses and orphanages. She might have her children if she dared.

"You won't mind? You are, after all, immortal. The affairs of a small family might seem petty."

Tasherit chuckled against her neck. "I have always loved cubs. I never had any of my own, before the bite, but I have spent time in the nurseries of ancient queens. You would make a better mother than they."

Primrose, pleased by such an accolade, rolled so she might kiss her werecat in gratitude.

Tasherit hugged her close. "I would give you the world, little one, if you asked it of me."

"Yes, but would you give up that fez?"

"No. It is a most excellent hat, such a nice long tassel."

So Primrose Tunstell made one last compromise on her moral choices in life, and her concern for appearances, and allowed the Turkish cap to stay.

SIXTEEN

Homeward Bound

Primrose presided over supper the next evening with only a modicum of residual melancholy. On any other first day of the year her thoughts would be filled with all the expectations she had not fulfilled – marriage, family, children, household. But in 1896, with the new century bearing down upon her, Primrose made the resolution to refrain from expectations, for herself and others.

I shall be a new woman, she thought. *And I shall have goals and wishes and hopes that are of my own making rather than my mother's. Or society's.*

Tasherit, sitting next to her at table, bestowed one of her cat-got-the-cream grins on her across the serving tray. *I could learn to love those smiles very much.*

Percy had managed, by dint of some very diligent research and a great many local bribes, to acquire aetherographic charts in Lima.

He was prodding Rue about where they should head next. "Shall I plot us a course northwards? To follow the pishtacos to California? It is never very easy to move latitudes, but I think it can be done with a large number of hops. Then we could cross the United States towards Boston and..."

His enthusiasm was a bit much all at once. The officers were all a little worse for the previous night's celebrations, with the exception of Percy, who seemed startlingly capable of holding his liquor.

Primrose understood her brother's urgency – they did need some kind of plan. They couldn't float over the Pacific Ocean near Lima indefinitely. But she wished Percy could have waited until after supper.

Rue forestalled his waffling. "Much as I should like to see our new pishtaco friends safely settled, I'm afraid we must return to London."

Primrose released an involuntary gasp. She felt part delighted and part terrified at this. Happy to be headed home after so many months away, but scared to know her new relationship might be exposed to her mother. Would be. Would likely *have* to be exposed.

She looked across the table at Percy. He gave her, of all things, a sympathetic smile. He had said that he would back her in this. *I will not lose all my family. I will still have my impossible brother.* Primrose wondered if Percy always had this awkward kindness under all his pomp and arrogance. He'd said last night, in a funny voice after too much cognac, that he liked how comfortable she was with herself now. Or, more precisely, what he'd said was: *Funny how it took a shape-shifter to show my sister how to fit her own skin.*

"So soon?" That was Rodrigo. He'd settled into attending dinners and officers' meetings alongside his wife in a way that no one found as disconcerting as they ought.

Primrose supposed, in the end, they must either choose to trust him utterly or keep him locked away forever. Which reminded her they still had an aether-pocket pirate imprisoned.

"Are we taking our friend the ladle pirate with us?" she asked.

Rue winced. "Oh, I forgot about him."

"And have you forgotten that I am wanted for treason in your country? Or I think I am, aren't I?" Rodrigo was justifiably cautious of his safety.

Rue shrugged. "Possibly. Difficult to know. We've been gone long enough for changes to occur. Next possible postal station, I'll send a message to my parents, both locations, and let them know our next few ports of call. Hopefully they can respond back and we'll get the lay of the political landscape before leaving this continent. Then if we have to, we'll leave you two behind."

Anitra and Rodrigo grimaced a little at that. Such a plan meant being left in the United States, most likely. And no one wanted that.

Rue looked at her cousin and his new wife. "I know it is not ideal, but I've another wedding I must attend, I'm afraid. It's vitally important that I not miss this one." Rue's face twisted in disgust. She wasn't one for highfalutin society gatherings. A wedding in London would be a great deal more elaborate and precedent riddled than the one they'd just enjoyed aboard *The Spotted Custard*.

Primrose tried to think whose wedding might be so important that they must return to London for it. She and Rue shared most of their acquaintances. It was odd for Rue to know of a wedding before Prim did. Especially as they had been out of communication with England for a month or so. It was even odder for Rue to be invited to attend festivities when Primrose was not.

Primrose decided to make a joke of it rather than take offence. "Rue dear, you know that Tasherit and I cannot publicly marry. If you're planning on launching us into society with a grand gesture..."

"No. Although now that you mention it..."

Quesnel looked up from where he'd been uncharacteristically silent over the cold sliced meat and biscuits.

Primrose noticed then that his face was quite red. He was even sweating slightly. It wasn't a hot evening by anyone's estimation.

Uh-oh, thought Prim.

"*Chérie*, spit it out," said the Frenchman to Rue, plucking at the tablecloth self-consciously.

Rue seemed to be enjoying his discomfort. Theirs was a very odd relationship. "Fine. Well. Not to mince words but this wedding, well, it is mine. My wedding. In London."

Primrose did her best impression of a dead fish. She had hoped, of course, but had rather resigned herself to her best friend living as an inamorata for the foreseeable future.

"To Quesnel, of course." Rue was now floundering a bit in the awkwardness of the utter silence around the table that had met her announcement.

"I should bally well hope so." Primrose found her tongue at last. "You've ruined his chances for anyone else." As if Quesnel were a maiden deflowered.

That broke the shock with chuckles.

Primrose was curious. "Why now? Why all of a sudden head us back to London for that?"

"Dama would never forgive us if we did it anywhere else."

"Nor would my mother," added Quesnel.

"And the timing is, well, necessary," added Rue, as if that alone explained her sudden decision.

Primrose felt suddenly adrift and alone.

"Oh," she said weakly, "is it? But you've been living happily in sin for so long. Not that I'm defending it, of course. Except that's now my fate, so I rather hoped we could continue to float along sinning differently but together."

"I did too." Rue reached over to grab Prim's hand. Her squeeze was reassuring in its familiarity. Just that gesture said so many things, held so many memories. *Come with me, Prim,* it said. *I promise we won't get into trouble. I'll be with you. It's only a little favour, Prim. Oh, but you're so good at acting, pretend with me, I'll take the blame. But Prim, it'll be fun. We'll do it together. Together. Together . . .*

"Then why?" Percy asked. "I mean why leg-shackle if you don't have to?" He looked at Quesnel, no doubt genuinely curious. He spent most of his time at any given ball avoiding all the unmarried ladies with a will.

Rue shrugged as if the answer were of no matter or particular importance. "I'm pregnant."

Primrose didn't like the wave of envy and sadness that hit her. She should be happy for her friend. Except that Rue looked rather more resigned than pleased.

"Quesnel and I were rather hoping we could persuade you and Tasherit to be godparents. It's not like either of us intend to give up *The Spotted Custard* and stop adventuring."

"You'll keep it aboard ship?" Prim felt her face tingling.

"Of course."

At which juncture Primrose burst into tears.

Tasherit was immediately upset with everyone and ran around attempting to solve the problem with more tea, a piece of cheese, and then some hair petting. Which, as Prim had her hair up, only messed with the arrangement and caused her to cry harder.

Rue pushed her chair back and crouched down in a way that Prim worried was rather more active than was healthy for a lady in her delicate condition.

"Please, Prim." Rue's face was a study in distressed hope.

Then Quesnel was standing behind her, a hand to Rue's shoulder, his normally cheerful face grave, watching Primrose intently.

And Tasherit was back on her other side, petting again, and Prim didn't mind so much that her hair had fallen down. Percy was standing up, leaning across the table, and grumbling at her not to be a ninny, but also wondering if a nice biscuit would cheer her up and setting it down gently in front of her. Further down the table Anitra watched her in sympathetic distress while Rodrigo went for water and a cold compress, in case Primrose was developing a case of histrionics.

Primrose realised they thought she was sad and overwrought with jealousy.

Rue said "Please, Prim" again, and then, "I can't do this without you. You know that. I won't be any good at it without you. We won't." She gestured to herself and Quesnel, and then all the others in the room.

It sounded like all those times before. Every time Rue had dragged Primrose into an adventure. *Together.* Primrose realised then that she had never regretted a single time. Certainly Rue got her into trouble, but it had always been fun, it had always been an adventure.

Primrose forced herself to speak, on a little gasp of hope. "We're going to have *a baby?*" She was certain her smile was as wide and as bright and as damp as the Pacific Ocean under a midday sun.

"We are." Rue's own smile answered hers.

"There, you see," said Tasherit, "I told you I would get you one."

"I rather think Rue and Quesnel deserve the credit," said Percy, sitting back down in his chair and sipping his tea. Now that he knew Prim's tears were not distress but joy, he returned to his old disinterested pompous self.

Rue let out a sigh, her tawny eyes intent on Prim's face. "You're happy about this?"

Primrose nodded. "Very."

Quesnel handed her a handkerchief, only slightly soot smudged. She dabbed her eyes.

Rue stood and smiled down at her. "Good, because you'll do most of the work once it's here. I depend upon you to take care of all the details. Nursery, nappies, nudibranch, whatever it is babies need. You'll organise everything?"

"Don't I always?" Primrose was already thinking about what needed to be done. Already considering the changes she would make to her household, for her family – what must be accomplished, and how she would do it, and how wonderful it would all be.

"Good," said Rue. Primrose could feel, in that one word, all her old friend's unshakable trust and love. "That's settled, then. Percy, take us home."

The story continues in...
RETICENCE

The Custard Protocol: Book Four

Coming in Summer 2019!

Acknowledgements

With grateful thanks to my most wonderful Pigeons. You know who you are.

extras

orbit

meet the author

Photo Credit: Vanessa Applegate

New York Times bestselling author GAIL CARRIGER writes to cope with being raised in obscurity by an expatriate Brit and an incurable curmudgeon. She escaped small town life and inadvertently acquired several degrees in Higher Learning. Ms. Carriger then traveled the historic cities of Europe, subsisting entirely on biscuits secreted in her handbag. She resides in the Colonies, surrounded by fantastic shoes, where she insists on tea imported from London.

if you enjoyed
COMPETENCE

look out for

SOULLESS

The Parasol Protectorate: Book One

by

Gail Carriger

Alexia Tarabotti is laboring under a great many social tribulations. First, she has no soul. Second, she's a spinster whose father is both Italian and dead. Third, she was rudely attacked by a vampire, breaking all standards of social etiquette.

Where to go from there? From bad to worse apparently, for Alexia accidentally kills the vampire—and then the appalling Lord

extras

Maccon (loud, messy, gorgeous, and werewolf) is sent by Queen Victoria to investigate.

With unexpected vampires appearing and expected vampires disappearing, everyone seems to believe Alexia is responsible. Can she figure out what is actually happening to London's high society? Will her soulless ability to negate supernatural powers prove useful or just plain embarrassing? Finally, who is the real enemy, and do they have treacle tart?

CHAPTER ONE

In Which Parasols Prove Useful

Miss Alexia Tarabotti was not enjoying her evening. Private balls were never more than middling amusements for spinsters, and Miss Tarabotti was not the kind of spinster who could garner even that much pleasure from the event. To put the pudding in the puff: she had retreated to the library, her favorite sanctuary in any house, only to happen upon an unexpected vampire.

She glared at the vampire.

For his part, the vampire seemed to feel that their encounter had improved his ball experience immeasurably. For there she sat, without escort, in a low-necked ball gown.

In this particular case, what he did not know *could* hurt him. For Miss Alexia had been born without a soul, which, as any decent vampire of good blooding knew, made her a lady to avoid most assiduously.

Yet he moved toward her, darkly shimmering out of the library shadows with feeding fangs ready. However, the moment he touched Miss Tarabotti, he was suddenly no longer darkly doing anything at all. He was simply standing there, the faint sounds of a string quartet in the background as he foolishly fished about with his tongue for fangs unaccountably mislaid.

Miss Tarabotti was not in the least surprised; soullessness always neutralized supernatural abilities. She issued the vampire a very dour look. Certainly, most daylight folk wouldn't peg her as anything less than a standard English prig, but had this man not even bothered to *read* the vampire's official abnormality roster for London and its greater environs?

The vampire recovered his equanimity quickly enough. He reared away from Alexia, knocking over a nearby tea trolley. Physical contact broken, his fangs reappeared. Clearly not the sharpest of prongs, he then darted forward from the neck like a serpent, diving in for another chomp.

"I say!" said Alexia to the vampire. "We have not even been introduced!"

Miss Tarabotti had never actually had a vampire try to bite her. She knew one or two by reputation, of course, and was friendly with Lord Akeldama. *Who was* not *friendly with Lord Akeldama?* But no vampire had ever actually attempted to *feed* on her before!

So Alexia, who abhorred violence, was forced to grab the miscreant by his nostrils, a delicate and therefore painful area, and shove him away. He stumbled over the fallen tea trolley, lost his balance in a manner astonishingly graceless for a vampire, and fell to the floor. He landed right on top of a plate of treacle tart.

Miss Tarabotti was most distressed by this. She was particularly fond of treacle tart and had been looking forward to consuming that precise plateful. She picked up her parasol. It was terribly tasteless for her to be carrying a parasol at an evening ball, but Miss Tarabotti rarely went anywhere without it. It was of a style entirely of her own devising: a black frilly confection with purple satin pansies sewn about, brass hardware, and buckshot in its silver tip.

She whacked the vampire right on top of the head with it as he tried to extract himself from his newly intimate relations with the tea trolley. The buckshot gave the brass parasol just enough heft to make a deliciously satisfying *thunk*.

"Manners!" instructed Miss Tarabotti.

The vampire howled in pain and sat back down on the treacle tart.

Alexia followed up her advantage with a vicious prod between the vampire's legs. His howl went quite a bit higher in pitch, and he crumpled into a fetal position. While Miss Tarabotti was a proper English young lady, aside from not having a soul and being half Italian, she did spend quite a bit more time than most other young ladies riding and walking and was therefore unexpectedly strong.

Miss Tarabotti leaped forward—as much as one could leap in full triple-layered underskirts, draped bustle, and ruffled taffeta top-skirt—and bent over the vampire. He was clutching at his indelicate bits and writhing about. The pain would not last long given his supernatural healing ability, but it hurt most decidedly in the interim.

Alexia pulled a long wooden hair stick out of her elaborate coiffure. Blushing at her own temerity, she ripped open his shirtfront, which was cheap and overly starched, and poked at his chest, right over the heart. Miss Tarabotti sported a particularly large and sharp hair stick. With her free hand, she made certain to touch his chest, as only physical contact would nullify his supernatural abilities.

"Desist that horrible noise immediately," she instructed the creature.

The vampire quit his squealing and lay perfectly still. His beautiful blue eyes watered slightly as he stared fixedly at the wooden hair stick. Or, as Alexia liked to call it, hair *stake*.

"Explain yourself!" Miss Tarabotti demanded, increasing the pressure.

"A thousand apologies." The vampire looked confused. "Who are you?" Tentatively he reached for his fangs. Gone.

To make her position perfectly clear, Alexia stopped touching him (though she kept her sharp hair stick in place). His fangs grew back.

He gasped in amazement. "*What* are you? I thought you were a lady, alone. It would be my right to feed, if you were left this carelethly unattended. Pleathe, I did not mean to prethume," he lisped around his fangs, real panic in his eyes.

Alexia, finding it hard not to laugh at the lisp, said, "There is no cause for you to be so overly dramatic. Your hive queen will have told you of my kind." She returned her hand to his chest once more. The vampire's fangs retracted.

He looked at her as though she had suddenly sprouted whiskers and hissed at him.

Miss Tarabotti was surprised. Supernatural creatures, be they vampires, werewolves, or ghosts, owed their existence to an overabundance of soul, an excess that refused to die. Most knew that others like Miss Tarabotti existed, born without any soul at all. The estimable Bureau of Unnatural Registry (BUR), a division of Her Majesty's Civil Service, called her ilk *preternatural*. Alexia thought the term nicely dignified. What vampires called her was far less complimentary. After all, preternaturals had once hunted *them,* and vampires had long memories. Natural, daylight persons were kept in the dark, so to speak, but any vampire worth his blood should know a preternatural's touch. This one's ignorance was untenable. Alexia said, as though to a very small child, "I am a *preternatural.*"

The vampire looked embarrassed. "Of course you are," he agreed, obviously still not quite comprehending. "Again, my apologies, lovely one. I am overwhelmed to meet you. You are my first"—he stumbled over the word—"preternatural." He frowned. "Not supernatural, not natural, of course! How foolish of me not to see the dichotomy." His eyes narrowed into craftiness. He was now studiously ignoring the hair stick and looking tenderly up into Alexia's face.

Miss Tarabotti knew full well her own feminine appeal. The kindest compliment her face could ever hope to garner was "exotic," never ' "lovely." Not that it had ever received either. Alexia figured that vampires, like all predators, were at their most charming when cornered.

The vampire's hands shot forward, going for her neck. Apparently, he had decided if he could not suck her blood, strangulation was an acceptable alternative. Alexia jerked back, at the same time pressing her hair stick into the creature's white flesh. It slid in about half an inch. The vampire reacted with a desperate wriggle that, even without superhuman strength, unbalanced Alexia in her heeled velvet dancing shoes. She fell back. He stood, roaring in pain, with her hair stick half in and half out of his chest.

Miss Tarabotti scrabbled for her parasol, rolling about inelegantly among the tea things, hoping her new dress would miss the fallen foodstuffs. She found the parasol and came upright, swinging it in a wide arc. Purely by chance, the heavy tip struck the end of her wooden hair stick, driving it straight into the vampire's heart.

The creature stood stock-still, a look of intense surprise on his handsome face. Then he fell backward onto the much-abused plate of treacle tart, flopping in a limp-overcooked-asparagus kind of way. His alabaster face turned a yellowish gray, as though he were afflicted with the jaundice, and he went still. Alexia's books called this end of the vampire life cycle *dissanimation*. Alexia, who thought the action astoundingly similar to a soufflé going flat, decided at that moment to call it the Grand Collapse.

She intended to waltz directly out of the library without anyone the wiser to her presence there. This would have resulted in the loss of her best hair stick and her well-deserved tea, as well as a good deal of drama. Unfortunately, a small group of young dandies came traipsing in at that precise moment. What young men of such dress were doing in a *library* was anyone's guess. Alexia felt the most likely explanation was that they had become lost while looking for the card room. Regardless, their presence forced her to pretend that she, too, had just discovered the dead vampire. With a resigned shrug, she screamed and collapsed into a faint.

She stayed resolutely fainted, despite the liberal application of smelling salts, which made her eyes water most tremendously, a cramp in the back of one knee, and the fact that her new ball gown was getting most awfully wrinkled. All its many layers of green trim, picked to the height of fashion in lightening shades to complement the cuirasse bodice, were being crushed into oblivion under her weight. The expected noises ensued: a good deal of yelling, much bustling about, and several loud clatters as one of the housemaids cleared away the fallen tea.

Then came the sound she had half anticipated, half dreaded. An authoritative voice cleared the library of both young dandies and all other interested parties who had flowed into the room upon discovery of the tableau. The voice instructed everyone to "get out!" while he "gained the particulars from the young lady" in tones that brooked no refusal.

Silence descended.

"Mark my words, I will use something much, much stronger than smelling salts," came a growl in Miss Tarabotti's left ear. The voice was low and tinged with a hint of Scotland. It would have caused Alexia to shiver and think primal monkey thoughts about moons and running far and fast, if she'd had a soul. Instead it caused her to sigh in exasperation and sit up.

"And a good evening to you, too, Lord Maccon. Lovely weather we are having for this time of year, is it not?" She patted at her hair, which was threatening to fall down without the hair stick in its proper place. Surreptitiously, she looked about for Lord Conall Maccon's second in command, Professor Lyall. Lord Maccon tended to maintain a much calmer temper when his Beta was present. But, then, as Alexia had come to comprehend, that appeared to be the main role of a Beta—especially one attached to Lord Maccon.

"Ah, Professor Lyall, how nice to see you again." She smiled in relief.

Professor Lyall, the Beta in question, was a slight, sandy-haired gentleman of indeterminate age and pleasant disposition, as agreeable, in fact, as his Alpha was sour. He grinned at her and doffed his hat, which was of first-class design and sensible material. His cravat was similarly subtle, for, while it was tied expertly, the knot was a humble one.

"Miss Tarabotti, how delicious to find ourselves in your company once more." His voice was soft and mild-mannered.

"Stop humoring her, Randolph," barked Lord Maccon. The fourth Earl of Woolsey was much larger than Professor Lyall and in possession of a near-permanent frown. Or at least he always seemed to be frowning when he was in the presence of Miss Alexia Tarabotti, ever since the hedgehog incident (which really, honestly, had not been her fault). He also had unreasonably pretty tawny eyes, mahogany-colored hair, and a particularly nice nose. The eyes were currently glaring at Alexia from a shockingly intimate distance.

"Why is it, Miss Tarabotti, every time I have to clean up a mess in a library, you just happen to be in the middle of it?" the earl demanded of her.

Alexia gave him a withering look and brushed down the front of her green taffeta gown, checking for bloodstains.

Lord Maccon appreciatively watched her do it. Miss Tarabotti might examine her face in the mirror each morning with a large degree of censure, but there was nothing at all wrong with her figure. He would have to have had far less soul and a good fewer urges not to notice that appetizing fact. Of course, she always went and spoiled the appeal by opening her mouth. In his humble experience, the world had yet to produce a more vexingly verbose female.

"Lovely but unnecessary," he said, indicating her efforts to brush away nonexistent blood drops.

Alexia reminded herself that Lord Maccon and his kind were only *just* civilized. One simply could not expect too much from them, especially under delicate circumstances such as these. Of course, that failed to explain Professor Lyall, who was always utterly urbane. She glanced with appreciation in the professor's direction.

Lord Maccon's frown intensified.

Miss Tarabotti considered that the lack of civilized behavior might be the sole provenance of Lord Maccon. Rumor had it, he had only lived in London a comparatively short while— and he had relocated from Scotland of all barbaric places.

The professor coughed delicately to get his Alpha's attention. The earl's yellow gaze focused on him with such intensity it should have actually burned. "Aye?"

Professor Lyall was crouched over the vampire, examining the hair stick with interest. He was poking about the wound, a spotless white lawn handkerchief wrapped around his hand.

"Very little mess, actually. Almost complete lack of blood spatter." He leaned forward and sniffed. "Definitely Westminster," he stated.

The Earl of Woolsey seemed to understand. He turned his piercing gaze onto the dead vampire. "He must have been very hungry."

Professor Lyall turned the body over. "What happened here?" He took out a small set of wooden tweezers from the pocket of his waistcoat and picked at the back of the vampire's trousers. He paused, rummaged about in his coat pockets, and produced a diminutive leather case. He clicked it open and removed a most bizarre pair of gogglelike things. They were gold in color with multiple lenses on one side, between which there appeared to be some kind of liquid. The contraption was also riddled with small knobs and dials. Professor Lyall propped the ridiculous things onto his nose and bent back over the vampire, twiddling at the dials expertly.

"Goodness gracious me," exclaimed Alexia, "what *are* you wearing? It looks like the unfortunate progeny of an illicit union between a pair of binoculars and some opera glasses. What on earth are they called, binocticals, spectoculars?"

The earl snorted his amusement and then tried to pretend he hadn't. "How about glassicals?" he suggested, apparently unable to resist a contribution. There was a twinkle in his eye as he said it that Alexia found rather unsettling.

Professor Lyall looked up from his examination and glared at the both of them. His right eye was hideously magnified. It was quite gruesome and made Alexia start involuntarily.

"These are my monocular cross-magnification lenses with spectra-modifier attachment, and they are invaluable. I will thank you not to mock them so openly." He turned once more to the task at hand.

"Oh." Miss Tarabotti was suitably impressed. "How do they work?" she inquired.

Professor Lyall looked back up at her, suddenly animated. "Well, you see, it is really quite interesting. By turning this little knob here, you can change the distance between the two panes of glass here, allowing the liquid to—"

The earl's groan interrupted him. "Don't get him started, Miss Tarabotti, or we will be here all night."

Looking slightly crestfallen, Professor Lyall turned back to the dead vampire. "Now, what *is* this substance all over his clothing?"

His boss, preferring the direct approach, resumed his frown and looked accusingly at Alexia. "What on God's green earth is that muck?"

Miss Tarabotti said, "Ah. Sadly, treacle tart. A tragic loss, I daresay." Her stomach chose that moment to growl in agreement. She would have colored gracefully with embarrassment had she not possessed the complexion of one of those "heathen Italians," as her mother said, who never colored, gracefully or otherwise. (Convincing her mother that Christianity had, to all intents and purposes, originated with the Italians, thus making them the exact opposite of heathen, was a waste of time and breath.) Alexia refused to apologize for the boisterousness of her stomach and favored Lord Maccon with a defiant glare. Her stomach was the reason she had sneaked away in the first place. Her mama had assured her there would be food at the ball. Yet all that appeared on offer when they arrived was a bowl of punch and some sadly wilted watercress. Never one to let her stomach get the better of her, Alexia had ordered tea from the butler and retreated to the library. Since she normally spent any ball lurking on the outskirts of the dance floor trying to look as though she did not want to be asked to waltz, tea was a welcome alternative. It was rude to order refreshments from someone else's staff, but when one was promised sandwiches and there was nothing but watercress, well, one must simply take matters into one's own hands!

Professor Lyall, kindhearted soul that he was, prattled on to no one in particular, pretending not to notice the rumbling of her stomach. Though of course he heard it. He had excellent hearing. *They* all did. He looked up from his examinations, his face all catawampus from the glassicals. "Starvation would explain why the vampire was desperate enough to try for Miss Tarabotti at a ball, rather than taking to the slums like the smart ones do when they get this bad."

Alexia grimaced. "No associated hive either."

Lord Maccon arched one black eyebrow, professing not to be impressed. "How could *you* possibly know *that*?"

Professor Lyall explained for both of them. "No need to be so direct with the young lady. A hive queen would never have let one of her brood get into such a famished condition. We must have a rove on our hands, one completely without ties to the local hive."

Alexia stood up, revealing to Lord Maccon that she had arranged her faint to rest comfortably against a fallen settee pillow. He grinned and then quickly hid it behind a frown when she looked at him suspiciously.

"I have a different theory." She gestured to the vampire's clothing. "Badly tied cravat and a cheap shirt? No hive worth its salt would let a larva like that out without dressing him properly for public appearance. I am surprised he was not stopped at the front entrance. The duchess's footman really ought to have spotted a cravat like *that* prior to the reception line and forcibly ejected the wearer. I suppose good staff is hard to come by with all the best ones becoming drones these days, but such a shirt!"

The Earl of Woolsey glared at her. "Cheap clothing is no excuse for killing a man."

"Mmm, that's what you say." Alexia evaluated Lord Maccon's perfectly tailored shirtfront and exquisitely tied cravat. His dark hair was a bit too long and shaggy to be de mode, and his face was not entirely clean-shaven, but he possessed enough hauteur to carry this lower-class roughness off without seeming scruffy. She was certain that his silver and black paisley cravat must be tied under sufferance. He probably preferred to wander about bare-chested at home. The idea made her shiver oddly. It must take a lot of effort to keep a man like him tidy. Not to mention well tailored. He was bigger than most. She had to give credit to his valet, who must be a particularly tolerant claviger.

Lord Maccon was normally quite patient. Like most of his kind, he had learned to be such in polite society. But Miss Tarabotti seemed to bring out the worst of his animal urges. "Stop trying to change the subject," he snapped, squirming under her calculated scrutiny. "Tell me what happened." He put on his BUR face and pulled out a small metal tube, stylus, and pot of clear liquid. He unrolled the tube with a small cranking device, clicked the top off the liquid, and dipped the stylus into it. It sizzled ominously.

Alexia bristled at his autocratic tone. "Do not give me instructions in that tone of voice, you..." she searched for a particularly insulting word, "puppy! I am jolly well not one of your pack."

if you enjoyed
COMPETENCE

look out for

THE IMMORTALS
Olympus Bound: Book One

by

Jordanna Max Brodsky

Manhattan has many secrets. Some are older than the city itself.

The city sleeps. Selene DiSilva walks her dog along the banks of the Hudson. She is alone—just the way she likes it. She doesn't believe in friends, and she doesn't speak to her family. Most of them are simply too dangerous.

In the predawn calm, Selene finds the body of a young woman washed ashore, gruesomely mutilated and wreathed in laurel.

Her ancient rage returns. And so does the memory of a promise she made long ago—when her name was Artemis.

CHAPTER 1

Punisher

Selene DiSilva crouched in a narrow alley between two run-down apartment buildings, watching the street. When she'd begun her vigil hours before, the smells of roasting chicken and frying plantains had wafted from the surrounding apartments. Families laughed and bickered, doors slammed, cars honked. But in the small hours of the morning, the only scents were those from the trashcans overflowing nearby, and the street before her lay nearly deserted. Even in the city that never slept, there were quiet corners like this: a forgotten neighborhood perched at Manhattan's northernmost tip. Here, most people obeyed the ancient human instinct to seek refuge from the dark. But not Selene—and not the man she'd been sent to hunt.

A single dark SUV rolled by, a wave of Caribbean hip-hop pouring through the open window to briefly shatter the silence. From her hiding place, Selene peered at the driver, but let him pass unmolested.

Later, a group of swaggering young men strolled along the street, laughing and shoving as they claimed the sidewalk for themselves. Selene watched them carefully but didn't move. Then two women passed her alley, speaking in slurred Spanish, their eyes purple with fatigue. She felt no empathy—as usual, she'd slept all day and only awoken with the moonrise.

Finally, a solitary figure appeared at the far end of the block. Long before she could see his face, Selene knew him by his stride. *Chin forward and shoulders high like he's looking for a fight,* she thought, *but only with someone he's sure he can beat.*

She glanced at the apartment building across the street— a wide 1920s façade, its art deco grandeur long since gone. A window on the third floor flickered blue behind thin curtains. Jackie Ortiz was awake and watching TV, just as Selene had instructed.

She stood up slowly as the man approached the building. Mario Velasquez. Medium height—shorter than her own six feet—but broad across the shoulders, his muscles bulkier than hers. He wore a rhinestone-studded cross on a thick gold chain around his neck and kept his hands shoved into the front pocket of his sweatshirt. She couldn't be sure if he was armed or not, but she'd find out soon enough.

She could see his face now, the same one she'd been stalking for a week: high cheekbones and a neat goatee, dark skin that made his light blue stare all the more alluring. *Once again,* she thought, *a woman falls for a pair of pretty eyes and never bothers to find out what's behind them.*

Mario stopped opposite Jackie's building. Looking up at her window, he pulled a cell phone from his pocket. Selene couldn't make out his murmured conversation, but she recognized the aggravation in the rising pitch of his voice. It wouldn't be long before he started throwing punches.

She let the tiniest of smiles cross her lips. She was, after all, going to enjoy this.

Mario stepped into the building's small vestibule. Through the cloudy glass of the front door, Selene watched him jab repeatedly at the buzzer for Jackie's apartment. Next to him stood a doorman's podium. *Just for show,* Selene knew. No lobby guard would appear to protect Jackie from her boyfriend. Her only defense was a weak lock on the building's inner door and the woman she'd hired to strike Mario down.

Selene crossed the street and waited just out of Mario's sight. *Come on, Jackie,* she urged silently. *Be brave.* The young woman appeared in the vestibule, closing the inner door behind her so that Mario couldn't get upstairs. Selene tensed, ready to spring forward. *But not yet, not yet.*

Jackie, short and skinny, looked even younger than her twenty-two years. She'd made a vain attempt to cover her swollen black eye with a smear of turquoise shadow. One hand nervously twirled a lock of dyed blond hair. She held her other arm across her body like a shield. Mario flashed her a smile and sneaked a quick kiss on her neck. Jackie shuddered— whether with delight or fear, Selene couldn't tell. Then he took a step closer, and the woman put a hand on his chest, pushing him away. He kept coming, backing her into a corner, still smiling despite Jackie's protests. He rested one hand possessively on her neck and hooked the other around the white leather belt at her waist, pulling her against him. Jackie struggled in his grip, her eyes darting back and forth, searching for Selene.

Just a moment more, Selene thought, *so the police have evidence.* Then it happened, quick as a snake bite: Mario slapped Jackie across the face.

Selene yanked open the outer door and put a light hand on Mario's shoulder. Still holding on to Jackie's belt, he turned to the intruder.

"Hey, Mario," Selene said with her best attempt at casual courtesy. She didn't want to antagonize him until Jackie was safe.

"Who the fuck are you?"

"You don't recognize me?" Selene gave him what she hoped was an alluring smile.

His defensiveness dissolved as quickly as it had appeared. He made a low sound of pleasure, like a man savoring some succulent morsel. Jackie slipped from his loosened grip as he turned all of his attention toward Selene. His eyes traveled appreciatively over her body, seeing past her loose cargo pants to the long, lean legs underneath. "If I'd nailed you, I think I'd remember." Unnoticed, Jackie scurried back through the inner door and pulled it shut behind her.

"Perhaps." Selene nodded with exaggerated thoughtfulness. "But considering the number of women you're currently sleeping with, perhaps not."

"What do you know about—"

"Lyla? Miriam? Fatima?" She ticked them off one by one on her fingers. "Raquel? Yolanda? And, of course, Jackie. Although you don't sleep with Jackie so much as beat her up, so I'm not sure I should count her."

Mario put his hand in his sweatshirt pocket and didn't draw it back out. *A knife,* Selene decided. *Hopefully not a gun.*

"You a cop?" he asked.

"Not at the moment."

"Then back away, lady. Mind your own business."

"It's my business to keep you away from her."

He smirked. "And how you going to do that?"

Selene drilled a right hook into his face, spinning him away, then a left into his kidney. With great satisfaction, she watched a line of bloody spittle drip from his mouth onto the floor as he doubled over. But Mario recovered quickly, coming upright with a long, serrated hunting knife in his hand. He barreled toward her. She sidestepped him easily, thrusting out a foot to send him stumbling forward into the opposite wall. Before he could regain his balance, she jabbed an elbow into his spine, bringing all her superior height to bear. Mario grunted and dropped the knife but stayed on his feet. Faster than she'd anticipated, he spun toward her and kicked her hard in the knee.

Biting back a yelp of pain, she fell, slamming the injured knee into the ground. He kicked again, striking her in the jaw. Her teeth sliced the inside of her cheek; she tasted blood. Cold panic rushed through her veins as a third kick smashed into her ribs, knocking the breath from her body. Vision wavering, she reached across the floor toward the fallen knife—Mario beat her to it, bringing the blade down in a slicing arc toward her face. She moved her head just in time to prevent losing her nose; the knife whistled through the air beside her ear and struck the tiled wall with a sharp ping.

"You're going to wish you hadn't gotten in my way, *puta*." He kicked her backward and kneeled over her body, pinning her in place. For decades, she'd been dreading this moment—the fight she couldn't win, the woman she couldn't protect. *Have I finally grown so weak that a mere man can defeat me?*

"Who do you think you are?" he demanded, raising the knife once more.

Selene grabbed his upraised wrist. "You wouldn't believe me if I told you," she gasped, her arm shaking with the effort of holding him off.

"Try me."

A hundred names came to mind, whispered in long-forgotten tongues, but she couldn't lay claim to a single one. Not any longer.

Mario laughed at her silence and waved the knife just out of her reach. "Don't even know your own name, huh? Guess it's true—the hot ones *are* dumb."

One look at his grinning face burned away Selene's self-pity. As he leaned forward, ready to strike, his rhinestone cross swayed above her. The symbol of everything she'd lost, everything she despised. She allowed herself a quick second to imagine grabbing it and punching it through his pretty blue eye. Then she hooked the base of the doorman's podium with her foot and brought it crashing down on Mario's head instead.

He collapsed, unconscious, on top of her.

Jackie rushed back into the vestibule. She stopped a few feet away from Mario, her hand to her mouth. "Did you kill him?"

"Unfortunately, no," Selene wheezed from beneath his bulk. To her dismay, it took Jackie's help to free her from the dead weight.

She slipped a length of wire from her pocket and tied Mario's wrists together.

Jackie stared at Selene's face, wincing. "Damn, you okay?"

Selene raised a hand to her throbbing jaw, wondering just how bad it looked.

"I already called the cops," Jackie went on, as if that would make Selene feel better.

"I told you to wait until I was gone," she said, more angrily than she'd intended.

"I saw him kicking you. Then I saw him holding that knife over you like he was going to slice off your eyebrows." Jackie put her hands on her hips. "Was I supposed to just let him carve you up?"

"Yes, that's exactly what you're supposed to do. I make myself the target so you don't have to." She looked at the red handprint on Jackie's cheek. "At least...not anymore."

"The cops will be here in five minutes. They're bringing an ambulance. You sure you shouldn't get your face looked at?"

"Don't worry about me. Just make sure to tell the cops that this time you're pressing charges. And tell Mario that if he ever threatens you again, the police are going to be the least of his worries."

Jackie looked down at her boyfriend. "He's not going to be a vegetable when he wakes up, is he?"

Selene just shrugged.

"I mean, I didn't think about that before, but the podium made this sound when it hit his head...like a *thunk*, like a wet *thunk*."

Selene stared at the young woman for a moment, a scowl creasing her forehead. "What're you doing?"

Jackie looked up. "I just—"

"You're worried about him."

"He's not just a—"

"Have you already forgotten our agreement?" Selene couldn't keep the acid from her voice. "I protect you, just like I protect all the women who come to me. And all I ask in return is two promises: You won't tell the cops about me, and you won't hook up with assholes again." Jackie opened her mouth to protest but Selene cut her off. "You want to get down on your knees and tell him you're sorry. I can see it in your face."

Jackie huffed indignantly. "I asked you to get him away from me, not to tell me what to feel."

Selene tried to summon the fury that had once defined her life. Instead, she just felt tired. She'd heard it all before—thousands of times over thousands of years. "If you go near Mario again, you're on your own," she said wearily, opening the door.

Limping down the sidewalk with her head down and shoulders hunched, she listened to the approaching sirens. She ran her fingers along the swollen bruise on her jaw and the tender spot on her ribs where she'd been kicked. The pain in her knee flared with every step she took. In the moment before she knocked the podium into Mario's head, she'd been in real danger, as vulnerable and helpless as the women it was her duty to protect. If he'd had a gun instead of a knife, Selene would be the one waiting for an ambulance.

And what would happen then? she wondered. *If a man put a bullet through my skull, would my tenuous hold on immortality finally rip free?*

She looked up at the moon, a hazy crescent just discernable between the buildings, heading toward its daily oblivion beneath the horizon. *And if I die—so what? The goddess Artemis vanished a long time ago. What's left of her is nothing but shadows and memories. Both disappear with time.*

Maybe I should, too.

Then, despite the balmy air, a sudden shiver crawled along her arms, as if from a distant shriek more felt than heard.

In another age, she might have recognized the sensation as a summons. She might have listened more closely to the prayer upon the wind. She might have heard the anguished cry of a woman in mortal danger, far away on the other side of the city, calling out for the goddess who might save her.

Now, Selene merely grimaced and zipped her leather jacket a little higher beneath her chin.

Follow us:

f /orbitbooksUS

𝕏 /orbitbooks

▶ /orbitbooks

Join our mailing list
to receive alerts on our
latest releases and deals.

orbitbooks.net

Enter our monthly
giveaway for the chance
to win some epic prizes.

orbitloot.com